Phantasmion

Phantasmion

A Fairy Tale

Sara Coleridge

MINT EDITIONS

Phantasmion: A Fairy Tale was first published in 1837.

This edition published by Mint Editions 2021.

ISBN 9781513280493 | E-ISBN 9781513285511

Published by Mint Editions®

MINT
EDITIONS

minteditionbooks.com

Publishing Director: Jennifer Newens
Design & Production: Rachel Lopez Metzger
Project Manager: Micaela Clark
Typesetting: Westchester Publishing Services

L'ENVOY OF PHANTASMION

Go, little book, and sing of love and beauty,
To tempt the worldling into fairy land;
Tell him that airy dreams are sacred duty,
Bring better wealth than aught his toils command—
Toils fraught with mickle harm.

But if thou meet some spirit high and tender, On blessed works
and noblest love intent,
Tell him that airy dreams of nature's splendour, With graver
thoughts and hallowed musings blent,
Prove no too earthly charm.

Contents

Preface

Phantasmion, the product of the enforced leisure on a sick bed of Sara Coleridge, was first given to the world in 1837; and although the book received warm and hearty commendation both privately and publicly from those who read it, the success which then attended it neither equalled in any degree its own singular merit, nor was what might have been expected, from the approbation the book met with at the hands of those best qualified to judge. I have always believed that this was in great measure owing to the mode of its publication. It was an expensive book, with no author's name, without a single illustration, and the edition was limited to two hundred and fifty copies. The publisher, Mr Pickering, doubted apparently the possibility of its being popular; and except that he printed it with all the care and beauty which marked every book he put forth, he seems almost to have determined that, as far as depended upon him, it should have no chance of becoming so. A small edition of a long fairy tale, by an unnamed author, published at nine shillings, had little chance in those days of forcing its way into general circulation. The few copies sold slowly, and were at length exhausted. The book has long been out of print; and even amongst men of letters, and men interested in the character and Admiring the genius of Sara Coleridge, it is almost unknown or forgotten.

The book, as now revived,appeals to a larger audience and a new generation; to readers who know the author, and who are already to some extent acquainted with the power, the grace, the refinement of her mind. They will be prepared to find in this, her only work of fiction, her longest continuous original composition, the delicate imagination, the melody of verse, the clear and pic turesque language, the virginal purity of conception, which are to be found in this book by those who look for them. Indeed, these things do not need searching for; they lie upon the surface.

It may be said that this is exaggerated language to use about a fairy tale, which is nothing but a fairy tale; into which no moral is intruded, the characters of which are slightly indicated only, and never elaborately de veloped; and which is itself an example of a kind of composition old-fashioned, out of date, and entirely at odds with the spirit and temper of the time we live in. No one, however, who reads this book through is likely to say that I have described it too favourably; and this edition is an attempt at least to ascertain whether it is not fitted for general readers, and may not achieve a general and lasting popularity.

Some time ago it would have been by no means super fluous to plead for fairy tales as entitled to a distinct and useful place in the cultivation of the intellect, and as having an important function to perform in a sensible and practical education. But this is hardly necessary now. We have, indeed, still too much of the directly moral and instructive tale, of stories wherein the interest turns upon small incidents of daily life, which are invested with a moral importance altogether unreal and exaggerated; the tendency of the whole tale being too often to foster a morbid self-introspection, and a diseased and effeminate religion. But there are signs of a healthy change; and if the number of good books, and books of what is called useful knowledge, is still somewhat overwhelming the use of works of pure fancy is at least, now generally admitted, and the good sense of culti vating the imagination is not disputed. Indeed, in England, and for most of us it would be hard-hearted to dispute it. When we think of the grim and unlovely lives, which the great body of the English people is doomed to lead, their dreary toil, their dull homes, their harsh surroundings, it is surely wise as well as merciful, to try to give them glimpses of things more beautiful and lofty than their daily life affords, and to enrich at least their minds with pictures of brighter scenes, and their hearts with happier thoughts, than are before them and within them, in the state in which their lot is for the most part cast. Phantasmion does not pretend to teach directly any moral lesson; it is not a sermon in disguise; but most people will be better and happier while they read it, and after they have read it too.

It stands alone, or almost alone, in fairy literature in the nature of its fancies, and in the extent and completeness of its narrative. Its supernatural beings have no English originals; perhaps indeed they have rather a German than an English character. The Legends of Number Nip, and the exquisite fancy of Undine are their nearest prototypes. But the various powers and spirits of earth, and sea, and sky, some gentle and comparatively weak, like Feydeleen the Flower Spirit, some stern and terrible, like Oloola the Spirit of the Storm; or Valhorga the gigantic Earth Spirit, have more of the bright and fresh Greek, or early Latin imagination in them than any other or later mythology.

The scenery of the tale is that of Cumberland and Westmorland, only under a brighter sky and with a softer climate. To me the descriptive power of it seems very uncommon, The characters are, as I have said, slightly drawn; the passion is not deep or strong; yet we are carried On by a very interesting story, and few readers but will regret when they end it. The English is pure and clear and vigorous. The verses are very lovely, always full of delicate fancy, sometimes rising into high imagination, and exhibiting, in the management of lyrical measures, often difficult and peculiar, the metrical melody and refinement, which in her case at least were an hereditary gift. As a rule, the poems are closely connected with the prose which surrounds them, and cannot without great disadvantage be taken out of their dramatic setting. It is not always so however; and many of them would be exquisite songs and lyrics if printed independently, and read as separate and unconnected poems Those beginning "One face alone," " The winds were whispering," and "Sylvan Stag securely play " (to take only two or three examples out of a number), are surely worthy of any great lyrical writer.

Indeed, the general literary excellence of the book fits it for all readers and all ages. The perfect purity of the story, its freshness, its beauty, its interest, fit it especially for the young With such readers at least, according to a limited experience, it. has been most successful The fairies and spirits of the book, its heroes and its witches, its maidens and its kings, have been, and may be again, household words with intelligent children, and may once more live, as they have lived already, in their minds, and give names and characters to their bright and pleasant play. The success of Phantasmion has hitherto been limited indeed, but within limits it has been complete. I would fain hope that there is in store for it a success not less complete, but far less limited.

It remains only to say why this Preface has been written. It is done at the request of those who have a much better right to do it, and who would have done much better; and because it is a pleasure to be connected, in however humble a sort, with one who was the teacher of my childhood, the friend of my youth and manhood, and who is now, in the decline of life, a precious, indeed a sacred memory.

John Duke Coleridge
Heath's Court, Ottery S. Mary
10th January 1874

I

The Fairy Potentilla appears to the young Prince Phantasmion

A young boy hid himself from his nurse in sport, and strayed all alone in the garden of his father, a rich and mighty prince; he followed the bees from flower to flower, and wandered further than he had ever gone before, till he came to the hollow tree where they hived, and watched them entering their storehouse laden with the treasures they had collected; he lay upon the turf, laughing and talking to himself, and, after a while, he plucked a long stiff blade of grass, and was about to thrust it in at the entrance of the hive, when a voice just audible above the murmur of the bees, cried "Phantasmion"! Now the child thought that his nurse was calling him in strange tones, and he started, saying, "Ah! Leeliba!" and looked round; but casting up his eyes he saw that there stood before him an ancient woman, slenderer in figure than his nurse, yet more firm and upright, and with a countenance which made him afraid. "What dost thou here, Phantasmion?" said the stranger to the little boy, and he made no answer: then she looked sweetly upon the child, for he was most beautiful, and she said to him, "Whom dost thou take me for?" and he replied, "At first I took thee for my nurse, but now I see plainly that thou art not like her." "And how am I different from thy nurse?" said the strange woman. The boy was about to answer, but he stopped short and blushed; then after a pause he said, "One thing that thou hast wings upon thy shoulders, and she has none." "Phantasmion!" she replied, "I am not like thy nurse: I can do that which is beyond her skill, great as thou thinkest it." At this the boy laughed, and said with a lively countenance, pointing to the hollow tree, "Could'st thou make the bees that have gone in there fly out of their hive all in one swarm?" The fairy staid not to answer, but touched the decayed trunk with her wand, and the bees poured out of their receptacle by thousands and thousands, and hung in a huge cluster from the branch of a sycamore; and as the child looked upon the swarm, it seemed to be composed of living diamonds, and glanced so brilliantly in the sunshine that it dazzled the sight. And the beautiful boy laughed aloud, and leaped into the air, and clapped his hands for joy. Then the fairy placed her wand within his little palm, saying, "Strike the tree, and say, 'Go in!' and they shall all enter the hive again." The cheeks of the young boy blushed brighter than ever, and his eyes sparkled, as he struck the hollow trunk with all his might, and cried, "Go in! Go in!!" No sooner had he done this than the whole multitude quitted the branch of the sycamore, and disappeared within the body of the tree.

Then the ancient woman said to the little prince, "Wilt thou give me that pomegranate?" and she pointed to the only ripe one which grew on a tree hard by. One member of the trunk of this pomegranate tree leaned forward, and invited the adventurous child to mount; he quickly crept along it, and having plucked the fruit which the fairy had pointed out, he turned round and tried to descend: but finding that he should slip if he attempted to return by the way he came, having measured the height from the ground with his eye, he boldly sprang at once from the bough to the turf below, and presented his prize to the stranger. With that she took it from his hand, and, looking kindly upon him, she said, "My little Phantasmion, thou needest no fairy now to work wonders for thee, being yet so young that all thou beholdest is new and marvellous in thine eyes. But the day must come when this happiness will fade away; when the stream, less clear than at its outset, will no longer return such bright reflections; then, if thou wilt repair to this pomegranate tree, and call upon the name of Potentilla, I will appear before thee, and exert all my power to renew the delights and wonders of thy childhood."

After speaking these words, Potentilla vanished; the child opened his eyes wide, and, now feeling afraid to be alone, he ran homeward as fast as possible, and in a little time heard the voice of his mother calling to him in quick tones; for she had outrun his nurse, who was also hastening in search of him. The child bounded up to her, and with breathless eagerness sought to describe the strange things which he had seen. "All the bees came out in a cluster," cried he, "and they were dressed in diamonds! thousands and millions of them hung together upon a branch! and I my own self made every one of the bees go back again into their hive, with the shining stick which the old woman lent me." "What old woman?" replied Queen Zalia to her little son; "was it one of the gardeners' wives?" "O no!" said he; "an old woman with wings on her shoulders, and she flew up and vanished away, like the bubbles which I blow through my pipe." "Thou hast been dreaming, my sweet boy," said his mother; "thou hast fallen asleep in the sunshine, and hast dreamt all this." "No, no! my mother," the child replied; "indeed, indeed it was quite unlike those dreams which I have at night. I wish the bees could speak that they might tell thee all about it, for they saw the winged woman as well as I."

II

Potentilla fulfils her promise to Phantasmion

Soon afterwards Phantasmion's fair mother, Zalia, fell sick and died. Her young son was kept from the chamber of death, and, roaming about the palace in search of her, he found a little child sitting on the floor of a lonely chamber, afraid to stir because he was by himself. "The people are all gone away," cried Phantasmion; "Come, I will take thee abroad to see the pretty flowers, now the sun shines so bright." The child was glad to have fresh air and company, and, holding fast by the older boy's hand, he sped along with short quick steps further than his tiny feet had ever carried him before, lisping about the bees and hornets, which, in his ignorance he would fain have caught, as they buzzed past him, and laughing merrily when his frolicsome guide led him right through a bed of feathered columbines, for the sake of seeing the urchin's rosy cheek brushed by soft blossoms and powdered with flower dust. At last they entered the queen's pleasure ground, where only one gardener remained, and he was sitting on the path, gathering berries in a basket. "Where is my mother?" cried the prince, leaping suddenly behind him; "hast thou hidden her away, old man?" "Thy mother is dead!" answered he, looking up in the boy's face; and it was the glance of his eye, more than the words he spoke, which made Phantasmion shudder. The menial smoothed his brow, and with humble courtesy offered a branch of crimson fruit to the young prince, who flung it on the ground, crying in a haughty tone, "How darest thou say that my mother is dead?" "Go to her chamber, and see;" replied the man sternly. "And how can I see her if she is dead?" rejoined the boy, with a tremulous laugh; "can I see the cloud of yesterday in yon clear sky? like clouds the dead vanish away, and we see them no more." Just then he spied the young child lying down, with the fruit-branch dropping out of his fingers, and his face buried in a flowery tuft. "What! hiding among the hearts-ease?" cried he; "ah! let me hide too." Then, putting his face close to that of his charge, "How cold the little cheek is!" he cried; "come, raise it up to the warm sun." Hearing these words the gardener turned the child's face upwards, and behold he was dead; his lips smeared with berry juice, and his pale swollen cheeks covered with purple spots! Then he held out the body to the startled boy, and showing the slack limbs and glazed eye, while his own shot fire like that of a panther:—"So look the dead," cried he, "ere they vanish away: just so Queen Zalia is looking!" Phantasmion shrieked, and hastening home, he met his mother's funeral procession going forth from the palace. The body was wrapped in a shroud, and black plumes nodded over the face; but he saw the dead hands, and the limbs stretched upon the bier. From that time forth he never spoke of Queen Zalia, but he often beheld her in dreams, and often he dreamed of the old man who told him she was dead, and who disappeared, on the same day, from the royal household.

Phantasmion grieved but little when his father died a year afterwards; for he scarcely knew King Dorimant's face, that warlike prince having been wholly engaged, since the birth of his child, in a fruitless search after mines of iron. It was commonly believed that ill success in this matter hastened his end; but the people about the palace well knew that he died of eating poisoned honey.

Thus Phantasmion was yet too young, when he inherited the throne of Palmland, to be a king in reality; and those who governed the land sought to keep him a child as long as possible. They prevented him from learning how to reign, but could not succeed in making him content with mere pomp and luxury; for his pleasures were so closely set that they hindered one another's growth, and, by the time that he attained to his full stature, nothing gratified him, except the society of a noble youth who came to visit his court from a foreign country, and who interested his mind by curious histories and glowing descriptions. Dariel of Tigridia was well skilled in the management of fruit trees and flowers; he had brought seeds of many fine sorts from distant lands, and at the desire of Phantasmion, he sowed them in the royal garden. One morning he came to the prince, saying, "The rare plant has put forth leaves; come and look at it!" "Earlier even than we expected!" cried the prince, rising joyfully from his seat. "I will not only see, but taste and try." The two youths took their way through a flowery labyrinth, talking much of the wondrous plant and the virtues of its leaves; but just as they were drawing nigh to the nook where it grew, several scorpions fastened all at once on Dariel's sandaled foot, and stung it with such violence, that, quitting his comrade's arm, he sprang into the air, and then fell prostrate under the towering lilies. Phantàsmion carried him to the palace, and placed him tenderly on a couch. After a time, seeing that he continued in a languishing state, he made an infusion of the leaves which his friend had so highly extolled, and silently gave it to Dariel instead of the drink which the physician had ordered; but, just as he expected to see the poor youth revived by this kind act, his head sank on the pillow, a blue tinge stole over his cheek, and, when the prince had gazed upon his altered face for a few minutes, he plainly saw that it told no longer of sickness, but of death. Not, however, till decay had wrought a still more ghastly change in Dariel's comely countenance, Phantasmion quitted the side of his couch; then, overpowered with sorrow, he roamed abroad, and sought the forest of lilies which his comrade's hand had reared: the sun was bright, the air fresh, but all that flowery multitude was drooping and ready to perish; cankerworms had gnawed their roots, and the wondrous plant itself had been attacked by such numbers of insects that scarce a trace of it remained.

This circumstance deepened the melancholy which had seized on the spirit of Phantasmion. He began to think that all persons and things connected with himself were doomed to misfortune; and when this channel of thought was once opened, a hundred rills poured into it at once, and filled it to the brim.

He reflected on the early deaths of his father and mother, as he had never reflected on them before: the black plumes and solemn tapers of the chamber where King Dorimant lay in state rose up before him, while Zalia stretched on her bier, and the strange man holding out his little comrade's body, visited him again as in the dreams of his childhood. These and other remembrances, grouped together under one aspect of gloom, all wore the same visionary twilight hue, and inspired the same sadness. He turned away from cheerful faces, and was constantly expecting to see the ghost of Dariel, a shadowy image of his swollen corse.

Phantasmion had spent many days in this state of dejection, when he wandered forth after a sleepless night, one clear morning, and, refreshed by the breath of early dawn, began to slumber under the boughs of a pomegranate tree. No sooner had he closed his eyes than the fairy, whom he had formerly seen on that very spot, seemed to stand there again. In his dream she touched him with her wand, and forthwith leafy branches, like those which drooped over him, sprouted from his shoulders; imperceptibly those branches changed into green wings and up he soared, feeling as if his whole body were inflated with air. As he floated along in the sky a group of angel faces shone before him: he surveyed them, and all were lovely, but one was far lovelier than the rest, and, while he gazed upon that countenance, it grew more and more exquisite, the others becoming indistinct and fading gradually away. Suddenly, like a balloon exhausted of air, down he dropped to the earth, and was snatched away from the vision. "Potentilla!" he cried aloud; starting up in the intensity of feeling, and stretching out both his hands, "Potentilla! help! help!" No sooner had he uttered that long forgotten name, than he opened his eyes, and saw the little old fairy smiling in his face. "Phantasmion," she said, "what shall I do for thee? I am queen of the insect realm, and powers like those which insects have, are mine to bestow." "Give me wings!" he cried; for still he had a vague hope that he might once more behold that heavenly face if he could but soar aloft.

Potentilla waved her wand, and soon the air was filled with butterflies, those angel insects pouring from every region of the heavens. Here came a long train arrayed in scarlet, waving up and down altogether like a flag of triumph; there floated a band clad in deep azure, and flanked on either side by troops in golden panoply. Some were like flights of green leaves, others twinkled in robes of softest blue besprent with silver, like young princesses at a festival; and, in front of the whole multitude, a gorgeous crowd, adorned with peacock eyes, flew round and round in a thousand starry wheels, while here and there one butterfly would flit aloof for a few moments, then sink into the circle and revolve indistinguishably with the rest: now the entire wheel flew off into splinters, now reconstructed itself at once, as if but a single life informed its several parts.

Again Potentilla waved her wand, and the bloomy throng descended on trees and shrubs, attiring every bough in fresh blossoms, which quivered without a breeze. Phantasmion saw that he was to choose from this profusion of specimens the wings that pleased him best, and he fixed on a set like those which he wore in his dream. The moment that Potentilla touched him with her wand a sensation of lightness ran throughout his body, and instantly afterwards he perceived that wings played on his shoulders, wings of golden green adorned with black embroidery: beneath an emerald coronet his radiant locks clustered in large soft rings, and wreathed themselves around his snowy forehead: robes of white silk floated over his buoyant limbs, and his full eyes, lately closed in languor, beamed with joyful expectation, while more than child-like bloom rose mantling to his cheek. Potentilla had seen an eagle teaching her young ones to fly, gradually widening her airy circles, and mounting in a spiral line that swelled as it rose, while the sun burnished her golden plumes; just so she flew before the winged youth, who timidly followed where she led the way, trembling in his first career when he saw the earth beneath him. But, gaining confidence, all at once he shot away from his guide, like a spark from a sky-rocket; he soared and gyred and darted on high, describing as many different figures as a skater on the ice, while from the groves and flowery meads below this choral strain resounded:—

See the bright stranger!
On wings of enchantment,
See how he soars!
Eagles! that high on the crest of the mountain,
Beyond where the cataracts gush from their fountain,
Look out o'er the sea and her glistering shores,
Cast your sun-gazing eyes on his pinions of light!
Behold how he glitters
Transcendently bright!
Whither, ah whither,
To what lofty region
His course will he bend?
See him! O, see him! the clouds overtaking,
As though the green earth he were blythely forsaking;
Ah now, in swift circles behold him descend!
Now again like a meteor he shoots through the sky,
Or a star glancing upward,
To sparkle on high!

SARA COLERIDGE

III

Phantasmion sees and hears strange things by the sea shore

Phantasmion left the shadows of earth behind him, while he soared so high that green fields, and blue waters, gardens, and groves, all melted into one, and even that heavenly sight which had first made him pray for wings was itself forgotten in the pleasure of flying. He thought it a delightful novelty to rush down upon the heron like the trained hawk, or aim a javelin at some bird of prey as she stooped upon her quarry; to whirl upward with the glede, drop down like a shot side by side with the jer-falcon, disperse the swallows in the midst of their aerial dances, or sweep the cope of heaven in pursuit of the swift: then hovering aloft in perfect stillness, with green pinions and floating robes, he attracted crowds of gazers, who marvelled how a bird of paradise could look so large at such a wondrous height. One fine clear day he flew southward to the ocean, and pursued a sea eagle to the highest ether. At first setting off he was rudely brushed by vultures, hurrying down to feast upon a carcase which lay rocking on the waves: he thrust among them with his drawn sword, and pushed onward, leaving a cloud of his delicate plumelets fluttering in the air. Having arrived at last where the atmosphere was too thin for anything but a bird to breathe, he hastily began to descend; but, faint and weary, scarce saw his way before him, and dropped full on the back of the eagle's mate, jerking out of her clutches a load of fish just caught for her young. Enraged at this loss, she pursued Phantasmion, and with her strong beak shattered one of his pinions ere he had time to gain a cliff towards which he was steering; so that, being no longer able to direct his course aright, he fell with violence, and lay stunned upon the rugged shore. While he leaned upon his arm, just recovering from the shock, and surveyed the ocean with dazzled eyes, he perceived a strange woman's form rising out of the waves, and gliding towards the beach: a wreath of living moving flowers, like sea-anemones, clung round her head, from which the slimy locks of whitish blue hung down till they met the waters; her skin was thick and glistering; there was a glaze upon it which made Phantasmion shiver; and, trailing her sinuous body beside the place where the youth lay, she cast a glance towards him, with her moony eyes of yellow green, at which his blood ran cold: but on she went, and turned round a crag which jutted into the sea beyond the fallen prince. Still scarce recovered, Phantasmion arose and leaned against the lower end of this rock, which, like a buttress, projected from the main body of the cliff; the shattered pinion drooped to the ground, while the wings on the left side were half-expanded, and lay languidly against the white stone, like a green branch amid unseasonable snow. And now other sounds caught his ear, beside the roar and hiss of advancing and retiring waves. He stood on tiptoe, and looking down into a recess on the other side of the rock, beheld the shape that had lately passed him, reclining on the shore, and staring up in the face of a lofty dame, who talked aloud with passionate tones and gestures. She whose voice Phantasmion heard stood with her back towards him; he saw not her face, but he observed that she wore purple robes and a jewelled crown. "Ah me!" she cried, "the beautiful Iarine! Glandreth has called her 'the beautiful Iarine:' teach me how to countervail the charms of this fair girl, and to secure the heart of Glandreth." To this the fishy woman made no reply, save a murmuring sound of laughter; whereat the crowned lady exclaimed, in a shrill voice, "Remember thy vow to the king, my father, when he caught thee in his toils upon the shore." Then the woman-fish replied, "Have I not redeemed that vow? Did I not lend thee spells to bewitch the heart of Albinian? and is it not through me that thou art Queen of this Land of Rocks? Without guerdon I will serve thee no longer." The crowned lady put her hands before her face, and groaned deeply. At length she made answer, "Be satisfied, Seshelma! the babe shall be thine. Help me to remove Iarine from the sight of Glandreth; help me to destroy the hostile house of Magnart, and thou shalt have thy desire." Then the crowned woman sate down below the rock, and listened to the words of her whom she called Seshelma, and the two seemed to be contriving some plot. Phantasmion could not understand all that was said, for Seshelma discoursed in a low gurgling murmur; but he heard her speak of poisonous fish, and of a charmed vessel, and of a damsel named Iarine. In the end she drew from an oyster-shell a glittering net, and offered it to her companion, who took it from her flabby hand, then rose, and, lifting up her embroidered train, went her way leisurely, as if absorbed in thought. But Seshelma returned into the sea, and, again rowing past Phantasmion, she looked up in his face with the same hideous leer which had chilled his blood before; then diving into the deeper water, she quickly disappeared.

Phantasmion stood for some time gazing on the flood, almost expecting that some new shape would rise out of it. He mused on what had passed, and could not help in some sort connecting it with his heavenly dream. A lady, young and beautiful, was hated and persecuted; powers of earth and sea were leagued against her. He pictured this fair Iarine with the countenance which he had beholden in the vision, and longed to find her and rescue her from peril.

The Prince now bethought him that he was a long way from his royal palace, having fallen on the borders of Rockland, a country adjoining his own dominions; he therefore hastened from the coast, holding up the disabled wing with his hand, and journeyed homeward on foot. After a night's sleep, he repaired to the pomegranate tree, but felt unable to express the imaginations that haunted his mind while Potentilla stood before him. He told the fairy, when she begged to know his pleasure, that he was tired of his butterfly pinions, and wished to try new experiments. "Make my feet," said he, "like those of flies, which climb up the mirrors or walk over the roof of my marble hall; enable me to follow wherever one of those insects can steal along." He had no sooner spoken thus than Potentilla removed the wings she had given him, and fitted to his feet the suckers of flies. This gift pleased Phantasmion well, and he spent the remainder of that day in gliding along the walls and over the vaulted ceilings of his palace, or scaling the pillar-like stems of the loftiest palm trees. Those who witnessed his feats were amazed; but it had been commonly believed that the race of the Palmland kings was under the protection of some mysterious being, and this tale, which had of late years been forgotten, was now recalled to mind with fresh awe and wonder.

IV

Phantasmion ascends the Mount of Eagles

Early the next morning, Phantasmion rode out to the Black Mountains, which divided his territories from Rockland, the realm of a neighbouring monarch; and, having arrived at the bottom of a steep hill, he alighted in order to climb the side of it. This was a precipice of solid rock, many hundred feet deep, which looked like a dark curtain let down from the sky, and till that hour had never been trodden by the foot of man. Strange was it to see him as he paused in the midst of the ascent, plucking a wild flower from a crevice; not sustained in the manner of a bird, with spread tail and half expanded pinions, but seemingly upborne by his own lightness, like a vapoury phantom. When the prince was a child, his mother had told him that a wreath of precious stones was hidden somewhere betwixt the top of this huge crag, and the summit of the hill beyond; she had hung it round the neck of her pet lamb in play, and, while she was plucking dainty herbs to regale her favourite, an eagle had carried away the lamb and its costly necklace to her young ones among the highest rocks. Phantasmion remembered this, and, in some faint hope of discovering the relic, wandered on, after he had gained the summit of the crag, till he came to a small round lake, which lay buried in shadow below a semicircle of rocks. Taking rest here for a few moments, he spied an eagle with something white in her talons, and soon he saw her fly across the pool and enter a recess amid the crags above. "This is one of those eyries," thought he, "where the eagles breed from age to age; I will invade their ancient house, and perhaps I may win back the prize which was plundered from mine." While he was beginning to ascend, the mother eagle flew forth again, so that Phantasmion was able to mark well the situation of the nest. With steady foot he climbed the crags above the tarn, till he arrived at the bottom of that loftier cliff, in the centre of which the eyry was embosomed; just as he reached this point, unexpected sounds met his ear: "The eaglets' cry is strangely like the wailing of a child," thought he; and, full of wonder, he glided up the front of the rock to the hollow where the nest was lodged, and there beheld an infant lying on its back unhurt, but screaming piteously, while two half-fledged eaglets were shrinking to the further part of the cavity, frightened by the clamours of their intended victim. Startled by this sight, the prince thought no more about the jewels, but took up the babe, which was clad in the fairest raiment, and now, having something beside himself to carry, was bent on returning by the easiest path. Accordingly, after having descended to the tarn again, he tracked the course of a rivulet which flowed from that darksome receptacle till it wandered away out of sight amid shaggy rocks; then, pausing to consider how he should proceed, again he heard a sound of lamentation, but it was softer and deeper than that which had proceeded from the eagle's nest. He listened, but the dashing of some hidden waterfall overpowered the voice, and for a moment he thought that fancy had deceived him; till once more it rose louder than those watery sounds, and then sank into silence.

Phantasmion wrapped the infant, now fast asleep, in his upper vest, and laid it on dry moss, under a jutting stone; he then followed the streamlet among the crags, and thus found his way to a nook, where it formed a series of cascades. Beside the lowest of these, a damsel sat weeping. She was so fair and exquisitely formed that, leaning against the black rock, she looked like those white figures that are cut in relief on the dark ground of an onyx. She was a prisoner amid the labyrinth of rocks, unable either to repass the precipitous road whereby she had incautiously ascended, or to climb the wall of rock which rose above her head, and over which the prince was airily advancing. A yew tree grew out of a cleft in the beetling crag, and from its twisted trunk Phantasmion looked down upon the damsel, and saw her cheeks wet with tears, and her luxuriant tresses curling amid the spray of the torrent; it seemed as if the waterfall mocked her distress, babbling while she wept bitterly, and crying, "Fair one, follow me! see how I leap down the precipice."

The rustling of boughs over-head made the fair girl look up, and seeing a bright face peering down amid the dark foliage of the tree, "Good youth," she exclaimed, "hast thou seen a babe upon this mountain? Hast thou seen an eagle carrying a young child to her nest?" "The infant is safe," replied Phantasmion; "I took him myself even now from the eyry, and he lies wrapped up in a silken garment under shelter of a rock." Then the youth swung himself down from the yew, and approached the damsel, who, overjoyed at these tidings, led him to the place where she had climbed up to reach the waterfall, thinking that she might find the eagle's nest within the chasm. Phantasmion offered to carry her to the bottom of the rock, and to prove with what ease it could be done, he darted up and down the steep cliff before her as firmly and fearlessly as if he were skimming over the plain. The lady looked astonished at his wondrous agility, and was somewhat alarmed when he carried her in his arms to the edge of the crag; but in a few moments he placed her in safety on the heather below, and hastened back to the jutting stone where he had left the baby. Phantasmion found the child still asleep, with the tears yet glistening on its placid cheek, and soon returned, holding it carefully to his breast; the damsel sprang forward to meet him; her countenance was no longer downcast, but beaming with joy and tender affection, and, as she stretched out her arms to receive the rescued babe, Phantasmion saw that her face was the same as that entrancing one which he had beheld in his dream. He suffered her to take the child, and gazed in silent ectasy while she was pressing it to her bosom. At last, after uttering many thanks, she bade him farewell, and was about to depart; Phantasmion would have attended her home, but, with earnest looks and words, she declined his courtesy, and began winding his way, in all haste, toward the further part of mountain. The prince followed her with his eye as she steadily descended a slope of smooth grass, the babe, now awake, showing its rosy face over her shoulder, while a gentle breeze uplifted her long wavy locks, brightened by the sunshine.

No sooner was she lost from his view, than Phantasmion, awaking from his trance, hastened in the direction which he had seen her take, and at length came in sight of a spreading vale, with a dusky lake in the centre of it. The damsel was no where to be seen; she had struck into a wood on the skirt of the hill, but, at the further end of the valley, companies of soldiers clad in mail were exercising themselves in a mock battle; they were too distant for the youth to discern their motions, but, the sun being reflected from their polished armour, a steady mass of lightning seemed to dwell upon the plain. Phantasmion's soul kindled at the sight, and he almost longed to run down and join these shining troops: but from the appearance of the sky he feared to be belated if he tarried longer, and in order that he might not miss his way, retraced his steps to the small round lake on the other side of the mountain.

At the time that he reached the tarn, a beam of light was resting on these waters, which were covered with shadows when he saw them last, and through the clear fluid a gemmy coronal was gleaming. Phantasmion

SARA COLERIDGE

waded into the pool, and plucked the splendid ornament from the ooze in which it was half buried; it was of exquisite workmanship, and represented a pomegranate branch, the leaves being made of emeralds, and the blossoms of burning rubies. The inner part bore this inscription in letters of gold: "The Queen of Palm-land."

Phantasmion placed the wreath in his girdle, and hastened to rejoin his attendants at the bottom of the hill. The suckers of his feet had imbibed a quantity of moisture, and being much fatigued, he scarce had strength to drag his clinging soles from that which they trode upon: so that he carried away many loose stones as he went along, and was in danger of being lamed ere he reached his horse.

On his way home, Phantasmion showed the wreath, which had once adorned the flaxen locks of Zalia, to an ancient noble, formerly his mother's guardian. The old man looked sorrowful at the sight of it, and said, "May the next queen of Palmland be happier than she who wore those jewels." "How sayst thou, Cyradis?" the youth replied: "didst thou not bid me visit the glades of my mother's native land, when Zalia was the gayest thing that sported under the green leaves?" "So it was with Zalia," Cyradis replied, "till she exchanged her wild-flower chaplets for a royal crown. Alas! thy father saw not how his fair queen was arrayed; he cared only for his kingdom, and grieved day and night that he could not aparison his army in solid brass and steel." "The King of Rockland has well-armed soldiers!" exclaimed Phantasmion, recollecting what he had seen from the mountain top. "He hath," replied Cyradis; "and a great-hearted general too, who seeks to enlarge the boundaries of Rockland on either side." These remarks, and a discourse which followed, made the son of Dorimant very thoughtful, and he sought next day to renew his conversation with Cyradis, but was informed that the ancient chief had returned to his own abode in the district of Gemmaura, where, in former days, Zalia, the orphan heiress of that territory, dwelt under the same roof with him. The prince pondered on the sudden departure of Cyradis, and began to suspect that the good old man had been forced away by those who wished their youthful sovereign to remain ignorant and careless of all that pertained to the government of the realm.

V

Phantasmion enters the Land of Rocks

The kingdom which Phantasmion had inherited from his ancestors abounded not only in palms, but in all kinds of grain and fruit trees, as well as in flocks and herds. The land flowed with milk and wine, oil and honey; but few metals or valuable stones had yet been discovered in its bosom. On the other hand the realm of Albinian, who reigned over a country separated from Palmland, partly by an extensive range of hills, called the Black Mountains, and partly by the river Mediana, which flowed from them to the sea on the right hand, was craggy and barren, rich only in metals, marbles, and other stones, and in materials for making glass and porcelain. The men of Rockland (so this wild country was called), were ingenious in mechanical devices and operations; the inhabitants of the fertile Land of Palms were given to agriculture, and had never acquired that skill in arts and manufactures, by which the neighbouring nation was distinguished. Anciently the two countries enriched and strengthened one another, but these friendly relations were exchanged for feuds and settled hostility during the reign of Dorimant. For that ambitious monarch cherished designs of rendering the Land of Rocks tributary to his kingdom, and, having been secretly informed of certain iron mines in a glen among the Black Mountains, he offered to yield his claim upon the hand of a fair lady whom Albinian had fallen desperately in love with, on condition that this narrow vale should be annexed to his crown. The king of Rockland unguardedly accepted these terms, but afterwards refused to ratify his part of the treaty, having learnt, as he declared, that Dorimant was covertly preparing to make war on his dominions. It was reported, however, that he had been influenced in this matter by the sorceress Queen of Tigridia, who foretold that a mighty conqueror should arise in a craggy vale among the Black Mountains containing veins of iron. Dorimant inveighed loudly against the bad faith of Albinian, which he secretly hoped he should soon be in a condition to punish; for, after deserting the lady to whom he had been betrothed, he espoused the heiress of Gemmaura, a district which lay between Palmland and the kingdom of Almaterra, fully expecting to find the desired metals in his new territory. But a spell seemed cast upon this region from the hour that it came into his hands, and, though he had reason to know that both iron and copper had once been found there, he died without discovering the object of his search. On his decease, however, the discord which he had sedulously fomented between his subjects and their neighbours did not subside; the first were very scantily supplied with instruments of war, and the others were dependent on the fields and pastures of a rich country called Almaterra; for needful sustenance; but so enduring was the enmity which the measures of Dorimant had excited betwixt the two nations, that no regard to interest could restore their former friendly intercourse.

Phantasmion revolved these things in his mind after hearing what fell from Cyradis; Dariel had formerly excited his curiosity concerning the Land of Rocks, and now he resolved to travel through it in disguise, for the sake of making observations relative to war, and still more from a hope of meeting with the lovely maiden whom he had rescued from her prison among the rocks.

When he presented himself before Potentilla, the fairy fixed her eyes on his countenance, and saw that there was more speculation in it than formerly. "Give me," said he, "the power to travel with great speed; yet, in such a way, that I may not outwardly appear to be thus gifted. Let me skip like the grasshoppers, and those insects which can go at one bound many hundred times their own length." Potentilla touched his thighs with her wand, and bade him try his new faculty; so Phantasmion gave a spring, and vaulted above a quarter of a mile, darting over a clump of young palm trees to alight in a verdant lawn.

The prince gave out that he was going to travel, and all the court imagined that he meant to visit Cyradis in Gemmaura, which he had never entered since the death of his mother. Before day-break he took horse, and sallied forth alone, habited after the fashion of Rockland, the language and customs of which country he had learnt from his nurse, and also from Dariel. He wore a vest of purple silk, embroidered with golden vine leaves: a jewelled girdle encircled his waist, and he exchanged his tiara for a cap adorned with a single arching feather of many hues. In his hand he carried a hollow reed of thin gold, with a serpent twisted round it; the folds of the snake held gold and jewels, and in the body of the wand a nutritious conserve was deposited. Thus equipped, Phantasmion rode forth to the river Mediana, the banks of which had formerly been fringed with olive-trees even to the skirts of the hills; now leafless stumps alone were to be seen by the river-side: the vineyards, which the prince passed on his way to the boundary stream, appeared to have been laid waste, for all the plants were lying on the ground, torn and trampled into the earth; and, in the rich pastures, for miles around, not a sheep or heifer was cropping the tall grass.

On the Rockland side of the stream, at the foot of a hill which ended the range of the Black Mountains, was a fortified town called Lathra. Phantasmion eyed the lofty walls and turrets and deep moat by which it was surrounded, and determined to overleap them all at a bound. He stood upright on the back of his steed, and impelled himself forward; in a moment he was shooting over the house-tops, and instantly afterwards a tremendous crash was in his ears, while fragments, sharp as glass, were entering into his flesh. The leaper had come down upon a stand of sumptuous porcelain exposed for sale; the owners all stood aghast while he endeavoured to glide away; but, soon recovering from their amazement, the whole crowd bustled after him, as a swarm of wasps rushes out indignantly when a stone has been flung by wanton children into their pensile nest, and all their delicate architecture has been crushed in a moment. They hem round the prince, the ring grows smaller and smaller; still each man waits for his neighbour to seize the mysterious culprit, and ere the circle has closed upon him, Phantasmion has sprung away, and, having cleared many a lofty edifice, he is now alighting in another quarter of the town. To avoid a fresh crowd which began to collect around him, he slipped into a large building, the door of which was standing ajar, and found that he had entered an armoury, the walls being covered with weapons fancifully arranged, and the floor with piles of bucklers and breast-plates. The attention of the prince was riveted by a magnificent sword which lay beside a suit of armour of extraordinary size. The master of the magazine, seeing his inquisitive countenance, told him that they belonged to Glandreth, who conquered the country of Tigridia for King Albinian. "And that large helmet, surmounted with a white plume, is that to be worn by the same person?" the youth inquired. "That too is for Glandreth," replied the keeper of the arms; "Queen Mandra placed those feathers in it with her own hand. Thou art from court, and must know more of courtly affairs than I; but it is plain to the whole country that the conqueror of Trigidia has ruled both the state and the queen's heart ever since the king grew decrepit."

Phantasmion went forth, and, leaving the town, advanced toward a field where men, wild beasts, and cattle appeared to be strangely mingled together. Drawing nigh to the scene of action, he perceived that a band of tigers were performing certain movements on signals given them by men with spears in their hands. Obedient to the word of command, they surrounded the sheep and kine, separated them into divisions, and drove them to different parts of the field with as much skill as a shepherd's dog will collect his master's flock on the mountains. A country-man was looking on by the side of Phantasmion. "I hear," said he, "that there is little booty to be got now in the tract about the river; doubtless our captains will march up to King Phantasmion's palace next, and see what can be made prize of there." "Aha!" cried Phantasmion, much startled, and ready to give one of his enormous leaps: he restrained himself, however, and carelessly observed, "I knew not that tigers were bred in this land." The rustic stared as he replied, "Sure thou hast heard how Malderyl, the queen's mother, sent them from Tigridia, where they abound in the brakes and forests?"

The prince made no reply, but directed his steps toward a woody knoll, which he espied at a distance; and, having reached the bottom of it, instead of slowly winding his way to the top, he gained it at one bound, and there stretched himself at full length on dry moss underneath the trees. "How have I been living," thought he, "like an animal in its winter burrow, wrapped in luxury, without hearing or seeing aught of what went on around me; I will spring back, to guard my palace; nay, I will make war upon Glandreth, and my numerous army shall cover the battle plain! Army! alas! can men armed with slings and cudgels deserve that name? No! it is best to pursue my original intent. I will survey this injurious, this faithless country, as an eagle eyes the flock on which he means to descend. I will make my way through Almaterra; Dariel was wont to say that a little effort would suffice to snap the ties which bind that state to this. Yes, yes, I will seek the king and the chiefs of the adjoining country, and, having gained allies there, I will return to my own kingdom, and be a monarch indeed." Instantly after Phantasmion had uttered these last words to himself, the small cunning eye of a serpent met his view: the creature looked in his face as if divining his very thoughts, while it lay coiled up under the fallen leaves of a bay tree. As soon as the prince raised his head, the snake began to move its forked tongue, and seemed to emit sparks of fire from its eyes; whereupon Phantasmion started from his mossy couch, and, having leaped from the top of the wooded hill to the plain below, found himself close upon that wide sheet of water which he had formerly seen from the craggy mountain, when he followed the steps of the departing damsel. Toward the banks of this lake he swiftly proceeded, and came opposite to a large island covered with tall trees of gloomy green, over which rose battlements and pinnacles and frowning towers. The waters of the lake seemed to be very deep, so dark was their aspect; and two craggy islets, at nearly equal distances, emerged from its bosom betwixt the large island and the shore. Phantasmion skipped to these isles of crag, one after another, and looked like some gay water-bird alighted on a rock with glistening plumage, as he stood on the dusky islet with his arched feather waving to and fro. From that station he had a fair view of the large island, and saw that, within its pebbly margin, there rose a fence of interwoven hollies, like a jasper colonnade on a white marble pavement. This firm bank Phantasmion was just able to attain by a leap, and no sooner had he gained it than his attention was arrested by a soft melancholy voice, liquid and musical as the chime of crystal cups thrilled by a dewy finger. He drew nigh the fence, and, though unable to catch a glimpse of the singer through the close hollies, he heard these words of the song:

Tho' I be young—ah! well-a-day!
I cannot love these opening flowers;
For they have each a kindly spray
To shelter them from suns and showers;
But I may pine, oppressed with grief,
Robbed of my dear protecting leaf.

Since thou art gone, my mother sweet,
I weep to see the fledging doves
Close nestling in a happy seat,
Each beside the breast it loves;
While I, uncared for, sink to rest,
Far, far from my fond mother's breast.

Sweet mother! in thy blessed sight
I too might blossom full and free;
Heaven then would beam with softer light;
But, could I rest upon thy knee
My drooping head, what need I care
How sickly pale and wan I were?

SARA COLERIDGE

My face I view in pools and brooks,
When garish suns full brightly shine;
Ah! me! think I, those blooming looks,
And that smooth brow can ne'er be mine!
Sad heart! I charge thee to express
More truly all thy deep distress.

Deceitful roses leave my cheek,
Soft lilies join those happy flowers,
Which nothing stirs but zephyr meek,
Which nought oppresses but sweet showers;
While she lies dead I grieve to be
More like those living flowers than she.

Here there was a pause in the soft strain, and Phantasmion, looking on the lake, descried some fishermen in a vessel just come within sight. He eagerly hailed them, and while they approached the shore, he heard the song thus continued:—

O, what to me are landscapes green,
With groves and vineyards sprinkled o'er,
And gardens where gay plants are seen
To form a daily changing floor?
I dream of waters and of waves,
The tide which thy sea-dwelling laves.

Dearly I love the hours of night,
When bashful stars have leave to shine;
For all my visions rise in light,
While sun-lit spectacles decline;
And with those stars they fade away,
Or look as glow-worms look by day.

VI

Phantasmion pays a second visit to the King's Island

Phantasmion leaped into the boat when it approached the shore, requesting the fishermen to convey him to the further end of the lake; and, while the vessel was receding, he listened in rapt attention to the music of that plaintive song which floated over the water, accompanied by the soft symphony of the dipping oars. His conductors eyed him in silent surprise; and, guessing that he was a person of condition, they held their peace, and continued to row from the island. When the melody was no longer audible, Phantasmion asked an old man who was sitting at the bottom of the boat, busy with his tackle, if he knew who it was that sang on the large wooded island. "Ay, marry!" replied he, "the voice was that of Iarine, the fair daughter of our king." "Iarine!" exclaimed the prince; "and dwells Iarine in yonder castle?" he inquired, pointing to the towers which were yet visible above the trees in the distance. "That is the summer abode of the queen and her aged consort," replied the old man. "Is the king aged?" rejoined Phantasmion. "He looks as if he were," answered the fisherman; "but that comes more of sickliness than of years. He is feeble in mind and body, but his wife reigns manfully in his stead, aided by a valiant general, and other helpers, belike, which to us are unknown and invisible." These last words were spoken in a low tone, and Phantasmion thought of the crowned lady and her strange companion on the seashore.

"I am a stranger in this land," observed he, after a while, "so long have I been absent from it; but, me-thinks, I recollect that the king had another wife before he espoused the Princess of Tigridia." "That beauteous dame," said the old man, "perished at sea, leaving the sweet Iarine to deplore her loss." "Has Queen Maudra children of her own?" the prince inquired. His informant replied, "she has two; and one of them is still a babe in his nurse's arms. This same infant was carried away by an eagle to its nest, on the highest peak of the Black Mountains, and the fair princess Iarine climbed up among the crags, and rescued him from the eyry. She had been playing with him in a field at the foot of the hill, when the fierce bird descended from the rocks to seize her little charge; and, in the evening, she reappeared with the babe in her arms, just as the king's household began to fear that both were lost for ever."

The island was now far in the distance, and the fisherman inquired where the princely stranger desired to be put on shore. Phantasmion asked the owner of the boat, if he could afford him hospitality for the rest of that day, and a night's lodging? and the old man made answer that he was able and willing to do so, even without the payment which the youth offered. His younger comrades now impelled the boat swiftly onward; and, passing a tiny tufted islet, over against which stood the fisherman's cottage on a pleasant green bank, the vessel was brought up to a little stone pier right opposite to the door of that lowly dwelling. Phantasmion entered the rustic abode, and partook of the humble fare which it afforded; then went forth again, having told the fisherman and his dame that he meant to return and rest under their roof that night. He wandered along the banks of the lake, directing his steps toward that part of them whence he could obtain a full view of the King's Island. And now the sun went down, and the lustre of a summer's day, which had drowned all things in a flood of hazy brightness, gave place to the distinct splendour of moonlight, when the hills looked like masses of ebony, and seemed for the first time to exhibit their true forms and bulk, while standing out in bold relief against the deep clear sky. Phantasmion gazed not on them, but kept looking towards the island; for the melancholy strain which he had lately heard there was yet sounding in his ears, and connected itself with the fair countenance which was constantly present to his mind. On the side of the wooded isle which he now beheld Phantasmion espied no verdurous wall of interlacing boughs, but a margin fringed with broad alders and bending willows. While his eye was fixed on that grove, he saw a small narrow boat issue from amid the boughs which drooped into the water, and flit across the lake. It was impelled by a youthful maiden, whose braided tresses shone in the moonlight. She entered a little inlet where the water looked black as pitch, the trees leaning over and hiding it from the moonbeams. Phantasmion stood in the shadow of the birchen grove, behind the narrow bay, and watched her motions. The damsel leaned over the edge of the boat, and dipped into the dusky basin a net that seemed to be composed of flaming wires. The prince expected to see those flames quenched, but they glowed and flashed in their liquid shrine like fiery water-snakes, illuminating the cove, and making the moonbeams that rested on the lake beyond appear of a greenish chrysolite colour. Shoals of little fish, with many coloured bodies, were attracted by the light: up they came, and crowded into the net, so that the maiden appeared to be catching live jewels instead of fish. When her net was full, the lady poured her draught of glittering fishes into a silver pitcher of water, which stood on the bench of the boat ready to receive them. Phantasmion gazed earnestly upon her, and knew that she was that same fair damsel whom he had met upon the mountain; but now she appeared more brightly beautiful than when he found her weeping beside the rushing cataract. Her face looked placid as marble; and those features, on which the ruddy light of the magical net was playing, seemed as if they ought never to have been cast in perishable clay. Dazzling in whiteness were the lady's rounded arms, extended over the pool; and her graceful neck, on which no jewels shone, was polished and smooth as alabaster, but with a look of soft downy depth which art cannot imitate. Her bright locks no longer floated to her waist, but were coiled round the back part of her head; even from her open brow the ringlets were strained away, and only a few tendrils, escaping from confinement, lay upon her cheeks and forehead.

Having filled her net once more, and loaded her pitcher, the damsel began to push the boat out of the cove by means of a long pole. While thus engaged, she looked up, and espying the figure of Phantasmion, as he stood under the birch trees just above the bay, she started and hastened her movements, then, flinging down the pole, she seized the oars, and began to row with all speed toward the island. This was done before Phantasmion had summoned resolution to speak or stir; now she was in the deep water, yet still within the limits of his vaulting powers, but he restrained himself from leaping into the lake. A little way further on was a vessel, which, by some accident, had got loose from its moorings, and was drifting about in the water; he leapt into it, and thus nearly upset the narrow skiff, which quivered with the sudden shock; but, when it steadied again, he caught up the oars and rowed to the wooded isle. Having arrived within a certain distance, he sprang to land among the willows, leaped over an alder grove, and beheld a maiden at the end of a long alley of cypresses, bearing on her head the silver pitcher, the polished surface of which reflected the moonlight. One arm supported the vessel, the other held aside her long white garments and disclosed her twinkling feet, brightened by the harmless flames of the magic net, which was grasped in the same hand that contained the folds of her light robe. Oh, what grace of motion was there! The black firs and cypresses which stood in the moonshine, stern and grand, like stony effigies of trees, the delicate acacias that hung their boughs in graceful attitudes, ready to sway to and fro on the slightest impulse, all seemed to recognize her as one of themselves, a being unsullied and perfect in the simplicity of nature. Something of this Phantasmion may have felt, but he thought not of trees or of moonshine, and knew not whether it were day or night; he was busily measuring the distance between himself and the damsel. But even as a silvery beam from a lamp, which some night passenger carries in his hand, will travel across the ceiling of an unlighted room, attracting the eye of one who sits idly musing in the darkness, so did the damsel gleam, glide, and vanish through the avenue of black shadows; and Phantasmion stood motionless, while swift thoughts were passing and repassing through his mind. He hesitated to follow the maiden along the walk which wound circularly about the island, but, espying a light amid the foliage, he darted through the trees into a smooth lawn, across which he beheld a tower separate from the main body of the castle. The lower half of this building was hidden by shrubs, but, just above the screen, projected a balcony, over the rails of which a lady in sumptuous attire was leaning, and looking eagerly down upon the path below; a diadem was on her brow, the rich train of her purple robe swept the marble platform, beads of gold were twined around her bony arms, while numerous carcanets and chains of sparkling jewels hung from her neck over the balusters. That lady's lineaments were queen-like, though harsh and worn: but hers was the aspect of no kindly dame, and on such a countenance of ungentle emotion the moon's calm ray seldom rests. "Iarine!" she exclaimed, "hast thou found them? quicken thy pace!" and now Phantasmion espied the damsel, with the pitcher on her head, mounting the higher steps of the balcony stairs; a moment afterwards she was gone, having entered the tower with the crowned lady; then, the door being closed, and the light of the inner apartment hidden, Phantasmion was left alone with the trees and the half shrouded moon. "That voice, that diadem, that gorgeous train!" exclaimed the youth; "full surely this is the passionate dame who sate discoursing with that strange woman of the deep. They spake of poisonous fish!—O, can this maiden, who looks too fair and good to dwell below the sky, can she be the base instrument of wicked wills? Nay, nay; she is herself beguiled, perchance to be the victim of treacherous hatred." He gazed on the dark tower, and had resolved to gain admittance by force or stratagem, when a file of armed men advanced through the trees into the lawn, talking loud and peering about, as if in search of some one. From a few words which came to his ear, Phantasmion guessed that he had been descried from the castle, and that the guard were come to lay hands on him. He glided off amid the trees, while the clouds were veiling the moon's light, and found his way, by the margin of the isle, to that same spot which he had visited in the morning; from the bank of pebbles he bounded to the first of the craggy islets, thence to the second, and from that again to the shore of the mainland.

The moon was driving off her veil when Phantasmion thus crossed the water; and, when he stood on the shore, having the woody knoll right before him, she had thrown it completely aside. The prince resolved on returning to the fisherman's hut by the side of the lake opposite to that which he had lately traversed, so that he should have gone completely round the whole sheet of water by the time that he reached the cottage, which from its situation he felt sure of recognizing.

He skirted the lake closely, being obliged now and then to leap over parts of the shore which it would have been troublesome to pass step by step, and in this way he came to a river, which he concluded was on its way to join the sea upon the right hand. The stream was wide where it issued out of the lake, and looked deep and turbid. Phantasmion prepared to spring across, but checked himself and paused for a few moments, surveying the opposite bank, and endeavouring to ascertain its nature. While standing thus on the river's brim, he felt something cold and slimy touching his foot between the straps of the sandals, and soon a slippery hand glided up his leg where it was bare, the tight vest having been rent by thorns during his journey. Phantasmion had no time to consider what this might be, for the touch was as that of a torpedo, and he had received an electrical shock which benumbed his whole body. While he stood stupified and motionless, again he felt the terrible hand grasping his leg, and attempting to drag him into the river. Then, throwing down the serpent wand, he hastily drew his sword, and smote that which was pulling at his leg; whereupon a hissing sound, such as a snake might send forth when crushed by a stone, issued from the water, which was tinged for a moment with blood. Phantasmion looked down and beheld the flat white face of the fishy woman, Seshelma, glistening in the moonlight; she leaned backward in the tide as if she were faint with pain, and her great glassy eyes appeared fixed and rigid; but, when they stared on him that had inflicted the wound,

SARA COLERIDGE

they seemed to express more of slow malice than of any keen sensation. Soon, however, she gathered strength, and turning about began to dive away into the deeper water. Phantasmion seized her blue locks, but they slipped out of his hand, while the air was filled with cries of menace or of mockery, and numberless grotesque visages, starting out of water, gleamed momently in the twilight. The prince staggered and fell, for he had received another severe shock; from which having at length recovered, he saw nothing but the image of the moon's face on the stream, and heard no sound but the soft full murmur of an unimpeded current, smoothly sweeping by.

VII

After passing the night in a thicket, Phantasmion talks with Telza, the nurse of Iarine

For some time after he had grasped the locks of Seshelma, Phantasmion felt as if his limbs were frozen; and, on attempting once more to spring across the river, he found that his leaping powers were suspended. No boat was at hand or to be seen within hail; he dared not trust himself in the waters of that haunted stream, but, feeling desirous of rest, he resolved to make his bed for the remainder of the night in a grove of oaks and beeches, a little way removed from the borders of the lake and river. On arriving in this thicket he seemed to have entered a dim chamber, so close and leafy were the boughs that composed it; and the moss on which he reclined, beneath the boughs of an oak, made an easy couch; but no sooner had he laid down than he seemed to hear the hum of a spinning-wheel, turned by some one in the dark; and the importunate bird, which produced that sound from her gaping throat, kept flying round his head and striking her wings together sonorously. After persevering in this course for some time, she would perch on a bough just above the prince's head, and utter two or three short sharp notes, as though a thorn were piercing her bosom. It was in vain to scare the bird away, for she still returned, and at last, in spite of her noise and restlessness, Phantasmion fell half asleep, and thus reposed till he was completely awakened by a still more impetuous clapping of pinions, and a vehement whistling close to his face. The youth arose, and, by a glimmer of the moon's light, which pierced the branchy covert, he descried a glistering snake, and the speckled night-jar, with her great bill wide open, pouring out her angry murmur over the silent reptile's head. He drew the sword from his girdle and cut the serpent in pieces; then, stooping down to examine its severed head, he espied a nest in a little hollow betwixt the roots of the oak tree, and thus discovered the cause of that poor bird's uneasiness. For she had first been driven from her nest by Phantasmion's approach, and was afterwards in trepidation at the appearance of the reptile. She imagined indeed that it came to suck her unprotected eggs, while the prince believed it to be some emissary of Seshelma, who seemed bent on procuring his death or driving him out of Rockland; and, when he had looked at the several pieces of the dead snake in a fuller light, and saw that it closely resembled that which prepared to attack him in the woody knoll, this opinion was strengthened.

The youth advanced a little further in the wood to climb a beech tree; and, when the night-jar was settled on her nest, he had stretched himself along one of its wide, flat boughs, the upper ones forming a canopy over his head. Here he slept till break of day, and was then roused by the twittering of birds all around him: when he first entered the grove it seemed to have no other inhabitants than the disturbed mother and himself; but now every tree was alive with chirping voices and moving pinions. Phantasmion was little inclined to join the vocal choir, being ill at ease in his whole frame; he felt so anxious indeed concerning his bodily condition, that he must needs climb further up the tree to make trial of his strength, and found it in some degree restored. From the top of the tall beech he cast his eyes over the lake, which wore a uniform colouring of sad blue, while motionless bars of grey cloud streaked the horizon, and all the landscape was revealed under a cold equalizing light. The youth at that hour felt a transitory despondence, and his beautiful visions seemed to have departed with the sublime shadows and spiritual splendour of midnight.

From his lofty station Phantasmion beheld the fisherman in his boat, and hailed him with a shout that woke the echoes, at the same time beckoning with his serpent wand. Well pleased was the old man to hear that salutation, having come out thus early in search of his guest, for whose safety he had begun to entertain some fear. The prince descended from the tree, and, repairing to the boat, which was soon brought to land, he seated himself at the stern, and requested to be conveyed to the cottage. He told his ancient host that he had been seized with cramp, and, feeling still much disordered, should be glad to remain under his roof till he should find himself in a condition to resume his journey. The old man renewed his former hospitable offers, and, rowing faster than he had done for many a day, quickly brought the vessel to the little stone pier. Passing the greensward, now wet with morning dew, Phantasmion entered the cottage, and was kindly welcomed by Telza, the fisherman's ancient dame who had stood on the landing-place, straining her eyes to ascertain whether the noble youth were with her husband, and as soon as she discerned him in the boat, had hastened within to prepare for his reception! Phantasmion was refreshed with the food which she set before him, and, happening to fix his eye on the porcelain vessels in which it was served, was told they were the gift of the princess Iarine, to whom Telza had been a fond and faithful nurse. No sooner was that subject opened, than the good old woman had more to say than she had time to utter, and the prince felt no desire to stir from her side while she enlarged on the charms of Iarine's babyhood. "In very truth," said she, "I was the luckiest nurse that ever rocked a cradle; and little need was there to rock the cradle of sweet Iarine. O! she would sleep so beautifully for hours together, without a start or a murmur, yet looking as lifesome all the while as that clear lake, which never seems so bright as when it sleeps in the sunshine! Then when it was her time to awake, in a moment she was full of smiles, her pretty eyes wide open suddenly, and sparkling like the little merry rivulets which never sleep at all. We thought she could not be meant to pass through this vale of tears, because she wept so little at the beginning of her pilgrimage; but now I fear she weeps enough, and more sadly and stealthily than she need ever have done in my arms." "Is it not several years since she lost her mother?" inquired the youth. "To me it seems but yesterday," Telza replied; "but to one so young as Iarine, the time must appear full long, and the loss might ere now have been forgotten, had it been kindly repaired." How did Queen Anthemmina meet her death?" said Phantasmion. "She perished at sea," was the answer, "in sailing to the Isle of Birds, where a gay entertainment was appointed to be held. I cannot tell thee all the rumours that were afloat at the time; but now I verily believe that evil spirits lent their aid in drowning that lady, for, since she sank beneath the waves, they, and they only, have ruled this land." "Was the first queen beautiful?" asked the prince. "O what could be more beautiful," exclaimed Telza, "unless it be her most fair child Iarine? I have her now before me, just as she appeared on the day of that ill-starred expedition. Her gleaming jetty tresses were bound with pearls; alas! she little thought how soon those pearls would be restored to the deep! and, wreathed around her snowy-white vest, was a garland of blue lilies fresh gathered from the lake. How well I remember the splendid lady raising her eyes to the child in my arms! 'My pretty one,' said she, 'are they not beautiful?' and she pointed to those starry flowers. Beautiful indeed were her blue eyes beneath black eyebrows; but soon they swam in tears, as if at that moment she had a presage of her doom. The sweet child had no presentiment; she laughed and hid her face behind me as I set her on the floor, though charmed to see her mother's festal ornaments; and O! how mirthfully she laughed again, when, lifting up a loose part of the lady's robe, she spied a silver vessel hanging by a silken cord!" Telza would have proceeded much longer in this strain, but the fisherman beckoned her away, and she left the cottage; whereupon Phantasmion stepped out of doors, and gazed upon the lake absorbed in thought. For many furlongs beyond the stone pier on which he seated himself, the smooth sod came close down to the edge of the water: and now that the sun shone brightly, the greensward and its reflection seemed all one piece. But soon that picture began to be filled with figures, which, emerging from a coppice, stole into the verdant foreground, while no steps were heard upon the noiseless turf. Palfreys, with courtly riders, were occupying the green space, and the mirror showed that one of them carried a silver vessel. Phantasmion looked up and saw that Telza had now joined the distant group, and that she was standing beside a lady who leaned forward on her steed to speak with her. In a few moments the train were winding through the coppice, while the fisherman's dame, smiling cheerfully, crossed the greensward and approached her guest, who was still sitting on the pier! "O that thou hadst seen my fair princess!" she cried. "The morning air has decked her cheeks with dazzling roses, and now she looks as lightsome as when she was my nurseling, and had never shed a tear." The face of the young prince grew deeply red at these words of Telza; and when she added, "The sweet lady is going to visit her mother's sister, the wife of Magnart, in Almaterra," he started from his seat and eagerly inquired what had become of the fisherman? "He is going to the King's island," replied the dame; and she pointed to his boat, which was yet within sight. Then the youth sate down upon the pier to watch for his return, and Telza seated herself by his side, hoping in the mean time to have him for a listener.

Looking at the island, which was just visible in the distance, she said in a low voice, "All the country believes that Albinian was bewitched when he wedded the daughter of Malderyl, whom Glandreth brought a captive from Tigridia. Scarce a month of that marriage had elapsed when the king fell into decrepitude, and Glandreth became the real sovereign of the land. My husband oft compares Queen Maudra to those evil spirits that allure men first and put them in bail afterwards."

"There is a little boy in the boat with thy helpmate," cried Phantasmion, when at last he beheld the fisherman coming from the island. "Yes," replied Telza, "that is Albinet, the king's eldest son. Iarine grieves to part with the poor child, and she prayed my husband to amuse him on the lake this fine morning. See there, he is guiding the rod which the young prince holds in his hand! Ah! now a fish comes out of the water, and poor Albinet fancies that he has caught it. How quietly the good old man drew his hand away, and left the rod and line, and the prize at the end of it, in the young one's possession!" "But the boy is lame!" cried the prince; "what strange motions he makes in trying to leap for joy!" "Till he was four years old," cried Telza, mournfully, "that child throve and grew like mown grass after the rain. One evening he played alone by the lake side, and from that hour he has been palsied and sickly. Home he came, looking all aghast, like one that had seen a spirit; and verily I believe that he met with something more than the damp air and biting gales of the season."

VIII

Phantasmion is guided by the fisherman to Polyanthida

Phantasmion was glad when he saw young Albinet lifted into a boat which was sent to take him back to the island; and he loudly hailed the kind old man, who attended to his summons, and was soon standing beside him on the stone peir. "My good host," cried the youth, "canst thou conduct me to the house of Magnart in Almaterra?" "That I can, right easily," the fisherman replied. "I oft go thither to sell fish; for we have a delicate sort in our lake which is found nowhere else, and the women of these parts have a choice method of preserving them with spices." "It is well," replied the youth; "I feel myself able to pursue my journey this very hour, and am desirous to reach the place I told thee of by the nearest road." "The nearest road," replied the old man, "is a rugged one; it lies among the Black Mountains; but it would bring thee to Almaterra some time before they who are winding through the plain will reach it." The prince was glad to become acquainted with the passes of the country; and still more he exulted in the hope of being speedily brought to the presence of the island princess. "Find me a good mule," cried he, "which cares not for rough ways; and as well as he plays his part shall I play mine."

Before the sun began to slant down his westerly path, Phantasmion and his ancient guide, seated on mules as sure-footed as rock-goats, but far more discreet and serious, were ascending a zig-zag road along a ridge of the Black Mountains. Telza had furnished them with provisions; the beasts knew every step of the journey even better than the guide; and thus the travellers wound their way for several days over the sides of hills and through bleak valleys, resting at night under the brow of a rock, or in the scanty shelter of weather-beaten pine trees.

At last they reached a deep gully, where the mountains reared their black fronts on either side, abrupt and steep, as if the double range had formerly been one, and had been split asunder by lightning. The blue sky formed a bright roof to these grim walls, which the sun vainly strove to illumine, and was the only sight that relieved the eye from sameness of gloom, except a rivulet which laboured along the bottom of the glen, meaning audibly in the summer silence, its weak voice intercepted by no sound of beast, or bird, or busy insect. "Yon falcon comes from Palmland," observed the guide. "See where she flies over the crags on the left hand. Doubtless her nest is hid among those airy battlements." "A wise bird!" cried the youth. "She keeps on the borders of a plentiful land, yet rears her young securely in a barren desert. This glen will be an utter solitude when we have left it." His comrade smiled as he answered, "Thinkest thou that we have no living neighbours but the falcon and her brood? Then come this way." Curious to know the meaning of the old man's smile, Phantasmion followed him to the edge of a pit, the black mouth of which he had taken for the shadow of rocks, and heard a noise as he approached like thunder imprisoned beneath his feet. The calm looks of his guide assured him that no earthquake was coming on; and, lying down, so as to bring his ear over the darksome gulf, he began to distinguish loud laments in divers languages, wicked words and piercing outcries, shouts of anger, accents of woe, and, mingled with tyrannical voices, the resonance of blows, the clank of chains, and the crashing of rocks—all these noises reverberated a hundred fold through the windings of the subterranean abode, and composed a whirlwind of sounds which smote the listener's ear with horror as it rolled upwards through the black abyss. "What place of torture is here?" exclaimed the youth, retreating from the chasm. "This is the famous iron mine," his guide made answer; "the same that caused such feuds between our king and his ancient ally. Glandreth discovered what riches these rocks contained while following his father's stray goats up the glen. Forthwith he stole across the hills into Palmland, and sold his secret to king Dorimant. This, and nought but this, was the foundation of his grandeur. Now he uses the mine both as a place of punishment and of safe custody: hither he sends his captives from foreign lands, all public malefactors, and all of every age and sex and rank who trespass against his lawless will." Phantasmion proceeded somewhat thoughtfully; but ere long he had ceased to think of Glandreth, how he began, or how he maintained his fortunes, and was musing on the bright lady Anthemmina, whom Dorimant had abandoned for the sake of this bleak vale, and whose wrongs he resented the more from having unconsciously clothed her with the form and countenance of Iarine.

The travellers continued to follow the stony path, and, on emerging at last from the mountain gorge, surveyed a prospect as little like the savage wilderness that had brought them to it, as the young monarch's dream of love and joy resembled the warlike projects by which he hoped to realize that soft and radiant vision. Turning round a broad rock they beheld the vale of Polyanthida, vested in sunny green, luxuriant with orange groves, meadows of golden bloom and sloping gardens, whence the rainbow might have borrowed all its colours. From the high ground where the travellers stood, they looked down upon a bright blue lake, partly girt by hills of soft wavy outline, clad in freshest verdure, to which an amethystine tinge was imparted by blossoms of the fragrant thyme. The skirts of these grassy hills were bathed by the water, while on the opposite side was a thick wood, stretching beyond the rocky shores, which looked as if they had been carved by a graver's chisel, and formed bays and promontories overhung, here and there, with knots of drooping trees. The well attired valley seemed to smile on the lake, which smiled radiantly in return, as a conscious beauty, beaming on her lover, causes his face to brighten with pleasure and hope. The little brook, too, which had murmured so fretfully in the darksome pass, now gushed with a wider stream, arrayed in sparkling white, and bounded to the lake, raising a gladsome cry as if of thankfulness at having escaped from those torturing rocks and that dreary prison. "Where is the mansion of Magnart?" inquired Phantasmion, charmed by the view of this delicious region. "Beyond that wood it rises," replied the fisherman; "verily, thou wilt find it as rich and noble a tenement as ever a groping miner found his way to. Time was when Magnart and Glandreth dwelt with their father in a lowlier hut than mine." "And how did they reach the height where we now see them?" asked Phantasmion. "Have I not told thee of the mine?" replied the fisherman. "Had they no natural gifts then?" inquired the youth; "did the mine supply hands as well as materials?" "Gifts!" cried the old man, warmly; "what need they natural gifts who have supernatural helpmates? moreover, they never scrupled to blast anything that stood in their way, and now I believe they would blast each other if the power answered to the will." Discoursing thus, the youthful king and his guide pursued their way down the slanting path into the flowery vestibule of Almaterra, and soon struck into the wood which lay between the lake and the dwelling of Magnart. They had not proceeded far in the woodland path when Phantasmion stopped short, listening to a voice which struck him as having some resemblance to that of Iarine; and looking down the wood he descried a graceful maiden throwing garlands around the neck of a white stag. At this sight the youth leaped from his mule, turned his glowing face to the old man, and hastily thanked him for his services, at the same time that he put into his girdle a handful of gold. "O, thou hast overpaid me!" cried the fisherman; "but shall I not guide thee to the goodly mansion?" "No!" said the prince: "only take charge of my mule, and return when thou wilt to the Black Lake, bearing a kind remembrance from me to thy good dame." The prince added a jewel for Telza to the gold already given to his guide, who, having by this time spied a lady in the wood, and thus gained a twilight glimpse of the youth's mind, bade him farewell, and proceeded to a neighbouring village.

Phantasmion advanced into the forest, and, looking from behind an oak tree, beheld the slender damsel caressing the stag, whose white hide was dappled with minute shadows from a branch of aspen, the sunbeams finding their way through the interstices of its delicate foliage. The lady had intermitted her melody, but now resumed it, addressing thus her happy comrade, who seemed to be conscious he was the subject of the strain:—

> Sylvan stag, securely play,
> 'Tis the sportful month of May,
> Till her music dies away
> Fear no huntsman's hollo;
> While the cowslip nods her head,
> While the fragrant blooms are shed
> O'er the turf which thou dost tread,
> None thy traces follow.

> In the odours wafted round,
> Those that breathe from thee are drowned;
> Echo voices not a sound,
> Fleet one, to dismay thee;
> On the budding beeches browse,
> None shall come the deer to rouse;
> Scattered leaves and broken boughs
> Shall not now betray thee.

> Sylvan deer, on branches fed,
> 'Mid the countless branches bred,
> Mimic branches on thy head
> With the rest are springing;

Smooth them on the russet bark,
Or the stem of cypress dark,
From whose top the woodland lark
Soars to heaven singing.

Here a livelier voice from another quarter of the forest, where the ground dipped into a dell, took up the strain and continued the song thus, as if in a spirit of gay mimicry:—

Bound along, or else be still,
Sportive roebuck, at thy will;
Wilding rose and woodbine fill
All the grove with sweetness,
Safely may thy gentle roe
O'er the piny hillocks go,
Every white-robed torrent's flow
Rivalling in fleetness.

Peaceful breaks for thee the dawn,
While thou lead'st thy skipping fawn,
Gentle hind, across the lawn
In the forest spreading;
Morn appears in sober vest,
Nor hath eve in roses drest,
By her purple hues exprest
Aught of thy blood-shedding.

The damsel was by this time seated on the projecting roots of a large tree, finishing a long wreath of flowers, while the stag lay beside her and seemed to watch her motions. She continued to murmur in a low key, but in unison with the voice which proceeded from the dell, and which was joined by one of deeper tone, in these latter verses:—

Milk-white doe, 'tis but the breeze
Rustling in the alder trees;
Slumber thou while honey-bees
Lull thee with their humming;
Though the ringdove's plaintive moan
Seem to tell of pleasure flown,

On thy couch with blossoms sown,
Fear no peril coming.

Thou amid the lilies laid,
Seem'st in lily vest array'd
Fann'd by gales which they have made
Sweet with their perfuming;
Primrose tufts impearl'd with dew;
Bells which heav'n has steep'd in blue
Lend the breeze their odours too,
All around thee blooming.

None shall come to scare thy dreams,
Save perchance the playful gleams;
Wake to quaff the cooling streams
Of the sunlit river;
Thou across the faithless tide
Needest not for safety glide,
Nor thy panting bosom hide
Where the grasses shiver.

When the joyous months are past,
Roses pine in autumn's blast,
When the violets breathe their last,
All that's sweet is flying:
Then the sylvan deer must fly,
'Mid the scatter'd blossoms lie,
Fall with falling leaves and die
When the flow'rs are dying.

But now the damsel seated under the tree, arose and began tripping towards the lake; as she went on she caught a glimpse of Phantasmion's figure among the trees, and sportively flung the stalks of flowers from her basket toward the place where he stood, crying aloud, "Come, brother, quit thy melancholy humour! thou wilt not lean all day against that gnarled oak when fair Iarine is seen amongst us." These words, and the countenance of the speaker, dissipated the illusion which had made Phantasmion's heart beat so tumultuously. Fair and sweet was that youthful maiden, but only so far like Iarine as the wild bloom

SARA COLERIDGE

of eglantine, dancing in every gale, resembles the splendid rose of a hundred petals. She took her way to a brake which was close beside the water, and Phantasmion resolved to follow her; for he surmised that she was one of Magnart's fair daughters, of whom Telza had spoken to him, and that by her he might be pleasantly introduced to the chief's household. Moving toward the brake he beheld the lady stoop down to gather marigolds, which grew far beneath the brambles, and he saw, what she could not see, a panther masked by those briars. The beast had now advanced one paw from behind the bush, and was touching the earth with his white bosom, about to spring on the stag, which seemed aware of its danger, as it stood between the panther and the unconscious fair one. That sight restored Phantasmion to all his former agility; from the place where he stood he leaped close up to the face of the glaring beast, which bounded back into the forest, and was out of sight ere the prince could draw his sword to despatch it. After vainly pursuing it to some distance, he returned to the brake, and saw the slender maiden lying in a swoon beside the brambles; her flaxen hair was caught among the thorns; the basket of flowers lay overturned upon the sod, and one crimson blossom rested beside her colourless cheek. The gentle stag was standing beside her, looking down lovingly on her wan countenance, while the gay garlands yet hung from his neck.

Phantasmion scooped water from the lake and sprinkled it upon her cheeks and brow. While he knelt beside her she revived, and blushed on beholding the bright countenance that bent over hers. She withdrew her eyes from his face, and they rested on a blue scarf, which was bound across his breast, and peeped from beneath his upper garment as he leaned forward. "Didst thou know Dariel of Palmland?" she inquired, looking earnestly at the figures embroidered on the scarf. "He was my dearest friend," replied Phantasmion. "And did he give thee that silken band?" asked the damsel fearfully. "Alas!" cried the youth, "I took it from my Dariel's corse, and now am wearing it for his beloved sake." The lady closed her eyes and would have fallen to the ground, but Phantasmion's extended arms received her, and, on recovering, she led the way to that hollow glade whence the two voices that chimed in with her sylvan song had proceeded.

The fair damsel advanced before the prince, who, on entering the shady dell, espied another beauteous maiden seated on the bank, with her eyes cast down upon a picture that lay in her lap, while a slender youth was twining a chaplet of dewy lilies of the vale amid her raven tresses. "Leucoia!" cried the maid, when she heard the rustle of leaves, but still without raising her eyes from the picture, "see what a lovely wreath our Karadan has been making, though not without my aid; he now vouchsafes to try it upon me, but I fear it will have lost it freshness ere Iarine comes to wear it." The youth had by this time dropped the chaplet on the ground, and was gazing with a bashful air on his sister's companion. And now the dark-haired lady caught sight of Phantasmion, and springing from her seat, came gaily forward, while the picture fell amid a heap of flowers. "My sister!" she exclaimed, "what has detained thee?" and so saying she cast a hasty look, with her bright black eyes, at the stranger.—"Zelneth," replied the damsel, "but for this noble youth I might never have returned at all;" and then she related how Phantasmion had driven away the panther. On hearing this tale the sprightly maiden melted into tears, and Karadan, forgetting his reserve, exclaimed, "Would that I had been with thee, dear Leucoia! I thought I had slain the last panther which lurked in the forest."

Phantasmion looked somewhat sternly on him who had been preparing a chaplet for the island maid; and Karadan appeared little delighted when the princely stranger, who called himself Semiro, a friend of their former guest Dariel, declared that he was bound for the house of Magnart. But Zelneth smiled blithely, her eyes yet glittering with tears, and thus she spoke: "The house of Magnart is the house of our father, and Karadan will guide thee to it, kind Semiro. Come, dearest Leucoia, what will our mother say when she hears of thy jeopardy? Thou art as delicate and as dearly prized as the frail bloom of wind flowers, which the first eager gale scatters abroad."

Then the fair maidens arm in arm proceeded to their stately home, and the stag was left browsing amid a herd of deer. Phantasmion followed them along the varied scenes of a wide pleasure-ground, and was conducted by Karadan to a splendid apartment, where a man of dignified aspect reclined on a sofa. This comely personage wore a head-dress adorned with jewels, and a superb scarf thrown over a pelisse composed of feather down, which gleamed with bright reflections, changing according to the play of light. The chief rose from his couch and courteously received the youth of noble demeanour, who was presented by his son. Karadan then hastily departed: a pang of jealous fear shot across the heart of Phantasmion as he quitted the apartment, but the expectant face of Magnart recalled his wandering thoughts, and all his warlike plan was once more brought to mind. With grateful gesture and flowing utterance he had soon told his story, professing that he was an envoy from Palmland, had travelled in disguise through the land of Rocks, and was sent to learn whether his sovereign might hope for aid from the kings and chiefs of Almaterra, should his country be invaded by its hostile neighbours. The countenance of Magnart brightened as Phantasmion spoke, and he received the tale exactly as it was told him, being apt to take all things which bore the image and superscription of his reigning desire, without a scrutiny. "Thy master's foes," cried he, "should be friends of mine; myself and Albinian married two daughters of Cleoras, son of Thalimer, and that king's mighty general is mine own brother. Nevertheless, I will not uphold Glandreth in his over-weening ambition: if he invades Palmland he shall have to encounter me, and I will speak on thy master's behalf with the heads of this realm." It was plain that not ambition displeased Magnart, but the success which that of a rival had met with. "Glandreth invaded Tigridia," said he, "on a mere pretext; and now, forsooth, he is puffed up with his conquest, and must give law to all the world. He threatens me doughtily, because I keep fast hold of Polyanthida in my wife's right. Who denies that one half was Anthemmina's portion? Ill befall them that put away the mother, and would rob the daughter of her inheritance! Safely will I guard it for that precious child till I can marry her to my eldest son."

Phantasmion was more startled by these last words than if they had proclaimed designs upon the Land of Palms; and Magnart, seeing the youth's darkened brow, began to protest that this marriage would make no change in his policy, and that Karadan would not fail to oppose any injustice which might be carried on in the name of his wife's father. But all his smooth words were as drops of hot lead to the feelings of his hearer, and, while the chief swore that he would leave no stone unturned to annul the alliance between Almaterra and the Land of Rocks, Phantasmion thought of nothing but how to prevent that between Iarine and Karadan. For this cause he thankfully accepted Magnart's invitation to pass that night under his roof. "We have not quite settled the matter yet," said the self-pleasing noble, as he led his guest to another apartment, there to repose till supper time. "Now Heaven forbid," thought Phantasmion, "that it be settled according to thy scheme! Could I but see the minds of the other parties—in this hope I tarry here." Having donned fresh robes he lay upon a sofa near an open door, that led into the garden, and, musing on what his host had let fall, watched the shades of evening sadden the landscape, while nightingales saluted her approach with varied song; till after a time, this strain, breathed forth more earnestly than theirs, was borne upon the breeze:

> One face alone, one face alone,
> These eyes require;
> But, when that longed-for sight is shown,
> What fatal fire
> Shoots through my veins a keen and liquid flame,
> That melts each fibre of my wasting frame
>
> One voice alone, one voice alone,
> I pine to hear;
> But, when its meek mellifluous tone
> Usurps mine ear,
> Those slavish chains about my soul are wound,
> Which ne'er, till death itself, can be unbound.
>
> One gentle hand, one gentle hand,
> I fain would hold;
> But, when it seems at my command,
> My own grows cold;
> Then low to earth I bend in sickly swoon,
> Like lilies drooping 'mid the blaze of noon.

The song ceased, but Phantasmion heard not the nightingales which still warbled in chorus. "The voice of Karadan," thought he, "a passionate rival! but sure that was no happy strain. He is gone; perhaps even now by her side. O what vantage ground he has!" Impelled by this agitating surmise, he advanced towards the other door, and met one who summoned him to Magnart's board.

He followed the messenger, and entering the sumptuous hall, surveyed a spectacle which would have chased all former visions from many a youthful mind. A pyramid of flame suspended from the roof drew out the deepest glow of crimson hangings, and they, in turn, cast rosy splendour on white marble pillars, images, and rich utensils, glittering all around: while over-head the lofty ceiling so vividly portrayed heaven's vault, that it seemed as if the buoyant forms that floated there, looking translucent amid golden ether, and spurning the clouds with their feet, were soon to vanish in the skyey depth. From the hand of one a posy was falling back to earth, and the scattered flowers, which caught the light as they descended, shone like meteors. In the centre of the hall stood a table covered with fruits, wines, and viands, contained in vessels of crystal and gold, among which was a taller one of silver. Arzene, the wife of Magnart, was seated at the board, apparelled as beseemed her queenly figure, which time had ripened into a new aspect of comeliness ere it had lost all the graces of youth. Zelneth sate next, with one full arm resting on the table, while the other held a chaplet of faded lily bells, which she was displaying to her mother when Phantasmion entered the hall. No tresses drooped over her cheek of rich carnation, or veiled the brilliance of her large and liquid eyes, but the raven hair that loosely waved around her head rested on the white expanse below in massy curls, like the volutes of a pillar, and, descending below the gilded cincture's deep recess, wandered along the falls and risings of her soft luxuriant form. Leucoia's figure, easy and graceful as the sapling ash, was seen bending over her mother's chair: her quiet eyes, gleaming through a shower of light ringlets, were fixed on the countenance of Zelneth, and one staid smile responded to the quick motions of her sister's face, which was incessantly rippling and sparkling beneath the breeze of mirthful fancy.

Karadan stood on the other side of Arzene, with his countenance turned away from the table: he held in his hand a javelin, and pretended to be wholly occupied in examining its sharp point, or trying the strength of the nether end by striking it against the marble floor; but half smiles and flitting blushes, which passed over his dark cheeks and brow, and beamed for a moment in his full black eye, evinced that the sallies of his blithe sister had not missed their mark. At the lower end of the board sate Magnart, and he too was smiling and showing so goodly an aspect, that how he gained Polyanthida by winning the heart of that noble heiress appeared to be no deep mystery. A blooming boy sate on his knee and leaned forward with both his arms on the table to catch the jests of Zelneth, at which he laughed louder than all the company, till, on spying Phantasmion, he sprung from his father's knee and ran up to him, exclaiming, "Our cousin is not come! Unkind Queen Maudra—." "Hermillian! hold thy peace!" cried Zelneth, while her brow assumed that lofty air which naturally belonged to it, but which the smiles of youth and gaiety were continually charming away. "Our beloved Iarine returned home of her own accord, when the messenger was sent to tell her of her father's illness." "All a false pretence, I dare be sworn!" murmured the boy as he quitted the apartment, rushing past the prince, whom at first he had taken for one of his familiar acquaintants.

The current of Phantasmion's blood seemed for a moment to be arrested by young Hermillian's announcement, but he made an effort to conceal his feelings, and when he looked on the graceful figure of Karadan, he almost felt glad that Iarine was not there to behold it too. Arzene courteously invited him to join the repast, and, seating himself at the table, he entered into discourse with her and her fair daughters. Zelneth continued her gay smiles, though more chary of her words than before the approach of the noble stranger; and Leucoia's soft brown eyes, that swam in silvery lustre, gazed on the youth when he spoke to others, but when he turned his bright glances on herself, were bashfully withdrawn to rest on the blue scarf still worn across his breast. Phantasmion talked with the damsels, and saw their beauty, but felt it no more than that of the sculptured nymphs which gleamed in white marble behind them.

"We cannot enjoy our cousin's sweet company," said the wife of Magnart, "but let us not forget the delicate conserve which the messenger brought us from her." "Karadan," cried Zelneth, "I warn thee not to taste Iarine's gift, thou wilt be sure to find it as bitter as wormwood." While the dark stripling allowed Arzene to pour some of the rich viand on his plate, his elder sister offered a portion of it to Phantasmion, who accepted her courtesy, well pleased to taste what had come from the hands of the Island princess. After eating a few mouthfuls of the conserve, he fixed his eyes on the vessel from which it had been taken: no sooner had he marked its resemblance to the silver pitcher into which he had seen Iarine pour the many-coloured fish, than his head swam dizzily, the brilliant lights and smiling faces danced before him, then vanished into darkness, and soon he sank fainting from his seat at the board. Karadan, who sat next him, and had been watching his actions instead of tasting the spicy food, held out his arms and prevented him from falling on the floor. Immediately after Phantasmion was surrounded by all who had been sitting round the table, and was borne by attendants, at the command of Arzene, to a luxurious chamber of the palace.

IX

KARADAN TAKES POSSESSION OF
THE SILVER PITCHER

P hantasmion remained without sense or motion for nearly an hour,
but, opening at length his heavy lids, he beheld faces bright and
soft bending over him, and felt as if he had awakened from the sleep
of death and beheld angels watching his reanimation. Arzene, when
she perceived that he was about to raise his head, made a sign to her
daughters and they glided out of the room, while the youth, ere he again
relapsed into unconsciousness, felt as if he had seen but the figures of
a dream. The lady now called to mind a sovereign antidote against
the effects of poison; this she administered, and seeing her patient
recover more thoroughly, she left him to court refreshing slumbers,
guests which, when they need to be courted, never come. The torpor
that lately possessed the prince was now exchanged for restlessness and
burning heat; he rose from his couch, and sought the fresh air from a
balcony which looked out on smooth turf, bounded by a sheet of water.
In the midst of the lawn stood Karadan embracing the silver pitcher
which had lately graced the supper table, as if in an ecstasy of joy; but
soon his looks and gestures changed; the pitcher fell from his arms; he
gazed upon it with a countenance of grief; he clasped his hands; and
his dark face up-turned to the clear calm sky, appeared to quiver with
emotion, while tears that filled his eyes glittered in the moonshine.
Toward his right hand was a tall cypress, on one of the higher boughs
of which an owl standing with his body erect, his wings closed, and his
plumage smooth as ivory, looking like a figure carved out of the wood
of the tree. When Karadan took up the fallen vessel and advanced to
the water's edge, this bird upreared the horn-like tuft upon his head,
and, light as thistle-down, he flew from the summit of the cypress to
a lower bough, only a few feet from the ground. Meantime the dark
youth cast the pitcher's glutinous contents on the grass, and, kneeling
down, immersed the vessel in the water not many paces from the
cypress tree. While he was employed in rinsing it, the owl quitted the
bough, and came hovering around him with such a soft smooth flight,
that the abstracted youth perceived not the bird till he saw its shadow

before him on the gleaming pool; then he lifted up his hand to scare it away, but, after eddying round the lawn with airy motion, it returned to the same spot and began to feed on the fishy mass which had been poured from the pitcher. A merry hoot, mimicking the owl's cry, burst from some part of the mansion: the bird seemed not to heed it, but Karadan started and hastened away, wrapping the pitcher in his loose garment.

Phantasmion's attention was now arrested by ringing laughter, and the name of Iarine uttered repeatedly in two different voices, one low and murmuring as the rustle of a willow grove in the wind, the other high and clear as the breeze that plays among the pendulous branches. He moved towards the place whence the sounds proceeded, and beheld the interior of an apartment on the same floor with that which he had quitted. The curtains in front of the chamber had been closed, but were now drawn partly aside to admit the air, and, through this open space, Phantasmion had glimpses of Zelneth and Leucoia, untwisting their platted hair beside a lofty mirror. Their words came distinctly to his ear as he stood under the awning beside the drapery of the apartment, but now they had changed the subject of discourse. "The picture!" cried Zelneth, "ah! I had forgotten! it must be lying in the wood." "Trampled beneath the hoofs of deer, mayhap," rejoined Leucoia, "or perchance, the hare has found it smooth enough to couch upon." "Well," replied her sister, "I would that Penselimer had no other perfidy than mine to complain of. He scarcely knows my face." "Yet how hast thou dwelt on his!" rejoined Leucoia; "how hast thou imagined the strain he is breathing forth, and heard the very sounds of the harp-chords which he seems to be striking! None but Penselimer, no living breathing lover—" "Dear Leucoia," cried Zelneth, "why remember dreams which even the dreamer has forgotten? I have ceased to be a child—" "Since this morning!" rejoined Leucoia in a low tone. Zelneth laughed, and with some hesitation she answered, "The visions of our earliest years soon fade away, or serve but to brighten the image of some real object, like forms of frost that shine in the chill morning, but, when the sun is high, are changed to dew-drops which sparkle on the firm green leaves." Leucoia sighed, and Zelneth said, with a glance of kindness, "Shall I ask Semiro to give thee that scarf, Leucoia?" "Hast thou such influence?" the maid replied. Zelneth looked up and perceived that Leùcoia strove to prevent a tear from descending upon her cheek. "Dear sister," she said, "thou art still tremulous from thy jeopardy in the morning. I had begun to think thou hadst forgotten Dariel, or remembered him only as I do." The tears now trickled down Leucoia's face and Zelneth hung over her in silence, seeming at a loss for words of comfort.

Phantasmion was about to retire, but at that moment Karadan entered the room, and the prince felt constrained to tarry. The youth lingered for a while by Leucoia's side, as if he had something to say or to hear spoken of; but the sisters were silent, and he was about to leave the room, when Zelneth laid her hand upon him, saying, "Stay, brother, and tell us what thou thinkest of Semiro? Hast thou ever seen a youth of more noble aspect?" "I have seen many comely faces ere now," replied the boy, "and some that are better worth studying than his." "The comeliness of Semiro's face may be seen without much study," answered the fair damsel with a smile; "but, dear Karadan," she added, "I have been thinking of that fearful beast which still lurks in the woodland. When the stranger is recovered, pray invite him to hunt the panther with thee." "Dost thou think I need his aid?" cried the youth warmly. "'Twere folly to reject so good a thing when it comes in thy way," replied the maiden. "What hindered him from despatching the beast this morning?" rejoined the dark youth. "Not want of manliness," cried Zelneth quickly; "Karadan, to judge from looks, I should say he would wield sword and lance better than thou." "That is as shall hereafter appear!" exclaimed the son of Magnart with flashing eye: at that moment he grasped his javelin and advanced further into the room, so that Phantasmion saw his countenance plainly. The prince began to glow, and, forgetful of everything but the menacing looks of Karadan, he laid his hand on the sword in his girdle, but, recollecting that he was unseen, he refrained from drawing it forth. "Yes, yes," cried the youth in a low smothered voice, "I am neither fit to win a lady's love, it seems, nor to do her manly service." Here Leucoia turned from the glass, with her fair dishevelled tresses in her hand, to look upon Karadan's flushed face, while Zelneth playfully sank on one knee, and, catching hold of her brother's robe, besought his pardon with arch humility in her smiling eyes. "Dear brother!" she cried, "I spake but in jest; what I think of thee in very truth—" "Nay, spare thy assurances, dear Zelneth," said Leucoia, "Karadan little cares how he looks in thy glass. If thou couldst assure him that Iarine will not prefer Semiro to Karadan, that anxious brow would become as smooth as this mirror." The blood was rapidly overspreading the face of the agitated youth as Leucoia spoke thus, and Zelneth, quickly rising from the floor, exclaimed, "Hath Semiro seen

Iarine then? how knowest thou that?" "I do but guess it," answered Leucoia; "certainly he seemed to know that we were expecting our cousin, and when he heard that she was not to come I saw him turn quite pale, and look as much distraught as thou and Karadan are looking now." Leucoia's hint had indeed banished all the gay looks and dimples from her sister's countenance, just as a pebble, flung into a pool, causes a crowd of circling insects and glancing fishes to disappear; but quickly they return, and as quickly did the face of Zelneth resume its easy brightness, while the eyes of Karadan seemed ready to overflow, and, to hide the tears that would not be repressed, without another word, he left the apartment.

When Karadan had withdrawn Phantasmion too retired, and sought the chamber he had quitted, where keen thoughts stimulated his mind till sleep suppressed them with imperceptible hand, and presented in their stead her strangely mingled pictures. But at early dawn those thoughts rose up again to awaken the sleeper; he left his couch, descended to the lawn by winding stairs that led from the balcony, and walked beside the shallow lake. Thence he roamed on to a rich garden where the flowers were still sleeping covered with dew, and the marble statues which gleamed in morning's timid light, now that living company was absent, seemed to share the beauties of their pleasant home with the lonely wanderer. Entering a dim alley, Phantasmion was struck by one still and graceful form, which, though not seen in front, appeared more perfect than any he had passed. It was crowned with fresh flowers and stood beside an arbour, the head thrown back, the arms uplifting an amber coloured urn, which glowed in light admitted at the end of the arched walk. Phantasmion admired the easy air with which those polished arms sustained their burden, the swan-like throat inclined a little to one side, and the full drapery flowing in soft curves from its deep and narrow zone. But sure those folds are not of marble! they undulate in a passing breeze, and glossy tresses gleam between the rose-wreath which partly hides them. "Is it clear?" cry voices from under the trees. "Clear as clearest amber," replied the fancied statue, turning round and showing the face of Zelneth. At sight of the prince her eyes brightened; smiling and whispering she gave the urn into the hand of Leucoia, who had come forth from the arbour, and now returned to her seat within, among heaps of rejected flowers and vessels of new wine.

A blush slightly tinged the prince's cheek as he greeted the fair

SARA COLERIDGE

daughter of Magnart, but it rose somewhat higher when young Hermillian, who sate at Leucoia's feet, looked up with eyes of wonder and exclaimed, "Well! here thou art, and neither of us need go far to serve thee! Dost thou see that yellow wine? It was prepared for Iarine, but thou art to drink it—to my sorrow. Not that I am sorry for thy being here; and let me tell thee, good Semiro, that I was the chief maker of the delicate beverage. Indeed now, sister! Did I not gather more than half the flowers? And I would have carried it to thy chamber too, but Zelneth cried, 'Peace, child! Dost think I will trust thee with it?' Yet other days I had need be shod with wings"——Here the prattler suddenly paused, struck by the altered looks of Phantasmion, who had relapsed into his former weakness, and now reeling forward fell upon the floor of the arbour close by his side. "O haste, Leucoia," cried Zelneth; "seek for some one to bear Semiro to the house." Leucoia departed, and soon returned with Karadan, who bore Phantasmion to a couch in one of the apartments of the mansion.

The youth quickly recovered from this slight renewal of former illness, and looking up he again beheld Zelneth. He now blushed more deeply than before, and a smile, which he could not suppress, played upon his lips when he saw the beautiful maiden standing a little way off, with her eyes timidly cast towards him. Alas for Zelneth! she is deceived by that bright smile, and takes for feelings like her own the glow of youthful fancy, which loves to feed on images of joy, and kindles at the sight of beauty, even while the heart lies still, as a bird beneath its mother's wing, "Take this juicy citron," said the damsel; "my mother sends it thee." In speaking these words, she cast a momentary glance at the stranger, then threw down her eyes while she offered him the fruit. Phantasmion took the citron and seemed intent on tearing it apart, but all the time he was thinking how he might lead the fair Zelneth to speak of Iarine. At last he resolved to break the spell which seemed binding him to silence; he took the hand of Zelneth, like one who is about to plead earnestly, and looking in her face with an animated expression, "Fairest maiden—" he said; but at those words he paused, having caught sight of another face reflected in an opposite mirror. It was that of Leucoia, who stood near the door behind the curtains of the couch; her head was drooping, and tears were about to flow from her pale face into her bosom; while Zelneth stood erect, with brightest bloom upon her cheek, and strove to hide her joy under an air of majesty. So after summer rains we see a stately flower raising its crimson disk to hail the sunshine, while underneath, the snowy bells of some frail plant lean forward on their bending stem, and still weep dew-drops. Leucoia stole away and Zelneth followed her, not casting a glance at the noble youth of whose heart she now felt secure.

X

Hermillian charges Karadan with
poisoning his owl

Phantasmion was musing on the demeanour of Zelneth and Leucoia when their mother approached him with a cup and phial in her hand. At sight of her the prince leaped lightly from his couch, and the lady exclaimed, as he made his courteous obeisance, "It glads me to find that thou hast more need of pleasant food than of bitter infusions; come with me, I pray thee, and partake of a simple repast." Phantasmion attended his gentle hostess to an apartment where Magnart and the household were already assembled, but the first object that struck his eye was young Hermillian. The boy refused the dainty fare which his sisters offered him, and stood with his back to the table, looking on the body of a large bird which lay motionless on his outspread palms, without a sign of life in its prominent eyes. "O, father! he never blinks in all this light!" cried the sorrowful child, his blooming cheeks flooded with a fresh gush of tears; "he is stone dead, and I know who it is that has killed him." Hermillian repaired to his father's side, and continued weeping and whispering in the ear of Magnart, who bent forward to listen, while Karadan kept his eyes fixed on the board in moody silence, and Arzene cast inquiring glances, first at one of her sons and then at the other. Phantasmion looked at the dead bird, and thought it was the same which fluttered over the head of Karadan the night before. New suspicions crossed his mind as he remembered the pitcher and its noxious contents: he took no heed of Zelneth, whose beaming eyes were fixed upon his countenance; nor thought for a moment of Leucoia, who watched to see whether that gaze was returned. "Speak aloud, Hermillian," cried Magnart, "I cannot understand this muttering." The child cast a side-long glance at Karadan; then, wrapping himself in the loose portion of his father's robe, he began his voluble story. "Last night," said he, "I made an outcry in my sleep, for I thought that an arrow whizzed through the air, and pierced my own poor owl to the heart. 'Go to sleep again,' said my nurse, 'the owls are hooting, and their noise has put this dream into thy head;'—but, as I would not be pacified, she took me to the window, that I might look out and see with my own eyes that he was alive and well." "How didst thou know it was thy owl?" said his father. "O! I know every feather of him," replied the child eagerly; "I first found him in his nest, nigh the top of an old tower, when he was covered with mere down, and, as soon as I looked in, he raised himself on his legs, puffed out his body and began to hiss at me, just as baby sister does when I offer to take away her playthings." "But what was the owl doing last night?" said Magnart. "Alas!" cried Hermillian, resuming his mournful countenance, "he was perched on a lower bough of the cypress near the pond, and up went the feathers of his head into a goodly ruff, while he bent forward and peered down on busy Karadan." "Be silent, foolish boy!" cried his brother sternly, and Arzene, who had been observing her son's troubled looks with surprise, beckoned to Hermillian; but Magnart said, "Nay, Karadan! let us hear how the owl met his death;" and the boy exclaimed, "He met his death by eating the conserve which Karadan threw out of the pitcher; I hooted to him over and over again, but he would not answer me, so eager was he to feast upon that poisonous food." "Prithee, mother, send him away," cried the dark youth; "how canst thou suffer him to babble so foolishly!" "Yes, Karadan," the younger boy rejoined, with a glance of defiance, which he cast over his father's shoulder, after having climbed the back of his chair, "and thou didst not taste a morsel of the mess thyself, though helped to it abundantly. Arzene commanded Hermillian to be silent, but she looked with a grave countenance at Magnart, and said, softly, "My husband, what thinkest thou of this?" "Indeed I think," replied he with a lofty smile, "that Iarine can send no dish wherein Maudra may not mingle poison. We must transplant that sweet flower to a happier soil: what sayest thou, Karadan?" His son and his guest both reddened at his speech, but on Karadan's cheek the flush subsided into deadly paleness. "Where is the pitcher, good wife?" cried Magnart, smiling; "has our eldest son stolen it? Thou seest what grievous charges are preferred against thee, Karadan." "Nay," replied Arzene, looking with persuasive mildness on the gloomy countenance of her son; "he has given me his jewelled cup in exchange for the pitcher, though I shall not be long in finding some excuse to give it him back again." "And I have neither cup nor pitcher," said Hermillian, appealing to his father; "and because Karadan is enamoured of Iarine, my harmless owl is to be sacrificed." "The eldest son," cried Zelneth, "has his mother's heart in fee, and other children may but hold the soil under him." "Yesterday," said Arzene, "some of you declared that I favoured my younger children!" Then she

SARA COLERIDGE

took her lute and thus she sang, while Hermillian, who needed no soft music to charm his melancholy away, was sitting on the ground and playing with her train:

Deem not that our eldest heir
Wins too much of love and care;
What a parent's heart can spare,
Who can measure truly?
Early crops were never found
To exhaust that fertile ground,
Still with riches 'twill abound,
Ever springing newly.

See in yonder plot of flowers
How the tallest lily towers,
Catching beams and kindly showers,
Which the heav'ns are shedding:
While the younger plants below
Less of suns and breezes know
Till beyond the shade they grow,
High and richly spreading.

She that latest leaves the nest,
Little fledging much carest,
Is not therefore loved the best,
Though the most protected;
Nor the gadding, daring child,
Oft reproved for antics wild,
Of our tenderness beguiled,
Or in thought neglected.

'Gainst the islet's rocky shore
Waves are beating evermore,
Yet with blooms 'tis scattered o'er,
Decked in softest lustre:
Nature favours it no less
Than the guarded still recess,
Where the birds for shelter press,
And the hare-bells cluster.

Arzene would have taken up another strain, all the good company being silent, though Magnart alone heeded the words of the song, but suddenly, as a rebounding ball, Hermillian leaped into the air: unheeded by any eye but his, the owl had risen from the floor, and sailing along the roof, silent as a snow-flake, disappeared under the arch of a lofty window. Arzene laid down the lute, well pleased to see the happy child bound through the lawn, clapping his hands and hallooing to the owl overhead, then swiftly pursue him into the grove, where he hastened to seek shelter from the sunny glare.

XI

PHANTASMION IS ENTERTAINED BY HIS HOST'S FAMILY IN THE GARDEN

Toward evening Phantasmion was seated beside Arzene in the farther part of the pleasure-ground: on the one hand light cascades twinkled athwart the foliage of a hanging orchard, on the other bright-eyed deer, followed by troops of fawns, tripped into the greensward from a darksome wood, then retiring to the sylvan covert, seemed to grow into that arborous landscape, as their branched antlers mingled with the boughs. Just in front of the bank where he sate, the children of Magnart danced round beds of blooming plants, which rose like bright embroidery from the shaven turf, or, forming one regular line, resembled a flower-spike on which the lower blossoms are fully blown, the others gradually greener and closer up to the sheathed bud which crowns the summit. Zelneth admired the forbearance of Semiro, who kept his seat beside the matron, believing it to be painfully practised for her sake; but, well disposed to tempt him out of this rigour, she approached a tree near the spot he occupied, and, snapping a twig from one of the branches, full half its foliage seemed to fly away; this was a bevy of green doves, which, sweeping rapidly before the prince's eye, proceeded to augment the verdure of an opposite shrub. Phantasmion smiled carelessly as he raised his eyes to the damsel, and that smile was more than returned by Zelneth, who yet lingered under the tree which the doves had deserted. Soon she was springing beside the cascades in the orchard knoll, her loose robe appearing by glimpses betwixt the leaves, white as those foamy streams. Now she bends over them to scoop the water in a shell, and now comes forth again, with the dripping vessel in her hand, attended by a train of squirrels. Go back, blithe squirrels, to your leafy haunts; it is more than a picture that Zelneth now dreams of, and the maiden has no heart to chase you round the lawns and groves. She laid the shell before Leucoia's stag, but he playfully threw it over with his horn, and wetted the foot of his fair mistress. Zelneth heard not her sister's mild reproach, but now grown weary of this game, where all the lover's part was supplied by fancy, she kneels down over against the bank to place flowers in a jar, and seems to be wholly occupied with the rich hues of amaranths and roses, while her softer cheek, on which Semiro perchance is gazing, surpasses the garden's pride in its deep crimson. But soon Iarine's name has caught her listening ear. "Were it not for Iarine," sighed the matron, "father and son might both sink into the grave." The maiden looked up, and saw that the eyes of the prince were eagerly fixed on Arzene; the damask rose, which now fell from her hand, still blushed bright red, but from Zelneth's cheek the hue of joy had faded. In haste she finished her task, and rising from the turf displayed before her mother the vase of various flowers. Arzene praised the well-formed group, and looked with silent pride on her beauteous daughter. "The spirit like the outward form!" Phantasmion murmured. Arzene thought he spoke of Zelneth, but he was far away on the Island of the Black Lake, and saw neither the flowers nor the fair trembler who held them. "Thou wert speaking of Albinet and Albinian," he rejoined; "how saidst thou that they are kept from sinking into the grave?" Zelneth retired, and approaching her sister, poured all that the vase contained upon the garden mould. Leucoia withdrew her vest, which was sprinkled by the water. "A second wetting from thy hand in one short hour!" said the maiden. "And what have the roses done that they must be turned adrift to wither?" "Why does our mother keep him listening to such tedious tales?" cried Zelneth. "Tedious to whom?" replied Leucoia. "If he finds them so he will not listen long."

Zelneth selected a few choice flowers from the heap which lay at her feet, joined graceful buds with half expanded blossoms, then with flushed cheek and fluttering heart, knelt down betwixt Arzene and the prince to fix the posy in her mother's girdle. Phantasmion was still hanging on the words of his hostess, and still the discourse was concerning Anthemmina's peerless child. "Magnart believes," pursued the dame, "that she silently loves our son; but, by Karadan's report, she thinks more of one who is dead and gone, than of those who live but to serve and worship her." Hitherto Zelneth had been studiously disposing the flowers in Arzene's bosom, but now she raised her eyes, and saw Phantasmion with rapt countenance gazing upward, as if he contemplated some glorious vision in the evening sky. Then she bowed her head, and one of her massy tresses fell upon the prince's hand. He started from his reverie, and beheld the lovely Zelneth looking at him with eyes full of love and sorrow, tears on her cheek, and her wild locks, which had broken from restraint, falling in careless abandonment to the ground where she knelt. Again he blushed and smiled, and his was a face on which smiles and blushes appeared to have a tenfold meaning, as sunny weather in a land of flowery waters and crystal meads seems tenfold sunnier than in a barren plain. Quickly as touchwood fires at a spark, while the flint from which it flew is cold as ever, poor Zelneth's heart kindled with sudden joy. Scorning her own distrust, scarce able to endure the tide of pleasure that overflowed her bosom, she rose and glided lightly over the lawn. Meantime, Phantasmion observed Leucoia leaning against a tree, with her eyes turned toward the bank where he sate beside Arzene. The dainty leaves collected for the stag had fallen to her feet: and he too seemed little to heed them, while his large mild eye was fondly fixed on the absent face of the damsel.

But Zelneth wandered on to a pool which gleamed betwixt the unbranched stems of trees like a mirror in its frame. And now she hears the sound for which her ear listens: she cannot be deceived; Semiro is tracing her footsteps. With tremulous limbs, which half refused to carry her forward, she gained the palm trees, and standing between them, eyed the waterfowl which flew out of the bordering wood, and caused a transient whirlpool in the glassy lake with sudden plunge, then made it roar and whiten as they rushed hither and thither on whirring wings. Ere the tumult had subsided, Phantasmion stood before Zelneth; his words were drowned in the hubbub of the waters; but he presented a letter cased in ivory, which the spouse of Magnart, to try his dispositions toward the dark-eyed maid, had charged him to lay before her. Zelneth had forgotten all men but one, and dreamed not that what he held in his hand reported of any heart but his own. With feigned reserve she turned away to caress a graceful bird in mantle of silver grey, which seemed to imitate some stately damsel as it trod the margin of the pool. "Pretty crane," said Zelneth, stroking its silky plumage, "what hast thou to say of thy fair mistress, Iarine? Has she never a thought to bestow upon the living! Wert thou not given to Karadan as an earnest of a better gift hereafter?" The letter in its carved case fell from Phantasmion's hand; his heart throbbed fast; he fell on his knees before the lady, and seizing her robe, exclaimed, "O! Zelneth, Zelneth, this is but one of thy jests? Karadan has not indeed won the heart of Iarine?" Zelneth looked upon his face, where passion was plainly pictured; but now she knew that not for her his cheek glowed, his lip quivered; and, when her eye sought the ground, she espied upon the ivory case, the letters of an unloved name. Pale and speechless she turned away, her heart swelling with sorrow. Midway between the pool and the flowery lawn she joined Leucoia, who, having seen Phantasmion throw himself at her sister's feet, expected to behold the maiden's face beaming with happiness. "I am weary," said Zelneth, in a languid tone; "let me lean on thee. O, sister he loves Iarine!" Then Leucoia saw that her first guesses were true, and became on a sudden fight eloquent, whispering a thousand consolations which she herself had a thousand times rejected. Phantasmion followed them to Arzene's bower, paid many abrupt courtesies to the sorrowful maiden, placed a lute in her hand, and scarce knowing what he said in his confusion, entreated her to sing. Zelneth swept the chords with hurried finger, then accompanied their expressive chime with these words:—

> *While the storm her bosom scourges,*
> *What can calm a troubled sea?*
> *Will the heaving, dashing surges,*
> *Tranquil through persuasion be?*
> *Rest, my soul, like frozen ocean!*
> *Let thy wavy tumult sleep!*
> *Rise no more in vexed commotion,*
> *Heedless where the gale may sweep.*

> *Clouds that have the light partaken,*
> *Round yon radiant planet rolled,*
> *Lingering in the west forsaken,*
> *Soon shall glimmer, wan and cold:*
> *All our thoughts are gay and golden,*
> *While the sun of hope they shroud;*
> *Those bright beams no more beholden,*
> *Turn again to watery cloud.*

> *He that scorns the smiling valley,*
> *Fragrant copse and gentle stream,*
> *Forth for distant heights to sally,*
> *Whence deceptive colours gleam;*
> *Late shall find that cold and dreary,*
> *'Tis but from afar they glow,*
> *Shall not when his feet are weary,*
> *Win the blossomed vale below.*

Having stolen a glance at Phantasmion, who was leaning against the arbour with his eyes fixed on the ground, Zelneth gave him back the lute, when all the company looked eagerly towards him. The prince played a soft prelude, then sang thus:—

Many a fountain cool and shady
May the traveller's eye invite;
One among them all, sweet lady,
Seems to flow for his delight:
In many a tree the wilding bee
Might safely hide her honeyed store;
One hive alone the bee will own,
She may not trust her sweets to more.

Say'st thou, "Can that maid be fairer?
"Shows her lip a livelier dye?
"Hath she treasures richer, rarer?
"Can she better love than I?"
What form'd the spell, I ne'er could tell,
But subtle must its working be,
Since from the hour, I felt its pow'r,
No fairer face I wish to see.

Light wing'd Zephyr, ere he settles
On the loveliest flower that blows,
Never stays to count thy petals,
Dear, delicious, fragrant rose!—
Her features bright elude my sight,
I know not how her tresses lie;
In fancy's maze my spirit plays,
When she with all her charms is nigh.

"Here is Karadan coming from the wood!" cried Arzene, rising, and Phantasmion, glad to leave the arbour, hastened away with her. Magnart, who had now come forth to see his guest, followed with the children, but Zelneth had fallen fainting among the branches of the bower, and Leucoia remained by her side. Ere the company returned to the spot they had left, the dark-eyed maid was weeping on her sister's bosom in that apartment where, from childhood, they had nightly reposed together. "O Leucoia!" she cried, "thy channel was once full, though now the stream is dried at the fountain: but mine has ever been despised, unvisited; the current winds another way, and will not flow there."

XII

AFTER MEETING WITH ADVENTURES IN THE WOOD, PHANTASMION GOES TO SEEK PENSELIMER

Thou hast not found the panther yet my son!" cried Magnart, as he met Karadan coming from the wood with a train of dogs at his heels, and the spoils of a wild beast hanging over his shoulder, "This is the hide of an ounce," pursued he, "I know it by the white ground." "The panther shall not escape me to-morrow," answered the youth, looking as if he would fain have avoided the company that greeted him, as he emerged from the outskirts of the forest. "Semiro will hunt with thee to-morrow," said his father, "Thou wilt not withstand this plea?" added he, turning to his guest, whom he had been urging to prolong his stay in Polyanthida. Upon that Karadan looked sternly at Phantasmion, and striking his spear on the ground, he said in a low, deep voice; "I pray thee, noble stranger, to accept my father's hospitality, but endanger not thy life by pursuing the same game with me." "Noble Karadan," rejoined Phantasmion, with a kindling eye and cheek, "I will pursue no game which I am not as free to follow as thou art; but danger to my life will never deter me from my just enterprise." Then checking himself at sight of Arzene's anxious face and Magnart's uplifted eyebrow, he added in a lighter tone, "surely I have some right to pursue this panther, for it was I who started it first—." "Thou knowest not who started it before thee," murmured Karadan; but at the urgent request of his mother he reluctantly appointed an hour to meet Phantasmion in the wood on the following day, and then hastened homeward, outstripping Magnart, who suited his pace to that of the young children, as well as the stranger youth who remained by the side of Arzene.

Next morning the prince accoutred himself for the chase, and partook of an early repast, at which neither Karadan nor his two elder sisters were present. Arzene looked less cheerily than usual, as she cast her eye round the board, and when Phantasmion set forth, she accompanied him through the lawn, speaking much of Karadan's over hardihood. Hermillian skipped by her side, and drank in more of the morning's balm than even the dewy flowers, which the sun seemed to paint with richer hues, while it stole their tears away. "When shall I be old enough to hunt?" exclaimed the boy, scattering the posy which he had been gathering with rapture: "Dear mother! before I am as tall as Karadan, I will be more venturous and rash than he!" At parting, Arzene placed in the hand of her guest a phial of the precious liquor, which had hastened his cure, bidding him administer the contents to himself or Karadan, should either of them receive a wound that day.

Phantasmion accepted the phial, as he had listened to the mother's story, with a courteous smile, and took his way to the brake, where Karadan had agreed to meet him. He looked around, and seeing no living creature in the wood, except deer and their fawns, he seated himself behind that screen of briars where he had formerly beheld the panther, and having tightened his sandal, began to examine the weapons with which Magnart had provided him. While thus employed, he heard sounds on the other side of the bushes; it seemed as if steps were approaching, then as if some one sate down upon the turf; soon after he saw the head of the white stag, the branches of his horns protruding beyond the shrubs which came down to the water's edge, and, ere he stooped to drink, Phantasmion caught a glance of his mild vigilant eye. From the top of an alder tree a thrush was pouring out the gladdest notes to soothe his patient mate, as she brooded on her nest in one of the brambles that overhung the water. But soon Leucoia's voice traversed the briary fence, and softly warbled these words:—

The captive bird with ardour sings,
Where no fond mate rewards the strain,
Yet, sure, to chant some solace brings,
Although he chants in vain:
But I my thoughts in bondage keep,
Lest he should hear who ne'er will heed,
And none shall see the tears I weep,
With whom 'twere vain to plead.

No glossy breast, no quivering plume,
Like fan unfurl'd to tempt the eye,
Reminds the prisoner of his doom,
Apart, yet all too nigh:
O would that in some shrouded place
I too were prison'd fancy free,

SARA COLERIDGE

And ne'er had seen that beaming face,
Which ne'er will beam on me!

When kindred birds fleet o'er the wave,
From yellow woods to green ones fly,
The captive hears the wild winds rave
Beneath a wint'ry sky!
And, when my lov'd one hence shall fleet,
Bleak, bleak will yonder heav'n appear,
The flowers will droop, no longer sweet,
And every leaf be sere.

Phantasmion hardly noted the meaning of Leucoia's song, but its melancholy murmur haunted his ear as he loitered along in search of Karadan, and it seemed to him as if he had heard the orphan Iarine lamenting that hapless mother, whose image her soul cherished so fondly. By the time that he had advanced some way into the forest, the sun was shining in full fervour, no cloud intercepted its beam, no breeze winnowed the warm air, and roused it from sleepy stillness. The lake, which gleamed through an open space between oaks and beeches, was all one fabric with the vaulted sky; and neither end of the lucid pile, though the lower was more shiny than the upper, contained a single fret or flaw. One little island was visible opposite the place where Phantasmion stood, and the weeping birches that grew upon its margin seemed to be intently studying their own images in the mirror; not one of their light leaflets moved upon its pliant stem. No rapid swallow skimmed over the water, now shooting aloft to snatch an insect, now wheeling round and soaring out of sight; but a lonely heron stood beneath those trees, and seemed as if he had fallen asleep over his task, as if the delicate perch might glance past him unobserved. The deer slumbered in the closest coverts, the birds had ceased to sing, all was profoundly silent, except that from a great distance among the trees, Phantasmion heard the cooing of a dove; but that, too, died away, and then no sound was audible but the murmur of a solitary bee over a bed of flowers, which loaded the sultry air with fragrance. This only moving object attracted the eye of the prince, as he sate beneath a broad-armed oak, wondering at the delay of Karadan; he watched the insect roving up and down among the hyacinths, which grew in countless multitudes far as eye could reach, till a drowsiness began to steal over him, and it seemed while he inhaled the odour of the blossoms, and viewed their soft colours, as if he saw a new flower gradually rising up from among the rest. Rousing himself to look more steadfastly at this strange appearance, he perceived that it was no flower, but an exquisite feminine form, which stood between his eye and the lake's deep azure. A breath would have separated the yellow tresses that lay upon her neck into a thousand diverging threads, as fine as gossamer; vivid bloom was on her cheek, her eyes were blue as the torquois, and her mantle was of the freshest green. A crown of dew-drops glittered on her brow when first she rose, but quickly melted away, and she held by a silken line a leash of butterflies. "Phantasmion!" she said, in a slender, sighing voice, "Phantasmion! thou lovest Iarine the daughter of Anthemmina! O how fair was Anthemmina when she plighted her faith to Penselimer! she was laden with beauty, like the trees of spring, that hide the green of their leaves with amethystine clusters, and garlands of yellow gold!" "Who art thou?" cried Phantasmion, "and why speakest thou thus to me?" The soft phantom replied, "I am Feydeleen, the Spirit of the Flowers; I love the house of Thalimer, but Karadan, to gain the charmed vessel, hath put his faith in other powers than mine. He loves Iarine;"—the spirit continued to murmur the names of Karadan, Iarine, and Anthemmina, but her breath appeared to be stifled. "Speak on!" said Phantasmion, "what hast thou to tell me of Karadan, Iarine, and of Anthemmina?" "Alas!" she feebly answered, "Oloola, the Spirit of the Blast!—go to Penselimer!— to the Deserted Palace!" the fading phantom waved her hand: "Even now," she murmured, "I feel her touch! it is like the hand of death!" While she yet spoke, the delicate colour faded from her cheek; her face began to shrivel; she hung her head; her whole form shrunk; then gradually sinking earth-ward, appeared to re-enter the ground whence it had arisen. While Phantasmion was yet gazing with fixed eyes, the trees, late so motionless, were bent by a rushing blast, which swept, as if in triumph, across the spot where Feydeleen had stood, disturbed the bosom of the glassy lake, then passed away, and soon every nodding hyacinth had ceased to sway upon its flexile stem. Even in the hot sunbeams the prince felt his blood chilled; he rose from his seat and felt an impulse to hasten out of the wood; but at that moment the deep silence of the forest was broken by clamorous yells, and the prolonged sound of a hunter's horn caused the sleeping deer to arise, and the birds to rush from the boughs they occupied, while the heron upon the island started up and sailed off to a distant shore.

Phantasmion passed swiftly on, and soon had sight of Karadan, who stood surrounded by vociferous dogs, with his javelin plunged in the body of a large panther. Indignant at this sight, the prince hurried through the trees, and, coming in front of the young huntsman, he saw that his countenance was full of joyful triumph, as he bent over the grim face of the expiring beast, and that drops of blood were slowly trickling from a wound in his hand into Iarine's pitcher, which he held up to receive them. So intent was he on this occupation, and on gazing at the panther, that he had not perceived the approach of his rival, who, stung with jealousy at what he beheld, and with remembrance of what the Flower Spirit had uttered, stood a little way off, eyeing him with fiery looks, and brandishing his stainless weapon, without knowing exactly in what terms to couch an accusation, or how to challenge one who was already wounded in combat. While he yet hesitated, the prince was struck by the sound of Leucoia's voice, crying "Karadan!" The maiden had heard her brother wind the horn, and, knowing by that signal that the beast was slain, she came flitting through the forest to the place of the encounter. Phantasmion gave up all thoughts of seeking a quarrel with Karadan when he saw his sister approach: he withdrew behind the broad trunk of a tree, and soon afterwards beheld Leucoia binding up her brother's wound with strips torn from her own garment, while the dogs leaped around fawning on the maiden, as if rejoiced at the aid that she rendered to their master. The lady's milk-white stag, fearless of the hounds, with which he had long been familiar, stood beside the bloody pard, and was the only one of the group who seemed to espy Phantasmion, as he lingered among the overarching trees of thickest foliage. "Karadan loves Iarine," were the words that rang in the prince's ear, as he retraced his steps through the forest; and, without re-entering Magnart's abode, he forthwith departed to find that of Penselimer, king of Almaterra.

XIII

Penselimer tells his story to Phantasmion

Phantasmion pursued his journey for several days in that rich land, travelling by leaps, whenever he could do so without attracting the gaze of the rustics, and taking refreshments in the humblest dwellings. He found that the peasant folks in general were quite unacquainted with the person of their king, though they had many strange tales to tell respecting him; but all the certain information in these matters which the prince gained, was, that he lived in retirement with Laona, the mother of Arzene and Anthemmina, the affairs of his kingdom being managed by Sanio, a wise and worthy man, who had been the friend of his father. The prince pursued his way, according to the directions he had received, till he found that blossomed orchards, gardens, and gay buildings, began to be less and less frequent, and it seemed as if, from the land of summer, he had stepped into November's dreary domain. At length he entered a tract which was full of fading flowers and trees, clad in the garb of autumn, and thence proceeded to a bleak and barren moor, where cold swamps, rocks encrusted with ashy pale lichens, or fringed with rustling fern, and twisted uncouth trunks, that looked like mummies of trees as they reclined in sepulchral cavities, were the only features of the stern landscape. One light-coloured object appeared in view just beneath a company of gaunt pine trees that straggled over a stony slope; this was a forlorn mountain ash, with foliage of transparent brightness. The wind came by fits, whistling through the pine grove, and, whenever it shook the fragile ash, a shower of yellow leaves fell from its delicate branches on the steely pool below. Those stagnant waters were agitated by the rough gale, and foaming waves for a moment were visible; then again, relapsing into torpor, they sullenly reflected the sullen sky and the wasting roan tree. Streaks of dull clouds covered great part of the heavens, but, just where the sun was sinking on the horizon, they showed a spectral whiteness, edged with faintest yellow and sea green. In the opposite quarter, the moon appeared like a wan face gradually kindling into life; she looked out from the sky in full splendour while Phantasmion was yet on his way; and, when he saw her beams resting on an ancient castle, surrounded by a moat and a high and thick wall, he knew that he beheld the domain of Penselimer. Arrived at the edge of the moat, he surveyed the barrier before him, and, having taken a good aim, leaped to the top of it, gained a sure footing on the wall, and waved his sword to an ancient domestic, who had espied him from a court-yard below. The old man gazed in astonishment at the youthful figure on the horizon, with nodding plume and glancing sword illumined by the moon-beams. Phantasmion proceeded along the top of the wall, looking down upon groves of cypresses and glistering laurels, till he came over-against a wide lawn which fronted the castle. Down into this grassy plain he leaped, and beheld straight before him an ancient yew tree which rose about the centre of it, casting a gigantic shadow on the moonlit sward. As the prince passed under this tree on his way to the castle, he perceived that a tall man, habited in a long black stole, was leaning over one of its broad arms, and looking from amid its dusky foliage, at the star bright sky. Just then a thin vapour was flitting across the moon; but soon Phantasmion beheld the side of the gazer's face in a clear light, and was struck with the majesty of his features, and the placid melancholy of their expression. He stood still, feeling assured that this was Penselimer, and considering how to proceed; when the man in the mourning robe turned round, and, having scanned his face, exclaimed reproachfully, "Ha! Dorimant; art thou come to render up the silver pitcher?" Phantasmion, who had been continually thinking of Iarine's silver pitcher ever since he first saw it in the hands of his rival, was too much struck with these words to make a prompt reply; but the lofty personage before him pointed to the moon: "Thou art come," said he, "from visiting the lady Anthemmina!" "King Penselimer," cried Phantasmion, a little confused, "I come from Palmland." "It is false," rejoined the monarch, in a tone of solemn indignation; "with my own eyes I saw thee descend from the sky, and alight on the hither side of those fir trees!" Then again he gazed upward at the moon: "I had been pleading with her all this evening," said he; "she was still silent and obdurate; she would not promise to restore the silver pitcher, but now I trust she has sent it by thy hand." "Noble Penselimer," cried the youth impetuously, "I know not what thou meanest by pointing to the sky, and speaking of a silver pitcher." "And perchance," rejoined the king, with a disdainful smile, "thou dost not behold the fair Anthemmina in heaven, and perchance she too will deny that she is at this moment looking down upon thee and me." "King

Penselimer," said Phantasmion, who now began to understand why the sovereign of Almaterra lived in retirement, "I see that fair dispenser of light as plainly as thou dost, and true it is that she has guided me to thy abode; but the lady Anthemmina I never beheld while she sojourned upon earth." "Art thou not mine enemy, Dorimant?" inquired the king earnestly, perusing the features of his youthful visitant. "Dorimant, king of Palmland, sleeps with his ancestors," replied the youth; "I know not why thou callest him thine enemy, nor how he can have injured thee concerning a silver pitcher?" "Ha, indeed!" said Penselimer, "then I will tell thee the whole story of my wrongs! But not here," he added, in a low voice, casting up his eyes to the moon, "lest she should hear the tale: it is my belief she often listens when shame or pride forbids her to reply." Then he moved away, and beckoned to Phantasmion, who followed him, as he strode across the loan, thinking of Iarine with the silver pitcher on her head, and Karadan pressing it to his bosom, and how the fishy woman by the sea-shore, and the bright fairy in the wood had both spoken of a charmed vessel. Penselimer conducted the youth to an apartment in the castle, where a fire upon the hearth cast its light on the walls, hung with dark paintings, and on a harp and other musical instruments which were scattered around. The king of Almaterra made Phantasmion take a seat opposite to one which he himself occupied, and began to speak thus: "There was a time when the beautiful Anthemmina looked graciously upon me, and told me every thought of her bosom: now she veils her face when I gaze upon it, and though I spend my life in assuring her that I seek only to be reconciled, she still persists in chilling silence." Phantasmion looked at the speaker and saw no haggard looks, no traces of anguish on his goodly face; clear and smooth was his high forehead, and the black locks that shadowed it were scarcely sprinkled with grey; but ever and anon his dark eye gave sudden flashes, like silent lightning on a gloomy summer's night. It seemed as if something were at work within, apart from the soul of Penselimer, something dangerous and irregular as lightning itself. Without returning the curious glance of Phantasmion, his eyes appearing fixed on vacancy, he proceeded thus: "One day the lady Anthemmina approached me, radiant with joy as with beauty, she held in her hand a silver pitcher, and placing it in mine, she said: 'Penselimer, while this charmed vessel remains in thy possession, no earthly power can deprive thee of me!' At these words I was full of astonishment; I threw myself on my knees before the stately virgin, and, receiving the

SARA COLERIDGE

pitcher, was unable to utter a word, but looked up eagerly in her face to seek an explanation. Anthemmina smiled, 'Dost thou believe the tale?' said she; 'truly thou may'st believe it. Feydeleen has answered my prayers, for she loves the house of Thalimer.' 'But Thallo, the king of this land,' cried I, 'whom thy father would have thee wed—is not he a descendant of Thalimer, as well as we two? 'Fear nothing from him,' the maid replied; 'Feydeleen, our guardian spirit, appeared to me as I watered the flowers, and in gazing at the bright phantom, I let the pitcher fall from my hands. 'Anthemmina,' she said, 'take up thy pitcher, and he in whose hands thou shalt place it can alone be thy husband; while he keeps it safe no other man can deprive him of thee.' The fairy vanished, and, looking down at my feet, I saw that my earthen pitcher was gone, and that this silver vessel, engraved with curious characters, was lying in its place. From the time that Anthemmina spoke thus I felt like a new creature, and ceased to tremble in the presence of Thallo, or of his young sister Zalia, whom my father would have had me espouse. I cared not who was called the sovereign of this land; the whole world seemed made for me since I possessed that charmed vessel; the rosy dawn, the noon day radiance, the gorgeous sunset, and the spangled firmament, all were but varied images of my inward bliss; to my exulting fancy they were but festal shows, set forth to celebrate my happiness with Anthemmina. Alas! alas! the glory of a sunset gradually gives way to darkness, and by slow degrees the magic spectacle of midnight passes from the heavens; but this radiance which surrounded me, and appeared to stream from a thousand sunny fountains was quenched as wholly and as suddenly as a man may extinguish one poor solitary taper! She took back again that precious gift, one that she had proffered me with such an overflowing measure of unhoped for tenderness; tricked me out of it by cruel art, and gave it to king Dorimant. I saw her place it in his hand. I saw his look of triumph as he held it aloft; more I could not see, for I fell on the ground senseless. O! why did I not pierce him to the heart, that base, perfidious man; doubly, nay, trebly perjured and faithless!" When Penselimer spoke thus, Phantasmion started up, and laid his hand on his sword, forgetting that the true spirit of Penselimer was not there to render account of his words. "My father was an honourable man," the youth exclaimed; "he hath a son at least who will maintain his honour." The king of Almaterra looked at him with majestic composure, as the fire threw its tremulous beam on his flushed countenance, for phantoms were realities to him, and external realities moved him less than phantoms. "How thy face recalls to me that fatal hour!" quoth he, "that hour when the aspect of my fate grew suddenly dark, as the glowing face of the deep will blacken in its whole extent when the wind rushes over it! for years I remained in a state of stupor; Thallo died, and I succeeded to my grandsire's throne; Dorimant delivered the pitcher to king Albinian, whom Cleoras forced Anthemmina to marry; the king of Palmland espoused Zalia, and annexed to his realm her inheritance of Gemmaura; all these events I learned with indifference, nothing roused me till tidings were brought that Anthemmina had perished at sea. Then I repaired to the shore, entered a boat, and roamed over the waste of waters, till at last I beheld my radiant mistress arise out of the waves. From the vessel's prow I stood gazing, and prayed aloud for wings that I might follow her into the sky; but a jeering voice issued from the deep, and seemed to utter these words, 'Where she is gone thou shalt never follow.' I looked down upon the waters and there beheld a round white glistering face, that seemed to be a hideous mockery of that celestial visage. It rose from the surface of the sea, and there stood before me a strange form, half fish, half woman, which held her arms aloft, and her body inclined in the posture of a dancing nymph, while she pointed with one hand at me, with the other at the newly risen Queen of Heaven; then with a burst of merriment she plunged amid the waves, which swallowed in the gurgling sounds of laughter." "And before this memorable night," said Phantasmion, "when Anthemmina took her station in heaven, didst thou never behold that bright orb which is beaming through yonder latticed window?" "Before that night," replied Penselimer, "I never beheld any heavenly orb which was fairer and brighter than the moon. But she, since then, has been so diminished, that I cannot distinguish her from the other stars." "And what has become of the pitcher?" said the prince. "That is the subject of my constant inquiry," replied Penselimer. "Albinian is not long for this world; could I regain possession of the charmed vessel, Anthemmina might yet be mine." While Penselimer spoke these words, an aged lady entered the apartment. "Laona," said the king, "hast thou heard any tidings of the silver pitcher?" "Not yet," replied the ancient dame in a gentle tone; "go now to repose, for Feydeleen will never help us to find the pitcher while the flowers are sleeping. To-morrow we will all renew our search more diligently."

When Penselimer had quitted the apartment, Laona looked earnestly in the face of Phantasmion, and said, "Art thou the son of Dorimant, king of Palmland?" "Even so," he answered. "Alas, then," rejoined the ancient lady, "why comest thou to Penselimer, and the mother of Anthemmina?" "Because I love Anthemmina's beautiful daughter," the ardent youth replied, "and in all truth and honour I seek to lay my crown at her feet. The Spirit of the Flowers knows my love, and she has sent me hither." "And hath she told thee where to find the charmed vessel?" inquired the dame. "Feydeleen decreed that after Anthemmina's time the fortunes of her child should depend upon it, as hers did before?" Phantasmion made no answer, being lost in thought, and Laona added, "Doubtless it is now at the bottom of the sea, for my ill starred child took it with her when she entered that fatal bark which never came to land again. Sweet Iarine knows nothing of this charm; she weeps when she looks on the wild waves of the ocean, but those tears are for her mother alone." Phantasmion felt certain that the pitcher so earnestly embraced by Karadan, must be this charmed vessel, which rendered him master of Iarine's fate, so far as to prevent her union with any one but himself. How he gained it, and how he might be dispossessed of it, were anxious thoughts which cast their shadow over the young prince's brow. Laona perceived his distress: "Come," she cried, "rest thou this night under our roof, and to-morrow we will consider if it be possible to find the pitcher. Since the Flower Spirit favours thy love, she will not suffer thee to seek in vain." Having spoken thus, she led her guest to a chamber of the castle.

When Phantasmion obtained sight of Laona the next morning, he inquired if she could direct him to the Deserted Palace. "Look out over the country," she replied; "below that hill which bounds the horizon thou wilt find the ancient abode of my husband: there we dwelt, with Arzene and Anthemmina, before Cleoras possessed the flowery vale which thou hast lately visited." "What a black cloud," exclaimed the youth, "is resting on the summit of the boundary eminence!" "That cloud," rejoined Laona, "overhangs the dwelling of the enchantress Melledine; she it is who has blasted this region, while Feydeleen vainly endeavours to counterwork her spells. Alas! that outward blasting is but a type of the desolation that she has brought on me and mine. Soon after the Spirit of the Flowers had blest Anthemmina and Penselimer with the hope of their happy union, my daughter met a woman whose face was covered with a shining veil, as she wandered, late in the evening, through an orchard that lies between the palace and the mountain. 'Come to this clear stream,' said the witch, 'and thou shalt see a strange sight.' Anthemmina looked into the water, and fancied that she there beheld the face of Dorimant, her cousin Zalia's suitor, hard by the image of her own. While she was gazing on the shadow in the brook, that wicked enchantress persuaded the maiden to drink out of a cup which she presented to her. No sooner had she tasted its contents than all her affections were transferred from Penselimer to him whose likeness she seemed to behold. Alas! no spell but that which beaming eyes contain was needed to turn Dorimant's fickle heart from Zalia to Anthemmina, and none but that of ambition caused him to break his faith with my faithless child, and again offer his hand to the heiress of Gemmaura." Phantasmion looked sorrowful and abashed, but could not feel anger against Laona, for she spoke as one in whom no affections remain, except such as are fit to live for ever. "Dorimant is dead," she added, "and Zalia and Anthemmina are at rest from their troubles. Penselimer yet lives, and—Hark! his lute is sounding from that gloomy cell, in which it is his pleasure to immure himself till the moon rises." Phantasmion listened and heard Penselimer sing thus:—

> *The sun may speed or loiter on his way.*
> *May veil his face in clouds or brightly glow;*
> *Too fast he moved to bring one fatal day,*
> *I ask not now if he be swift or slow.*

> *I have a region, bathed in joyous beams,*
> *Where he hath never gilded fruit or flower,*
> *Hath ne'er lit up the glad perennial streams,*
> *Nor tinged the foliage of an Autumn bower.*

> *Then hail the twilight cave, the silent dell,*
> *That boast no beams, no music of their own;*
> *Bright pictures of the past around me dwell,*
> *Where nothing whispers that the past is flown.*

The eyes of Laona shone in tears for a moment, but no strong emotion disturbed the serene sadness of her brow. "Alas!" she said, "his are but mockeries of woe, that dwell in the wild brain and never touch the heart. Yet hark again!—" Penselimer was singing,

> *Grief's heavy hand hath sway'd the lute;*
> *'Tis henceforth mute:*

Though pleasure woo, the strings no more respond
To touches light as fond,
Silenced as if by an enchanter's wand.

Do thou brace up each slackened chord,
Love, gentle lord;
Then shall the lute pour grateful melodies
On every breeze,
Strains that celestial choristers may please.

XIV

Phantasmion visits the deserted palace

Having received the blessing of Laona, Phantasmion departed, and, just as the castle towers were sinking out of sight, remembered that he ought to have inquired for the abode of Sanio. Eager, however, to explore Anthemmina's ancient dwelling-place, he hastened forward, now running, now leaping, yet sometimes forgetting even to move, in his deep thoughts concerning past and future events. The sky was clear in every part, except right before him on the horizon; there the dark mass hung so steadily, that it looked more like a black sea than a cloud. At last he reached a smiling peninsula in the sullen ocean of the waste: "Here at least," thought he, "Melledine has not turned the leaves yellow when they ought to be green: here the Flower Spirit hath her way." Phantasmion passed the mossy stones which of yore had formed an outer wall, and now inclosed a neighbourhood of snakes and lizards, and proceeded to a wilderness where commonest weeds up-reared their heads among rare flowers, and towered, and swelled, and blossomed, and seeded, casting out their branches on every side in unassailed prosperity and tranquil pomp. There the soft hyacinth and rich carnation were overtopped by thistles, the full peony blushed among tall grass half hidden, and a solitary arch, that once had been a gateway, was crested with the prim larkspur and spruce jonquil. Over against a green mound, from which the wild goats bounded at his approach, Phantasmion discerned an imperfect outline of two apartments; the first was tapestried with jessamine, and tenanted by owls, who stared with no hospitable looks upon the stranger as he entered their abode; a shallow pool floored the second, reflecting the ruined walls with its arched windows and carved ornaments, over which the eglantine waved its lithe branches, still perhaps to wave them in the gale, when that phantom edifice should have fallen under its breath. Phantasmion paused not here, but went on to find the brook spoken of by Laona, passing orchards where the unpruned boughs were bending under crowded birds and fruit, till, through the close undergrowth, in parts quite impervious, he perceived a stream which flowed through a vaulted opening at the base of a lofty rock, then wandered away to the right

SARA COLERIDGE

hand. Above that rock was a succession of crags, the highest veiled in darkness; and this was the cloud-capped height which he had seen from the castle. Phantasmion approached the stream close to the archway, and, looking on its waters, discerned his own colourless shadow, and nothing more: but, on stooping to bathe his temples in the brook, he perceived beyond the shadow, a picture of himself as vivid and seemingly substantial as that which the finest mirror might have presented. It was not looking as his natural face would have done in a glass at that moment, for his countenance was thoughtful, and bore traces of tears; but the countenance of the picture appeared to be radiant with joy and love. It did not gaze on him that gazed on it, but on another object in the watery depth, the graceful figure of a damsel, holding up a silver pitcher so that it concealed her face, which was bowed down upon her bosom. While the youth still examined the picture, it gradually faded, and he saw only the sparkling sands in the bed of the river; but, ere he turned away his eyes, those very sands had formed themselves into characters, making the names of Dorimant and Anthemmina, Iarine and Phantasmion. Again they were mingled together, and, while he thought to decypher them as before, a tinkling melody rang out from the rocks overhead. It seemed as if they were musical stones touched by some invisible hand with a silver hammer, and soon they seemed to speak thus:

> *Life and light, Anthemna bright,*
> *Ere thy knell these rocks shall ring,*
> *Joy and power, a gladdening dower,*
> *Thou shalt shower on Palmland's king.*
> *Floor of coral, roof of beryl,*
> *Thou shalt find afar from peril,*
> *While thy lovely child is dwelling*
> *Where the palm and vine are swelling,*
> *Crystal streams around her welling,*
> *All the land her virtue telling.*
> *Life and light, Anthemna bright,*
> *Thou to Palmland's king art bringing:*
> *Richest dower, fairest flower*
> *Is from thee for Palmland springing.*

"That king of Palmland is Phantasmion!" exclaimed the youth in ecstacy; "and the watery picture is my likeness, only like Dorimant as I resemble my father. Anthemmina's fair child is mine,—but how am I to gain the charmed vessel?" Full of joyous agitation, he strayed along the margin of the brook, and after a time stooped down to drink; but, ere he had fully slaked his thirst, a cry issued from the opposite bank, while sudden brightness fell upon the water. Phantasmion at first imagined that he had heard the voice and saw the shadow of a king-fisher, whose emerald wings and breast of ardent gold were casting that rainbow gleam on the smooth current; but looking up he espied the green mantle of Feydeleen, floating behind her in a transient breeze, as she leaned from a grove of rushes over the stream, to which her silken bodice, in hue like the honied nectary of a blossom, was imparting its yellow tinge. No sooner had the fairy caught Phantasmion's eye than she pointed up the river to the place where he had beheld the vision, and lo! there was Karadan with his face bent over the waters while the silver pitcher stood on the ground beside him. "Now will I wrestle with thee for that pitcher!" Phatasmion would have cried, but the words died on his lips: an irresistible drowsiness came over him, and down he sank in slumber beside a shady willow. Soon however a gale of sharp fragrance awakened him, and he raised his head; the air had become thick and misty; and Karadan was lifting in both hands a heavy stone, as if for the purpose of crushing the pitcher to atoms. Phantasmion strove to speak, but again sleep surprised him; thought vanished from his mind as the stream from his eye, and with closed lids he fell back under the canopy of the willow. When he next awoke, the clouds that lately capped the mountain had descended to its base, and all was darkness; yet in this darkness there were spasms and slower pulses of light, which, here and there, unveiled the rocks and the river; and one of these discovered Karadan standing bewildered, his right hand raised before his face, as if to repel the mist, and the pitcher hanging from his left. Thereupon, with a shout, Phantasmion rushed forward to attack his rival; but, even as he advanced, the light was swallowed up, and all the force and fury of his onset were bestowed on the stem of a birch tree, while Karadan's misguided weapon was striking a volley of sparks out of the flinty rock, in a cleft of which the tree grew. But soon Phantasmion started back, struck by a plaintive scream close to his ear. Then came the flickering light, and revealed the birch tree which he had so fiercely assaulted, its long pendant boughs laden with moisture, and blood drops trickling down its silver skin. And next, eyes of steady flame were glaring upon him from a hole in the rock, and, while the darkness came on again,

SARA COLERIDGE

he heard a rustle overhead, and then perceived wings as of white fire sweeping onward. While these sights were presenting themselves, the youth imagined that he had wounded some living female frame, and thereby exasperated a demon who kept watch over the imprisoned object of his love; but a second cry from the goblin as he sailed away, and the sense of a slight wound about the bosom, soon made it clear that he had but startled an owl from its hiding place, and stained a senseless trunk with his own blood. After this interruption, he raged about in search of Karadan, on whom at last he fell with an impetuosity which made the pitcher fly out of his hand, and flung the youth himself with stunning force upon the ground, while his own sword was shivered in the encounter. He was bending forward, and groping for his rival, when something plucked him back; at the same time the cloud was rent, and admitted a bright beam just over the spot where the pitcher lay. Again he sprang to seize the vessel, but it was snatched away into the darkness. Doubly baffled at having lost both the prize and his enemy, Phantasmion stood motionless, until he perceived, straight before him, a dim figure glimmering gigantically through a thinner part of the mist. Then, as a great serpent gathers all his might to crush a buffalo of unusual size and strength, letting fall his broken sword, and rushing onward, Phantasmion coiled himself with vast force around his foe; but a loud and bitter cry, followed by earnest words of supplication, induced him to relax his grasp, and, on the outskirts of the mist, he now beheld a woman's form, writhing on the ground, and twisting the ends of a silvery veil which covered her face. On one side all was yet dark; on the other the archway was visible, and, beneath it, an ivory boat, to which a team of swans was fastened. The pitcher had rolled to the side of the brook; Phantasmion caught it up, dipped it in the stream, and, urged by thirst, drank deeply. No sooner had he done so than sleep once more seized him, occupying his senses as fast as vapours in a storm envelope a mountain. He was about to examine a scroll, which he had taken out of the vessel; it fell from his hand, while the pitcher slipped from his bosom; he sank down in deep slumber, with his face toward the stream, and heard neither the voice of Karadan in the cloud, nor the mournful dirge of the swans, which bewailed their lady's anguish with strains that might have preluded their own death, and were given back from under the archway with more and more distant echoes.

On awaking he saw that a gray-haired man had hold of his arm. He started up: boat, swans, and veiled lady were out of sight; the scroll lay upon the ground before him, but the pitcher was gone. "Who has robbed me of the silver pitcher?" exclaimed Phantasmion, looking wildly upon the old man. "One who seemed half inclined to take thy life also," he replied. "When I came hither, he was standing over thee, dagger in hand, yet appeared irresolute." "Which way went he?" cried the youth. "Nay, it were vain to follow him," the ancient man replied; "he set out many an hour ago." "And took the pitcher with him!" exclaimed the prince. "On espying me," resumed the stranger, "he thrust his dagger into his belt, caught up a silver vessel, and went his way. Since that time I have been vainly striving to awaken thee: I guess thou hast been drinking these waters, which flow from the enchanted domain of Melledine, and are well known to produce unnatural sleep. Had I left thee alone in this neighbourhood of spells and sorceries, thou mightest have suffered worse than the loss of a pitcher." "I owe thee many thanks," replied Phantasmion. "Perchance thou canst tell me where I may find Sanio, the king's minister." "Thou hast found Sanio already," rejoined the grey-haired man; "for I am he."

Phantasmion now observed that the air was clear, the cloud confined to the mountain top, and that all around looked as when he first came thither, save that the sun was in a different quarter of the sky. Placing the scroll in his bosom, he led the discourse to Penselimer. "Ay! there flows the stream," quoth Sanio, "which ruined him and this poor kingdom. Yet it is my belief that Anthemmina would never have seen Dorimant's face in the waters, had it not first been pictured in her own fickle heart." "They say that Anthemmina's child is fair and faithful too," interposed Phantasmion. Sanio smiled: "You that are young," he said, "search the past only to illustrate the present; while for us that are old the present has little interest, except as it reflects the past,—alas, how dully! Yes; Anthemmina had a daughter by Albinian, whom she married, after rendering Penselimer unfit to govern either wife or kingdom." "He has no heir," said Phantasmion; "will the son of Arzene succeed him in his throne?" "I would fain have it otherwise," the old man replied. "I have loved Penselimer from a boy, as I loved his father before him. It is for this cause that I repair hither to call on Melledine, and entreat her to bestow some charmed cup or potent herb, that may restore him to his senses. "Melledine!" exclaimed the prince with emotion; "can the hot blast of the desert be persuaded to bear health upon its wing?" Sanio hung his head: "Strong desire," he said, "has deceived me also: lest I should be further deceived, I will go hence."

Phantasmion accompanied the ancient noble through the tangled grove, cutting a way for him amid the bushes; and, when those impediments were past, he spoke of his mission, and of the succours promised by Magnart. "Hope little from him," Sanio made answer, "and trust him with little. Such as he will smile and take in all, and give out nothing but what is noxious,—like glittering bogs, the warmer the sun shines on them, the colder is the air which they exhale!" "This lord of Polyanthida is the counterpart of his ambitious brother, then," Phantasmion observed. "A true copy," replied the minister, "in all but his fine points, and shining qualities. Magnart's train hath no eyes in it; yet he loves to unfurl it as widely as if it portrayed the starry heavens; and rears his crest and sweeps the ground with even more pride and consequence than his brother peacock." "I have heard," said the prince, "that Glandreth is plotting with Maudra to ascend the throne of Albinian at his decease, and moreover to unite Palmland with his dominions." "And art thou ignorant," said the old man, "that his ships are, even now, hovering about the coasts of thy country? We know it well, for they carry off sheep and kine from the land of Palms, and convey them to the plain of Tigridia, which borders on this realm as well as on Rockland." "Then," cried the young monarch, "it is the interest of Almaterra to unite with us against our warlike neighbours: for they will soon be independent of all that her luxuriant fields produce." "To second you," the old man replied, "but not to begin the war. If I were as young as Penselimer, and he as sane as I am, we might move faster in this enterprise. Palmland has a youthful monarch, led him lead the way."

XV

Phantasmion returns to Palmland

Sanio guided his youthful companion to a solitary mansion where he had left his attendants, and the fellow wanderers rested there that night; but, before the aged man had left his chamber, Phantasmion was far upon his road, leaping from field to field, and only stopping to inquire his way and procure food. He slept that night in the shelter of an orange grove, having left the desolate region far behind him; and thus he fared till the blooming vale of Polyanthida came in view. He did not take the road which led to Magnart's mansion, but passed through a valley betwixt the green hills on the further side of the lake and those rugged mountains which overbrowed them. Here he entered a cottage, and exchanged a fine jewel for a bow and quiver, on hearing the huntsman, to whom they belonged, describe the sport which might be had, by an expert climber, in shooting rock-goats on the Black Mountains. Over those wild hills Phantasmion resolved to take his homeward way; he left Polyanthida, and leaped up the crags, passing far above the valley of mines, and crossing the whole of that mountain district, through which he had already travelled, at a much quicker rate than when he wound his way along the lower ridges and stony dells with the fisherman. The contents of a light case, which he had replenished in the huntsman's cottage, satisfied his hunger, and, when that failed, he had recourse to the conserve inclosed in his serpent wand. As he vaulted from rock to rock many an ibex gazed at him with terrified eyes, and one, leaping down a precipice to get beyond his reach, was dashed to pieces.

At last he gained the lofty Mount of Eagles, where Iarine had been imprisoned among the crags. As he was climbing more than half way toward the top, and had turned away from gazing on the Black lake in the vale below, he beheld a herd of rock goats in a hollow just above him, and soon, one of the number quitting his companions, placed himself at the edge of a jutting crag. "How like a child's toy that creature looks!" thought the prince, "while he thus stands out against the wide back ground of the sky!" A moment afterward his arrow whizzed through the air, but the ibex had leaped from the crag, and there stood in his place a man with a plumed crest, who had been ascending from the vale of the Black Lake and had hitherto been hidden from view by projecting rocks. The shaft would have hit his forehead as he climbed the crag, had the air remained as tranquil as before; but a strong gust arose and made it slant over the precipice, whence the ibex had leaped. The plumed man made no pause but waved his hand aloft, as if communing with some one in the air, and continued swiftly to ascend the hill.

Phantasmion hasting forward reached the topmost peak of the mountain by the time that the sun had descended, and, while he sought to obtain a view of his own royal domain, beheld, on a peak over against him, the man from whom his shaft had glanced aside. He was of great size and stature, and wore a plume of glossy white feathers which fluttered in the gale, and now shone, now glimmered, as the moon was visible by snatches betwixt the hurrying clouds. Beside him stood a woman's form, with streaming dusky locks, which the wind raised above her head, and she was pointing to the sea, where it gleamed beyond the dark inland waters like a cloudless part of the sky, and to some vessels off the coast of Palmland. Suddenly she unfurled her wide transparent wings, which had been lying motionless over her shoulders, and floated away on the wind which blew toward the Land of Rocks. "This is Glandreth!" cried Phantasmion; "I know that plumed crest; and he hath for his counsellor Oloola, the Spirit of the Blast!" Gradually the wind died away, the moon shone brightly, Phantasmion saw the figure of Oloola, like a white-winged bird in the distance, and Glandreth intently surveying that fair country which he hoped to make his own. The youth knelt down, he set his arrow in the bow, and fixed his eye on Glandreth, who stood quite motionless absorbed in contemplation. "Now," thought he, "at this moment could I lay him level with the earth, and his schemes should fall with him." Then he cried aloud, "Nay, nay! hereafter will I meet him face face." He was about to rise, when a violent blast tore the bow and arrow out of his hand, and, eddying round and round, lifted him on high, then suffered him to fall upon the stony soil as gently as a nurse can lay her infant charge upon a carpeted floor. Phantasmion looked up and beheld a speck in the heavens right over his head. It vanished at the moment when Glandreth disappeared descending the peak on the side toward the vale of the Black Lake.

The prince went on to find a sheltered nook which he had remembered seeing beside the shadowy tarn. There he slept peaceably, forgetting Glandreth and Oloola, and seeing only the angelic face of Iarine as it looked when she beheld in his arms the lost infant. At dawn he descended the hill toward the Land of Palms, and saw the sun light up the white sails of those pirate vessels of which Glandreth had communed with Oloola. He entered a herdsman's hut below the mountain, to obtain refreshments: here a damsel was sitting in company with a youth from the palace, and Phantasmion heard them talk about a council which was to be holden that day concerning the king's absence: so he induced this page, who had never seen his face before, to lend him his horse, and travelling at full speed he reached the palace soon after the ancient men were assembled.

Not tarrying to change his wayworn garments he entered the hall of state in the midst of a vehement harangue; on catching the tenor of which he paused, and held up his hand to those who had recognised him to forbid their announcing his name. "At this moment," said the speaker, "Phantasmion is exploring the central regions, or revelling in the sequestered caves of ocean, or visiting the stars with some arch spirit; and there, no doubt, he takes sage counsel, and learns things of deep concernment to his realm upon earth." Scarce had these words fallen from his lips, when he perceived the young monarch looking at him with a keen composed countenance, while the other chiefs were full of perturbation, as he stood betwixt himself and the throne. Then all the assembly rose, the brother of Cyradis exclaiming, "Our king appears, and his gainsayers are put to silence:" the presumptuous chief did homage with the rest of the elders, and Phantasmion ascended the vacant throne. Thence he addressed the council, relating all he had learned during his absence which concerned the welfare of his country, and appearing no more like him who till then had been called the sovereign of Palmland, than a tree full robed in leaf and blossom resembles the same tree ere a bud is unfolded; for he was clothed with majesty, and spoke like one who desired and deserved to be a king.

XVI

Phantasmion rescues the infant brother of Iarine

On the evening of the day on which Phantasmion returned to his palace, he conferred with Potentilla beside the pomegranate tree, and, showing her the scroll that fell from the silver pitcher, "What is this?" he asked. The Fairy similed disdainfully as she read aloud, "A record of the agreement betwixt Seshelma and Karadan, the son of Magnart." "Seshelma!" exclaimed the youth; "wherefore does she hate me, and serve mine enemies?" "She hates thee," replied Potentilla, "because an ancestor of thine poisoned the waters of a certain spring, and for the same cause she will hate thy remotest descendants." "But how is she in league with Karadan?" inquired the prince; "is she not Maudra's servant?" Potentilla made answer: "Karadan may have offered some higher bribe, or perhaps she only serves him out of wayward malice. Be that as it may, Maudra is but the press that toils to crush the fruit and keeps the empty skins alone, while the juice flows down below. 'I will bring poisonous fish into the lake,' Seshelma said to her; let Iarine send them to the house of Magnart in Anthemmina's pitcher, which I brought thee from the ocean. So thine enemies will perish, and the charmed vessel will fall into the hand of the steward. But Glandreth will scorn Iarine, believing that she has poisoned her own kindred for the sake of that low-born favourite.' This plot she framed in order that Karadan might get possession of the charmed vessel; and how Maudra has been cheated concerning the fish thou thyself well knowest." "They caused sickness indeed," cried the prince, "but not death. Then it was the water-witch," he continued, "who brought Anthemmina's pitcher from the bottom of the sea?" Potentilla made no reply to this question, and, when Phantasmion spoke of Oloola, she trembled, and was silent. At length, however, she said, "Be thou guided by me, and I will serve thee against all thy foes without guerdon. Dorimant scorned my words, and I left him to his fate." So saying, the Fairy flew away in the form of a chafer, and the prince fancied that he could distinguish her deep droning sounds when her form was hidden among the foliage. It was now very dark, and Phantasmion returned to the palace through groves and alleys, where the stars, shining athwart the leafy boughs, appeared like funeral tapers. "How did my father perish!" thought the youth, musing on the last words of Potentilla; "was it not surmised that he ate poisoned honey?" Phantasmion shuddered: "Shall I seek aid," he said, "from beings like these, freakish and sudden as children, yet steadfast in revenge as the sternest of mankind."

But when the young monarch arose with the sun other thoughts possessed his soul. He remembered the pirate vessels which were plundering the fair plains of Palmland; he conceived a project of driving them from the coast without delay; and, seeking the pomegranate tree, exclaimed to Potentilla, at the moment she made herself visible, "Once more give me wings! make me able to fly over the sea, and dive deep into its bosom!" The Fairy touched him with her wand, and, in exchange for his leaping powers, Phantasmion received those of a water-beetle; his body was cased in black mail, and he was furnished with ample means of flight. No sooner was this work performed, and his head surmounted with the crest and fiery eyes of a sea-dragon carved on a helmet, than, having expanded his hard black upper wings with sudden snap, and unfurled the soft silvery pinions that lay beneath, till they stretched far beyond their dark wing-cases, he flew off to the ocean, filling the air with a loud humming and droning, which, when it mingled with the dash of waves below, produced a noise like that of a great water-wheel. But, when the wind sank, and the sea was at perfect rest, he descended and played upon its surface. As one that slides on ice runs a few steps, and is then borne along the crystal floor without exertion, so did Phantasmion, in his new method of swimming, give a few strokes to the water, then dart on smoothly over the waveless flood, while his jetty corslet now twinkled in the sun like mother of pearl, now blackened suddenly, as if a shadow had fallen upon it. Then down he dived, and walked at the bottom of the sea as long as he could remain there without taking breath. Having enjoyed enough of this pastime, he went in search of the ships that were plundering his subjects' cattle. Espying one at a little distance, he flew towards it, plunged under water, and came up close beside the vessel, the deck of which was crowded with sheep and goats. Great was the perplexity of the crew as they watched the winged swimmer emerge from the deep: the dragon's head rose first, then came to view the curly locks, white brow, and animated eyes of a fair youth, then those vast insect pinions, and that strange coat of mail. A large net was straightway brought by one of the sailors, but Phantasmion rushed up into the air amid the roar of waters, uttering loud threats and denunciations. He hovered aloft, and made as if he would enter the ship, but the crew, taking him for a demon sent to carry some of them away into a place of torment, with one accord set up a yell of terror; the captain, who had climbed the mast, thence to survey the monster in the deep, brandished his sword; the sheep and goats huddled together, one over the back of the other, and all the spears and pitchforks which the men had used in their marauding expeditions, were turned upward, so that the deck bristled with iron points. Phantasmion wheeled suddenly round, and snatched away the sword of the captain, who, endeavouring to make a rapid retreat, tumbled into the sea. The youth plunged after him, as an osprey plunges after a fish, and would have landed him on the deck of the vessel, but the sailors, stupified with fright, remained in the same attitude as before, and the serried spears were still held aloft to oppose his entrance. Phantasmion therefore relaxed his grasp, and let the captain fall back again into the water, then violently shaking his wings, though not a particle of moisture adhered to them, he soared away, having first proclaimed aloud that he should speedily return with his armed legions to punish the plunderers. They did not await the execution of the threat, but hastily the whole pirate fleet cleared the coast of Palmland, and, proceeding along that of the adjacent realm, conveyed their booty to the plains of Tigridia.

Meanwhile Phantasmion resolved to steer his course towards the Black Lake, and to return home over the Mount of Eagles. He held such a lofty course that his form was not discernible from below; but, having reached the Rockland shore, he desired to rest, and softly alighted not far from the spot where he had first seen Seshelmer and the consort of Albinian. A remembrance of that strange incident prompted him to approach the low projecting cliff, and, leaning against it, to look down into the cave. Having done this he started, for there, on the same rock which she had formerly occupied, sate the queen, with an infant asleep upon her lap. The tide had reached the train of her long robe, and was dashing it to and fro, but Maudra, heedless of her, sumptuous garment, gazed with looks of anguish on the little child, which slumbered peacefully on her knee. The sea was calm and glittered; but if a fish leaped up, or a sea bird dipped into the water, a shuddering came over her frame, and she looked upon the tranquil ocean with a countenance of despair. A few tears trickled from her eyes on the face of the infant, which started, roused by their heat, then, breathing a soft sigh, resigned itself again to sleep, while the breeze just lifted up and down the delicate rings of flaxen hair that lay in clusters on its innocent head, and tinged with the faint pink of May blossoms the upturned cheek, which till then had been colourless, but round and lovely as a gleaming pearl. Maudra took the diadem from her burning brow, and would have dashed it against the rock, but checked herself through fear of awakening the sleeper, and let it fall on the soft bed of sand. Then, in a low lulling tone, she sang these words:—

> O sleep, my babe, hear not the rippling wave,
> Nor feel the breeze that round thee lingering strays
> To drink thy balmy breath,
> And sigh one long farewell.
>
> Soon shall it mourn above thy wat'ry bed,
> And whisper to me, on the wave-beat shore,
> Deep murm'ring in reproach,
> Thy sad untimely fate.
>
> Ere those dear eyes had opened on the light,
> In vain to plead, thy coming life was sold,
> O! wakened but to sleep,
> Whence it can wake no more!
>
> A thousand and a thousand silken leaves
> The tufted beech unfolds in early spring,
> All clad in tenderest green,
> All of the self same shape:
>
> A thousand infant faces, soft and sweet,
> Each year sends forth, yet every mother views
> Her last not least beloved
> Like its dear self alone.
>
> No musing mind hath ever yet foreshaped
> The face to-morrow's sun shall first reveal,
> No heart hath e'er conceived
> What love that face will bring.

SARA COLERIDGE

O sleep, my babe, nor heed how mourns the gale
To part with thy soft locks and fragrant breath,
As when it deeply sighs
O'er autumn's latest bloom.

But now Phantasmion's heart begins to swell, and he feels impatient of his strange disguise, for Iarine enters the recess and fondly bends over the sleeping infant. No sooner had Maudra looked upon that angel face than her own assumed an expression of malignity, all her worst passions being roused by the soft splendour of the maiden's beauty. She bade Iarine take the infant boy and walk with him close to the water, that he might be refreshed by the mild sea breezes. "Soon I will join thee," she said, "and Glandreth will come to conduct us to the boat, and across the lake to the castle. Iarine took the babe in her arms, but spite of all her care, he opened his blue eyes, and, smiling on his mother, encircled her finger, which she had holden up to enjoin silence, in playful pertinacity with his fairy hand. Iarine unclasped it, and, casting a look of wonder on the agitated countenance of the queen, she hastily withdrew. Till the damsel and her charge were out of sight, Maudra stood fixed and rigid, leaning against a rock; when they were no longer visible from the cavern, her form collapsed, and she sank upon the ground with closed eyes.

Phantasmion sprang into the air, and the sound of his large pinions was like the whirring of an albatross. He flew over the sea-shore and hovered above the spot where the damsel was pacing the sands. Iarine took him for some large eagle, and held the child aloft to show him the great bird which was wheeling about high over head. Then with the rapidity of lightning he slanted downward, and dived into the sea, his form being rendered indistinguishable by the swiftness of his flight. Iarine was astonished, and stood waiting to behold the strange bird reappear, while the baby pointed to the place where it had rushed into the sea, and lay back in the arms of his fair nurse, laughing merrily, and believing that what he saw was a game of hide and seek, carried on for his amusement. But Phantasmion has caught sight of Seshelma lurking in the water, and now he sees her dart onward, now emerge, and approach the maiden. At that moment he rose from the waves, and, before the extended arms of Seshelma had grasped their prey, he had snatched it from the hands of Iarine, and, violently spurning the face of the woman-fish with his mail-clad foot, he soared aloft, and became as a speck in the vault of heaven.

Before he winged his way homeward, Phantasmion descended once more, to take a last look at the distressed Iarine. Poised on his outspread wings, he beheld her with her heavenly face thrown upward, and her white arms outstretched, as if she had forgotten all fear, and were imploring him that had seized the infant to restore it. Some one approaches her on the sandy shore; by his stately port and plume of waving feathers, Phantasmion knows him to be Glandreth. Iarine still gazes on the sky, and points to the hovering youth. And now he beheld Maudra rushing across the sands; she utters a loud shriek as she looks at the sky; she tears her hair and flings herself upon the ground; then, arising, she hastens to the side of Glandreth, points at Iarine, and seems to be accusing her to him. The innocent maiden clasps her hands and still keeps her eye on the infant.

Phantasmion dared tarry no longer; he used his wings vigorously, and scarcely paused till he had arrived at the pomegranate tree, where he was divested, by Potentilla, of his wings and other strange accoutrements. He then carried the infant to his nurse, Leeliba, and bade her bring him up with as much secresy as possible. For the remainder of the day the child drooped like a bird newly placed in a cage, and looked strangely on his nurse when he awoke the next morning; but, ere many hours were over, he was smiling in the arms of the youth who had twice preserved him from death, and seemed ready to spring away, and catch the wild colt, which the attendants brought to gambol for his amusement.

XVII

Phantasmion meets with Iarine and Albinet on the banks of the Black Lake

Phantasmion again sought an interview with the fairy, and told her that he desired above all things to win the heart of Iarine, and to confound his enemy Glandreth. Potentilla replied, "Go then to the Black Lake, offer thyself as cup-bearer to Queen Maudra, and with my aid thou shalt accomplish both these projects." Having spoken thus she turned to the bough of a plane tree, where a cicada was pertinaciously chirping, as if it would bear a part in the discourse. She touched the insect, and it gradually expanded to a vast magnitude, while the sound of its drum grew rapidly louder and louder, till at last it seemed about to split, with its vibrations, the broad trunk and stout arms of the tree on which it stood. Phantasmion exclaimed, "With such an instrument as this I might roam at night through the forests, and make the wild beasts fly on all sides." "Ay," replied Potentilla, "and with an instrument like this thou shalt terrify the soul of Glandreth; for I will whisper such a warning in his ear that when he hears that sound, he shall believe his last hour to be at hand." Phantasmion embraced the fairy's scheme with ardour, feeling confident that he should not fail in executing his part of it. Potentilla placed the drum in the forepart of his body, and showed him by what slight imperceptible motions he might draw forth the full powers of the instrument; then, removing her wand to his shoulders, she endued them with wings that might be closely folded down lengthwise, and concealed beneath his loose upper vest.

Having entrusted the affairs of his kingdom to the brother of Cyradis, and the royal scion to that of his ancient nurse, he attired himself in garments denoting the office he meant to assume; they were embroidered at the edge with green vine leaves and clusters of purple grapes. Thus equipped he set forth, flying many a league till he reached the valley of the Black Lake, and stayed to rest on a large tree where he was hidden by the abundant foliage. When he arrived at this station, the King's Island, and the whole sheet of water in which it stood, was wrapped in a thick fog, only the edge of the lake being visible beyond the vapoury curtain, like a rim of lurid steel. Phantasmion looked out from amid the boughs, and, after a time, began to perceive a small ghost-like vessel advancing through the mist. It contained two figures, faint and shadowy, a young boy moving the oars, and, standing beside him, a damsel clad in white robes, and wearing a crown of star-shaped azure lilies, which gleamed within the misty veil. Slowly the boat made way, gradually the figures grew in distinctness, and, as the lake looked clearer, and the radiant face of Iarine came closer, it seemed to the prince that she, and not the dull red orb on high, was pouring brightness through the sullen mist. Young Albinet, now weary of his task, resigned the oars: skilfully the maiden drew the boat to land, then leaping on the shore she held up both her arms of gleaming whiteness, and lifted the lame child out of the boat. "Sister," said the boy, "thou wast kind to come with me when nobody else would venture out. The finest summer days often begin thus. Let us sit down here and see the white curtain draw up from the lake." Iarine seated herself beside young Albinet on a bank below the tree where Phantasmion was concealed, and soon the child began to amuse himself with plucking purple flags, and sticking the blossoms all about her dress, and here and there amid the labyrinth of her locks. Now he would lift up those tresses, and spread them abroad in the faint sunshine, till they glittered like a tissue of golden threads, now heap them together in full masses, which looked as deep and mellow as rich wine in the cask. "Sister," said the child, "why wilt thou always wear those cold blue water lilies? Red and yellow flowers are livelier than blue ones." "I love them because my mother loved them," said Iarine. "Dost thou think she wears such a crown as this now?" said Albinet, softly, looking up at the sky. "The flowers she wears," replied the maiden, "are such as will never fade." "Heaven must be very full of flowers," cried he, "if new ones come and yet the old ones never go away. I hope it is not like that picture of a sunny garden which never changes; I hope there are half opened buds in heaven, Iarine, and merry milk white lambs." "Heaven is happiness," the maid replied; "all that can make us happy we shall meet with there." "I wish," said Albinet, with a sigh, "that we could get thither without going down into the dark grave. Is there no lightsome road to heaven, up in the open air?" "My mother never went into the grave;" said Iarine, "she was buried in the waves of the sea." "O, from the sea," said Albinet, "it must be easy enough to climb up into the sky, for I myself have marked the very place where it meets the water. When this fog clears away, if I could get to the top of that tree, and look intently, perchance I might descry some very minute trace of the beginning of heaven. Dear Iarine, these are no heavenly flowers, for they are drooping already: I will throw them into the lake to send away the fog." So saying, he pulled the chaplet from his sister's brow, and flung it into the water, when a large dark bird suddenly rose from one of the craggy islets, and rushed onward, appearing vast and indistinct as it loomed through the mist. Albinet shrieked aloud, and fell upon the ground writhing; Iarine hung over him tenderly, and, when he recovered, she pointed to the dark bird, which now stood on the shore in full view. "There is the goblin," she said; "no goblins but such as that will ever come near thee and me." The pale boy smiled, and, hiding his face in his sister's lap, entreated her to soothe him for a while with one of her soft melodies, and, while the fog was rapidly dispersing, she sang words like these:—

How gladsome is a child, and how perfect is his mirth,
How brilliant to his eye are the daylight shows of earth!
But Oh! how black and strange are the shadows in his sight,
What phantoms hover round him in the darkness of the night!

Away, ye gloomy visions, I charge ye hence away,
Nor scare the simple heart that without ye were so gay;
Alas! when you are gone with all your ghastly crew,
What sights of glowing splendour will fade away with you!

He'll see the gloomy sky, and know 'tis here decreed,
That sunshine follow every storm, and light to shade succeed,
No more he'll dread the tempest, nor tremble in the dark,
Nor soar on wings of fancy far beyond the soaring lark.

I love thee, little brother, when smiles are on thy face,
I love thy eager merriment, thy never failing grace:
But when the shadow darkens thee and chills thy timid breast,
I'd watch from eve till day-break that thou might'st be at rest.

"I dreamt that we were in the grave," said Albinet, roused by his sister from sobbing sleep; "and I began to cry: but, behold, it was only a passage, and there was light at the other end." "What have we to do with the grave?" said Iarine, in a sprightly tone: "we can never be laid under ground, only our worn garments. The earth is nature's wardrobe; for out of it every living thing and every tree and plant receive apparel. Ere we go hence we must replace our garments in the great receptacle, that the old materials may serve to make new clothes for other creatures." Albinet looked at his pining limb: "I will have finer clothes than these in heaven," he said, "and such as fit me better." "Think of our garden favourite," said the maid again; "when the streaked petals and shining leaves and upright stem all disappeared, was the dear lily dead?" 'No, no,' she might have cried from under ground, 'though all you ever saw me has gone to dust, yet I am still alive, and soon shall have fresh raiment fit to appear in; unless the spring proves faithless.'" Albinet clasped his sister's hand joyfully: "We too shall be fresh clothed," he cried, "and better clothed, because our spring will be in a far finer soil and climate. Ha, ha! who knows but these bodies of ours may be the bulbs out of which our heavenly bodies are to spring, as that caterpillar is the bulb of a butterfly, and the poor dry acorn of a branching oak?"

Then full of smiles he ran away to gather blossoms that grew in the lake, the vapours having all cleared off; but soon returning, "Sister," he cried, "I cannot reach the queen of the whole company; pray come and lend a hand." Iarine had begun to read a letter with deep attention, yet now she rose, and placing stones in the water, erected a little bridge to the floating colony of flowers. But just as she was about to gather one, Albinet screamed aloud, for he had heard the sound of the magical drum, which the prince struck against the branch of a tree in bending forward to look at Iarine. The maid was startled, her foot slipped from the stone, and, looking up, she beheld Phantasmion, with light wings unfurled, gazing at her from the middle of a broad leafy bough. She knew his face, and remembering how strangely it had appeared to her twice before, she believed the youth was some wizard or guileful spirit, and springing to the bank and catching hold of her little brother, she hastened away as fast as his feeble limbs would allow him to keep pace with her. Phantasmion lightly fluttered down from the tree, and, fanning the air with his delicate pinions, quickly overtook Iarine and the terrified child. At that instant he lowered his wings, folding them down over his shoulder, and kneeling before the princess, held out a cup to show what office he sought, and intreated her to favour his suit with the queen. Albinet clasped his sister round the waist, and hid his face, that he might not see the object which excited his terror; but the fears of Iarine almost melted away while Phantasmion spoke, and looking at his noble countenance, she could not but yield to the faith which it inspired. "I cannot speak for queen Maudra," she replied, "but thou shalt be conducted to her presence and mayst have an answer from herself." She then returned with young Albinet to the boat, which she had over-passed in her sudden alarm, and was soon on her way to the island. Phantasmion went to gather up the flower which had fallen from her hand into the lake, and, at the same time, espied the letter floating by its side. The name of Semiro and that of Karadan caught his eye as it lay open before him, and guessing that it came from Zelneth, he read what follows while he waited for the boat from the island:—"Beware of him, dearest Iarine, for it is reported that he deals in magic; yes, powerful magic, and I believe the charge. Our house has never seemed like itself since he entered it; Karadan is more despairing than ever, and Leucoia grieves twice as much for her lost love as she did before the enchanter came among us. She seems to have sat too long in the sun; her cheeks are like a bleached primrose born near midsummer. And oh! what a sun-bright visage beamed on us lately!

"My cousin, beware of him, if he comes into thy presence; be not deceived by his heavenly brow, nor his noble countenance, nor his deep sweet voice, nor his gallant bearing: above all, be not deluded by his smile: that smile I know to be his most pernicious spell. It banishes all natural smiles from the place where it has once appeared; it is a light that puts out all other lights, and, vanishing, leaves darkness behind it.

"Our father avers that Semiro was no envoy from Palmland, but a spy sent by Glandreth. Oh folly! Semiro never came from any dominions but his own, whether they be of earth or of some other sphere. Arzene is wroth with him, for the sake of her dear son: that he sought Karadan's blood, I believe not; but if he seeks to rob him of that which he values more, thy love, he does far worse. I beseech thee let him not succeed in this, Iarine; let him not work spells on thee, as thou valuest thy good name. I grieve that any suspicion should rest on that; but strange rumours will fly abroad unless thou hearkenest to the suit of Karadan. Pity indeed should incline thee to this; better have nipped his passion in the bud, than suffer the flower to blow in vain, wasting the percious juices of the tree. I could not act thus cruelly, even toward a wicked sorcerer, if I were loved by him as thou art by Karadan. Alas! no one, whose love I care for, will ever love me thus; yet, loved or unloved, I remain thy loving cousin, Zelneth."

XVIII

PHANTASMION MAKES USE OF
HIS MAGICAL DRUM

Phantasmion thanked Zelneth in his heart for that warning letter, which seemed so well fitted to defeat its own purpose, and by the time that a boat had arrived to transport him whither his heart was bound, he had concealed his wings under a cloak, and every aspiring thought under a countenance of humility and reserve. The queen, when she beheld him, was pleased with the opportunity of engaging so handsome a cup-bearer, and, being engrossed with the image of Glandreth, observed no beauty in him which might not belong to men of lowly station. "He looks sedate yet quick," thought she; "I may find him the more useful; at all events he will be a goodly piece of furniture, becoming a palace."

That day a high feast was holden at the castle, and Phantasmion attended in his place amid the crowd of domestic servants. He placed himself right opposite to Glandreth, and read his face more keenly than any one at the board. He saw the courtier bend forward to address the queen with soft volubility, prolonged smile, and gently suspended eyelid, then, absolving himself from the mimic task, on a sudden resume his lofty port and natural countenance, every smile gone, every muscle braced up, and none but stern thoughts legible on his brow, at one end of the table sate poor Albinian, the mock effigy of a king, his white locks incessantly shaken by the palsied motions of his head. Now and then he muttered a few words which no one tried to understand but Iarine; she, brightest and loveliest, safe beside him, devoting all her looks and words to the afflicted man; but from her heavenly face he turned away, by a miserable fascination, to watch his gaudy queen and the proud injurious noble. Phantasmion could see his eye flash and his teeth chatter with impotent rage, when others perceived none but the twitches of disease in that distorted face. And now Glandreth has fixed his ardent eye upon the beautiful princess; but silent reproaches, deeper than any but an angel face could have expressed, were all her answer, and looking back to Maudra he spied suspicion on her lowering brow. He refrained from casting another glance upon Iarine, and renewed his discourse to the queen, leaning forward and addressing her with all the tender confidence of a favourite: "Last night I had the strangest dream," said he; "'tis well I have few fears;" then dropping his voice, and looking expressly at Maudra, he added, "there is but one being on earth who holds me in awe." "Tell me thy dream," answered the queen with a smile; "I did not think thou hadst been a dreamer; but the dreams of some are worth more than the waking thoughts of others." "I dreamed," said he, "that I heard a thundering sound, which gradually grew louder and louder, till I thought it would shatter myself and all around me with its violence. I started from my couch, expecting, forsooth, to be swallowed up by an earthquake; but all was still and silent; I lay down to sleep, and had no sooner pressed the pillow than these words were breathed into my ear: 'Glandreth, when thou hearest that sound again, prepare to die.'" Maudra listened to this story with a face full of smiles, believing that it was a feigned tale, intended to elicit from her some mark of favour. She poured out a cup of sparkling wine, and bade Phantasmion present it to Glandreth. "Long mayst thou live," she cried, "and never cease to prosper till dreams like these become true prophecies!" When that service was performed, the graceful cup-bearer took his station behind the noble guest, and, just as he was raising the wine-cup to his lips, having answered the queen's pledge, Phantasmion produced a long, loud, swelling peal from his gong, which vibrated across the back of Glandreth's stately chair through every fibre of his frame, and caused him to spill the contents of the goblet into his bosom. The queen started from her seat with clasped hands, and the whole company were full of amazement. Is that an idiot smile which distends Albinian's face, while he stares upon Glandreth?—to Phantasmion it seemed the expression of gratified hatred. Meantime the proud chief sate trembling, and vainly strove to recover the careless air with which he had related his dream. But Phantasmion perceived that the soft eyes of Iarine were bent on him with a regretful look, that seemed to say, "Zelneth speaks truly; that beaming face and princely aspect are the disguise of a sorcerer." No one else appeared to guess whence the sounds had proceeded; most of the company had listened to the story of the dream; they cast unpiteous glances on the haughty warrior, and all agreed with one consent that the noise they heard could never have been produced by any instrument which the hand of man had fashioned. Glandreth frowned, and it seemed doubtful whether alarm or anger spoke loudest in his heart.

Phantasmion retired among the domestics, and, wandering, while day declined, through the woods on the island, he espied, between the foliage, a twinkling light upon the lake. He uncovered his wings, flew up to a tree, and, looking down upon the gleaming pebbles of the shore in the clear moonlight, espied the dark face of Karadan, who, at that moment, was leaning on a pole, in the act of bringing his boat to land. In a few moments he took up the silver pitcher, leaped upon the shore, and looked and listened, as if expecting some one from the castle; then he seated himself on a turfy bank, just below the prince, and while he embraced the charmed vessel, softly murmured these words:—

> *I tremble when with look benign*
> *Thou tak'st my offer'd hand in thine,*
> *Lest passion-breathing words of mine*
> *The charm should break:*
> *And friendly smiles be forced to fly,*
> *Like soft reflections of the sky,*
> *Which, when rude gales are sweeping by,*
> *Desert the lake.*

> *Of late I saw thee in a dream;*
> *The day-star pour'd his hottest beam,*
> *And thou, a cool refreshing stream,*
> *Did'st brightly run:*
> *The trees where thou wert pleased to flow,*
> *Threw out their flowers, a glorious show,*
> *While I, too distant doomed to grow,*
> *Pined in the sun.*

> *By no life-giving moisture fed,*
> *A wasted tree, I bow'd my head,*
> *My sallow leaves and blossoms shed*
> *On earth's green breast:*
> *And silent pray'd the slumbering wind,*
> *The lake, thy tarrying place, might find,*
> *And waft my leaves, with breathings kind,*
> *There, there, to rest.*

Phantasmion had now taken his resolution; he was about to spring from his place of concealment and contend with Karadan for the pitcher, but his motions were suddenly arrested, when he beheld Iarine, clad in flowing garments as she sate at the feast, advance through the trees to meet the son of Magnart, and he then became all eagerness to hear what discourse would follow between them. His heart began to sink, and he felt more alarmed for the success of his hopes than he had ever done since he first beheld Iarine.

The dark youth threw himself on his knees before the princess, and laid hold of her robe, as if to secure her stay till he had gained courage to speak. "Karadan," said the maiden, "I received thy message; say quickly what thou hast to tell me, for I have little time to tarry here." "Iarine," said the youth, "I have a relic in my possession which once belonged to thy mother." "Dear cousin," replied she, "hast thou come thus far to gratify that fond wish of my heart? Give me the relic, and I will bless thee for ever." "Thou canst indeed bless me for ever," exclaimed the youth, fervently, "but not with words alone, dear as thy words have ever been to me. Oh let deeds follow, or thy gentlest words will come in vain, as the dew falls on plants that waste inwardly, having a worm at the core." "Nay, Karadan, speak not thus;" answered the maiden, "thou hast no worm at the core, but a sound heart, a gallant heart, which will carry thee through a thousand noble enterprises." "O lady, sweet cousin," cried the youth, "my grief is a jest to thee. If thou couldst understand but half the intensity of my anguish, I know that, out of tenderness and compassion, thou wouldst learn to love me." "Not as thou desirest, Karadan;" replied the maid; "why wouldst thou force me to promise what I never can perform?" "If thou hadst promised to love me," answered Karadan, eagerly, "even that thou couldst perform. Virtue and kindliness are thy very being, thy every thought and feeling is informed by them. Promise that thou wilt try to love me, and I will go hence the happiest man that ever loved and hoped. That sky, which lately looked so bare and void, now shines with multitudes of stars; and barren plains, which seem to have no germs of life within them, how soon are they covered with flourishing herbs and groves where the birds nestle! Only try to love me, and thy heart, sweet lady, will prove as great a change as this." "Dear cousin," answered the maid, "we have duties enough which nature imposes; for a heart like mine I am sure they are sufficient; never let us make a duty of love." A change came over Karadan's face, and his eye shot fire, as he exclaimed, "Thou art more than usually resolute! perchance thou hast seen a youth from Palmland." Iarine was silent. "Yes, yes!" pursued Karadan with vehemence, "a youth like the sun, as my sister blazons him; to thee, no doubt, he seems not less radiant. Oh, he is the rising sun, and I the gloomy night that must retire when he approaches!" "Give me the relic, good cousin," replied the maid, "and I will show favour to no youth from Palmland." Karadan seized the pitcher, and holding it up, he exclaimed, "Tell him that I have the charmed vessel on which thy fate depends. Tell him that thou thyself hast made it mine: tell him that I will hide it where it shall never more be found, and then let him fight with me till one or both of us perish!" Karadan pressed the pitcher close to his bosom, while his countenance this moment seemed glowing with passion, the next, darkening in despair. Phantasmion again prepared to spring forward, and challenge him for the pitcher, but restrained himself once more when he beheld Glandreth emerge from the shady wood, into the clear moonlight which gleamed upon the lake and pebbly shore. On espying the youth and the maid he suddenly stopped, holding up his hand, as if in astonishment. "Iarine!" exclaimed he, "the princess Iarine! Fair lady, let me lead thee to the castle; thou art looked for by the queen: she would wonder indeed to see thee in such company at such an hour." At these words, Karadan, whose face Glandreth had not yet seen, rushed forward. "Proud man!" he cried, "my kinswoman owes thee no explanation: my father is her natural guardian, and not thou." "What, Karadan!" exclaimed Glandreth, "Hast thou ventured hither? Hence, and bear my defiance to Magnart." "I will bear no message from thee," replied the youth: "I have a sword here, and can stand in my father's place." "Hast thou a life to spare, mad youth?" replied Glandreth, contemptuously. "Away! when I am in second childhood I will fight with thee!" "I have a life to spare!" vociferated Karadan: "Do I not know thy wickedness against the mother of Iarine? Art thou not in my power? Glandreth approached Karadan, who was trembling with passion, and bending down his hand, which held the sword with a mighty grasp, he pointed to the sky, while, in deep low tones, he murmured, "Rash Karadan, look yonder! Hast thou forgotten that form?" Phantasmion and the son of Magnart both raised their eyes to the sky, and beheld the dim outline of a winged figure, with the hand outstretched, and pointing to Karadan, while from that outstretched hand lightnings appeared to radiate in quivering lines along the starry vault, at the same time a shuddering passed across the lake, and over all the woods in which it was embosomed. Like a stranded vessel, that, after tossing in violent agitation, runs aground upon rocks, Karadan sank silently to the earth, Iarine covered her face with her hands, and even Phantasmion's heart was chilled with fear.

He still gazed upward, and observed the form grow fainter and fainter, till it finally vanished; Karadan, too raised his drooping head, and saw Glandreth seize both hands of the fair princess, and smile triumphantly in her face. Then, forgetting everything but vengeance, he sprang to his feet, and dashed the silver pitcher against the forehead of the insulting chieftain: at that same moment the Isle resounded, and all the distant hills re-echoed the tremendous roar of the magical drum, during the reverberations of which, Phantasmion leaped forward, full of life, hope, and energy, feeling ready to encounter a world in arms.

Glandreth, stunned by the blow, but far more overpowered by the terrific sounds, which he believed to be the heralds of his death, lay motionless on the shore, his face streaming with blood. The dark youth gazed in perturbation upon the young king of Palmland. "Sorcerer!" at length he exclaimed, "wilt thou come betwixt me and my foe with spells and witcheries?" "I am no sorcerer!" cried Phantasmion, glowing with indignation; "but it is the most fiendish of all that practice sorcery in whom thou puttest thy trust! How speaks 'the Record betwixt Seshelma and Karadan, son of Magnart?'" "How came that Record into thy hands, thou robber?" Karadan retorted—"Didst thou not attempt to steal this vessel which I purchased with my own gold?" "Thou shalt purchase it with steel as well as with gold," cried Phantasmion, drawing his sword, "come on, there is light enough here to fight by." Karadan flung the pitcher into the boat, and beckoned his antagonist to a firm space of smooth turf, clear from trees; there they fought in the moonlight, guiding their weapons with deadly resolution,—Phantasmion inspired by hope as well as love and courage, Karadan with no ally to second those feelings but despair. The calm lake reflected their bright blades, hard by the image of the waning moon, which lay motionless on its bosom. Iarine fled to the castle, and soon the combatants heard earnest voices and hurrying footsteps of persons who came to separate them. Both paused at once. "Let us meet again!" cried Phantasmion; here is my pledge!" and throwing his mantle, which lay upon the ground, on the arm of Karadan, he plunged into the depths of the wood, while his adversary leaped into the boat, made it skim round the Island, and was out of sight from that part of the shore when the armed men reached it. The soldiers sought about, and found no one but Glandreth, who was just roused from his swoon, and sat upright, gazing around him with blood-stained face and looks of bewildered fury.

XIX

Glandreth is more than ever amazed and discomfited by the noise of the magic drum

Phantasmion stole away through the woods till he came into the midst of a jovial company who were carousing in the open air. These were the pages and other servants of the royal household; they had heard the awful voice of the gong, and were making haste to drown their fears in wine. "The mighty general," they cried, "who dreams only of war and conquest, how sober he looked at that spirit-quelling sound!" "Did ye mark," said one, "how Queen Maudra started from her chair; there was little sobriety in her demeanour, I trow." "Now I warrant," cried a saucy page, after having renewed his courage with a deep draught, "while she is planting arbours, entwined with passion flowers and jessamine, wherein to enjoy the converse of Glandreth, when Albinian lies low, he has been looking out for a stronghold on the frontiers, where he may keep her under garrison as far from his palace of pleasure as possible." "One good thing will come to pass in those days," cried another; "Iarine will be queen instead of Maudra." "Hurra! hurra!" shouted the revellers: "The moon shall be queen in heaven, and bright Iarine upon earth." "Hush, hush!" exclaimed an old wine bibber, who was lying under the rose bushes, "let the moon hear nothing about it yet, nor Maudra either, but mark my words,"—here a burst of merriment drowned his sage discourse, but when the uproar had subsided he raised his flushed face among the pure cool roses, and stammered out, "Depend on it that young Iarine would rather drink the waters of the sea than marry that wicked miner and underminer, who caused Anthemmina to drink them." "When Albinian dies," cried a sprightly page, "the heads of the land shall all be young and handsome. None but a fit spouse for Iarine shall be our king." The revellers cast their eyes on Phantasmion. "Come," said one, "take this fine fellow, pour some royal blood into his veins, and he shall be the man." Thereupon they crowded round the prince, placed a chaplet on his brow, and made him drink out of many a sparkling bowl, till he caught their spirit, and joined them in a blithe chorus after this sort:—

Ne'er ask where knaves are mining.
While the nectar plants are twining:
To pull up the vine
They never incline,
With all their deep designing.

O, ne'er for the dead sit weeping,
Their graves the dews are steeping;
And founts of mirth
Spring up from the earth,
Where they are at peace and sleeping.

Away with studious learning,
When heaven's bright lamps are burning:
In the glorious art
That gladdens the heart,
We cannot be more discerning.

Forget the blood that gushes
Where the fiery war-horse rushes:
The blood that glows,
As it brightly flows,
Is making us chant like thrushes.

When burdened troops advancing,
In cumbrous mail are glancing,
With garlands crowned
We reel around,
While the earth and sky are dancing.

Phantasmion escaped from this boon company, and, having entered the castle, espied Glandreth and the queen communing together in a vaulted passage. The chieftain bent his head, and slowly retired to his chamber; but Maudra beckoned to Phantasmion, and bade him keep watch in the balcony adjoining Glandreth's apartment, that he might render assistance to the wounded warrior in the night if it were needed. The prince obeyed this order with alacrity; he crept to the appointed station, displaced a party of bats, and looked down on his late comrades, most of whom had now fallen asleep among their cups. Glandreth was neither drinking nor sleeping, but drawing a chart of Palmland; with his face bent over the table, he had lifted up his pen to mark the very spot where his invading host was to enter the country, at that same point of time when the young monarch, pressing his drum close to the wall, produced an indescribable and intolerable din, which not only made the apartment of Glandreth rock and resound like a belfry, but circulated around the castle, till every dome, and tower, and vault, rang again, and the whole edifice appeared to be a sounding cymbal in the hand of some mighty musician. Phantasmion crouched down, and, peeping through the rails of the balcony, was amused to see that the whole party of sleepers, lately scattered up and down among the bushes, had started to their feet, and were all standing in one attitude, every head thrown back, every right arm upraised, while rooks, bats, owls, and swallows, day birds and night birds, were flying about in confusion, and the howling of dogs, from various quarters of the island, sounded as if an enemy had entered the precincts.

After having observed the effects produced without the castle for a little time, the prince resolved to enter Glandreth's chamber, under pretence of obeying Maudra's command. Accordingly, stealing in from the balcony he found all as still as death. He advanced farther into the apartment, and beheld the strong man lying upon the floor, his eyes fixed, his cheeks livid, and the wound upon his forehead sending forth a fresh stream of blood. Maudra knelt beside him, with a pale, horror-stricken face: a lamp, which had fallen from her hand, lay burning on the floor, and cast a lurid gleam on the blotted map just beside it, and on those two ghastly visages, while the moon's milder light admitted through the window, illumined the rose-crowned head of the royal youth, and his light, half-raised wings, from which his upper vest had slipped aside.

Maudra was too much absorbed to observe Phantasmion; he glided away, and, passing into another part of the castle, where a lamp shone from the roof, he beheld Albinian standing outside his chamber door, with a wild exultation in his blear eyes. On seeing Phantasmion, he began eagerly to mutter and gesticulate, pointing along the passage, as if to inquire what had become of Maudra. The youth was too wary to throw light upon this subject, but making a low obeisance, hastened on, and entered a gloomy passage into which a feeble light was shining from a window at one end: and now he heard soft irregular steps approaching; some one, little and light, ran against him; by an involuntary motion he erected his gauzy wings, which caught the faint rays from the high window, while the rest of his figure was shadowy and obscure. A shrill scream pierced those darksome recesses, then a door opened at a little distance, and, swift as a coney hies to his hole in the rock, young Albinet, with his bare feet and loose vest, hurried into Iarine's unlighted chamber. Phantasmion stood at the door, and between the pauses of the boy's eager story, uttered amidst loud sobs, he heard her soothing tones and mild remonstrances. "Let me stay here," said the child at length. "I am happy even in the dark when close to thee. But O, sister, would that we lived where there is no night for almost half the year! In those lands, when the sun does set, a throng of purple meteors play his part in the sky. The very ground too is luminous, and reflects the moonbeams from its snowy surface." "Those lands have more light than heat," said Iarine; "thou dost not love the cold." "In heaven there will be neither cold nor darkness," he answered, after a pause; "but, alas! now I think on it, up in the sky we shall be close to the dreadful thunder, and there it will sound as loud as that terrible din which is bellowing in my ears even yet." "Thunder comes from the clouds;" the maid replied, "our dwelling will be far beyond the clouds that frown upon this earth. There will be no vexing noises, no dull silence, no shade but the shadows of bright blossomed trees with sunshine all round about them. But sleep, now—" "O, sleep is scared away for ever," sighed Albinet; "never, never to come nigh these walls again!" A few moments afterwards Phantasmion heard the soft, regular breathing, which told that his fearful spirit had ceased to strive with itself; then, having laid himself down beside that chamber-door, he too fell asleep, and dreamed right pleasantly.

XX

GLANDRETH QUITS THE ISLAND,
AND PHANTASMION OBTAINS AN INTERVIEW
WITH IARINE

When Phantasmion awoke in the dim passage, he heard the inmates of the chamber greeting the dawn with this song:—

How high yon lark is heavenward borne!
Yet, ere again she hails the morn,
Beyond where birds can wing their way
Our souls may soar to endless day,
May hear the heavenly choirs rejoice,
While earth still echoes to her voice.

A waveless flood, supremely bright,
Has drown'd the myriad isles of light;
But ere that ocean ebb'd away,
The shadowy gulf their forms betray:
Above the stars our course may run,
'Mid beams unborrow'd from the sun.

In this day's light what flowers will bloom,
What insects quit the self-made womb!
But ere the bud its leaves unfold,
The gorgeous fly his plumes of gold,
On fairer wings we too may glide,
Where youth and joy no ills betide.

Then come, while yet we linger here,
Fit thoughts for that celestial sphere,
A heart which under keenest light,
May bear the gaze of spirits bright,
Who all things know, and nought endure
That is not holy, just and pure.

"Now for fresh thoughts and fresh deeds!" cried the youth, starting up, when the strain ceased, and doffing his withered chaplet; but ere these glowing resolves had taken any fixed shape, forth came Iarine, hand in hand with Albinet, throwing light from the chamber full in his face: then starting at the sight of him, she hurried away, and soon had entered Maudra's apartment. Phantasmion stood in a recess, and in a little time, the young boy, going out on some errand, left the door ajar, so that he now beheld the interior of the apartment, where Iarine was dressing the queen's hair, and beheld her lovely form as she bent over the task, and her face reflected in the mirror above that of Maudra. The step-dame surveyed her own too faithful portrait, and the more she gazed, the more she was dissatisfied with those bleak remains of pristine splendour. A deeper shade seemed to fall over her sunken eyes, and the hollows that lay beneath them, so that the reflection, and that which was reflected, mutually increased each other's gloom; while the soft image of Iarine's unconscious face beamed on in pensive beauty. Maudra pulled away her dishevelled locks from the lily hand that held them, and, scowling upon the maiden, said, "Thy tresses are too thick, Iarine: no wonder my work stands still, when thou hast such a multitude of gadding tendrils to cultivate: if thou wert a child of mine I should have them pruned much closer." The damsel understood this hint, and, while her tears fell fast, cut one after another of her sunny ringlets, and let them fall upon the ground, while Maudra looked sternly on, and never seemed to think that she had done enough. Phantasmion's blood was rising. Albinet, at this moment ran back into his mother's room, and seeing what Iarine was about, stopped short in his career. Then, looking greatly astonished, he held her hand, and plaintively inquired, "What! art thou shearing away all thy locks which our poor father loves to play with?" Iarine whispered, "Hush! it is by the queen's command." Upon which Albinet looked full in Maudra's face, and exclaimed, "O, mother? what harm can Iarine's ringlets do to thee?" The haughty woman turned away from her child's inquiring gaze, and muttered in a low tone to the damsel, "Have a care that no one else plays with them, but thy doting father, or this poor fool." Albinet began to gather up the scattered tresses, while Iarine hastened to close the door, having caught a glimpse of Phantasmion's eager face in the mirror.

Afterwards the prince went forth, and saw Glandreth at a little distance, hurrying to the lake, with pale disordered looks, and still the chart of the realm he meant to conquer, was in his hand. "Terrified yet unsubdued!" exclaimed the youth; and when his enemy's boat was midway between the island and the opposite bank, he knelt upon the ground, and drew forth from his body a hollow noise, which was conveyed over the water with great force, to the chieftain's ear; then he saw Glandreth drop the oar, and let the vessel drift at random.

But Phantasmion arose. "I will not break the calm of this sunshiny hour," he cried, "with more loud peals. O that these gentle-trilling birds, and that soft breeze, could plead for me with my coy mistress!" Possessed by such thoughts, he wandered about the flower-beds, and through many a pleasant copse, in hopes that he might find her, but still disappointed, he sadly cried, "O, harsh step-dame, to keep Iarine out of the sunshine on such a day as this!" At length he approached that ancient tower, detached from the main building, whither he had seen the maiden ascend, the night she caught the poisonous fish. Now it cast a black shadow in the midst of the sunny garden: a thousand bees were busy there, but not one murmured over the flowers which lay in that shade; no butterfly flitted across to reach the golden blossoms that basked in the warm rays beyond. The entrance to the tower was open; he went in, and, going up the dark winding stairs, he heard the voice of Albinet: "I dare not play in the garden," the boy was saying, "for fear of the stranger youth." A soft reply which followed was not audible, and Phantasmion mounted a little higher. "Indeed now, sister, I did see his wings," rejoined Albinet; "he hides them by day under his cloak. O, sister, sister, perhaps it was he that flew away with our baby brother." "Dear child, I cannot let thee in," replied the soft voice of Iarine; "the door is locked, and thy mother has the key." "Alas! alas!" cried the child; "it is so dark here!—if I had wings I would fly in at the window which opens upon the lawn." Phantasmion descended the stairs, and soon discovered the window spoken of by Albinet, then loosing his wings, he flew up to it, and, looking into the apartment, beheld the maiden at work on a superb vest, which lay floating in ample folds over her lap, while Albinet was crying from without, "Sing, sing, Iarine; keep singing, that I may hear thy voice." As soon as the damsel espied Phantasmion entering at the window, she turned her face to the door, bent over her task with renewed assiduity, and began singing aloud. The prince attempted to describe the ardour of his passion, to explain his conduct, and entreat the beautiful princess to exchange that gloomy tower for the throne of Palmland: but he wasted his eloquence on deaf ears; Iarine kept singing, over and over again, in concert with Albinet, a few verses which her mother had taught her, and nothing would she reply but this:—

> *Newts and blindworms do no wrong,*
> *Spotted snakes from guilt are clear;*
> *Smiles and sighs, a dang'rous throng,*
> *Gentle spirit these I fear;*
> *Guard me from those looks of light,*
> *Which only shine to blast the sight.*

"Do I blast thy sight, cruel Iarine?" exclaimed the youth; and renewed his passionate prayers, which were interrupted with words like these:

> *Serpents' tongues have ne'er been known*
> *Simple maid from peace to sever,*
> *But the voice whose thrilling tone*
> *Tells of love that lasts for ever,*
> *Gentle spirit—*

"O, gentle spirit, plead my cause!" exclaimed the youth, "and dissipate this strange illusion. Look up, fairest Iarine; I only borrowed wings that I might fly to thee, but take this sword, and cut them in pieces if thou wilt." The maid still kept her eyes on a wreath of corn poppies which she was embroidering, nor stole one look at the kingly brow with its black arches, that inclined towards her in persuasive humility, nor at the radiant eyes of the enamoured youth, cast down beseechingly under their full lids and shadowy eye-lashes; but still she sang on, with Albinet:—

> *Beetles black will never charm me,*
> *Spiders weave no snares for me,*
> *Thorny hedge-hogs cannot harm me,*
> *But the brow where heaven I see,*
> *Catching beams from sunny eyes,—*
> *Guard me from that bright disguise!*

As the prince drew nearer to the damsel, she pressed closer to the door, trembling all over, and singing more and more earnestly, and at last she knelt down, wrapping the silken garment round her head and face and her whole figure, till she was completely enveloped. Thus baffled and utterly disappointed, Phantasmion stood still, and clasping his hands, exclaimed, "O fatal disguise! O fatal magic arts that have undone me!" Thrown off her guard by the earnest tone in which this was uttered, Iarine let the robe fall from her head, and looked up, somewhat fearfully, in the face of the youth who stood at a little distance. His eyes met hers, he uttered not a word, but again the maid felt irresistibly persuaded that truth as well as beauty beamed from his countenance. A spell seemed to hold them both silent and motionless, but the spell is broken, for a feeble knocking is heard at the partition wall, and Iarine starts up to obey that summons, letting Maudra's unfinished robe fall upon the ground. She opened a door, and discovered Albinian with his head resting on a harp, of which some strings were broken. Iarine braced them up, and the greyhaired man began feebly to move the chords, murmuring an old melody, the burden of which was scarce intelligible to the prince; but when the damsel joined in the strain, he distinguished words like these:

> *The winds were whispering, the waters glistering,*
> *A bay-tree shaded a sun-lit stream;*
> *Blasts came blighting, the bay-tree smiting,*
> *When leaf and flower, like a morning dream,*
> *Vanished suddenly.*

> *The winds yet whisper, the waters glister,*
> *And softly below the bay-tree glide;*
> *Vain is their cherishing, for, slowly perishing,*
> *It doth but cumber the river side.*
> *Leafless in summer-time.*

XXI

Phantasmion joins Iarine on the lake

Phantasmion continued to gaze on Iarine, unperceived by her father, whose face was turned in an opposite direction, till he heard a key turn in the lock, and the voice of Maudra speaking to Albinet. Then he quitted the tower as he had entered it, and roamed about the island, pondering how he might obtain another interview with the princess. That day he poured out wine for a noble company, but Glandreth was absent, and Maudra's glances fell upon his empty chair, while Iarine seemed afraid to raise her downcast eyes, lest they should meet those of a present lover. The banquet being ended, Phantasmion repaired to the lake side, and, looking out for Glandreth or Karadan, beheld only the light skiffs of the castle guests lying at anchor in the bay, their gay streamers rustling in a gentle breeze. Albinet sate and looked at them with tearful eyes; it seemed as if he loved to hear the varied intonations of his childish grief, so long drawn out was his sobbing and sighing. "I wish that breeze would rise to a tempest ere to-morrow's dawn," he murmured; "my sister is to be upon the lake when the sun rises; and woe's me! I am not to be with her."

Phantasmion's heart beat high with the thought of a scheme which these words suggested; he dreamed of it, sleeping and waking through the night, and by daybreak the next morning he was hovering over the lake. There all was solitary and silent; Iarine was not come; he flew back again to listen at her chamber window, and at last was so far carried away that he softly entered, and hung over her, like a guardian spirit, while she yet slept. Then he taxed himself to examine the separate charms which made up that sum of beauty, the graceful flowing line in which the whole was contained, the full eye, gently slanting at the outer side like a dove's, the soft gradation of colour, from locks of golden brown to the dark thread-like eyebrow and still blacker lashes, which, parting from fair white lids, appeared like foliage of a yew-branch laden with a pile of snow. It seemed as if the hand that streaks the tulip and the iris, and traces jetty lines down many a milk-white petal, had just finished painting that exquisite picture, and left it with every tint bright and fresh as new blown flowers. But hush! those eyes will quickly open, and the prince dares not wait to see them unclosed! He repassed the window, and, soaring upward, placed himself beside the pinnacles of the castle.

From the top of the highest tower he watched Iarine as she went leisurely across the lawn, till she disappeared in a grove between the castle and the lake; and, full of impatience he still waited, with outspread wings, till the prow of her light shallop darted forth from the dark green alders that clustered on the shore; then, plying his ready sails, he launched into the air, swept over the lawn and grove, and, wheeling round the boat, alighted just in front of the beautiful damsel, who dropped the oars and sate motionless when she saw him arriving. "Ah, leave me!" she cried, "I must needs be alone; the queen bade me go unaccompanied to meet a messenger, and receive some token or message for her." "And wilt thou be the blind servant of her wicked will, rather than reign in my fair land?" replied Phantasmion; "nay, sweet princess, thou shalt go with me, and never return to give an account of thy embassy." Then he seized the oars, and, turning the boat, made it fly over the waters like a swallow traversing the sky; Iarine sought in vain to arrest his movements; gaily the youth smiled, when her hand was laid on his strong arm, as if the snow would seek to impede the course of the torrent on which it falls. "My father!" she cried, "alas! my father! Thou hast taken his infant child, and wilt thou rob him of me also?" "I took that child to place him in safety," answered the young monarch; and I will place thee in more than safety: thou shalt be a queen, and reign over all my subjects, as now thou dost over my heart." "Karadan hast promised to aid my father against Glandreth," said Iarine. "What is his aid compared to mine?" exclaimed the youth; "and what his love compared to that I bear thee?" "He is my mother's kinsman," replied the maid; "my father loves him as he never will love thee; and for his sake I must shun thee, and seek to love him." "Would it be less difficult to love me than him?" cried the prince, "must thou shun me ere thou canst love him? O, if this be true, a thousand enemies and rivals shall never prevail against me!" Abandoning the oar he seized Iarine's hand, but with the one still left at liberty she pointed to the sky: "See what clouds," she said, "have gathered on the mountain-top! how threatening they are! how rapidly they are overspreading the heavens!" She had scarce finished speaking, when the hills, the shores, and the island were shrouded in vapour, while the lurid waters glimmered in a flickering twilight. Lightning rent the clouds on the mountain head, and disclosed the black rocks beneath them; instantly they closed again,

SARA COLERIDGE

but, at that signal flash, thunder and a boisterous wind raised their loud voices together, one like sullen threats rising louder and louder into fury, the other like the prolonged scream of maniac rage. A skiff which tossed at a distance, its white sails fluttering as the wings of a tempest-beaten dove, was the last object visible on the dusky horizon. Phantasmion surveyed the sky, in the centre of which he seemed to discern one cloud blacker than all the rest, and round it a faint edge of lighter hue; on that dark mass the youth could not help gazing, it seemed so like the shroud of a winged form; here and there might be the outstretched pinions, and, above these, the head and floating hair. While his face was upturned, a sheet of lightning overspread the cope of heaven: dizzy and half-blinded he cast down his eyes upon the lake, and there beheld the glistering face of Seshelma, upraised by the side of the boat, while her hands were extended to catch Iarine. Phantasmion seized the oar, and driving it betwixt the water-witch and the vessel, he thrust her away, then uplifted it again to strike her with all his force; but, like an otter, she darted under the waves, and soon her bubbling laugh was heard at a little distance, amid the voices of the storm. Still the boat goes onward, riding up and down the waves, at each descent seeming about to enter the deep, yet again mounting to the summit of the billow. It drives toward the foot of the lake, and soon approaches the skiff which has been seen on the horizon. Karadan is standing at the prow! vainly does he stretch out his arms and call upon Seshelma; she cannot bring about that meeting which her arts contrived, for a mightier power than hers presides over the storm. The dark youth beholds Iarine and Phantasmion together; he may not look upon them long; the skiff is going down; it sinks! "O save him!" exclaims the maid; and Phantasmion leaps into the tumbling element. It is a desperate enterprise; those wings, not made for the water, now only encumber him, and Karadan clings round his body with the clasp of a drowning man. Long did he struggle, but in vain: he and his rival were nigh sinking together, when a vessel, conducted by the old fisherman from the lower end of the lake, arrived in time to save them from death. In a little while they were rescued from the waves, and laid at the bottom of the wide bark, where the crew surrounded them, intent on their restoration, and none save the aged husband of Telza, bestowed a thought on the damsel in the narrow boat.

But the storm now abated, and Iarine, waving her hand to the fisherman, in token that she needed no help, slowly pursued her way homewards. On the horizon of the plain, beyond the foot of the lake, a border of pale brightness was visible; it seemed to show that there was a silver firmament behind those tumultuous volumes of cloud which had remained unmoved throughout the chaos of the storm. The maid was alone, but for herself she felt no fear; she thought not of Karadan or of Glandreth, of the water witch or of an angry step-dame; she was thinking only of Phantasmion. Her love had hitherto been as a distant strain of music, scarce noted by one that is busily occupied; but now the harmony sounds fuller and more distinct; it will be heard, and the hum of many voices falls into an undersong. With reluctance she recedes from the vessel where she lately saw him taken in, dripping and senseless. That bark was filled with servants of Magnart, who had been despatched from Polyanthida in search of their master's son. Learning from the old fisherman that he had gone upon the lake, they ventured through the storm, guided by the old man, in the direction of the island, whither they supposed he might have taken his course. Phantasmion recovered wholly while Karadan was but just beginning to revive, and, while the men in the boat were still bending around the dark youth, he took flight from the stern, and hastened to rejoin Iarine.

Black clouds were yet rolled around the body of the hills, while the head of the lake and one side of the island were still thickly veiled with mist; but the sun began to gild the peaks of the mountains, and a vivid rainbow spanned the waters, which now lay motionless and inky black, as if a trance had succeeded to violent agitation. Again Phantasmion stood by the side of Iarine: with moist wings he hovered over the boat, when the maid looked up and continued to ply the oars without speaking: but there was a smile on her face, and the youth entered the narrow vessel. Ere that splendid phantom which bent around them had faded away, Iarine and Phantasmion were bound to each other by the strongest ties that words can form; clouds or sunshine might reign without, but their faith was to remain like the dial, which stands fixed and changeless, while day and night roll on, and can but brighten or darken its face as they are passing over it. Now the youth feels that perfect satisfaction in the present hour which lulls in its tranquil ecstacy, all hope, all effort, all reflection, all forecast; even the certain knowledge that the dream must dissolve, cannot lessen its charm, that joyfulness of feeling which thought has no power to shake. He took from beneath his girdle the chaplet which had been worn by Zalia, and on which was inscribed, "The Queen of Palmland." He showed her the ruby flowers with their leaves of emerald, and the lady smiled, but turned away, and again pointed to the heavens. "How strange it is," she said, "that those wreaths of vapour are yet lying on the lake, when every cloud has left the mountain, and almost all have melted from the sky!" Phantasmion cast his eyes around and saw that the welkin was clear, except above the vapoury mass to which Iarine pointed; there he descried the same noticeable cloud which he had gazed upon in the beginning of the tempest; it was in the form of a cross, and the shape was more conspicuous now that it was alone in the sky. "Let us fear nothing," cried the youth; "these clouds too will disperse like the rest, and we shall have perfect sunshine." Scarce had he spoken thus, and placed the chaplet on Iarine's brow, when a boat shot forth from the dark mist. Glandreth was standing at the prow, and that vessel was followed by a train of others, which, at his command, surrounded Phantasmion and Iarine.

In a few moments the youth was bound with cords which fastened his arms and delicate pinions to his body, and, while Glandreth's armed men were dragging him away to the Castle, he beheld the chieftain conducting Iarine to the shore, then Maudra hidden among the trees, jealously watching his actions, then the drooping Albinian with his lame child on their way to the lake side. Albinet pulled his father's arm as Phantasmion passed him. "Look at his shoulders," he said; "now see his wings by daylight!" The cross-formed cloud had disappeared, and the sky seemed an endless depth of sunny blue when Phantasmion was hidden from daylight in a subterranean vault of the castle.

XXII

Phantasmion escapes from prison and presents himself to Iarine in disguise

Dark and cold was the place in which Phantasmion was confined, and such as might have chilled a less ardent temper than his, but he paced the stone floor, like a leopard in a cage, devising plans of escape, and nursing hopes of vengeance. He had now leisure to review the events of the morning, and now he surmised that Maudra had sent Iarine to meet Karadan at the suggestion of her wily counsellor, because she desired, at any cost, to remove her from the eyes of Glandreth; that the dark youth had planned to carry her away, and that their schemes and his own had been frustrated by the intervention of Oloola. "The spirit of the storm cannot conquer the heart of Iarine!" cried he; "other things may change for the better, and that will never change for the worse."

Thus he hoped and triumphed, but no food was given him, and his limbs were painfully pinioned, so that after a certain length of time he sank on the floor, exhausted and spiritless. His eyes were fixed in anguish on the massy door, at the top of the stone steps, by which he had descended into the dungeon, when he heard the bolts withdrawn and, in a few moments, Glandreth stood before him, sumptuously attired, and with a flaming lamp in his hand. "King of Palmland," said he, with a smile, "why hast thou chosen to conceal from a brother chief thy rank and dignity?" "A brother chief!" exclaimed the captive, in high disdain. "I know thee now," pursued Glandreth, "and can offer terms suitable to thy rank. Deign to read that scroll: I may not tarry to hear thy reply, for I must visit my fair mistress Iarine, who will brook delay on my part worse than thou wilt. Early to-morrow thou shalt see me again, and the light of the sun also, if thou approvest the conditions." So saying, he placed the lamp and the scroll on the ground beside the prisoner, and without loosing his bands, or giving him a morsel of food, quitted the dungeon. Phantasmion began to peruse the writing laid before him by his adversary, and found only such proposals as roused his indignation. "No!" he exclaimed aloud, "rather than yield half my kingdom, and what I value more than the whole of it, my claim on the hand of Iarine, let the floor of this dungeon be my death-bed! here let me perish since Potentilla does not come to my aid." Just as he had spoken thus, Phantasmion beheld a multitude of saw-flies with yellow bodies and black heads, flitting toward the light of the lamp; along with them came numbers of wasps, and the youth shrank as he beheld the mingled swarm approaching himself. He had little cause for fear; they alighted on the cords that bound his arms and wings, and setting resolutely to work, the wasps with their jaws, the flies with their rasping instruments, they severed the tough threads, till the prisoner, by a single effort, snapped the weakened bands; at that moment his arms were stretched at full length, and his wings broke forth like the tender leaves of a tree when released from their gummy sheath. Away flew the whole company of wasps and flies, and while they were disappearing by the narrow space between the bottom of the door and the top of the stairs, Phantasmion perceived a host of bees entering on the opposite side. They flew to a corner of the roof, and holding up the lamp, he saw that waxen combs were suspended above his head, and that the bees were there depositing the honey which they had just collected in the gardens of the island. Phantasmion now acknowledged that he had not been neglected by Potentilla, who had been employed in his service ever since he entered the dungeon. He soon gained possession of the luscious store, which the bees abandoned at his approach; and having feasted on the honey, found his strength and his hopes return together, nay, felt as jocund as one that has drunk new wine. In this mood he passed the remainder of the night, and when a few faint rays of the dawn found their way beneath the door into his gloomy abode, he ascended the steps to examine a painted roll which Glandreth had let fall as he left the dungeon; it was all emblazoned with gay devices, in the midst of which Phantasmion read these lines:—

> *False Love, too long thou hast delay'd,*
> *Too late I make my choice;*
> *Yet win for me that precious maid,*
> *And bid my heart rejoice:*
> *Then shall mine eyes shoot youthful fire,*
> *My cheek with triumph glow,*
> *And other maids that glance desire,*
> *Which I on one bestow.*

Make her with smile divinely bland
Beam sunshine o'er my face,
And Time shall touch with gentlest hand
What she hath deigned to grace;
O'er scanty locks full wreaths I'll wear;
No wrinkled brow to shade,
For joy will smooth the furrows there,
Which earlier griefs have made.

Though sports of youth be tedious toil,
When youth has pass'd away,
I'll cast aside the martial spoil
With her light locks to play;
Yea, turn, sweet maid, from tented field
To rove where dew-drops shine,
Nor care what hand the sceptre wield,
So thou wilt grant me thine.

Before the lamp expired, Phantasmion fed its flame with this testimony of his rival's passion, then re-ascended the steps, and stationed himself beside the door. Hearing a key thrust into the rock he hovered about it, on balanced wings, face downward, and while Glandreth was beginning to descend, rushed past him out of the dungeon. The fugitive played his vans faster and faster, till he had cleared the island, then away over the lake he floated through clear fields of air, as if borne along by the breeze, without a movement of his outspread pinions.

He alighted in the midst of that thicket where he had formerly spent the night, and looked about with momentary dread to see that no snake yet lurked there. Scarcely had he finished hiding his wings, when the fisherman's ancient dame come in sight, and, being startled at his unexpected appearance, let her bundle of sticks fall to the ground. The youth accosted her kindly, and began to collect her scattered burden, while she seized the opportunity of chatting and asking questions. "Thou hast travelled far since we saw thee last," she cried; "but there is no city in Almaterra so well worth going to see as the capital of this country, Diamantha." "How knowest thou that I have not been to see it?" said the prince, with a smile. "I think thou wouldst hardly come away," said Telza, "just as the court are going thither." "Are they going thither?" inquired the prince; "ah! methinks, I heard tell of this; and when will they set out?" "This very day," replied the dame; "come to my cottage and thou wilt see them pass." By the time that Phantasmion reached a rising ground, just beyond that lowly cot, the royal train might be seen winding along the vale; and, long after they were out of sight, he stood looking after them wrapped in thought. Telza marked his countenance. "The last time thou wert here," said she, "our lovely princess passed by: truly till thou hast seen her thou hast not set eyes on the fairest thing in Rockland."

Phantasmion partook once more of Telza's hospitality, and learned from the fisherman, her husband, that Glandreth was not travelling with the King and Queen, but was still at the Island. Forthwith he resolved to follow Iarine, and, taking leave of the aged pair, pursued his journey alone; but presently, fearing that he might stray out of the right course, he looked about for some one to guide or direct him. So doing he espied a number of tall peasant girls with baskets on their heads, and saw them sit down by the way-side to eat their provisions. "Who are these lofty maidens?" inquired the youth. A passing countryman, to whom he had spoken, made answer, "They come from a certain glen, and are bound for a neighbouring town, where they expect to sell the fruit in their baskets: some of them will not need to go so far, for this evening they will overtake the royal household who are already encamped at no great distance." Phantasmion approached one of the damsels: "Are all the women of your valley as tall as thou and thy comrades, fair maiden?" he said. "No women are so tall as those of our glen," she replied; "and no fruit is so fine as that which we gather on the tops of our hills. Prithee taste and buy." "I will buy thy whole basket," answered he, "if I may purchase thy cloak and headgear too:—and how might I procure the secresy of thy comrades, were I to go along with them thus disguised?" That affair was quickly despatched by the mountain maiden, who dighted the prince in her upper vest and muffling head dress, placed her basket on his head, and departed to a cottage hard by with more gold in her hand than the baskets of all the company were like to gain. The prince went on with the rest of the band, and, about evening, espied a number of tents erected at the entrance of a wood. The women were soon dispersed among them, eager to gain purchasers for their fruit, and Phantasmion, having learnt that the princess was wandering in the forest, hastily went in search of her, followed by some of his new associates. Soon he hears a rustling amid the leaves, a bird falls from its lofty perch, and young Albinet shouts for joy. "Sister!" he cried, "my little bow and arrows will shoot as well as the longest and strongest in the land." "I prithee aim not at me, young archer!" cried a voice from amid the trees; "nor take me for a white heron or long-necked crane!" Phantasmion hastened on. The voice was at some distance, but believing it to be that of Iarine he wondered at such lively tones. Soon he entered a glade, where three white-robed damsels were standing beside a rivulet; the first who was looking toward the wood was Zelneth; Iarine and Leucoia were talking together at a little distance. The youth drew his head-dress, which he had begun to push aside, close over his face, while his comrades offered their fruit to the lady. "Here are the tall mountaineers," cried she, "with their pleasant cloud-berries; let us sit beside that elder tree and eat the dainty fruit." Phantasmion was by this time kneeling before Iarine and vainly endeavouring to catch her eye, unperceived by Leucoia; but Zelneth called him away to place the fruit in his basket on broad leaves which grew near the brook, and, while this repast was eaten, the maidens' talk went on. "I have little doubt," said Iarine, "that we shall find Karadan at Diamantha, near the northern palace. Arzene's heart may soon be set at ease." "Nay," cried Zelneth, "it is more likely that we shall find him about the Black Lake, for it was there that he escaped again from those who were sent to bring him home." "Was he imprisoned in the dark vault of the tower, or in the castle?" "Karadan imprisoned!" said Iarine. "I meant that other youth, of whom thou and Zelneth were speaking," replied her cousin. "He was confined in the tower," answered Iarine with tears, "and perhaps he is a prisoner still." "And thou didst nothing to set him free!" exclaimed Zelneth: "I would have died"—here the damsel checked her hasty speech, struck by an eager countenance which reminded her of Semiro. But Phantasmion turned away, and the startling likeness was forgotten when Iarine offered her a key, and in an earnest tone rejoined, "Then go thou to the Island, and open his prison door." "I am ready to attend thee, Zelneth," cried Leucoia, quickly rising from her seat. "Why didst thou not release the captive thyself?" said Zelneth, as she took the key. "I was prevented by the queen," Iarine replied; "she met me as I descended the steps of the tower, where I had discovered it beneath the tapestry, and, full of misplaced suspicion, angrily sent me to my chamber." "And thou wilt seek for Karadan," said Zelneth, "while we perform this charitable errand?" "O hasten to perform it this very hour," exclaimed the lovely princess. "Yon cloud above the wood is yet full of radiance, and even when the sun declines, it is pleasant travelling by the softer beams of the moon." "Which will not rise this night, sweet cousin," Zelneth made reply. "For that favouring countenance we may vainly pray, as luckless Karadan does for thine."

Then the three slender damsels and the manlike mountaineers with their princely companion quitted the lawn and pursued their way through the wood. "Come, Albinet! we are returning!" cried Iarine, but the boy, with a laugh, went and hid himself among the underwood. Phantasmion kept by the side of Iarine, and, when Zelneth and Leucoia stepped forward, he pulled her robe. The princess looked up in surprise, but at that moment the dark-eyed maiden turned back to address her cousin;—"What will our mother think of this journey?" she cried, "and, after all, what thanks shall I earn?" "A thousand thanks!" said Iarine, blushing deeply, "From thee, but not from him!" murmured Zelneth. "I will never repine," Iarine answered, "whatever guerdon he offers thee." Zelneth smiled and again stepped forward with Leucoia; Phantasmion once more touched Iarine's robe and whispered, "I am here; and subject to no will but thine." Joy now animated her trembling frame, and when Zelneth addressed her once more she wondered at the glow of happiness that mantled on her cheek. "Unhappy Karadan!" sighed the maiden. "Hush!" cried Iarine; "my father is approaching." Then Leucoia impatiently beckoned to Zelneth: "Come, sister," she cried, "if thou art resolved on this journey we must mount our steeds without delay."

The daughters of Magnart now departed, after taking leave of their kinswoman, who remained within the wood, and beheld the crimson sun half sunk below the distant plain, betwixt bare shafts of trees, which looked like pillars of ebony. Over their rugged roots Albinian was slowly advancing, his thin white locks just tinged with red by the sunbeams. Glandreth and his armed band were close behind, their casques glittering brightly, while their shadows blackened the ground. The chief strode on before them, passing Zelneth and Leucoia without a glance, for he had discerned Iarine in the wood. With firm step and lofty port he came, while the tottering Albinian hurried on when he perceived his approach, and went to lean upon the lady's arm. "Give me the hand of the fair princess, thy daughter," said Glandreth, "and thou shalt have a firmer support than she alone can give." The old man's face appeared convulsed with inward passion; he strove to speak, but words failing him, shook his head and waved the chief away.

Glandreth, incensed by the refusal of Albinian, impetuously took the lady's hand from his, and the feeble man, overthrown by that sudden movement, fell to the earth. Iarine turned her indignant eye upon the proud usurper, and would have knelt by the side of Albinian, but the chief detained her hand, till Phantasmion leaning forward from the group of damsels, forced him to release it, seizing his arm with no friendly grasp. Astonished that a woman could assault him thus, he turned about and was wounded at that moment in the cheek by a small arrow which flew from the underwood. Then believing himself surrounded by concealed enemies, he shouted to his armed men, who were still in the back ground. They hastened into the wood, but scarcely had they entered it, when a cloud descended from on high and hung, like a canopy, over the tops of the tall trees. That canopy was composed of innumerable winged insects: every moment it grew thicker and thicker, and the soldiers groped about in total darkness, unable to find their chief. He, meantime, was battling with armies of moths, which, as fast as he cut them away with his sword, continued to swarm around him undiminished, and soon his men at arms were engaged in like manner: they ran against the trees, and straggled in all directions into the wood, trying to escape from their countless antagonists. Phantasmion seized by mistake, the robe of Albinian, who was clinging to Iarine, and whispered in his ear. "My fairest, dost thou still love the stranger from Palmland?" a low groan was the only answer to this fond inquiry. The youth let go his hold and rushed away to a little distance; there the cloud of insects dispersed right above his head, and, looking up into the clear space, he beheld Potentilla, cloaked in wide moth wings, hovering aloft. She beckoned to Phantasmion; he dropped his feminine garb, and soaring upwards, floated by the side of his guardian Fairy through the dim grey sky. By the time that both were out of sight, the wood was free from insects: the sun's flaming ball had sunk, and no moon had arisen; but one large star was shooting its diamond rays just over the top of a sable fir tree.

XXIII

POTENTILLA WEAVES A WONDROUS WEB
FOR PHANTASMION

Potentilla guided Phantasmion to the chief palace of Rockland, situate between the sea and Diamantha, after he had procured the dress of a peasant by the way. The travellers rested in an orange grove, and, when the prince besought Potentilla to deliver Iarine from the power of Glandreth and Maudra, she made answer, "To-morrow, the courtly company will arrive at this place. I cannot give thee troops of horse and men in armour to meet them; but I will exhibit a strange spectacle, and while the crowd are gazing at it thou mayest carry off the princess to the sea shore. There the son of Magnart hath a skiff in readiness; for he still hopes to win Iarine, and carry her to a secret bower in Nemoroso. This vessel, if thou art beforehand with him, may transport thy fair one and thee to Palmland."

The heart of Phantasmion bounded with joyful expectation when he heard the fairy speak thus. He donned his rustic disguise, took a pruning hook in his hand, and, when he saw any one approach, seemed to be busy among the shrubs. He fed on the fruits of the garden, and at night lay down to sleep in a clump of trees, close by the principal entrance to the royal domain. Right in front of that gate, at the top of a gentle ascent, over which the road led to the Diamanthine palace, was a triumphal arch of light architecture, erected to commemorate the conquest of Tigridia, but now overgrown with climbing plants and decked with their gay blossoms. Phantasmion had not reposed long when he was awakened by an eager dream: he thought he saw the royal procession enter the great gate and advance toward the archway. One by one the company seemed to be pacing along; Iarine passes, but still he is chained to the turf where he lies; the damsel floats on,—she gains the arch, but just as she is about to disappear Phantasmion starts up. The dream has vanished, but the scene remains, and, by the pale light of the midnight sky, he discerns a strange object under the festive fabric: a spider, as big as a wolf, is wheeling round and round within the circuit of the lofty arch, spinning and weaving as she goes. The frame-work of her giant web is formed, the warp is laid out, and now she is travelling round and round to fill in the gummy woof. Not long afterwards Phantasmion beheld the fairy artisan depart, in the manner of spiders, shooting long lines into the air, and seeming to fly without wings. Upwards she travels, and now she darts across the moon's bow, and now she is a black spot in the midst of a twinkling constellation. Phantasmion slept again, and the first object that struck his newly opened eyes was the magic web, looking like a wheel of fire in the rosy light of morning. Anon those flames expired: every spoke and cross-thread appeared to be a shining icicle, and the whole might have been taken for a crystal net; but soon the elastic substance began to undulate beneath a gentle breeze, and all the scarlet blossoms which flaunted over it were softly heaved up and down. Phantasmion feared that the delicate apparition would melt away before the travellers arrived, but the sun, as it grew stronger and stronger, had no power to dissolve that fabric, and, while a crowd was advancing from the palace to view it close at hand, the courtly train, being suddenly arrested on entering the great gate by this unexpected sight, and utterly forgetful of every other object, stood gazing in wonder at the magic web. Phantasmion easily recognized Iarine amid a bevy of damsels, though she and all of them were veiled from head to foot. He shaded his brow with his peasant's cap, and, approaching the princess, eagerly whispered, "Come with me and I will explain this wonder." The lady started, threw down her veil, which she had partly drawn aside to survey the spectacle, and, after a few moments' hesitation, stole away into the wide plain beyond the precincts of the palace. Phantasmion followed, full of hope and joy, and beheld Iarine, fleet as an antelope, speeding across the moor. She had gained some ground at first, and, so swiftly did she bound along, that the youth came not up with her till she had sunk down among the trees of a shady copse. Great was his surprise when he arrived here to find the princess, her veil thrown off, clad in the habit of a shepherdess, with a crook in her hand. "Wherefore is this disguise?" he cried, and why hast thou fled hither? on the sea coast we shall find a vessel wherein we may sail to Palmland, and thence up the great river to my very palace gates." Iarine replied, "My heart is thine, and yet I may not go with thee; I am bound by a vow to make a pilgrimage elsewhere; the strongest proof of love which thou canst give will be to let me instantly depart and ask not whither I am going." Phantasmion felt like one who has dreamt of golden fruit, and, waking, sees what he had dreamt of glowing nigh, but finds his arms fettered, his feet fastened to the ground. "This device of thine," she said, "has enabled me to escape, just as I had begun to despair of what I so anxiously desired. If my enterprise succeeds, I shall owe that happiness to thee." Cheerily the maiden spoke, yet could not choose but weep, while Phantasmion remained speechless and tearful, looking in her face with imploring eyes, as if he hoped by the mute eloquence of his grief to melt away her resolution. Iarine cut off one of her long ringlets, tied it round the arm of the sorrowful youth, and smiling playfully yet tenderly, bound him with that silken fetter to the branch of a shrub. "Farewell!" she said, "when next we meet thou mayest fasten the chain on me, and, if it binds me to thyself, believe that I will gladly wear it even to my life's end." Then she took up her shepherd's crook, and hastened away, nor turned her head till her motions were scarce to be discerned by him she left behind through the dimness of distance. Phantasmion sought not to follow her, but, long after she was out of sight, he stood in the same attitude as when she disappeared, clasping the glossy ringlet in unconscious hands.

At length he moved away, and wandering along with uncertain steps, found himself once more beside the archway. It was now past noon-day, and all the gazers had dispersed; but still the mystic web remained, and, while he was looking at it with sorrowful eyes, he saw a beautiful bird called a chinquis fly into it, and become entangled in its meshes. While it fluttered there he recognized it as one which he had been wont to caress and feed in Palmland, and which had gained the name of the moon-bird, from the sky-blue moons or mirrors which adorned its wings and train. "Poor bird," said the prince, "thou hast followed me hither out of love! thou shalt not perish in these toils, if I can set thee at liberty." He threw off his upper vest, fanned the air lightly with his pinions, and, forgetting the supernatural strength and tenacity of Potentilla's work, laboured to free the bird till he himself became entangled, and struggling to disengage his wings was only the more firmly glued to the web. Thus he hung, suspended in the centre of the arch, with the moon-bird by his side, while a set of rustics who beheld him from the open gate, believed him to be some deity that presided over the feathered tribes, and gazed at his wings in silent wonder. All his struggles to escape were vain, till a large eagle, rushing upon the moon-bird, became likewise entangled in the toils. He with his strong pinions shook the net so violently, that at last it was rent asunder: aloft he flew with great part of the web clinging to his back, and Phantasmion was dashed upon the ground. For some moments he lay under the triumphal arch with his eyes closed and his senses gone; but, coming to himself, he beheld the pretty moon-bird hovering affectionately over him. Then he arose, drew on his cloak, and hastened out of the royal precincts; having gained a lonely place, he tried his wings, but, finding they were too much injured to sustain him aloft, except during very short flights, full of sorrow and perplexity, he took his way to the seashore.

Karadan had gone thither before him; Karadan stood on the rocky beach, and raising to his lips a trumpet-formed shell, produced a sound in which the tones of the wind, as it whistles through a crevice, were combined with the deep, full, swelling voice of many waters. The blast was borne over the liquid plain, and soon a woman's form arose from the ocean; the setting sun threw its orange glow on the bloodless visage of Seshelma, as onward she came, cleaving the amber flood; a smile widened her flat face and glittered in her yellow eyes, unshaded by lashes, and, thus illumined, her countenance looked like that of a demon brightened by surrounding flames. "Where is Iarine?" exclaimed Karadan; "hath my rival carried her away, and have thy promises come to this?" "Iarine is gone to Nemorosa," replied the sorceress, "and he to whom she has given her heart is not far off." At these words Seshelma smiled maliciously upon Karadan, and the youth uttered a deep groan. "Accursed be the day," he cried, "when I entered into a league with thee! Iarine loves my rival and what fruit have I of this wicked bond?" "Do my bidding as heretofore," said the woman-fish, "and thou shalt banish thy rival from the maiden's heart." "Away! cried Karadan impatiently; "thy promises are but vain lures." "What!" was the reply; "have I not put into thy hands the silver pitcher?" "That is true," cried the youth; "what hast thou to propose?" "The king of Palmland," she answered, "hath Iarine's infant brother secreted in his palace: place that child in my power, and I will cause the maiden to believe that Phantasmion has delivered him to me. Agree to this, and I will transport thee to his royal domain long before he can return to it: thou shalt travel swiftly by the sea and up the large river which flows past the palace of Palmland to enter the ocean." Cold drops stood on Karadan's brow while he debated within himself on this proposal; at last he exclaimed, "O never will I betray the child that Iarine loves to this monster! One sacrifice I have promised; to gain that heavenly maid, I have made a vow which renders me unworthy to possess her. Surely I have never loved aright." Seshelma laughed, and that long drawn jeering laugh blended with the

SARA COLERIDGE

bubble and hiss of the waters and died into the piping of the wind: but no angry emotion ruffled the glazed surface of her face, as she fronted the youth's agitated countenance. "Do as thou wilt," she replied; "perchance thou art wise to cease contending in this cause, for who can alter the fixed purposes of fate? There are spirits of the flood that can see into futurity."—"Did they tell thee of her I love?" interrupted Karadan with vehemence; "shall the maid be mine?" "Never!" answered Seshelma, and again she laughed, while it seemed as if her laugh was re-echoed by a lurking train under the waters, till it passed off into the noises of the ocean. "Treacherous fiend!" Karadan shrieked aloud, "shall Phantasmion possess Iarine? Dost thou answer, yes? unsay that word and I will come and dwell with thee, all hideous as thou art, in dark and breathless caves for ever!" Furiously he rushed forward and seized her extended arm, whereat a lightning flash of electricity shot through his frame; his impotent grasp relaxed; he stood motionless, cramped in every muscle, and with anguish-stricken eyes, bent in fixed stare upon the deep, beheld the enchantress holding up her hands in mockery, while she retreated backwards through the ocean, leisurely rocking up and down with the waves, as if she resigned herself, like a drifting vessel, to their guidance.

XXIV

PHANTASMION RETURNS TO
PALMLAND BY SEA

Meantime Phantasmion approached the sea shore by a thickly wooded gorge, the lovely Chinquis flying by his side or before him, then rushing up among the trees to play hide and seek with her master, as she had been wont to do in the groves of Palmland. From between the last rocks of the valley appeared a small portion of the sea, in the midst of which, a little skiff moved on the dark waves with white sails gleaming in the twilight. The moon-bird paused not with Phantasmion to note that object, but skimming on, now hither now thither, with careless waste of motion, flew unawares against the face of Karadan, as he turned an angle of the winding road. The youth, being suddenly startled in his miserable mood, lifted an angry hand and smote the bird with such force that it fell to the ground; whereupon Phantasmion sprang forward, and the two princely rivals stood face to face. "Well met!" cried the young king of Palmland; "I have not come hither in vain, since I have encountered thee. Let us fight now for that pitcher which hangs to thy girdle." "So be it!" cried Karadan, hastily unfastening the vessel; "I will show thee a good place, smooth and light." He hurried on, till, coming within a stone's throw of a chasm amid the rocks, he raised his hand to fling the pitcher down that dark abyss, hoping thus to prevent its falling to the lot of his rival, let the event of the conflict be what it might. But Phantasmion, springing forward, stayed his arm; the pitcher fell at his feet; Karadan in desperation drew his dagger, and was rushing on his unguarded adversary, when the moon-bird, which had risen from the ground unobserved, flew upon him and darted her beak into his eye. A stream of blood gushed down his cheek; he was still feeble from the effects of Seshelma's touch, and, overpowered by this second blow, he fell fainting on the ground. Phantasmion resolved to secure the pitcher, and fight with Karadan on some future opportunity; he began to draw it from under the body of the youth, who opened his eyes and groaned deeply, but had not strength to stir. The prince saw that his lips moved, but no articulate sounds reached the listener's ear. He desisted for a moment, then renewed his attempt, and, pulling out the pitcher, sought to place it under his cloak, but the handle slipped out of his fingers; he took it up again, but the same thing happened; then he would have seized the vessel by the lip, but, like those insects which elude the grasp with their finely polished cases or pliant hair, it still glided away; he might as well have tried to hold quicksilver, and, after many vain attempts, he began to suspect that he was foiled by some invisible being. "Can Seshelma prevail here," he cried, "among rocks and trees and flowery banks?" Phantasmion cast his eyes around him on all sides; at a little distance from the place where he stood grew a tall branching plant, sheeted with blossoms, which at this evening hour were newly opened, when other plants had closed their dewy cups and bells. At mid-day the hue of those flowers would have looked wan and spiritless; but now that the sky was sobered, now that scarlet and crimson began to blacken, while blue, lilac, and green were growing all alike, the silver yellow gleam of the broad disk, which gathered in the light, like eyes of night birds, had a noticeable lustre, and they seemed to be the beautiful spectres of blossoms that had perished in the day. Just above that luminous plant appeared another spectre, yet more softly resplendent. It was the Fairy Feydeleen, with warning hand outstretched toward the youth of Palmland. "Phantasmion!" she whispered, "the tears of Arzene have prevailed, and, even against thee, I must guard her truant son. Go hence, I beseech thee, and trouble him no more." The young monarch obeyed; he proceeded down the glen, and, looking back, ere the path turned away, beheld the delicate fairy pouring balm from a chalice on the eyes of Karadan.

And now Phantasmion has entered the little skiff, and is about to leave those hostile shores, when on the summit of the cliff, high over-head, he beholds two figures, the indistinct lineaments of which, seen through the dusk, fill his soul with apprehension. That stony outline of an armed form, sharp as the rugged rock, and that soft quivering plume belong to none but Glandreth, while, on the other side, vast wings upraised, and moveless, bespeak the presence of Oloola. She points to an eagle that flies overhead with threads of network hanging from its feathers. It is the one that rent Potentilla's web; Glandreth looks after the bird, then eagerly renews his discourse; what words he uttered were inaudible to Phantasmion, but the gale brought to his ear Oloola's resonant reply. "Phantasmion has not carried her away; she is gone to seek a spring of healing waters; for the sake of Albinian and of Albinet, she roams afar." The youth listened eagerly: Glandreth's discourse was a dull murmur, but Oloola spake again, and her words appeared to have been blown through a trumpet. "While Phantasmion goes in search of Iarine, Glandreth shall conquer the Land of Palms." Then Glandreth shouted for joy till all the rocks reechoed, and Phantasmion saw that Oloola had disappeared from the cliff. He was still watching Glandreth and listening to the uproar which his voice raised along the shore, when the little vessel in which he stood was suddenly lifted up and whirled about in the air, while the sea dashed and roared and eddied underneath, as if a waterspout had fallen on the spot. The moon-bird, having no power to resist that blast, eddied round and round without the vessel; but gradually the wind fell, the sea grew smooth, and the fragile bark settled on the water, as a falcon sinks to her nest after wheeling about restlessly in the air. Meantime Phantasmion heard a voice on high, and it sent these words to his ear, "I swore to serve him till Anthemmina's dying day."

The moon is up, and two large stars, bright spots of light, appear as if they had dropped out of her beaming crescent; Phantasmion admires not the moon, nor fancies an invisible chain by which those pendant gems may be linked to her golden bow. The chinquis rests upon the mast and sleeps in the moonlight, her splendid train, with all its mirrors, reflecting the mild rays of night: but the Prince of Palmland gazes not on her: in thought he is following the lovely pilgrim through dangerous woods and wilds. Thus he coasted along, coming to land now and then for provisions, till he reached Palmland, and sailed up the principal river to his own abode. Weary and dispirited, he reached his palace gates, and scarce had arrived at the pomegranate tree when the faithful chinquis, which had never wholly recovered Karadan's blow, fell dead at his feet. Phantasmion sate upon the ground, and shed tears over the lifeless bird: but Potentilla came behind him and cheerily exclaimed, "Weep no more for the dead, but take thought for the living." The prince looked up; "I have gained the heart of Iarine," said he; "but I cannot make her my wife because of Glandreth and Karadan." Potentilla replied, "Surely my aid has availed thee somewhat; perchance it may enable thee to gain still more."

XXV

Iarine visits the house of Malderyl in company with Penselimer

While Phantasmion sailed homeward, Iarine was wandering through the wilds of Tigridia, at every hut where she obtained food and shelter, inquiring, as if by chance, concerning the situation of Malderyl's mansion, but telling no one that she was thither bound. Could the sweet feelings and glad thoughts, which she excited wherever she went among the pastoral people of the land, have sprung up into visible flowers, it would have been seen that she left a blooming track behind her, and, like the sun, drew virtue from the coldest soil. One evening she entered a green dell between woods, where a shepherd was conducting his sheep to the fold: a youth who accompanied her knew this old man, and having commended her to his care departed, to the great distress of the maiden, who feared lest wild beasts should attack him on his way home as the shades of night came on. The shepherd tried to lessen her fears by relating how Ulander of Nemorosa had thinned the tiger inhabitants of the land. "In these woods," said he, "I doubt if a brindled coat remains, for here it was that the huntsman chief and his comrades procured a band of tigerlings for Queen Maudra. I wish this country paid no other tribute to the barren Land of Rocks than that. Here the parents were murdered, and the young preserved to flesh their teeth on the subjects of king Phantasmion." While the old man stood talking to Iarine, describing with lively gestures the battle of tigers, the braying of horns, the crashing of boughs, and the yelling of wounded beasts, many of his sheep, as if glad to steal away from the oft-told tale, had straggled into the woody glen, which was full of soft herbage, and Iarine offered to guard the main body of his flock while he went in search of the truants; so thanking her for that courtesy, taking a weapon of defence from his girdle, and placing his crook in her hand, he hastened away. The lovely princess led the flock slowly onward till she arrived at a stream, which crossed the dell, and had been swollen by sudden rains to a torrent: here she paused, waiting for the shepherd, and, while the sheep eyed the water, thinking, perchance of a ford lower down, where they had crossed in the morning, Iarine's mind had travelled back to her father and Albinet, thence to her baby brother, and all the time was not wholly absent from Phantasmion. At last she began to think that the old man was long away, and looked up with pleasure when she heard footsteps advancing; but he who now stood before her was more like a king than a rustic swain; his attire, though black, was costly, his countenance abstracted and grave. He stopped to look at Iarine, as she lifted up a dripping lamb which had slipped into the water, and, seeing that she eyed him anxiously, as if desirous yet afraid to speak (for indeed she wished to inquire whether he had seen the shepherd,) his eye lit up with expectation, and in an eager tone he exclaimed;—"Hast thou aught to tell me of the silver pitcher? Surely thou art akin to Anthemmina, for there is something in thy face like hers." Iarine was startled at being accosted thus, but in a few minutes felt assured that she must be in company with Penselimer of Almaterra. "I know not what has become of the silver pitcher;" she said; "would that I could hear tidings of it! But meantime I feel anxious lest the shepherd whose flock I am guarding, may have met some accident in yonder wood." "I trust he has not fallen in with a tiger," said the king, "such a fell beast as lately carried off my horse at noonday." Then, taking a javelin from his belt, he hastened in the direction which Iarine pointed out, and soon the maiden saw him return followed by the truant sheep, and bearing in his arms the old shepherd, who had fallen down a ravine, formed by a recent flood, and so disabled himself. He directed Iarine to a shallower part of the stream where her fleecy charge were able to pass over. She penned the sheep in the fold while Penselimer carried their owner to his cottage; then, repairing to that rustic abode, she assisted the shepherd's daughter to tend his wounds and prepare the evening meal.

Penselimer sate beside the hearth, seeing forms in the fire which appeared to no one but himself; for as soon as he had placed the old man in safety, his thoughts had all flown back to the silver pitcher. When Iarine's employment was over, and she too sate down, he offered, out of courtesy, to guard her during the rest of her journey, and hearing in what direction she must proceed, declared that he should lose no time in attending her, as the way she spoke of would bring him to the house of Malderyl, whither he desired to go. There was a damsel in the cottage, who had bashfully drawn back when the strangers entered; while Iarine was helping the shepherd lass, she took the maiden's wheel into a corner and span; but hearing Penselimer speak in a low voice of Malderyl, she stayed both hand and foot, and leaned forward to catch the words of his discourse. Iarine, then first beholding her countenance by the fire light, felt a sudden glow of alarm, so much did it resemble that of Karadan: the passionate black eye, the brow, the dark skin, all seemed his, and just such a green and crimson roll as he commonly wore, concealed her locks. The shy damsel seeing herself noted, resumed her spinning, and Iarine smiled at her own suspicion when she saw her thus quietly employed.

Early the next morning the princess went forth again in company with Penselimer, who related the story of his unfortunate love for Anthemmina; then at length she understood how her own fate depended on the silver pitcher, and saw that Karadan had told no feigned tale when he showed it her upon the Island. Penselimer did not observe her sorrowful countenance, but continued talking of himself. "It is strange," said he, with the smiling face of a child that wears his newest, finest suit; "that I, who am the most unhappy among men, should be the envy of beings who dwell on high. The truth is, they hate me on account of Anthemmina, foreseeing that I shall regain her love if I can but find the pitcher. Therefore they watch me with their bright eyes incessantly; and even at this hour, though I cannot see them, I well know that they are keenly observing me." Iarine cast up her blue eyes to the sky, with a look of pity and wonder. "Their unheard-of persecutions," added he, "excited the compassion of the veiled lady Melledine, who bade me repair to her sister Malderyl, and gave me good hope that, through her, I should regain what I had lost." The maiden rejoiced on hearing Melledine's name, and surmised that Penselimer was to recover his lost senses by means of the blessed spring of which she herself was in search.

The travellers rested at noon beside a stream, and Iarine sought to persuade her companion that the notions which he dwelt upon were shadows of no substance, echoes of no sound, like those sights and voices which the disordered eye and ear create within themselves, unmoved by any outward thing. But Penselimer calmly replied: "Sweet lady (for it is plain to me that thou art no shepherdess), if the mirror of my mind did indeed play false, as thy speech infers, how vain it were to lay the truth before me! For I must either be incapable of seeing it at all, or must see it distorted and discoloured through the flaws and stains of the glass. That Anthemmina dwells in yonder sky seems to me as plain as that I view thy beauteous face, and heard thee just now declare that she lies under the wave. But this is one of the tricks of my persecutors:

go where I may, a report has still preceded me that I am mad." Just as Penselimer spoke thus, a fawn gambolled past Iarine; the damsel was tempted to pursue it a little way down the stream, and, running by a leafy covert, she caught a glimpse of the brown girl, who span at the cottage; but passing that way again she saw no one there.

The travellers went on their way, and Iarine, finding that all the thoughts which a sane mind can suggest to one that is diseased will take the hue of the receptacle, as colourless waters turn blue or green when poured into certain channels, rather sought, by gentle ingenuity, to make him conceive happy imaginations, than presented them to him, and no longer combated errors which were as invulnerable as they were easy to hit. Both rested at a goatherd's cottage that night, and, in passing through the little orchard attached to it, when she set forth early the next day, Iarine beheld the dark maiden, wrapped in a cloak and sleeping under a tree. The swarthy cheek and black eyebrow again fixed her attention, but, as she gazed, the girl awoke, and, beholding Iarine, covered her face with her garment. Penselimer now joined his fair comrade, and the maiden, in some perplexity, pursued her way. At noon she beheld the house of Malderyl, situate on the lowest ridge of a conical mountain, which towered alone upon the plain, and showed from its rugged brow on one side pastoral plains, interspersed with woods and hollow glades, full of giant reeds and tree-like ferns, on the other the endless forest of Nemorosa, which Glandreth had never subdued. The mansion itself and the wall around it were hewn out of a rock. "Whither shall I conduct thee?" said Penselimer to his companion when they reached the foot of the hill. "I must go whither thou art going," she said, "even to the house of Malderyl; for I too seek the presence of the ancient queen, but was bound not to speak of this till I approached her threshold." Penselimer blew a horn which hung at the outer gate of the mansion, as soon as he reached it, and started at the loud sound which ensued, and which all the rocks above and below echoed. A raven flew from a beetling crag, overhead just as a rugged churl admitted the strangers: other domestics then appeared and conducted them to the apartment where their mistress sate at the summit of a tower. Malderyl was seated in a carved chair, the brown arms and upright back of which resembled her own figure, dried and stiffened, but not enfeebled by age. Her face appeared of bronze, all but the rapid eye, like a lambent flame, shining and restless; her heart was dead as the leathern girdle that covered it, her brain ever in motion, like the sands of the hour

SARA COLERIDGE

glass that stood before her on the table. She was clad in robes of purple and scarlet, and wore upon her head a crown of golden spikes. Iarine felt appalled when Malderyl desired that Penselimer would wait in the ante-room while she conferred with the maiden, but, summoning courage, presented an ivory tablet on which her name was inscribed, with curious cyphers underneath. Malderyl, after a glance at the writing, told her that she must go alone to the spring and impart the secret to no one. The maiden having agreed to this condition, she placed in her hand a light bucket and chain with a leathern bottle, at the same time giving her certain directions, and Iarine took her leave with many thanks, delighted to think how much of the precious water the skin would contain. No sooner was she out of hearing than Malderyl turned her keen eyes on the melancholy king, who had entered at one door as Iarine disappeared by another. "Penselimer," she said, "he who robs thee of thy right is Phantasmion, king of Palmland." "The son of Dorimant!" he exclaimed, with kindling eye. On each side of the queen's footstool a dwarfish figure was crouching; Iarine had scarcely observed them, and by Penselimer they had been taken for appendages to the grotesque imagery of her wooden chair, but when the queen touched one of them with her foot, up he sprang, and fixed upon Penselimer a pair of toad's eyes ringed with scarlet: at the same instant the other dwarf raised his pointed face, in which the eye-holes were mere points, laid out his broad flat hands, and put forward the side of his head as if to hear rather than see what was going on. While Penselimer viewed these objects with surprise, Malderyl began to mutter, and soon both they and the whole apartment were obscured, clouds creeping over the vaulted roof and veiling the wide crystal windows. A fiery light then rose up on the opposite wall, and Penselimer beheld, in many-coloured flame, a picture of Phantasmion, standing over Karadan, and striving to secure the enchanted vessel. When the king beheld that image of Anthemmina's pitcher in silvery light, he rushed forward and would have clutched it from the wall; but, lo! it was, impalpable as fires that hover over a marsh, and a loud puffing noise arose from below, that seemed to be an expression, either of pain or mockery. Thereat Penselimer looking down, espied the toad-like dwarf, whose body he had squeezed against the wall, with his great mouth wide open, and a slimy liquid oozing from every pore of his wrinkled skin. A hollow laugh echoed from the chair of Malderyl, who was wrapped in darkness, and the crystal windows of the tower tinkled with her mirth. "Is it thus thou rewardest those that serve thee, noble monarch?" she said. "Swartho has shown thee thine enemy by the power of his art, and in return thou art trampling him under foot." Penselimer drew back, and was incensed, when he recognised the face of Phantasmion, to find that the youth, to whom he had related his story, was King Dorimant's son, not doubting that he had visited him solely to obtain an account of the silver pitcher. "Transport me to Palmland," exclaimed the king, "and furnish me with armour." "Nay," answered the crafty witch, "if thou goest now to Palmland, thou wilt miss thine enemy, and in case of meeting him on the road wouldst fail to know him, for he is disguised by the Fairy Potentilla." "Show me his likeness," rejoined the king, "as he appears at this moment." The sorceress bade Swartho comply with that request, and straightway he brought so strange a phantom before the eyes of Penselimer, so all unlike any adversary which he had ever dreamt of, that for a moment he stood aghast. But, ere the grim figure faded away, and light once more succeeded to darkness, his courage returned, and, kneeling before the ancient queen, he besought her to arm him, so that he might fitly encounter such a formidable foe. "What guerdon shall I have from thee for such service?" inquired Malderyl. "What wouldst thou have?" the king replied. "If thou conquerest Phantasmion," said the queen, "thou shalt bestow half of Palmland on my young kinsman Ulander." The king willingly acceded to this proposal, and also agreed that if he died without issue, Ulander should inherit Almaterra. In a little time afterwards Malderyl had provided him with a horse and armour, and a plumed casque, as like as possible to those of Glandreth, whose stature was scarce loftier than his own, and bade him repair to the mansion of that aspiring chief, on the confines of Rockland, Tigridia and Almaterra. "By the time that thou arrivest there," said she, "Phantasmion will have reached the same place, under a feigned character, for the sake of encountering the great enemy of his kingdom in single combat. Thou shalt bear a letter from me to Glandreth; he will easily be persuaded to let thee accept the challenge in his name, when he knows that thou, being furnished with enchanted armour, in addition to thy own great skill and might, art more certain to defeat the King of Palmland even than his valiant self."

Thus forewarned, Penselimer departed, full of joy and confidence, expecting soon to have the disposal of Phantasmion's life and kingdom, and to obtain the more valuable pitcher for himself.

XXVI

Iarine has a fearful adventure on the mountain

Malderyl was sitting under the outer wall of her abode, looking after the king of Almaterra, as he rode down the hill, when the dark damsel kneeled at her feet and placed in her hand a withered branch. "Thou comest from Melledine!" said Malderyl; "who art thou, and what has passed betwixt thee and the veiled lady?" "I am Zelneth; daughter of Magnart," said the damsel, taking the roll from her head, and letting her jetty ringlets fall down to her waist. "This is not my natural colour," added she, putting up her white hand to her swarthy cheek; "I stained my face that no one might know me as I travelled to thy house. Melledine I met with on the King's Island, and she sent me to thee." "Wherefore?" said Malderyl, feigning ignorance of what she knew full well. "To find my sister Leucoia," replied Zelneth, while a bright blush glowed through her tawny mask. "Then return to thy home," said Malderyl, "for there thou wilt be more likely to learn tidings of Leucoia than here." Zelneth cast her eyes on the ground, as she replied in a whisper, "Where can I learn tidings of Phantasmion, son of Dorimant? I do confess that for his sake also I am come to thee." Malderyl's searching glance was now exchanged for a look which encouraged Zelneth to proceed in her disclosure: she told the story of her love for Phantasmion, and how she had set forth to free him from prison. "It was midnight," she said, "when we reached the Island, and straightway, repairing to the darksome vault, and putting the key into the lock, I found the bolts already withdrawn. I descended and sought in all the subterranean chambers, but found no trace of him whom I hoped to meet. Just as I emerged from the vault my lamp threw its light on a lady covered with a veil which gleamed in the darkness. "Dost thou seek Phantasmion of Palmland?" she said; "this morning his prison door was unlocked by the king's daughter." Then I knew that Iarine had deceived me, and, recollecting the lofty mountaineer who kept by her side in the wood, I clearly saw for what reason she had sent me away. While I was weeping on my pillow that night, the veiled lady entered my room, and offered me a cup, one draught from which, as she averred, would make me cease to love and cease to feel such sorrow. But starting up I promptly answered, "Ask me not to drown the remembrance either of those I love or those I hate: rather offer me a charm by which I may gain the heart of Phantasmion, and triumph over my false rival." Then she bade me repair to thee in secret, bearing a token from her, and placing a withered branch in my hand she left me to repose. Early the next day I sought Leucoia, but she was nowhere to be found, and I could not doubt that she drank of the forgetful cup and followed Melledine. In all haste I crossed the mountains, and travelled on to the house of a shepherd in Tigridia. There I dismissed all my attendants, bidding them repair to Arzene, and tell her that I hoped soon to return home with my brother and sister. I had not long been under the shepherd's roof when King Penselimer and the princess Iarine arrived at the same cottage. Alas! even here perhaps, the daughter of Anthemmina has forestalled me, and I cannot weep with sweet Leucoia, for she has been carried away!" Tears flowed down the face of Zelneth, streaking the stains that hid her lovely skin. Malderyl smiled: "Have no fear," she said, "touching Iarine and Leucoia: neither shall cross thy path." "But is Leucoia safe and happy?" said Zelneth, tenderly. "Safer than a pearl five fathoms deep," said Malderyl; "and happy enough, though not so blest as thou shalt be ere long, come with me to my cavern in the forest; and if I do not quickly bring Phantasmion to thy feet, in that secret dwelling, I will hide my head there for the remainder of my life." Zelneth trode on air when she heard Malderyl speak thus: she washed herself white in a pure fountain, and joyfully accompanied the sorceress queen to her cave in the woods.

Iarine meantime wound along the mountain, scarce pausing for a moment to survey the sylvan prospect before her, but going steadily on till she found the well, in a hollow betwixt two rocky ridges. This dale was clothed with herbage, converted into stone by the overflowings of the spring; and the breeze when it swept the valley, stirred not a leaf that grew there. Joyfully the maiden smiled when she saw these manifest signs of the water's potency, and imagined that it would brace and strengthen her father's quivering frame even as it had enabled the tremulous reeds and blades of grass to stand firm against the wind. With a fragment of rock in her hand she ascended the petrified mound that encased the spring, and, having flung her burden into the well, kneeled down and listened for the noise described by Malderyl, who had told her that the waters were commonly out of reach; that she must throw a heavy stone into the pit, whereupon they would gradually rise higher and higher, till at last they might be taken up by the bucket; that when she heard a noise like stifled thunder she must listen carefully till it changed to that of bubbling and hissing; then regardless of the fumes which would pour from the mouth of the pit, she must let down her bucket and fill quickly, ere the water sank again out of her reach. And now Iarine has caught the sound, and with a beating heart she applies her ear close to the opening, in spite of the hot vapours with which she begins to be enveloped: such indeed was the effect upon her frame that she felt as if she must quickly dissolve and trickle into the well or float away to the sky in subtle steam; yet still she listened, holding her breath lest she should fail to hear the sign, and miss the right moment. But, just as the hissing noise commenced, just as she was about to raise her head and lower the bucket, a youth leaped forward, caught her suddenly in his arms, and rushed away to a distance from the shining mound; and, scarce had he placed the maiden on her feet, when the volumes of steam sent forth from the pit were succeeded by a column of boiling water, which rose higher than the dark rocks behind it, and, falling in foaming curves quickly deluged the surrounding vale. The fountain continued to play before Iarine, mounting higher and higher as if it would sweep down the clouds,—a pile of rainbow splendour with a crest of a thousand feathers as white as snow;—and, while she watched it in speechless amazement, the young huntsman gazed upon her face in equal wonder, and almost equal agitation. "What didst thou at the boiling well?" at length he inquired. "I have been cruelly deceived," the maid replied, and then began to relate how she had been beguiled into undertaking her pilgrimage.

"One night," she said, "I was working for my stepmother in a lonely tower; the evening shades came on, I dropped my needle, being unable to distinguish the colours of the embroidery, and, hearing my silver pheasant tap at the window, I hastened to let her in. But, when I rose, the bird was not at the casement, and looking out, I saw that she had fallen to the ground, with an arrow in her breast. Then I hastened down the steps of the tower and bent over my favourite." "O, surely, she revived!" replied the youth, fixing his eyes, full of tenderest rapture, upon Iarine, as if to say that looks of pity from her face were enough to heal any wound. "Nay," replied the maiden, "my bird seemed stone dead; but, raising my tearful eyes, I saw a lady wrapped in a shining veil, with a vial in her hand. Pure water from this tiny vessel she poured on the face of the bird, when suddenly I saw the glazed eye relume within its scarlet rim, the ruffled feathers expand and show their finest gloss, like silken streamers swollen with the wind, and, rising from the ground, my graceful favourite took her highest flight, clearing the tower, and sinking down into the grove beyond. I turned to thank the lady in the shining veil, but she was gone, and never again did I behold her, till one night when I sallied forth to free a prisoner from the lonely tower." "A prisoner!" said the youth, "and thou wast going to set him free!" Iarine blushed as she pursued her story. "On that night I met the same veiled lady in the grove, betwixt the castle and the tower: 'Wilt thou save strangers,' she said, 'and do nothing for those that are near to thee, for poor Albinian and his sickly son?' Then I besought her to tell me how I might serve them, and she bade me seek the fountain-head of that water with which she had restored the dying bird. 'How shall I find it?' I eagerly replied. 'Go to Queen Malderyl,' she answered, 'bearing this token from me; but tell no one whither thou art bound, or on what errand; unless thou goest in secret, she will not reveal the salutary spring.' Then, placing an ivory tablet in my hand, again she disappeared." "And didst thou free the prisoner?" the young huntsman anxiously inquired. Iarine paused, then answered, "I trust he is now at liberty, though not through me." "And thou hast taken this long pilgrimage," cried the enamoured youth, "all for thy father's and thy brother's sake!—and the cruel queen gave thee that bucket, and would have sent thee to destruction?" "O for a swift steed!" cried Iarine, "to travel day and night till I reached the Diamanthine Palace." "Come with me!" exclaimed the youth, seizing her hand, "even here we are not in safety."

The maiden now perceived volumes of smoke far above the watery column; they rose from a high peak, and soon were changed to spiral flames, which occupied the vault of heaven just over the foaming fountain. Iarine kept pace with the speed of her conductor: soon they reached the grove below the hill where the young huntsman had left his horse to follow a goat among the rocks: he placed the princess hastily on his steed, and mounting before her, never ceased urging him forward, till he was in the very bosom of the forest. "We are going farther from Rockland!" exclaimed the maid, in sorrow. "Trust to me," the youth replied; "this way will sooner bring thee home than to retrace thy steps." Iarine was bewildered by the ocean of trees into which they were launched, but hoped that she should emerge from it in time, and find herself in some territory not far distant from Rockland. It was almost dark in the shady track through which the young huntsman threaded his way he had left his bow near the boiling fountain, so that the quiver at his shoulder would have been of little avail, had one of the panthers, whose bright eyes glared from under the dark branches, felt courage for an attack; but at his approach they bounded away, leaping from tree to tree. At last Iarine began to catch bright gleams and moving objects through the foliage, and soon her conductor came upon the skirts of a wide pleasure ground, on the slope of a hill crowned by a goodly palace, which, from glittering spires and gay enamelled windows, reflected the rays of the sun, just then about to sink on the opposite woody horizon. Below the mansion were hanging gardens of rich flowers, intersected with rivulets, which ran among the beds of roses, like tears down a bright blushing face. On a lawn at the foot of the hill a band of youths and maidens were dancing: these had no sooner espied the noble huntsman than they came forward in a body to cast their wreaths at his feet, and, by their festive cries and salutations, Iarine learned that her companion was Ulander, chief of Nemorosa. The maiden entered his dwelling still beguiled by hopes that she was on the way to Rockland, but soon discovered that her being restored to the arms of her father depended on a condition which even love for him could never strengthen her to fulfil. As Ulander's bride she might revisit her native country, but else was doomed to brook the fruitless penance of distasteful courtship in a foreign land. Day after day she complied with every request of her adorer, save that alone to which all his petitions tended; she flew by his side on the light steed, pierced the pard, or lynx, or savage deer, and, while the forest rang with praises of the graceful huntress, and Ulander, kneeling, declared that she excelled in skill and courage even as in loveliness, the gentle maiden longed to fly with those she pursued, and either escape or perish. From her chamber in Ulander's palace she looked out over the undulating forest of Nemorosa, which appeared like a wavy ocean fixed in stillness by an enchanter's wand: for gold or silver gleams, when the sun shone, there was a gilded verdure, and, when the breezes blew, for ocean's purple frown, a ripple of green leaves. But care darkened the shadows of the scene for her, and sickening hope tinted the mellow foliage. Now she thought of Phantasmion; of him she had so resolutely quitted, whose pursuit she had almost feared; now she repined at that multitude of trees, which seemed to interpose an endless barrier betwixt them, and gazed for hours on the woodland prospect, still faintly hoping, deeply longing, to see him rise with the morning star from the skirts of the forest, or sail from the golden east with brightened wings over the green expanse.

On a tufted knoll behind the palace Ulander was carving Iarine's name upon a cypress with a spear's point, when, hearing her soft voice among the trees beyond, he dropped the implement, and, resting his head against a bough, listened with grieved heart to these numbers:—

> *He came unlook'd for, undesir'd*
> *A sun-rise in the northern sky:*
> *More than the brighest dawn admir'd,*
> *To shine and then for ever fly.*
>
> *His love, conferr'd without a claim,*
> *Perchance was like the fitful blaze,*
> *Which lives to light a steadier flame,*
> *And, while that strengthens, fast decays.*
>
> *Glad fawn along the forest springing,*
> *Gay birds that breeze-like stir the leaves,*
> *Why hither haste, no message bringing,*
> *To solace one that deeply grieves?*
>
> *Thou star that dost the skies adorn,*
> *So brightly heralding the day,*
> *Bring one more welcome than the morn,*
> *Or still in night's dark prison stay.*

XXVII

Phantasmion goes to fight Glandreth and encounters Penselimer

W hile Phantasmion seeks Iarine, Glandreth shall conquer the Land of Psalms!" "Surely," thought the young monarch, "Oloola is secretly on my side, and those words, which were blown to my ear as with the blast of a trumpet, were meant to give me warning. Not only this kingdom but Iarine herself will never be securely mine while my enemy lives and triumphs." After a conference with Potentilla he informed his council that, as Glandreth alone endangered the safety of the realm, and to conquer him would be to extinguish the war at once, he had resolved on defying him to single combat, and purposed to announce himself, in the challenge, as a puissant warrior, sent by the king of Palmland to encounter the mighty general of Albinian. He had already given orders for raising an army, and guarding the sea coast with a numerous fleet; there were hosts of brave men at his disposal, but the want of metal armour was one which no ingenuity could supply, and rendered his subjects ill fitted to contend with the men of Rockland, who had iron without as well as firm sinews within. This consideration only heightened Phantasmion's desire to encounter Glandreth, and seeking the pomegranate tree, at the first peep of dawn, he besought Potentilla to produce that powerful armour with which she had offered to furnish him. She struck the earth, and brought before the eyes of Phantasmion a pair of warrior ants which fought ferociously till both were exhausted. "How sayest thou?" said Potentilla; "wilt thou be armed like these pugnacious insects?" The youth having readily consented, she laid her wand upon his head, then bade him strike it with his dagger. He did so, and found it perfectly impenetrable; but, looking with eager curiosity into a clear pool near by, he started at the portentous shadow of his insect helmet, It displayed a moveable crest in the shape of jagged awl-shaped jaws, with which, if other weapons failed, a terrible wound might be inflicted, while the face and breast of the wearer appeared to be cased in a substance tough as horn, yet hard as brass. The youth was still surveying his figure, not without dismay, little thinking that the picture of it was at that same moment before the eyes of Penselimer in the house of Malderyl, when Potentilla placed in his hand the sting of a scorpion increased to the size of the largest scimetar, and taught him how the fearful weapon was to be used. "But thou wilt rid me of this disguise as soon as the fight is over?" said Phantasmion. Potentilla smiling replied, "It might stand thee in good stead whither thou art going. Malderyl has a young kinsman who pursues fair damsels more earnestly than the bright-eyed antelope and silver coated hind. The constancy of thy mistress may be strongly assailed in the country of Ulander." "How sayest thou?" exclaimed Phantasmion, but the fairy disappeared, leaving him wrapped in thought and gazing on vacancy, till the sting of an ant upon his right foot admonished him to set off without delay. Forthwith he concealed his face and the upper part of his body with a mask and a cloak, which, at the fairy's suggestion, he had brought to the interview, mounted his horse, and through rugged passes among the Black Mountains travelled toward the house of Glandreth.

His adversary, meantime, had been pondering over the defiance from Palmland, when Penselimer arrived bearing the letter of Malderyl. On perusing this crafty epistle, Glandreth was well content that the king of Almaterra should stand in his place, and fight his enemy with charmed weapons, resolving in the meanwhile to lead his well-trained forces into the realm he so much desired to invade. He would not even await the event of the conflict, but stole away, after pompously accepting the challenge, and, while Phantasmion was traversing Rockland, Glandreth was on his way to the Land of Palms.

The combatants met on a wide plain before Glandreth's castle, in the presence of a large assembly. Phantasmion looked at the sky, and satisfied himself that it was perfectly clear; then he cast his eyes on his adversary, and thought that Glandreth, though of noble port and stature, was by no means so broad-built a man as he had formerly imagined. The king of Almaterra, meantime, could scarce turn his attention from Phantasmion's woollen cloak, which lay on the ground; for though it was only wrapped about the serpent wand, and a silver cup, he imagined that it concealed nothing less than Anthemmina's pitcher. But now the trumpet sounded, and great was the astonishment both of Phantasmion and an amphitheatre of spectators, to see Penselimer's panoply drip all over, then fall into furrows; and, lastly, trickle away in many a bubbling stream, as if he were but a waxen warrior, and melted at the very breath of his antagonist. Such was the effect of Malderyl's treachery, such the power of her muttered charm, that Penselimer quickly stood bare in the sight of all men, his helmet with its visor and his uplifted blade alone remaining for a season firm. When drops began to fall from the end of that weapon also, he indignantly rushed upon Phantasmion; but no sooner had he felt the point of the scorpion sword, than, uttering a loud cry, he sank senseless on the ground, with the magic weapon sticking fast in his side.

At the same moment that he fell, Phantasmion's fairy accoutrements vanished, and, when with loud shouts Penselimer was removed from the field, he procured fresh armour, and challenged every warrior present to stand in Glandreth's place; but all declining the combat, he forthwith departed to roam in search of Iarine. And now that deeds of arms no more engaged his thoughts, they centred wholly in that fair and pious maid, whose image beamed on all sides of his solitary path; and this was one of many strains with which he addressed her:

> Yon changeful cloud will soon thy aspect wear—
> So bright it grows:—and now, by light winds shaken,
> O ever seen yet ne'er to be o'ertaken!
> Those waving branches seem thy billowy hair.
> The cypress glades recall thy pensive air;
> Slow rills, that wind like snakes amid the grass,
> Thine eye's mild sparkle fling me as they pass,
> Yet murmuring cry, This fruitless quest forbear!
> Nay e'en amid the cataract's loud storm,
> Where foamy torrents from the crags are leaping,
> Methinks I catch swift glimpses of thy form,
> Thy robe's light folds in airy tumult sweeping;
> Then silent are the falls: 'mid colours warm
> Gleams the bright maze beneath their splendour sleeping.

XXVIII

PHANTASMION IS DETAINED IN MALDERYL'S CAVE

Phantasmion pursued the same track which his gentle princess had taken through Tigridia, and excited curiosity in all who beheld him by his noble aspect and kingly air. The first discourse of his cottage hosts was ever concerning the fair pilgrim, Iarine, and this tale was sure to be followed by an animated history of Ulander as its counterpart. Phantasmion glowed and trembled when he heard those names wedded in description, and scarce dared inquire about Nemorosa lest he should hear some unwelcome eulogy on the graces of its youthful chief. Thus he fared, tracing his lady's footsteps to the house of Malderyl, where he learned that the ancient queen had repaired to the forest with a most beautiful maiden. His heart beat higher than ever at this intelligence: a most beautiful maiden could be no other than Iarine, and it seemed plain as the sun at noon-day that Malderyl was bent on securing so rich a prize for her young kinsman Ulander. He wound along the bottom of the mountain, and left his horse, before night-fall, at the cottage of a goatherd, thinking that he could best proceed on foot through the tangled forest to find Malderyl's retreat. Provided as he was with good armour, and dauntless courage, he feared neither man nor beast, but anxious thoughts and surmises crowded on his mind, like swarms of stinging gnats, the pertinacity of which no efforts were sufficient to repel. Just as his mental fever had reached its height, and had begun to bring, even before his visual eye, a graceful huntsman kneeling at the feet of Iarine, in whose face a smile seemed to dawn, but whether of cold courtesy or nascent love he vainly strove to distinguish,—a voice whispered, seemingly from underground, "Dost thou seek Iarine? she dwells with Ulander: and—the loveliest of all maidens is in Malderyl's cave." Phantasmion shivered, and an instant afterwards his veins could scarce contain their scalding currents. "Iarine with Ulander in Malderyl's cave!" "Surely," thought he, "that was not the mere voice of my delirium." Then he began to rave and shout aloud, as if the forest could hear him, "Where is the cave? where is the cave? O these huge trees, that stretch their giant arms, and point on all sides, how they too madden me!"

Flinging away his cloak, he rushed on wildly till he was stopped by close underwood, growing over a swamp. Here again a voice rose to his ear, crying, "Iarine dwells with Ulander; seek the beauty in Malderyl's cave." Phantasmion now looked down and perceived a strange figure, but could not see either its form or features clearly from the dimness of the place. "Do thou show me the way, whoever thou art," cried the youth, franticly waving his sword. At these words Malderyl's toad-like dwarf leaped from amid the bushes, and skipped on before Phantasmion, who followed him till the shadowy path was faintly illumined by what appeared in the distance like two huge eyes of fire. "Those are openings in front of Malderyl's rocky tenement," said the dwarf; "their light will guide thee thither." Phantasmion looked at his good steel blade, then hastened on, and entered the cavern by a winding passage. He paused at the threshold, and saw no graceful hunter youth, but a wrinkled crone, in queenly attire, bending over the flames of a well-heaped hearth, and carefully inspecting the contents of a wide vessel, which simmered amid the blaze, and filled the cave with odorous inebriating fumes. Beside her stood the glowing and beautiful Zelneth, her glossy raven locks carelessly flung back from her white forehead, and her splendid eyes intent upon the work that was going on. She held in both hands a crystal bowl, into which Malderyl began to pour some of the rosy liquid scooped from the cauldron, when Phantasmion appeared and caused such alarm in the damsel's mind, that the vessel would have fallen to the ground, if her companion had not taken it from her. "King of Palmland," said the aged queen, "thou art welcome; be seated, and take off thy cumbrous armour." Muttering within herself she touched the head of the youth, as he bent forward to look after Zelneth, who had retreated to the inner part of the cave, when his crested helmet vanished, and soon the hyacinthine locks and goodly countenance of Phantasmion were revealed by the red light of the flames. Then Zelneth uttered a cry of astonishment and exclaimed, "O Malderyl! is this a delusion of magic, or do I look upon the very face of him I love?" "Dost thou still love Phantasmion, best and loveliest?" cried the youth, rushing forward to throw himself on his knees, his whole soul possessed with the image of Iarine; but, looking up and beholding Zelneth, her bright face beaming with transport, her fair form almost appearing to expand from the joy of her bosom, he started away with a countenance of deep disappointment! "Zelneth, daughter of Magnart!" he exclaimed, in a sorrowful tone; "O tell me, hast thou lately seen thy kinswoman Iarine?"

The damsel turned away without speaking, and, while tears gushed between the ivory fingers that strove to conceal them, Malderyl, who still bent over the cauldron answered in her stead. "Iarine was gaily hunting the deer," said she, "by the side of her betrothed Ulander, when Zelneth came to my house in search of Leucoia. Iarine, pretending to serve her parent, deserts him for a lover, while this maiden faces a thousand dangers for her sister's sake, and loves with constancy, though hopeless of a return." Zelneth flung her white arms around Malderyl, and, hiding her head, she gently cried with half suppressed sobs, "O speak no more! Phantasmion will win back his beauteous bride, and Zelneth would rather die than trouble his happiness." The youth's brain had been half unsettled by feverish suspicions together with bodily fatigue, and now the steams of the liquor doubled its confusion: he turned away and would have rushed out into the forest, to seek his rival, but the cavern appeared to be full of passages winding in every direction, and he found it impossible to hit upon the one by which he had entered. "Take thy rest here to-night," said Malderyl; "thou wilt never find the Sylvan Palace in the dark, and to-morrow, or a month hence, Iarine may still be found at the house of Ulander,—if thou must indeed go fight for that gathered lily, with tarnished leaf and tainted fragrance." At another time Phantasmion would have flamed at those words like a fire fresh fuelled, but now the luscious vapours were stealing over his senses; he was gazing unconsciously upon Zelneth, as she stood a little behind Malderyl with arms pensively crossed and downcast face, shaded on each side by drooping locks. He retired to a recess in the cavern, and tried to think again his former thoughts and purposes; but insensibly they floated away. His rage against Ulander seemed to dissolve, or turn into its opposite, and he vainly sought to keep firm hold of that or any other feeling. Zelneth approached with the crystal basin in her hands, and said to him, as he sate in the shadow, "Malderyl has been preparing a precious liquor for my beloved parents, it takes away all sense of toil and pain." She stood with her face half turned away, yet holding the vessel within Phantasmion's reach. He put out his hand towards it, gazing all the time on the damsel; but with a sudden effort, he drew it back again, and turned his face to the rocky wall. Zelneth sipped the liquid, then cried to the aged woman, who was busy about the fire, stirring and skimming the cauldron. "Malderyl, add nothing more; it cannot be better. I will fetch the jars in which it must stand this night." She left the crystal basin on a table of rock, just opposite to Phantasmion:

he saw the liquor lie glowing and creaming in the bowl, like melted rubies frothed with pearl; he inhaled its sweet bewildering odour, and, scarce knowing what he did, the youth raised it to his lips and drank deeply. In a moment he was electrified with delight, a rapturous tranquillity pervading his whole frame: he felt intoxicated with pleasure which sprang from no cause and tended to no object, yet was ever ready to be reflected and multiplied from all objects around: he seemed incapable of thinking, and happier than any thought could make him. Zelneth returned from the further part of the cavern, bringing jars in her hand; in the eyes of the spell-bound prince, she now appeared to be glorified by a supernatural light of beauty; joy streamed from every line of her face and form into the joyful heart of the prince, as light shoots from the surface of smooth water back towards its heavenly source. All thought of Zelneth, all thought of Iarine, all remembrance of the past, all anticipation of the future, were completely suspended: he only knew that he was gazing on a sun of loveliness, in which a thousand beauties seemed to converge, while the feelings inspired by his own heavenly maid were mingled with his new sensations, though the object of them was veiled in his memory by a dazzling mist. Zelneth retired again into the dark recess to fetch more vessels, while Phantasmion, reclining on a smooth low rock, with his head sunk into a mossy hollow, beheld fantastic petrifactions, which hung from the ceiling, illuminated by the fire-light. He gazed upon them in ecstacy, and felt as if the transport of his bosom, which invested them with splendour, was derived from these unmeaning forms, till Zelneth, again presenting herself, occupied his whole fancy, and seemed once more to be the fountain of all his glad sensations. The damsel now ventured to cast her eyes upon him, and, seeing the bowl by his side, was sure that he had drunk the charmed liquor; eagerly she perused his countenance, and, reading the deepest fascination of love in every line of it, she let the jar fall upon the floor. "He is mine!" she whispered, clasping her hands; "O, Malderyl, is this all thy work? Have I no part in it? But will not the enchantment fade? Will Phantasmion love Zelneth forever?" He heard the words, and smiled on her who spoke them, but spoke not himself, his eyes being heavy with sleep. As an infant lies in its cradle, watching every motion of her whom he loves fondly, but unconsciously free from the burden of esteem, and obligation of gratitude, so Phantasmion followed with his eyes the beautiful Zelneth, and saw her prepare a couch for him on the floor of the cavern. She heaped up sweet scented withered leaves, and strewed over them the skins of wolves and flowing fur of lynxes; Phantasmion sank down upon the soft bed, and was speedily wrapped in slumber. Zelneth kneeled beside him, gazing on his gentle and noble countenance, as the fire-light irradiated his fair brow, where all the soft blue veins were traceable under a smooth surface, and his bright youthful cheek reclining amid the spoils of savage animals, and surrounded by the black walls and shadowy hollows of the cavern. Already she fancied herself the flower-crowned bride of Phantasmion, and breathed in a soft lulling melody this happy strain:—

> I was a brook in straitest channel pent,
> Forcing 'mid rocks and stones my toilsome way,
> A scanty brook in wandering well-nigh spent;
> But now with thee, rich stream, conjoin'd I stray,
> Through golden meads the river sweeps along,
> Murmuring its deep full joy in gentlest undersong.
>
> I crept through desert moor and gloomy glade,
> My waters ever vex'd, yet sad and slow,
> My waters ever steep'd in baleful shade:
> But, whilst with thee, rich stream, conjoined I flow,
> E'en in swift course the river seems to rest,
> Blue sky, bright bloom and verdure imag'd on its breast.
>
> And, whilst with thee I roam through regions bright,
> Beneath kind love's serene and gladsome sky,
> A thousand happy things that seek the light,
> Till now in darkest shadow forc'd to lie,
> Up through the illumin'd waters nimbly run,
> To shew their forms and hues in the all revealing sun.

Singing thus she fell asleep, and, when her eyes were fast sealed in slumber, Phantasmion heard a shrill voice crying:—"Awake, young prince of Palmland, awake!" He raised his head and saw Malderyl sitting on the floor, an urn by her side, a branch of red berries on her lap, her fingers wet with purple juice. The crown she lately wore was thrown aside, her eyes shot fire, and Phantasmion knew that the face he now looked upon, was the very face of the strange old man, who told him of his mother's death. A shadowy form hovers aloft: it is the spirit of the poisoned child: Phantasmion remembers that swoollen spotted cheek as if he had seen it but yesterday. "Beware, young prince of Palmland!" the wan spectre cries, and, unmoved at Malderyl's awful threats, with sullen eye and obstinate finger still points to the purple berries that lie beside the urn. "Witch! Murderess!" exclaimed Phantasmion, starting up; but while he strove to free his feet from the coverings of the couch, Malderyl stirred the cauldron till fumes filled the cave, and entered every pore and inlet of the youth's body. He sank down again and scarce had pressed the furry pillow, when Zelneth met his eye, Zelneth, smiling in sleep, her head inclined on one ivory shoulder and her soft white arm extended over the skin of a black wolf. The charm resumed its power, the murderess and the ghastly spectre vanished from his sight, and dreaming only of lilied meads, bright streams, and perfect loveliness, he lay in deep repose within the rugged cavern.

XXIX

Phantasmion is disenchanted by Oloola

From the witch's cavern subterranean passages conducted into a delicious garden, embosomed in the forest, and surrounded by a double fence of lofty trees. Here the prince found himself when he awoke in the morning: bright wreaths of an acacia bower drooped over his head; flowers blushed, and streamlets glittered far as eye could reach; a splendid picture was hung out before him, and Zelneth, placed at coy distance, appeared the very subject of the piece. Phantasmion sprang from his odorous couch, and approaching the damsel, seemed to tread on air. No trace of the warning vision remained in his memory, and now that the charm had taken into its alliance the refreshment of sleep, he was transported with a still more exquisite delirium than on the preceding evening. He felt it to be his turn to speak, while Zelneth was speechless with happiness, drinking in his fluent love-discourse, as if it were a rill which ever gratified, but never removed, the pleasurable thirst it excited, while to him their volubility seemed in itself an enjoyment, and resembled the soft lapse of the brimming rivulet which wandered past his feet to visit a thousand flowery knots and odorous copses. Phantasmion scarce noted anything stedfastly, or considered whence it arose, or what it betokened: but sitting by the side of Zelneth, and pouring himself forth in admiration of her charms, he ever and anon caught glimpses of Feydeleen's flowerlike face, darting smiles from corners of the bower, dim with the shadow of clustered roses, while now and then her fingers came like a twinkling butterfly, and scattered over the head of the delighted maiden a shower of light petals from the frailest and most transitory blossoms. Zelneth saw not Feydeleen, nor anything but Phantasmion: she rose from her seat to fetch a well-filled urn, which had been placed in the arbour: it was the vessel which contained the poisoned juice, and the moment so long watched for by Malderyl seemed about to arrive. The sorceress leans forward over a leafy bough: Phantasmion's glance for a moment is diverted from the maid, and that prominent eye-ball, flashing amid the foliage, brings dim recollections to his mind; but Malderyl sinks back to her hiding place, and the youth turns to gaze on Zelneth, who stands smiling before him, with a crystal goblet in her left hand. "Wilt thou drink once more," she said, "and promise to be mine for ever?" Phantasmion threw himself on his knees, ready to utter vows of eternal love and faithfulness, having forgotten those he had made to Iarine, as if they had been characters formed in ice, which a hot sun had melted away. At the same moment, his tongue was arrested and the blood appeared to stagnate in his veins; the air had become piercing cold, and filled with white vapour; the brook ceased to murmur, and the birds to sing; the waters were congealed, the leaves and flowers wan and drooping, the branches encrusted with hoary rime. But the eyes of Phantasmion were fixed on Zelneth! motionless she stood, one arm raising aloft the urn, from whose lip an icicle depended, the other holding the empty crystal goblet, now no longer grasped but glued to the powerless palm. She was frozen to the ground: the glowing carnation of her cheek had faded to palest lilac: a deathy blueness tinged her brow of pearl, and crept over her bosom; wreaths of frost curled around her stiffened jetty ringlets; her arms looked brittle and crystalline; while those dark orbs that lately almost eluded the sight by their lifesome motion, had a dull shine upon them, like eyes of glass, and seemed fixed in their marble sockets. Phantasmion would have risen and approached the damsel, but strove in vain to move one step nearer to her statue-like form. His heart beat fearfully, but every other part of his frame was beginning to lose power and sensation: his head was fixed on one side; his knee clung to the earth, and no longer perceived its coldness; the fingers of his extended hand were cramped into one, and felt as if they touched each other through velvet: he seemed to be fast changing into a form of ice. On a sudden the sky grew black, showers of stony hail came rushing on between him and his fair companion, he was wrapped round about in a sheet of snow, while blasts which he found it impossible to resist, carried him to the further end of the garden, prostrated the tall fence of trees with interwoven branches, and continued to impel him onward for many a mile and many a league, till at length, when the wind lulled, he sank upon the open plain far beyond the Forest of Nemorosa, his blood moving rapidly and his limbs stiff with exertion.

Phantasmion had fallen under the shelter of massy walls overgrown with ivy, the wreck of a palace where Trigridia's monarchs had dwelt from age to age. Here the husband of Malderyl and her son Sylvalad had been treacherously murdered when Glandreth invaded the land, and Maudra her daughter, becoming enamoured of the blood-stained hero, followed him as a voluntary captive. The two sons of Sylvalad had been brought up by the widowed queen; one had perished in a far country, the other, whose name was Ulander, bore sway in the woodland fastnesses, where his father had ruled before him, but was too wild and careless to attempt the recovery of his whole inheritance. The wind had relented, the sky was disclosing more and more of its blue dome, snakes and lizards came forth to glitter in the sun, and the solitary bird that hides its nest under grey ruins, sought food in the moistened herbage, enjoying, amid the desolation of that ancient abode, the pleasures of a dear though transient home. Still the breeze lingering round Phantasmion, playing with his wet robe, and gently shaking the particles of snow from his redundant locks. Plaintive sounds issued from different parts of the building, as if a penitent lover were uttering meek confessions mingled with regret, and from within the pile some solemn instrument sent forth a deep slow melody of former days. While it yet was proceeding the youth heard a voice that seemed to be just above his head. "Phantasmion," it whispered, "what dost thou here, while faithful Iarine wanders in Nemorosa?" Soon afterwards the same voice appeared to come from a higher point, it was accompanied with a noise of light wings fanning the air, and to the youth's anxious ear it seemed to say, "Phantasmion must seek Iarine while Glandreth conquers the Land of Palms." After these words were spoken the solemn music swelled into a fuller tone, then sank into silence. Phantasmion started up and saw the pinnacles of the edifice gilded, here and there, by partial beams, which struggled forth from amid disorderly heaps of dark vapour. Just beyond the battlements of a black tower, he beholds transparent pinions, spread to their vast extent, with the sun glittering through them. A moment afterwards they recede; Oloola dives among the clouds on which those golden wings shed radiance. On she goes, sweeping the sky, as a shearer sweeps away the fleeces of the new-shorn flock; and now she is indistinguishable from the mass that moves along with her, and now both she and the clouds themselves are gone, leaving the cope of heaven pure and resplendent, as if it were cut out of a single sapphire, through which a powerful sun was pouring its diffusive light.

XXX

Zelneth is carried to the Sylvan palace, whither Phantasmion goes in search of Iarine

The storm which followed that intense frost had beaten on the rigid form of Zelneth unfelt, unseen; but now the charm was broken, the stony locks fell loose, all gemmed with dewdrops gleaming in the soft sunlight, and, even as thawing streams break forth into sound and motion, so the damsel moved and spoke once more, and sparkled with returning life. She roamed about the garden where Feydeleen had revived the drooping flowers, and breathed new vigour into their languid stems. The fairy looked at her pitifully from amid the leaves, and fondly whispered, "Kings shall sue for Zelneth, and Zelneth shall cause the ardent lover to forget his first love." The maiden heard not, heeded not, but continued her weeping, or murmured laments like these:—

By the storm invaded
Ere thy arch was wrought,
Rainbow, thou hast faded
Like a gladsome thought,
And ne'er may'st shine aloft in all earth's colours fraught.

Insect tranced for ever
In thy pendent bed,
Which the breezes sever
From its fragile thread,
Thou ne'er shalt burst thy cell and crumpled pinions spread.

Lily born and nourish'd
'Mid the waters cold,
Where thy green leaves flourish'd,
On the sunburnt mould
How canst thou rear thy stem and sallow buds unfold?

Snowy cloud suspended
O'er the orb of light,
With its radiance blended
Ne'er to glisten bright,
It sinks, and thou grow'st black beneath the wings of night.

Malderyl had been stricken to the earth by the rapid tempest, and there she lay muttering and making hideous faces: the green-vested fairy gleamed past her, as a lizard glances past a fallen log, then, pointing with dewy finger at Zelneth, "Malderyl," she said, "when wilt thou weep again? Ah! thou art old and sapless, past the luxury of tears."

A harsh voice uttering the name of Iarine caused Zelneth to raise her head, and looking up she saw the dwarf Herva seated beside the ancient woman, his sharp visage turned towards her, and each flat paddle arm spread out. "How long since?" cried Malderyl, angrily. "Yester morn," said he, "I was about to climb the high wall that girds Ulander's domain, when lo! the damsel Iarine, armed with bow and quiver, appeared on the top of it: she saw not me, as I crouched beneath, but leaped over my head on the soft moss, then, swift as a roe, she darted through the wood." Zelneth turned away wringing her hands, for she gathered that Iarine had escaped from Ulander, though she could not catch all that the dwarf muttered. "And where hast thou been loitering?" cried Malderyl, fiercely; but the next moment her thoughts were engaged by the other dwarf, who came limping in, with open mouth, to tell his tale. "Mistress," he said, "she is at the goatherd's cottage, and her father is there also!" "How?" cried Malderyl, "the palsied King Albinian?" "Even so," replied the dwarf; "strong love, or perhaps the approach of death, counteracted his disease so far, that he stole away from the palace, followed Iarine's footsteps, and this morning came to thy house on the hill, inquiring for his daughter. I guided him to the boiling fount—" "Right!" cried Malderyl: "he has cumbered the earth long enough; and how did he escape?" "He was saved by his daughter, who had got away from the Sylvan Palace," replied Swartho, "and took her way across the hill, doubtless because it was the shortest and best known to her. Entering the stony dell, she espied Albinian lying just under the mound of the well, where he had sunk down exhausted. The maiden rescued him from that dangerous place, dragging him away in her arms; but, if the goatherd had not come within call, she would scarce have reached the bottom of the hill by this time. Now

SARA COLERIDGE

both are under his roof, and Albinian seems to be on his death-bed." "Didst thou follow them?" said the witch. "I should have done so," the dwarf answered, "but, no sooner did the goatherd relieve Iarine of Albinian's weight, than she took the bow from her shoulder, an arrow from the case, and made this wound in my heel." The body of Swartho puffed up as he spoke, and the flaming circle of his dilated eye appeared to grow wider and redder. "Coward!" exclaimed Malderyl, with a laugh, "thou shalt have a worse wound in thy face presently." "Nay, mistress! hear what I did further," replied the dwarf; "after a while I repaired to the cottage garden, and there learned from a boy, who has lived with the goatherd ever since his wife and child perished together in a burning shower on the mountain, that Iarine will be close to the cavern this evening. I know the exact spot whither she means to repair, a patch of berry-bearing plants, just under the hollow sycamore, in which a squirrel has made his nest. She has been once there already to gather fruit for her father; and, ere it is dark, she will come again for a fresh supply." Malderyl arose. "Well! get ye both into the cavern," she said, "and be ready when I call." The dwarfs retired, and their ancient mistress approached Zelneth, who sate upon the ground with her streaming locks around her, silently watering the turf with tears. "Oloola brought the frost and raised the storm," said Malderyl; "she favours Glandreth and hates his enemies; for his sake she persecutes the son of Dorimant, and she will separate him from Iarine as well as from thee. Take courage: I will devise a plan—" "Away!" cried the damsel, scornfully; "thou hast neither skill nor foresight. Why didst thou bring us into the garden under the open sky? Oloola could have worked us no ill in the cavern." Malderyl's eye lightened at this taunt, but Zelneth saw not its vengeful flash, and relapsed into silence. Imperceptibly, however, as a snow shower changes into rain, her sullen mood relented, and Malderyl found an opportunity to propose her plan. "Iarine," she said, "is at the goatherd's cottage"—"Where Phantasmion will find her," cried Zelneth, impetuously. "He shall never find her again," replied the witch, "if thou wilt consent to a brief disguise, and brave a slight peril." Zelneth fixed her brightening eyes on her evil counsellor. "Thou hast some skill," she said, while the last tear fell from her cheek: "tell me what peril, what disguise thou art thinking of." Malderyl brought from the cavern a panther's skin. "It is but to dress thyself in this gay garb," she said; "then to sit crouching on the bough of a tree hard by here, and, when Iarine comes under it, and is busily engaged in gathering berries, suddenly to show thyself and leap down by her side. When she attempts to fly, thou and the dwarfs shall intercept her return to the cottage, and I, meantime, will beckon her into the cavern, whence she shall not come out till she consents to marry Ulander. My kinsman shall meet her here, and thou shalt repair to the Sylvan Palace, where Phantasmion will be sure to go in search of Iarine." "She sent me to the Island," murmured Zelneth, "to release one who was standing by her side at that moment." "I will take good care that she shall not escape," added Malderyl. "Thou shalt see me run out with a chafing-dish in my hand, to stupefy her senses by the smoke of burning herbs. But come! either reject the scheme, or prepare to do thy part in it; for she will be here presently." Zelneth took up the skin, without knowing how to put it on, but Malderyl adjusted it so well that the lady's speaking eyes looked through holes which had formerly contained the bestial ones of a panther. Strangely now indeed they sparkled under a shaggy brow and upright ears, which the original wearer could move and bend at will. Zelneth in her childish days had been wont to follow the squirrels up many a well-branched tree. She loved to wind her way among the boughs, overcoming a series of delightful dangers, till she could place her fairy foot betwixt the topmost fork, proud to find herself at such a dizzy height, and glad to have in prospect the pleasing adventure of descent. But such sports of the vacant mind and lithe limbs had fallen into disuse, and, though the sycamore was easy to climb, slowly and timorously she crept up to her lurking place, and still more violently her heart palpitated when she saw Iarine approach with her basket, and kneel down to collect the fruit which grew on tiny bushes under the tree. While the eyes of the gentle princess were busily engaged upon the ground, those of Zelneth, anxious and fearful, were gazing at her from above. The bough shook as with trembling limbs she began to creep forward, after the manner of a wild cat, and all the crisp leaves and branches made a rustling noise. Iarine started, and looking up espied the pretended panther peeping down from the bough, whence she had scarce summoned resolution to spring. Unhappy Zelneth! she had not reckoned on her cousin's newly acquired skill in archery, nor on that matchless bow, the amorous chieftain's gift, which now hung at her shoulder. On seeing the damsel prepare to shoot she uttered a loud cry, and strove to turn about, but, ere she could escape the arrow was in her side. Iarine, hearing Ulander's voice from a distance, stayed not to examine the false panther, which had fallen to the ground, but glided swiftly through the wood, while the dwarfs, who were stationed to prevent her return, panic-stricken at what they had witnessed, and at the approach of the royal huntsman, crouched among the brush-wood, and Malderyl, her form half hidden by wreaths of smoke from the censer in her hand, stood laughing at the entrance of the cave, till at last she fell upon the ground, overpowered by the fumes she had heedlessly inhaled. Meantime, Ulander, who had been roaming in search of his fair fugitive, drew nigh the patch of berry-bearing plants, and there found Zelneth, prostrate on the ground, with the skin of a wild beast covering the lower part of her body: for by this time she had freed her head and neck from the cumbrous disguise. Astonished both by her beauty and the strange state in which he found her, the youth alighted from his horse, and asked what savage hand had inflicted that wound in her side, whence the blood was flowing. Zelneth pointed to the panther's skin still hanging about her feet, then sank into a swoon, her disengaged arm falling powerless on her shaggy spoils. The chieftain forgot Iarine while he gazed on her fair countenance; he gently removed the skin, placed the fainting damsel on her horse, and conveyed her with all care and tenderness to his princely home. But though the travellers went at so leisurely a pace, that the night was far gone when they arrived there, the motion of the horse inflamed the lady's wound, which would soon have healed but for this aggravation. Fever seized the hapless maid, and Ulander found with sorrow that his love had proved as injurious to Zelneth, as it had been irksome and greivous to Iarine.

Not long after the chief of Nemorosa reached his mansion, Phantasmion arrived there also. The influence of the magic draught over his spirit had been destroyed by Oloola's counteracting spell, the mist dispersed, and Iarine's image again shone forth in sunny splendour, while that of Zelneth, late so radiant, showed like the vanishing moon with her weak superfluous light. But the last words of Oloola had cast him into a reverie. Glandreth had fallen by his hand: how then should Glandreth conquer the Land of Palms? Had the voice a hidden meaning, or no meaning at all? He had heard that Glandreth formerly sued for the hand of Iarine's mother, that Oloola loved the bold and beautiful chieftain, and made a solemn vow to be his friend and minister till Anthemmina's dying day. "And now that they two are dead," thought he, "perchance Oloola befriends Phantasmion; or it may be that, like the winds of heaven, she follows no settled course, to sport with human hopes and purposes her only plan." Raising his eyes from the ground he saw Malderyl's mansion upon the brow of the conical mountain, just visible in the distance, and thither he resolved to go and inquire again for Iarine. On reaching the gate Phantasmion made the rocks resound with his loud summons, and, ere the echoes had ceased, the porter and his grisly beard stood before him. "Hast thou seen any other maiden," cried the youth, "beside her who went to the woods with thy mistress?" "None since she was here," the porter replied. "But, just before she arrived, there came a shepherdess in company with a man of high degree. Her face was shaded with a hood, and she went forth alone, having a bucket and a bottle in her hand. Surprized to see the way she took, I watched her while she ascended that steep upward path. And on she went, so wondrous, fleet, and graceful, that, when she gained yon cloudy summit, I thought within myself, "Is this a shepherdess or an angel going back into the sky?" Phantasmion hastened up the steep track to which the servant of Malderyl pointed, and wound along the mountain till he met an old man who was driving on goats before him. He stopped when the youth approached his flock. "Thou art a stranger by thy garb," said he; "dost thou know of the boiling fount, and the volcanic fires, which oft break forth on that part of the mountain to which thou art proceding? Daily I climb this hill"—"And didst thou lately see a damsel here," the youth inquired, "in the habit of a shepherdess?" "Yes, truly," answered he; "and I meant to give her warning, but she waved me off with her hand, and sped along so fast that even my goats could scarce have followed her. She entered the stony dell, which lies beyond the rocks, and there no doubt she perished." Phantasmion rushed away, passed the rocks, and entered the dell where the fountain was playing. He stood motionless at the entrance of the hollow till the water subsided, then approached the mound, and an icy chill seized his heart when he beheld a leathern bottle petrified on the edge of the well, with a bucket and chain lying close beside it. Believing that Iarine had been overtaken by the force of the waters, and had so lost her life, he sought about in desperation, expecting to find her fair body among the other petrifactions; but, seeing no trace of any such thing, he imagined that she had fallen into the well, and lying down on the edge of it, resolved there to remain and await destruction. Many times he was tempted to throw himself into the dark abyss, and, when he called on the name of Iarine, he thought that fierce voices answered him. In this condition he remained till the moon rose and threw her cold beams over the stony dell; when, turning his eye once again toward the bucket, he descried the steel point of a petrified arrow shining a little beyond it. Instantly it struck him that this shaft had fallen from the quiver of some huntsman, perhaps Ulander himself, and that he might have borne Iarine away, either alive or dead. Roused by this thought he started up, hurried down the hill, and, about daybreak, knocked at the goatherd's cottage. The host of Albinian and Iarine came out with his finger on his lips. "There is a dying man in my house," quoth he, "I may not ask thee to enter. Thy steed has been taken care of. Thou wilt find him in yonder shed beside the marigolds." The goatherd having re-entered, Phantasmion found his good horse, which recognised him with signs of pleasure, but, so greatly exhausted was he, that, instead of mounting, he sank down by his side, and slept with his feet among the marigolds, and his head on the neck of the gentle beast. Ere he awoke at mid day, one of Ulander's train came nigh and stopped his horse in admiration of the young monarch and his goodly steed, whose quick eye seemed to say, "Pass on, I pray thee, and disturb him not." The huntsman's cheek was fresh and glowing, while that of the slumberer looked pale amid the sunshine and the gleams of his golden bed. "Art thou Ulander?" said Phantasmion starting up. "I would I were," the youth replied, with a smile: "not for his crown and palace, but for the sake of a most fair damsel, worthy of both, by whose side he is kneeling." "Wilt thou guide me to that palace?" cried the young king of Palmland, his burning cheeks and scintillating eyes turned full on the huntsman. "It is my home," the youth answered, "and I can show thee the shortest road to it." Phantasmion was quickly mounted, he and his guide went at full speed, whenever the road permitted, and, ere the light began to fade, he entered the abode of Ulander.

XXXI

Phantasmion leaves the Sylvan palace and Zelneth receives succour from Feydeleen

Phantasmion demanded to see the chief of Nemorosa, and was conducted to a spacious apartment, the couches and seats of which were covered with brindled or spotted skins, the walls with horns of deer and rock-goats fancifully arranged. There, under a high canopy adorned with branching antlers, lay the wounded Zelneth, her limbs motionless, her eyes closed in death-like languor, while the young chieftain was raising her from the couch in his arms, and trying, by a thousand assiduities, to elicit signs of life and looks of recognition. So a child, grieved to see his rarest flower, the milk-white fox-glove, with its whole spire of bells, newly blown, extended on the earth, sets himself to support the crushed stem which his own heedless foot has beaten down. But all in vain; for, leaning on the prop, it hastens to decay, no longer able to imbibe the dews that fall around it, withered by that sun which lately nourished its firm stalk and bursting blossoms. Ulander saw not the young king of Palmland till he had entered the apartment, and stood midway between the door and the couch, gazing intently on Zelneth. But, when he did at last perceive his presence, the chieftain started, uttering an exclamation; roused by which the damsel opened her eyes, and seeing Phantasmion, leaped wildly from the couch, with crimsoning cheek and eyes of delirious brightness; but, her strength soon deserting her, she fell forward, looking still more lifeless than when she lay on the couch upreared in the arms of the sylvan chieftain. Ulander looked on with sullen surprise, while Phantasmion carried Zelneth to the couch, and laid her on the tiger skins with which it was covered. "Who art thou?" he said; "art thou the brother of this maiden?" "I am bound to her by no near ties," replied Phantasmion, with haste: "she came to greet me as one who had received hospitality at her father's house." "Why then hast thou come hither," rejoined the chieftain, "breaking in upon my privacy without leave asked?" "I came in search of another," replied the youth, in some confusion; "I came to inquire for this fair damsel's kinswoman, the princess Iarine." "Iarine!" exclaimed

Ulander; "she it was that wounded this lovely maid. I found her bleeding in the midst of the forest, and she accuses Iarine of the cruel deed. That name, and one other, inarticulately murmured, are the only words she has spoken since she entered here." "Iarine accused of a cruel deed!" exclaimed Phantasmion: "here is more witchery, more wickedness and deceit!"—The chieftain held up his finger, then pointing to the maid, "Look there!" he cried, in a low stifled voice; vex not her parting spirit by violent words." Phantasmion held his peace, and drawing nigh to look on Zelneth, he felt assured that her soul had abandoned its fair tenement for ever. The crisp and glossy tresses that flowed to her waist seemed yet instinct with life; in all their wonted beauty they curled around the full white arm that lay so dead and motionless by her side: but mournful was the stillness of her long black eye-lashes, which seemed now laid to rest forever on that smooth cheek whence every life-like tint had vanished, as the warm light of morning fades from a snow-clad hill, leaving it as coldly white as pure and polished marble. Ulander wept aloud; Phantasmion mused in sorrowful silence. Till now he had never looked on Zelneth as on a bright flower, doomed to wither, but had felt as if she were like the glittering stars that shine unaltered, while a thousand roses bloom and perish.

At last he recollected what befel him in the house of Magnart. "Perchance the damsel is but entranced," he said; "I myself once lay thus for many an hour." Ulander raised his head, and, starting from his knees, approached Phantasmion. "Didst thou lie motionless?" he cried; "was thy breath suspended, were thy cheeks as pale as these?" Phantasmion poured balm into the heart of Ulander by the answers he gave to all his eager questions, and soon the chieftain called to mind how his ancient kinswoman, Malderyl, had cured one of his train who lay insensible after a wound received from a wild boar. The two youths were now standing together by the couch, the hand of Phantasmion locked in that of Ulander, who frankly told all he knew of Iarine, how he loved and lost her, and how he was on the way to consult Malderyl in the cavern concerning the fair princess, when his thoughts were suddenly absorbed by the distress and beauty of Zelneth. "But now," says he, "I will go forthwith to fetch the Queen of Tigridia: she hath great skill in medicine, and in other arts too. Me she loves well, and at my entreaty she will restore this maid, and perchance discover to thee the retreat of Iarine." Right glad was Phantasmion to accept Ulander's intercession with one whose evil powers were not to be averted by sword and spear;

he zealously offered to keep watch by the body of Zelneth and to defend it, with the danger of his life, against a host of her kinsmen, should they come to take it away. Having accepted his courtesy, Ulander kissed the damsel's cold hand as it lay upon the couch, and sighed to see it no longer withdrawn as heretofore; then with looks of deep anxiety he hastened away. After his departure Phantasmion read these lines which he found traced on a tablet, but whether addressed to Zelneth or Iarine seemed uncertain:—

I thought by tears thy soul to move
Since smiles had proved in vain;
But I from thee no smiles of love,
Nor tears of pity gain:
Now, now I could not smile perforce
A sceptred queen to please:
Yet tears will take th' accustom'd course
Till time their fountain freeze.

My life is dedicate to thee,
My service wholly thine;
But what fair fruit can grace the tree
Till suns vouchsafe to shine?
Thou art my sun, thy looks are light,
O cast me not in shade!
Beam forth ere summer takes its flight,
And all my honours fade.

When, torn by sudden gusty flaw,
The fragile harp lies mute,
Its tenderest tones the wind can draw
From many another lute;
But when this beating heart lies still,
Each chord relax'd in death,
What other shall so deeply thrill,
So tremble at thy breath?

But the dark hours came on; no lamp shed light on the silent face of Zelneth, when a train of damsels entered from the garden, with lighted tapers, and baskets of night-blowing flowers in their hands. They sang a dirge over the maiden, then covered her body with those blossoms of greenish white or palest yellow, stuck their tapers around the canopy, and slowly departed, leaving the chamber filled with an aromatic fragrance. Phantasmion had retired to the further end of the apartment, where the horns of an elk threw their wide shadow on the marble floor, and from that station he watched the mourners while they performed their gentle rites, then softly stole away. At last the door was closed, but one of the train yet lingered under the canopy, her flower-basket resting on the couch. Phantasmion, as he drew forward, beheld her countenance by the light of the tapers, which threw a tender gleam over the pale flowers, the still features of Zelneth, and the bright aerial visage that shone above them. "Feydeleen!" cried the prince, "can Zelneth be restored? and O! where is Iarine?" "Leave Zelneth in my care," she answered, "and seek thou the domain of Melledine, there to find and rescue her that is lost for thy sake." Phantasmion was about to reply with eagerness, but the nightly exhalations of so many overpowered his senses, and he sank on the floor, motionless and pale as the fair damsel who lay stretched upon the couch.

No sooner had he become thus entranced, than his guardian spirit stood beside him. "Feydeleen!" she exclaimed, "is it not enough to have deprived Phantasmion of the pitcher? wherefore hast thou dealt with him thus?" The soft Fairy smiled on Potentilla, and, with words and tones like the warm breeze that unbinds the frozen earth, she persuaded her not only to forgive what was past, but to make a compact with herself, whereby all whom they both loved should in the end be gainers. Potentilla called for her light car, drawn by dragon-flies, and having increased both to a convenient size by magic power, conveyed away the fainting prince, through the murky air, while Feydeleen remained alone by the side of Zelneth.

As a plant that seems irrecoverably withered revives at the first shower, swells out its flaccid leaves, and stretches them forth to catch the kindly moisture, so was Zelneth restored by the salutary dews and airs which the kind spirit shed around her. Gradually a tender bloom suffused her cheek, gentle breathing returned, the damsel raised herself from the couch, holding out her hand, as if to welcome some one, while her lids were yet fast sealed, then fell back upon her pillow in deep refreshing slumber. But, when a thousand flowers were opening their soft eyes upon the dawn, those of Zelneth were unclosed, and up she sprang, scattering on the floor the blossoms which had been so plentifully strewed on her seeming corse; they were now drooping, while she was upraised in health and lifesome beauty. Alas! Phantasmion had disappeared, and all the apartment was silent and solitary, till a fawn ran in from the open door, through which, ere the cock crew, Potentilla had carried him away. She went forth, and caught a glimpse of Feydeleen, who was just entering a tufted grove with a chalice in her hand. Zelneth followed, and, kneeling on the ground, under the embowered branches, besought her to declare why Phantasmion had left her side, and whither he was gone. A slender voice came from amid the myrtles, and it spoke thus: "Phantasmion left Zelneth to seek Iarine." "And shall I never more regain his heart?" the maid exclaimed. Again the soft voice, breathing gales of perfume, gently but clearly answered in these words: "Henceforth Phantasmion's heart will never swerve from Iarine." Zelneth continued to listen, while tears chased one another down her upraised face, but the only voice she now heard, was that of a turtle cooing to his mate, with soft notes long dwelt upon, in the depth of the wood. Then she strove to turn her heart against the bright youth of Palmland, and grieved to find how much more love than pride had mastery there. While her mind was full of such thoughts, she heard a slight rustling; something had fallen from the branches beside the place where she sate, and, straight before her, she espied the picture of Penselimer, with its eyes looking at hers, and seeming to convey, in their passionate melancholy, an expression of reproach. From the hour that it fell from her lap, when she first beheld Phantasmion, Zelneth had scarce bestowed a thought on this idol of her childhood, which Anthemmina, when her heart was estranged from Penselimer, had carelessly hung around her baby neck. Now she took it up by the chain of pearls to which it was fastened, and sighed, as she gazed on the well-known lineaments, for the free heart and enamoured fancy of former times, when she rejected many an unpleasing suitor, for the sake, as she loved to imagine, of the noble Penselimer. Zelneth raised her eyes, on being accosted in a shrill voice, and shuddered to behold Malderyl approaching her with a cup. "Ulander brought me to thy couch," said the ancient queen, "where we found plenty of withered flowers but no entranced maiden; and soon my young kinsman, rushing to the door, beheld thee bound lightly over the lawn. I could have restored thee to health, had thy malady continued, and, even now, I would have thee drink this cup, lest it should return with the evening dews." Zelneth suspected that the liquor presented to her was some of that which had been prepared in the cavern, and that Malderyl's design was to make her return the chieftain's passion; nevertheless she took the cup and slowly drank, with her eyes fixed on the features of Penselimer. Scarce had the magic draught pervaded her frame than the portrait assumed a new aspect: it seemed fairer, nobler than Phantasmion himself; love for the king of Palmland seemed absorbed into a larger emotion, as the last wave is swelled by those which have gone before. Her visions of childhood rose again in all their keen aerial colours; the realities she had since experienced melted into indistinctness; their forms were gone, but still their glow remained, and filled the atmosphere of memory with warmth and golden light. Ulander advanced from amid the trees, where he had hitherto been shrouded, and, seeing her face bright with smiles, when she returned his salutation, he inwardly rejoiced, vowing eternal gratitude to Malderyl, by whose endeavours he fully believed that Zelneth looked upon him thus. Formerly his enamoured looks and words, which the maid lacked strength to repel, seemed to hasten her spirit's flight; now they fell upon her occupied mind like rain-drops on marble, which glitters amid the shower and remains unsoftened. Both were equally possessed with gladsome fancies, and confident in the success of their hopes, when they rode into the forest, ere noon-day, followed by a train of huntsmen, Zelneth indulging her steed in all his graceful vagaries, and Ulander fondly hoping that for long years to come she would thus disport herself by his side. "Kings shall sue for Zelneth, and for her the ardent lover shall forget his first love." Feydeleen breathed this prophecy once more in Zelneth's ear, as she passed under the branches. Now it was no longer unheard or unheeded; the damsel applied it to Penselimer, and joyfully expected that he would soon appear to rescue her from durance.

XXXII

Phantasmion enters the sunless valley

A night and a day had elapsed since Phantasmion left the domain of Ulander, when, roused from his trance, he found himself descending through the sky. Then he sate upright, and saw right before him, fanning the twilight air, the gauzy wings of dragon-flies, while those of Potentilla, who stood upright on the seat of the car, were playing above his head. The moon had not yet risen, but, when he came to the ground, and leaped upon the turf, he perceived a shining circlet in the sky, and had no sooner looked upon it, than it began to descend, widening, swelling, and brightening as it sank. The tract where Phantasmion stood first glimmered, then gleamed, and lastly shone with more than noon-day splendour in many-coloured light, while gradually the features of the scene stole upon his eye, and soon he recognised the skeleton palace, where owls peeped forth from bowers of ivy, the ruined hall with its watery floor and rose-crowned window, and the wild pleasure ground in all its flush of blossoms. The Deserted Palace, and the space in front of it, were encircled by a vast hoop of cold flame, produced by innumerable fire flies. Phantasmion turned to Potentilla, who was leaning back in the car, over which her wings reclined, and smiling at his looks of wonder. "Wilt thou go with me," she said, "to rescue a lost maiden from the sunless valley?" "Instantly," cried Phantasmion. "Wherefore do we tarry?" "Recruit thy strength," replied the Fairy, "with what is provided in the car, then drink from this vial which Feydeleen gave me for thy use. It will ward off the drowsy influences of Melledine's abode. Phantasmion obeyed, and, while his eyes were brightening with the effect of the Flower Fairy's gift, Potentilla, from the seat of the car, touched his head and shoulders with her wand, then waved him after her as she soared aloft. The next moment he was flying through the air, his head surrounded with a halo of intense light, his dragon-fly wings and whole body beaming with a keen lustre, which varied from chrysolite to vivid green, passing off into the deepest azure, and thence into amethystine purple. Potentilla flew on before, with the wings and radient head of a lantern-fly, and the clouds of luminous insects followed. As the whole mass went undulating along, they looked like a fiery river, flowing athwart the sky, and so proceeded, till just as the moon rose, they overpassed the wall of rock which bounded Melledine's domain. "This region," said Potentilla, "by the spells of the enchantress, who dwells here, is perpetually hidden from the sun's light: the whole valley is girt on every side by rugged mountains, and, during the day, it is shrouded by an opaque fog." Phantasmion followed his guide above the black vapours, to a point over the centre of the valley, while the fire-flies, high over head, appeared once more like a circular constellation. Thence he saw the pitchy cloud splitting in the middle, and shrinking more and more, on every side, till at last it was heaped in huge scrolls on the mountain tops. While the moon and stars in full splendour were thus revealed to waking eyes below, Phantasmion beheld their beams reflected from the enlightened vale, from lily fields and groves of gleaming foliage, pastures whitened with straying flocks, and one wide sheet of water.

As he descended he heard no sound but that of the owls, hooting to one another from yew trees and ivy-mantled rocks, the sonorous notes of those at hand receiving clear but slender responses from others at a distance. Coming yet lower, he began to catch the nightingale's upper notes, and next the sound of flowing waters and the gurgling of brooks. Potentilla waved her wand, and the luminous procession, which now following in the form of a serpent, quenched its radiance, and became suddenly as black as ink. Phantasmion underwent the same change, and followed his guide, who alone retained her light, to the abode of Melledine. The enchantress was busily employed in gathering herbs, on which the moonbeams rested, seeking them by the side of a rivulet which wandered through a meadow, silvered with white flowers. A damsel delicately fair and slender, with flaxen locks that floated to her taper waist, was following Melledine, and leading by a silver chain a milk-white stag, the hoofs and horns of which appeared to be also of silver. On his back the deer carried a pannier, filled with flowers and herbs, which the damsel received from the enchantress, and deposited there. Thus they proceeded, moving contrary to the course of the brook, till they arrived at a rocky knoll, where the same rivulet formed a little cataract, splitting, like a ravelled skein, into divers shining threads, here gliding in clear lapse over a smooth-faced stone, there skipping from rock to rock enveloped with foam, here narrow as a spindle, there spreading like a garment puffed out by the wind. Melledine was stopping over the united streams, when Potentilla ranged her legions right above the meadow and watery knoll: the head of the enchantress was crowned with white poppies and a shining veil, thrown back from her face, covered her kneeling form. Surprised at the shade which darkened the rivulet and its flowery banks, she looked straight up to the sky, disclosing a face of goodly features but black as ebony. Gazing thus she beheld Phantasmion all irradiated with purple light descending under the cloud, and in an instant afterwards the pitchy mass became a flaming pavilion. Then, blinded and amazed, she fell upon the ground, covering her face with her veil, and muttering disjointed spells, without power to repeat any at full length. Phantasmion alighted on the hillock, and Potentilla, hovering over his head, called on Melledine to deliver up the damsel whom she kept a captive in her sunless domain. She, meantime, was hasting away with the white stag, and soon entered a cypress grove, through which the rivulet held its way. Melledine hesitated to promise obedience, but when the air blackened with swarms of stinging insects, and the ground with locusts, she consented to yield up the captive maid, and to conduct her to the Deserted Palace through the pass whereby she entered the valley. No sooner was this promise given than the locusts rose into the air: Potentilla secured Melledine by chains, which were hidden under her glittering raiment, and with which she was wont to bind her victims: this being done, the whole swarm flew away along with the other insects, till they disappeared in the distance. Phantasmion had no sooner witnessed the submission of Melledine, than he pursued the damsel into the dark wood. As he rushed along, casting phosphoric splendour on the sombre foliage around, the nightingales hushed their songs, and the owls shrank away, letting down the curtains of their prominent eyes. At last he obtained sight of the damsel; she, after flitting on before him for some time, being now unable to go any further, stood in the pathway, leaning on the white stag, who had suited his pace to that of the lady, and restrained his steps when he saw that her powers of flight were exhausted.

The damsel clung to her mild companion, hiding her face against his neck, till the pursuer, having arrived where she stood, took her hand and gently cried, "Look up, my fair one! it is Phantasmion." At these words he withdrew the dazzling radiance which streamed from his whole person, leaving his head only encircled with a diadem of softened rays. Then the lady raised her face, and Phantasmion saw that it was Leucoia, the sister of Zelneth. Ill-fated maid; she had drunk the oblivious draught of Melledine, had not only forgotten her parents and pleasant home, but ceased to pine for the noble stranger, whose image had occupied her soul, a beautiful poison tree, that spread abroad its glistering boughs and blighted every other growth. But now Phantasmion's illumined face, radiant with love and beauty, suddenly cast a flood of light on forms and hues of memory, which magic power had obscured, but never obliterated; again she loves, again her stilled bosom is roused to emotion, and, full of tears and blushes, she once more hides her face on the stag's neck. Phantasmion himself was overwhelmed with trouble and perplexity; Leucoia's heart he had never cared to fathom, but he now suspected that she, and not Iarine, was the lost maiden whom he had been sent to deliver. "Hast thou not found the daughter of Albinian?" he cried, turning to Potentilla, as she came through the grove, leading the sullen Melledine by her chain. "O tell me whither to go in search of her!" "Seek not here for the lovely princess," she replied: "but free Leucoia from captivity, and Feydeleen will lend her aid to make Iarine thine." "What power has Feydeleen?" cried Phantasmion, "and why must I do her behest?" "Hast thou forgotten the silver pitcher?" Potentilla replied; "without Feydeleen's good will thou canst never obtain the hand of her whom thou lovest." "Doubtless Ulander will be sent to rescue my lost maiden?" exclaimed the youth. "Nay," replied the fairy, "Ulander cares for no one now but dark-eyed Zelneth." Leucoia had been weeping silently, while the stag looked in her face with eyes full of tenderness; Phantasmion even fancied he saw a tear glisten there, and that he had seen that countenance before, if these were not illusions of his dazzled sight. But at Zelneth's name the maid looked up with an enquiring glance. "Knowest thou aught of my sister?" she said. "Zelneth went to seek for thee in the forest of Nemorosa," the youth replied: "there she was wounded by an arrow, and now lies, I fear, in evil plight at the house of the young chief Ulander." When Leucoia heard this her heart was oppressed by a crowd of sad emotions, and, throwing herself on her knees before Phantasmion, "Take me hence, I beseech thee," she cried; "I will not keep thee long upon the road, but travel, night and day, to reach my home." Phantasmion declared that he was ready to conduct the damsel whither she desired to go. He raised her from the earth, and placed her upon the back of the stag: Melledine showed the way to the borders of a lake, and Phantasmion followed, leading Leucoia's gentle steed by the silver chain.

XXXIII

Phantasmion rescues Leucoia
from captivity

Having reached the banks of the wide sheet of water which Phantasmion had seen from on high, the company entered a mother-of-pearl boat, which was drawn by a team of swans, a full grown pair in front of the vessel, then three yokes of younger ones, each couple being smaller than that behind, while a single tiny cygnet floated on before. Doves fastened to the stern by silken cords and studs of diamond fluttered round the gleaming skiff, and hastened its progress, while they lulled the air with their downy pinions. The fire-fly constellation was reflected, together with the moon, on the calm waters, forming now a belt across her disk, now a ring which inclosed and shone beyond it: white peacocks spread their snowy trains over the dark foliage that overhung the lake, white cormorants occupied the rocks, and alabaster images of herons cast their still reflections on the pool. A tiger emerging from the recesses of the wood came to drink the cool wave, after sleeping in his lair during the close heat of the darksome day; and he too was colourless and gleaming as a ghost. Anon a white bird of paradise rose from the trees, and flew with slow undulating motion over the lake, first crossing the moon's bright image, then sinking amid blossoms, downy and drooping as her own light plumage, like a snow-flake descended into a wreath of snow. The tiger was drinking at the end of a little promontory as the skiff passed by: a reflection on the water made him look up, when beholding the youth's illumined visage, he suddenly rushed back again into the depths of the grove. The company in the vessel were all silent and thoughtful, Leucoia's fair stag lay beside her feet, Potentilla sate at the helm with Melledine's chain in her hand, while the captive crouched beneath, her ebon face bowed forward. Phantasmion leaning over the prow cast such bright gleams upon the waters, that the silver-scaled fishes leaped up, attracted by a stronger light than had ever penetrated their liquid haunts before. The pensive eyes of Leucoia were bent upon the youth's averted face: she longed not for green fields and sunshine, but would fain have dwelt with him in that gleaming vale for ever. Melledine drew nigh the stag, and would have rested her head upon his lily side, but when he shrank away she leaned against the edge of the boat, and began to murmur a soft melody. The tone of her voice was inexpressibly sweet, and such was her power that it seemed to proceed from the woods and waters and all places except the skiff. For at the time her words were inaudible, but, at last, Phantasmion, ceased to watch the leaping fishes, and listened unconsciously to these numbers:—

Blest is the tarn which towering cliffs o'ershade,
Which, cradled deep within the mountain's breast
Nor voices loud, nor dashing oars invade:
Yet e'en the tarn enjoys no perfect rest,
For oft the angry skies her peace molest,
With them she frowns, gives back the lightning's glare,
Then rages wildly in the troubled air.

This calmer lake, which potent spells protect,
Lies dimly slumbering through the fires of day,
And when yon skies, with chaste resplendence decked,
Shine forth in all their stateliest array,
O then she wakes to glitter bright as they,
And view the face of heaven's benignant queen
Still looking down on hers with smile serene!

What cruel cares the maiden's heart assail,
Who loves, but fears no deep-felt love to gain,
Or, having gain'd it, fears that love will fail!
My power can soothe to rest her wakeful pain,
Till none but calm delicious dreams remain,
And, while sweet tears her easy pillow steep,
She yields that dream of bliss to ever welcome sleep.

While the strain proceeded, a pleasing stupor stole over Phantasmion, in spite of the antidote supplied by Feydeleen; he began to dream with his eyes open, and beheld the face of Iarine in that of Leucoia. He fancied himself on the Black Lake, and the radiance of the moon seemed to his eyes the same soft sunlight which had shone upon his last interview with the island princess. Potentilla had been busily plying her pinions, and broke the silence of night with a continuous hum, which seemed to tell of open flowers and glancing sunbeams: now her wings of gauze hung sleepily down, her lamp languished, one hand dropped the helm, the other resigned the chain, and bending forward, she nodded over the stern. Then Melledine raised her head, and, fixing her eyes upon Phantasmion's face, continued her melodious incantations, accompanied by the soft noise of downy wings and of the gliding vessel. Meanwhile, as she waved her hand, a mist gradually rose all round the skiff, and on its silvery tissue the rays of the moon painted a vivid rainbow, which rested on either side among darksome groves and shady waters, while, betwixt the arch, an island, and the grey towers of an ancient castle, appeared to loom through the vapoury veil. Then Phantasmion dreamed that all which had passed, since he plighted his faith to Iarine under the sunny rainbow, was but a dream: he took from his bosom her glossy ringlet, which had been twined with rubies to form a crown for his brow, and placing it on Leucoia's head, while he whispered vows of changeless love, he bade her wear it for his sake till she was queen of Palmland. Melledine looked earnestly at Leucoia, with her finger on her lips, and entreated her, in low breathed strains of melody, to bear at least a silent part in this deception. And, if the maiden loved Phantasmion while his countenance was unimpassioned, how still more loveable did he now appear, when his looks and tones expressed the deepest tenderness! But her spirit was free from magic influence, and, having just recovered from the treacherous spell, she was less subject to its power. "Never," she said, "shall Phantasmion, for my unworthy sake, be hidden from the sun's light; false Melledine's subtle sleights shall all prove vain." The enchantress had by this time turned the skiff, the doves fanned the air with redoubled vigour, and the swans rowed swiftly on toward the head of the lake. Leucoia took a loosened peg, which had fastened one of the dove-cords into the skiff, and was about to prick the relaxed palm of Potentilla, which lay half open beside her lap; when the vigilant fairy, who had only been feigning slumber, quickly rose, her flames all rekindled, and snatching the peg from Leucoia, plunged it up to the diamond head in the arm of Melledine which was guiding the rudder. Stung with pain, the enchantress uttered one loud piercing shriek: such a sound had never escaped her lips till then, such a sound had never before been heard in the gleaming valley. The peacocks which sate in multitudes on the trees around the lake, unfurling their eyeless trains to the moonbeams, echoed that scream till the mountains rang again, and instantly afterwards the fiery constellation descended from on high to hang over Melledine's head in the guise of a comet, that flamed and quivered just aloft with painful splendour. Dazzled and stunned, she sank to the bottom of the skiff, veiling her head and pressing her palms closely over her muffled ears. While Potentilla resumed the rudder and put the vessel back into its former course, Phantasmion, now thoroughly awakened, looked in confusion at the chaplet of Iarine's hair which twined the flaxen locks of Leucoia. The damsel took it from her head, and with a gentle smile and glistening eye, restored it to him: that done, the stag, which had been standing by her side with wild looks ever since Melledine turned the skiff, lay down at her feet and rested peacefully as before.

After awhile the boat entered a river, by which the waters of the lake partly flowed off. The swans held on their course till they arrived at a steep wall of cliff, against the lower part of which a cloud was resting. Here they stopped, and Potentilla having pulled Melledine by the chain, she rose, and, waving her hand, caused the cloud to soar from the base to the middle of the rock, discovering an archway, through which the stream flowed and disappeared amid the windings of the passage. Leucoia embraced her gentle stag as they entered the gloomy vault; Phantasmion covered himself with redoubled brightness, and cast his many-coloured radiance on the expanded wings and arched necks of the swans, while on before and around the gliding boat all was black shadow, save where the fire-flies made a golden line in the dark wave, or, soaring up, illumined the roof of the vault, enkindling many a sparry rock, which never reflected one bright ray before. At last the damsel's now unwonted eyes were smitten by a faint sunbeam; the birds moved with renewed vigour, hastening toward the genial light, and soon a picture, delicate and minute from distance, presented itself to the eyes of the voyagers, who once more beheld the varied green of trees opposed to the deep blue of the sky, and all the landscape bathed in golden radiance. Melledine seemed blasted by the sight, and crouched with her face to the stern, closely wrapped in her veil. Meantime the halo which surrounded Phantasmion faded away, and his wings disappeared: but heedless of the change he sate, gazing into the stream, while the swans lowered their expanded sails, and Leucoia leaped ashore with her white stag; for once more he beheld his watery image with that of a damsel holding up a pitcher before her face. And now for the first time he observed, in the faint background of the picture, a prostrate form, with the aspect of one dying or dead. "Why renew this vision?" said he to the enchantress, pulling her chain; "whom wouldst thou now delude?" The prisoner replied that what had deceived Anthemmina was no work of hers, but produced by a spirit of the waters, who had the faculty of fore-showing future scenes. While she yet spoke it faded away; all quitted the skiff, and, at a signal from Melledine, the swans disappeared under the darksome vault.

XXXIV

Phantasmion hears the second part of Penselimer's story

Potentilla bade Phantasmion follow the stream that flowed from Melledine's domain till it entered a large river. "There," said she, "thou shalt find one who will convey thee and thy company to a dell not far, from Leucoia's home. Offer the gem that clasps thy sleeve to the boatman, and he will receive you all without delay." Then her form changed, and he knew not if she were gone, or still flitted around him among the gilded flies and feathery gnats that hummed in the sunshine.

As they proceeded, Phantasmion heard the rocks resound from a distance, above the murmur of the brook, the course of which they were following: sometimes he thought they rang Anthemmina's knell with melancholy falls, and then again their merry tinkling chime seemed fitter to express the happiest espousals. Soon after those sounds ceased to be audible, having arrived where the waters met, and espied an old man in a boat, he plucked the jewel from his sleeve, and ran toward him holding it up to sparkle in the rays of the sun. On a nearer view he saw that the conductor provided by his guardian Fairy was no other than the ancient fisherman of the Black Lake, who clasped his hands for joy as soon as he knew the prince. "The messenger might have told thy name," he cried, "instead of offering hire." "What messenger?" inquired the youth. "She with bright wings," he answered, "who met me in the watery dell, and bade me hasten hither with this boat. Was it not on thy account she promised that I should win by the journey more than my fish had ever earned in Polyanthida? or was it all a dream?" Phantasmion replied that, if it were, he had dreamed to a good purpose, and, having placed his companions in the vessel, he took an oar, and seated himself beside the fisherman, who felt right glad to see him turn the boat, and begin rowing down the stream. They made great way with little effort, the full tide bearing them so rapidly forward, that the rich meads of Almaterra flew by like dreams, while each new scene had carried its colours into the next, ere the eye had time to distinguish it. Now and then they came to land for refreshment, and added the juicy fruits of the river side to their other provisions: such delays Phantasmion yielded to courtesy, though but ill pleased to see the stream run by his idle boat. Nor did Leucoia wish to linger long upon the way, for she had now resolved on following her sister to the chieftain's palace, if her mother's consent could be gained; and the more her heart reproached her with Zelneth's wound, and Arzene's anguish, the less she felt the pangs of unrequited love.

It was now the end of the third day, and night hung over the voyagers: white moths, flitting by, reflected feeble gleams of light at intervals, and once the eyes of the wild cat glared amid branches that deepened the darkness of the waters by their shade. Leucoia slept with a tear on her cheek, lulled by the chant of nightingales; Melledine lay still, and heaved no breath; Phantasmion rowed on in silence, while the old man, from whose failing hand he had taken the oar slumbered heavily at his feet. He was thinking whether Potentilla still watched over him, when a ring of fire-flies suddenly encircled the black visage of the enchantress, and revealed the workings of her sullen face. In a few moments they rose with shrouded light, and a well known voice was heard to sing thus:—

> *What means that darkly-working brow,*
> *Melledine?*
> *Whose heart-stings art thou wresting now,*
> *Melledine?*
> *The dearest pleasure follows pain,*
> *But thou with grief shalt aye remain,*
> *And for thyself hast forged the chain,*
> *Melledine!*

"Those gauzy wings!" muttered the fisherman, disturbed, but not awakened, by the fairy's shrill pipe. He slept in peace, while she thus proceeded in a softer tone:—

> *Ah, dream of sullen skies no more,*
> *Sad Leucoia!*
> *The roughest ocean hath a shore,*
> *Sweet Leucoia!*
> *A stedfast shore the billows kiss,*
> *And oft some fancied joy to miss,*
> *Prepares the heart for higher bliss,*
> *Young Leucoia!*

SARA COLERIDGE

By daybreak the vessel was gliding near a field, which the river all but surrounded. Bright green was that field, sun-bright its liquid fence, and brightly shone its groups of giant lilies, their glossy leaves full fed with moisture, their painted petals vying with the painted insect, which seemed in rivalry to rest its wings beside them. Round this fair semi-isle Phantasmion steered his boat, and saw that just beyond its farthest angle a narrower stream, which flowed beneath high woody banks, joined company with the river, losing itself in the stronger current as childhood steals imperceptibly into vigorous youth. Guessing that this new comer issued from the lake near Magnart's mansion, he concluded that here was the place to which the fairy had directed him, and was preparing to land on the meadow when his ear caught the melody of a harp, floating along the hidden course of the tributary stream. The sounds approached quickly from a distance, and now were interpreted by the varying tones of a voice, which it seemed to him that he had formerly heard with the same accompaniment. He fixed his eye on the spot where the rivers met, and soon beheld a skiff, with silken streamer, glide from among the trees. It made for the meadow, and, when he had ascertained by whom it was occupied, he took up the oars, and, having awakened the fisherman, began to look about for a landing place. Leucoia still lay fast asleep, with her head towards the prow; she had been dreaming of Zelneth, and seemed to roam in search of her through tangled wilds; but, when the sounds of the harp came thrilling across the waters, they wrought new images into the dream. That kingly portrait, once her sister's idol, appeared to gleam upon her lonesome path; but, when she stooped towards it, the picture had become a living shape, while the frame rose into high trees, between the golden shafts of which the monarch sate before her, singing and playing on his harp. This vision was dissolved by the slight shock of the boat coming to shore, and no sooner were her eyes opened than they discerned the very object of her dream, Penselimer himself, with his hand upon the strings of the harp, which he had just ceased to sound, while on he came, betwixt the drooping trees that overhung the river. And Zelneth stands beside him! Zelneth herself, with outstretched arms, and eager look, and face not pale and languishing, but full of bloom and triumph, as before the days of her unprosperous love. And who is she that bends towards the long lost maid with deeper and more melancholy fondness? Is it Arzene? Ah yes! that mild maternal brow is none but hers: Leucoia is soon folded in her mother's arms, and feels that now indeed she has attained a peaceful haven.

When the happy tears and embraces of this meeting were over, Arzene retired with her daughters to another part of the dell, where a tent had been pitched among the trees for their reception, and harnessed steeds were in readiness to carry them home by land. Then Penselimer, finding himself alone with Phantasmion in the island meadow (for the old man was a little way off with his vessel), accosted him in the friendliest manner, smiling, and saying with a perfectly rational air,—"I owe thee many thanks, young king of Palmland; by thy hand I have been restored to reason." The youth looked astonished at these words. "That thou art a changed man," he answered, "I see plainly; but how I can have wrought the change I see not, and were thy looks no less wild than thy speech, I should hold thee as far from reason as ever." "Hear the second part of my story," said Penselimer, "as thou hast formerly heard the first: I will soon show what part thou hast played in my adventures, unknown to thyself." Phantasmion delivered Melledine to the attendants, and heard the king of Almaterra relate how the ebon-faced enchantress had tempted him to seek the house of Malderyl, what had befallen him there, how he personated his enemy, fought with him in that disguise, and was wounded by the magic weapon, but not mortally, as all supposed." "And whither went Glandreth?" exclaimed Phantasmion, Oloola's prophecy rushing into his mind, "did he invade the land of Palms?" "I thought not of him," replied the monarch; for days, indeed, I lay incapable of thought, and, when my senses returned, was racked with grievous pangs; but this bodily suffering proved the cure of my better part, which, like the dyer's tincture, underwent the fire till it became clear, glowing, and resplendent. Reason rose, as it were, from the dead, and now in my true being I began to live once more. Again the stars shone forth in their own brightness, again the breezes blew with their own freshness, self, shrinking within its natural limits, no longer sicklied the whole face of outward things, as vapours veil with one same lurid hue, earth, sky, and water; my spirit ceased to multiply itself by a thousand vain reflections, but grew and spread through nourishment from without.

"While I was in this happy state, feeling as if my soul were a thing apart from its mortal frame, yet with my head sunken among the pillows from utter weakness, Albinian's queen drew near, weeping bitterly, and calling me by the name of Glandreth; while, at the same time, methought there was a soft bright face on the other side of the bed, which peeped from behind the curtains, and seemed to be smiling at her in derision. Wondering if these were but spectres of delirium, I raised myself up a little, when Maudra, beholding my face, cried aloud, and hurried from the apartment. Then that other bright visitant, growing more distinct, showed herself to be the fairy Feydeleen, and bade me hasten to Nemorosa, where a lady of the house of Thalimer was detained against her will. As she gave the command, the Flower Spirit imparted the power of obeying it, such enlivening odours and salutary dews she scattered round me ere she disappeared. I arose, feeling that my wounds were healed, and took my way, sane in body and mind, through the country of Malderyl. Entering Nemorosa during the heat of the day, I was allured to a shady covert by the sound of falling waters, and there I spied a dark and slender youth holding a silver vessel under a scanty rill which spouted over the rocks. At the first glance I felt assured that this vessel was Anthemmina's pitcher, but, before I had resolved whether to claim it or no, the dark youth mounted his horse and rode away. 'Anthemmina is dead,' thought I, 'and if any malignant power imagines that by this sight he may lure me back again to my former dreams, he has missed his purpose; but, for the sake of Anthemmina's lovely child, I will see into what hands the charm has fallen.'" Phantasmion was now listening with a fixed eye and troubled heart, for he doubted not that Karadan was the youth with the pitcher, and that he had gone in search of Iarine to Nemorosa. "I followed him," pursued Penselimer, "but he had ridden out of sight, and, while I was considering which way to take, a strange object arrested my attention. Below the green oaks of the forest, grew the stump of a black thorn, which seemed to have been blighted, for not a single leaf remained upon its uncouth boughs. The tree was split into a double trunk, one portion of which reclined upon the ground, while the other stood upright, and, toward the top, shot forth a solitary pair of branches. Casting my eyes adown the forest, I beheld the branches change into the horns of a stag, the upright stem put on the appearance of a deer's head and towering neck, while that which lay upon the ground swelled out into a body covered with a spotted hide. I rushed forward to examine this marvel, when the creature started up on legs newly formed, perhaps from the roots of the thorn bush, and flew before me, while I eagerly followed, spurring the sides of my fleet horse to overtake him. Bounding on with huge leaps, he came at last upon a company of hunters, the most noticeable of whom was one that wore a panther skin around his loins, and on his yellow hair a crown of golden oak leaves. No sooner had, this goodly youth espied the giant stag, than off he flew, followed by all his train with whoop and hollo. One fair huntress alone remained, gazing bashfully at me, with such looks as might have made me pause on the road to paradise," "And this fair huntress," cried Phantasmion, "was Zelneth, daughter of Magnart; she whom Feydeleen sent thee to deliver, she who was destined to replace all that thou hadst lost in Anthemmina?" "Even so," rejoined Penselimer; "at first I thought she was Anthemmina herself, restored in all her bloom and beauty. And thus we stood silent and motionless, till the shouts of the distant huntsmen began to die upon the ear. Then she fled with me, and, on better knowledge of the sweet lady's features, I found they had an expression all their own, and one for its own sake most worthy to be loved. Fair indeed were the still eyes of Anthemmina, gleaming amid cloudy tresses; seen in the light, they showed as many exquisite shades of colour as a mountain pool; but those of Zelneth sparkle so with life and meaning, that we think less of them than of the eloquent tales they tell. How her love was bestowed on me I marvel; she was but a laughing babe—"

"Think me no babe now!" cried Zelneth, softly approaching, and smiling away some little confusion at sight of the younger prince; "sooth to say, I have not yet found thee much older and wiser than myself. I should scarce quarrel with these few grey hairs," she added in a lower tone, "if they did not remind me of the years that I have missed thy love." With a brightened countenance Penselimer finished his story. "It was dusk," he cried, "when we entered Magnart's garden; Arzene ran from the threshold to welcome us, but Zelneth greeted her with tears. 'Think not that I bring Leucoia,' she cried; 'I hoped to find her with thee, but the tone of thy voice tells me that thou art still bereaved.' While the sad mother wept on Zelneth's bosom, Feydeleen gleamed upon my sight just under those moon-shiny blossoms that droop over the porch. 'Weep no more,' she cried, in soothing accents, 'but seek the long lost maiden in the watery dell'" "Didst thou see her?" asked Zelneth. "As plainly as I see thee now," replied the king, fixing his pensive eyes on the sprightly maid; "and methought she drew a white violet from her bosom." "Ah, my sister's flower!" the lady cried; "mine eyes must have been dimmed with tears. I only heard her voice. And said she not that a spirit of the wood protects Leucoia, and that this same spirit lent her power to raise the sylvan phantom that brought thee to my aid?" "Methought so," the king replied; "but, lady, let me place thee on thy steed, or the sun will reach his journey's end while we are delaying ours."

Then they all rose to depart, and, after bidding farewell to the friendly fisherman, Phantasmion rode with Zelneth and Penselimer toward the mansion of Magnart, relating his adventures in the Sunless Valley by the way.

XXXV

Phantasmion meets a numerous company at the mansion of Magnart

Meanwhile Arzene and her train were hastening homewards with fair Leucoia, whose snow-white stag tripped on in front of the company, as if delighted to carry a rider that so befitted his own graceful form. At times the maid turned to exchange smiles with Arzene, and see what watchful eyes were ever bent on her, then she flew forward again, surveying with new delight the vale of Polyanthida, and every object brightened by the beams of day. At last her father's mansion came in sight, and the damsel bounded on, waving aloft a white mantle, and casting up her eyes to a little mount within the walls, where her young brothers and sisters were assembled to watch the advancing company. Thus she approached the principal entrance, while the children were skipping down the hill, and beheld, not far from the gateway, an ancient woman seated in a car, to which leopards were harnessed. The heads of the beasts were held by a youth, who had himself somewhat of a wild and sylvan air, but not unmixed with gentleness and lofty grace. He was listening to the words of a dwarf, who stood in front of the car, and grasped the reins with his left hand, while with his right he pointed at Leucoia. But when the damsel's fair stag came nigh the leopards, he started, and rushed through the open gate by which the children had passed to meet Arzene. The youth stepped forward, but could not overtake the fugitive till he had reached the top of that woody hillock which overlooked the road. There, holding the reins of her sylvan steed, he told the lady that his name was Ulander, that he had come to Polyanthida under the guidance of his sage kinswoman Malderyl in search of her lovely sister Zelneth, whom he sought in marriage, and who had been carried away from his forest realm just when he hoped she would become his bride. "Tell me now," cried he, looking out over the road with glowing cheek, "is not that my betrothed lady who comes in front of the troop?" "A betrothed lady comes there, but not thine, I think," replied Leucoia, with a pitying smile. "O no, I cannot be deceived!" exclaimed the lover; "what damsel rides with such youthful spirit, such queenly grace, as my fair Zelneth? O yes! and surely that is Phantasmion of Palmland who comes on before!" Ulander cast his sparkling eyes upon Leucoia's face, and marked its pensive air. "But who is he that keeps by the side of Zelneth?" the chieftain next inquired. "That is the king of this country," she answered. "And wherefore comes he to Polyanthida?" asked the youth. "To celebrate his nuptials, as I guess," Leucoia made reply. Ulander smiled when he beheld her blushing cheek, and asked in a courteous whisper if she were to be the bride. "O no!" she answered; "Penselimer seeks the hand of Zelneth, who had indeed betrothed herself to him, as I can witness, before she went to seek for me in thy far country." Struck by these unexpected tidings, Ulander dropped the reins, and sank upon the ground; but soon recovering, he saw the gentle eyes of the stag and of Leucoia fixed upon his face: the one was standing near him, while the other kneeled by his side. The lady's gentle countenance tempted Ulander to pour forth all his sorrow to her, and even while he spoke, her looks of pity stole into his heart, and softened the bitterness of that grief which he described so eloquently. But now Arzene appeared, climbing the hill with young Hermillian and all her blooming train. The chieftain was still telling his tale with passionate gestures to Leucoia, who leaned upon her stag, and felt her own griefs assuaged by the tears that flowed for Ulander. Arzene accosted the youth, and made him the same courteous proffer of hospitality which had been already accepted by his ancient kinswoman. He gladly consented to be her guest, and accompanied the wife and daughter of Magnart to a pleasant bank shaded by trees, and spread with wines, and fruits, and dainty viands, by Arzene's command. Ulander kept by the side of Leucoia, continuing his discourse as much for the sake of the listener as the subject; for, while he beheld her gentle smiles, and soft retreating eyes, new thoughts and wishes began to arise in his bosom. Insensibly he ceased to think of Zelneth; but, caressing Leucoia's silver-coated stag, observed how fair he would look among the glades of Nemorosa. "Wilt thou go to that far land?" quoth the damsel playfully to her favourite. "Fair mistress," replied the chieftain, answering for him, "without thee I should pine and perish; let us both dwell there together." At that moment the stag raised his soft bright eye, and looked at Leucoia, as if he adopted what was said in his name.

Arzene and the ancient queen were now sitting on a bank; the white deer came to browse beside them, ever and anon looking up in the face of Malderyl, who scowled and shuddered as she met his gentle gaze. Ulander among the trees at a little distance was teaching Leucoia how to shoot, when Zelneth, followed by her noble companions, entered the grove. With light steps she approached her sister; but, on a sudden, beheld the chieftain of Nemorosa bending his bow under a laurel. At that sight she uttered an exclamation of surprise, and drew back hastily to the side of Penselimer. Then she approached the bank to salute young Hermillian, who was twining his mother's hair with honeysuckle, and started, when the face of Malderyl presented itself to her view.

Soon afterwards the whole company assembled in Magnart's princely hall, but, while the guests were gaily entertained, their gentle hostess sighed for one that was absent, and wondered whether Karadan had joined his father in Rockland. Ulander had ceased to sigh, and appeared so all intent upon winning Leucoia's grace that Zelneth addressed him with one of her archest smiles, and inquired what had become of the panther's skin which he used to wear for her sake. She blushed when the youth whispered that he did but follow her example; had not she too forgotten for whose sake she once wore it? Afterwards, however, he drew a remnant of the hide from beneath his vest to spread it under Leucoia's feet, then cast upon the spotty carpet his crown of golden oak leaves, which Zelneth took up, and twined among her sister's ringlets.

Amid these and other such pleasantries the evening shades stole on, when Melledine dismissed her gloom, and joined insensibly in the general mirth. Next Malderyl rose, and with meaning glances, besought the Lady of the Sunless Vale for that oblivious charm which her kinsman stood in need of; at the same time she placed a chalice in her hand, and Melledine, taking forth a vial, poured the contents therein, and delivered the cup to Ulander. But he fixed his eyes on Leucoia, as she sate considering the coronal which now she held in her hand, and, declaring that he had no flames in his bosom which he desired to extinguish, poured out the liquor on the marble floor. Then Malderyl complimented the bashful maid on having gained a most experienced suitor, one so well seasoned to love's variable clime that he might now endure its worst vicissitudes; and, flinging stones that rebounded from one point to another, annoyed all present by hints at Ulander's passion for Zelneth, and his worship of Iarine. While the youth himself maintained a blushing silence, Melledine pretended to take his part. "Methinks I can spy good reasons for his last change," said she, "I know of a song which fits this case well"—"A song!" cried Malderyl; let us hear it; thy voice may have more persuasion than thy words." Phantasmion was absorbed in thought of Iarine, and Leucoia engaged by the silent courtship of her sylvan lover, when this wily proposal was made; so, without opposition from them, the veiled lady held up her fettered arms, where she stood in the midst of the hall, and, with expressive gestures, began to sing thus in the person of Ulander:

Methought I wander'd dimly on,
But few faint stars above me shone,
When Love drew near;
"The night," said he, "is dark and damp,
To guide thy steps receive this lamp
Of crystal clear."

Love lent his torch,—with ready hand
The splendid lamp, by his command,
I strove to light;
But strove in vain; no flame arose,
Unchanged, unfired as moonlit snows,
It sparkled bright.

Again on wings as swift as thought
The boy a glittering cresset brought
Of sunny gold:
Full sure 'twas worth a monarch's gaze,
And how I toil'd to make it blaze
Can scarce be told.

Depriv'd of hope I stood perplex'd,
And, through my tears, what offer'd next
Obscurely floated:
One other lamp Love bade me take,
Mine eyes its colour, size, or make,
But little noted;

Till soon (what joys my soul inspire!)
From far within a steady fire
Soft upward steals;
And O how many a tender hue,
What lines to loveliest nature true,
That beam reveals!

Now what reck I of burnish'd gold,
Or crystal cast in statelier mould?—
This lamp be mine,
Which makes my path where'er I go,
With warm reflected colours glow,
And light divine.

Gradually Melledine's voice, together with the fumes of the liquor which had been spilled upon the floor, infected the hearers with drowsiness, and, as the song proceeded, the scenes it pictured stole upon their misted eyes: first dim star-light, then Love with a torch and lamp and beamy smile emerging from a wood, till at last a crowd of witching faces, and bright torches, and lamps of a thousand shapes and colours, lit and unlit, waved along before them in endless succession. Even the enamoured chief could no longer look upon the very face of Leucoia, but beheld a lucid image of it with closed lids. The maid herself scarce inquired whether she were indeed the lamp that was kindling at Ulander's touch, and, though lately proof against Melledine's charm, now nodded under the influence of this doubly potent spell. Phantasmion kept his eyes open longer than the rest, and perceived that Malderyl was loosing the fetters from his captive's feet and hands, but was too fast held in drowsy bands to prevent her liberation, and, ere it was fully effected, he too lay slumbering on the floor. A new sun had just dawned when he started up and saw its rays brightening the crimson cushions around, and the fair faces which reclined on them; but the enchantresses were gone. With small hope of recovering his prisoner he rushed into the garden, and, passing toward the chief entrance through a shady avenue, beheld the traces of panthers' feet on the humid soil. But beyond the trees and the gate, in open sunshine, not a foot-mark was to be seen upon the firm dry earth; and, when he looked at the contracted shadows of cattle on the verdurous plain, and saw the broad blue sky, where a carolling bird was the only speck of darkness, he felt as if drowsy charms, and sunless vales, and sable visages were but dreams of a long dim night.

XXXVI

Ulander conducts Leucoia to the forest

There was something in the face of the huntsman chief which brought to Leucoia's mind young Dariel of Tigridia. The maid had loved and suffered silently, so that, when she listened to the suit of Ulander, Arzene thought she gave her hand to him who had first touched her heart. The nuptials of Zelneth and Leucoia were celebrated in their native vale, and Sanio, Penselimer's trusty minister, being present at the festivities, was the first to inform the king of Palmland that Glandreth had invaded his dominions, and was now occupying them with a powerful army. Forthwith a league was struck betwixt the three sovereigns, who resolved to unite hand and heart against the common enemy, to drive the invaders from Palmland, to free Almaterra from dependence on the Land of Rocks, to protect the right of Albinian's son, and to place Ulander on the throne of his ancestors. Phantasmion resolved on secretly entering Gemmaura, that district which had been annexed to Palmland by the union of Zalia and Dorimant, for the sake of raising the spirits of the inhabitants by his presence and stirring them against the foe. It was settled that Penselimer, meantime, should divide his forces, that one part, in company with the foresters of Nemorosa, should fall upon Rockland, while the other, having joined Phantasmion in Gemmaura, which was yet free from the foreign troops, should unite with such an army as he could muster to drive the invaders from the Land of Palms. With these allies Phantasmion would have felt sure to triumph but for the lack of metal armour, which damped his subjects' martial prowess. Neither could the king of Almaterra supply the deficiency, for all the steel and brass which his people had in use they derived from Rockland, having neither mines nor skilful smiths among themselves. Magnart could not be called upon to fulfil his big promises, for he had entered Rockland with all the men he had at command, under pretence of securing Albinian's throne, against his brother's selfish schemes, for the boy Albinet. He desired to have his eldest son with him in this expedition, and to bring about his marriage with Iarine; but the youth and the maid were both missing, and no one could inform him where to seek for either. Penselimer's queen was eager to raise a powerful army in behalf of Phantasmion, not from any lingering remnant of love for him, but that her kingly spouse might appear important in the eyes of all men: Leucoia dreaded warfare, but from gratitude to her deliverer she felt anxious that he should be enabled to regain his kingdom.

While Phantasmion journeyed on towards his mother's country, which lay betwixt Almaterra and Palmland, full of grief to think that he must again travel away from Iarine, Penselimer conducted Zelneth to his castle with regal pomp, and Ulander's gentle bride accompanied her spouse to Nemorosa. The wife of Magnart went with Leucoia on her journey; for having heard Penselimer's tale, she could not doubt that the youth who carried a silver pitcher was her beloved son, and purposed to make inquiry in every house on the borders of the forest till she traced him out. After many disappointments in this quest she entered the goatherd's cottage, and there heard tidings which made her resolve to shape her course toward the sea. Arzene had left home with no attendants of her own, and now that she was to part company with her son and daughter, Leucoia bade the chieftain guard her through the dangerous forest. Ulander, though somewhat loth, obeyed his bride's behest, and, to show his zeal and devotion, attended her mother, leaving Leucoia at the goatherd's cottage. The lady asked many questions of her host concerning his late guests. She had already heard him relate to Arzene how a beautiful young maid and her aged sire abode under his roof, how the old man died, and the damsel departed with a tall dark youth who bore a silver pitcher. Now he spoke more minutely of these matters, and showed the jewels which his guests had given him. Leucoia felt certain that the decrepit man of whom he spake must have been Iarine's father, and full of tender thoughts, she wandered forth alone to view the hollow in the rocks where his body had been deposited. Passing through a part of the wood she espied the fair white stag browsing among the trees a little way off, and, fearing that he might stray too far, she went to lead him back toward the cottage. On she tripped, calling him by his name in silver tones; but, ere she reached his side, two dwarfs rushed out upon her from behind some bushes, and, while one pinioned her arms, the other bound them with cords, then both together placed her at the bottom of a car drawn by leopards, wherein the ancient queen of Tigridia was seated. "Swartho," said Malderyl, to one of these monsters, putting the reins into his hand, "dost thou see how yon white deer stands terror-stricken? Drive up to him: if he awaits our approach I will throw this noose round his neck, and take him to the gardens of the cavern." Swartho's toad eyes gleamed strangely while his mistress spoke, and, as he stared in affright, the scarlet ring flamed out all round; but, without answering a word, he shook the reins and drove up to the stag. Leucoia was lying stupified at Malderyl's feet, the witch stood erect, the object of attack appeared as motionless as if it were a marble effigy placed there to decorate the glade. But no sooner had Malderyl cast her loop round his neck than she dropped the cord and shrieked aloud: it was no stag, but a tiger with glaring eyeballs and terrific jaws, around which her noose was hanging. With a roar that shook the forest he sprang upon the leopards, and, at that moment, Ulander appeared in sight. Perceiving the jeopardy of his kinswoman he rushed on with his javelin uplifted: but, no sooner had he approached the car, than the tiger vanished. Ulander beheld his own Leucoia lying bound at the feet of Malderyl, and the hideous dwarf crouching like a nightmare on her breast. In a moment he had severed the cords that bound her arms, and would have spitted the monster with his spear, but a voice that seemed to be made up of many sweet voices, so powerful and mellow it sounded, was heard to speak thus; "Take home thy gentle bride, Ulander, and let the dwarf and Malderyl go unhurt. Fear nothing for Leucoia: she may wander securely, by day or night, amid the loneliest recesses of this forest. The Spirit of the Woods protects her, and destined the maid from childhood for thy bride. Go, Malderyl! in vain wouldst thou seek to overthrow my plans: fly to thy mountain abode, and lurk no longer in the shadow of these boughs, weaving deceits and treacheries." While the voice continued, every bird was silent, every leaf motionless on the spray; but, when it ceased, a murmur ran through the forest, as if the whole expanse of foliage were swept by one strong transient gale, and all the feathered inmates of the wood burst forth at once into a choral melody. Leucoia leaped upon the turf, then Malderyl drove her leopards through an opposite quarter of the forest, and soon was hidden from view amid leafy oaks and beeches. The lady by Ulander's side pursued a different course: wherever she passed, the birds crowded to the boughs, even the trees themselves appeared to be saluting her with lowered branches, and a troop of white fawns, like snow-drops, such as had never been seen in that region before, skipped around and preceded her steps.

But when the wedded pair arrived at the Sylvan Palace, Ulander saw, to his astonishment, that its precincts were enlarged, that a fence of tall trees which formerly bounded one end of it was now removed, and a delicious pleasure ground, watered by a clear stream, laid open to the view. This was Malderyl's garden, which the Spirit of the Wood had thus added to the domain of Ulander, having taken off the spells which had hitherto hedged it round. The Witch's cavern was yet standing, but soon afterwards an earthquake laid it in ruins, and the place it had occupied became a rocky channel, where the river, diverted from its ancient bed, flowed roughly, flashing and raving in its broken course, as if indignant at the remembrance of deeds once perpetrated there.

XXXVII

After the death of Albinian Iarine leaves the Goatherd's cottage

While the daughters of Magnart were surrounded with festal pomp and pleasure, Iarine watched her father's dying bed, and, so deeply was her heart engaged by his wants, and sufferings, that the season of Albinian's mortal sickness, with its slightly varied stages, its melancholy hopes and transient restorations, remained imprinted on her mind like a vivid chart, which the eye surveys at once all equally distinct and clear from the beginning to the end.

Just before his death, Albinian spoke of Maudra and Anthemmina; for in this time of natural decay his speech was wholly restored. "It was a fearful retribution," he said, "that she to whom I denied my hand and heart, (alas too hastily promised,) should be enabled to bewitch my spirit with an amorous infatuation, and afterwards my body with unnatural weakness. But O, the beauty of Anthemmina might have done away stronger traces from the heart than Maudra ever left on mine!" Iarine sighed, and still more sadly she felt when Albinian spoke further. "Weakly and wrongfully," he said, "I accepted the fair hand which a father offered me, and that gift brought after it a train of evils which clung to the receiver even after the gift itself had been taken away. Dorimant was in all her thoughts, Dorimant was in her nightly dreams: when, wrapped in slumber, she uttered the name of Dorimant, sleep deserted my pillow; one fatal image haunted the unloved husband and the regretful wife. But thou, Iarine, wast the child of that marriage; thy beauty brings only blessing and happiness; thou hast loved me here, and where I go thy love will follow me." While he spoke thus, the old man's withered face began to expand and brighten, his mind being filled with the one only thought on which it could dwell with perfect complacency. He imagined blissful regions, where Maudra and Anthemmina could wreck his peace no more, where Iarine, with brave Karadan, who from boyhood had shown him reverence, might dwell for ever in his sight. But soon that vision faded, while sad remembrances and anticipations cast their deep shadows over his soul. Iarine saw that his countenance was disturbed, though no new words had been spoken, as a lake appears ruffled on the surface while not a breath of air is stirring abroad, and the valesmen imagine a wind under the waters. Albinian was thinking of Albinet, left in Glandreth's power, of his infant boy in the palace of Palmland, and, worse than all, of Iarine plighted to the son of Dorimant. "Father!" said the maid, reading part of his thoughts, "thy children have noble and brave defenders: me they may survive as well as thee, but while I tarry here below I will watch those children with a mother's care; and rich indeed will be my reward when I receive thy thanks hereafter, and hear thy sons declare that I faithfully discharged my trust!" These soothing images found no entrance to the spirit of Albinian; Dorimant and Anthemmina, Iarine and Phantasmion, linked together in eternal bliss! Alas! alas! earth had been a scene of sorrow to the dying man, and heaven, he feared, would be no heaven for him. He pressed the hand of his daughter, and, even while the dews of death stood on his forehead, his sunken eyes appeared to glow and be projected by the force of passion. "Promise to marry Karadan, thy dear mother's kinsman," he cried, with struggling utterance; "then I shall die in peace:" at that moment the unhappy maiden longed to die too, and dwell with both her parents in realms above. She remained silent, while tears flooded her cheeks, and her whole frame trembled. With a faint groan Albinian abandoned her gentle hand, and instantly afterwards he ceased to breathe. Iarine closed his eyes and knelt beside the bed with her face bowed down in sorrow.

She had remained for some time in this posture lost to all outward sights and sounds, when a well known voice roused her from abstraction. Iarine lifted up her eyes, dim with tears, and beheld the silver pitcher of Anthemmina gleaming in the light admitted by a narrow casement at one end of the rustic chamber. He who held it now advanced from the door, and she saw the dark face and slim figure of Karadan. "Is he dead?" cried the youth, gazing sorrowfully on the couch: "O, say not that he is gone for ever! I have here a blessed medicine, which the kind spirit has given me at my earnest prayer: I myself have felt its wondrous potency." "It comes too late!" replied the maid, with fresh-flowing tears: "charms and witcheries can have no power upon him now, for good or evil." "Woe is me!" exclaimed the youth, "it would have restored him to health and vigour! How long have I been wandering bewildered in this land of trees! O would that Feydeleen had shown me thy abode before!" "Many thanks to thee, Karadan!" exclaimed the damsel fervently; "thou hast ever loved and honoured my father!" Karadan wept, and stood looking with a countenance of grief on the face of Albinian; at last he said, in a low voice, "Thy father loved me too, and fain would have had me for a son. Were thou and I united in marriage, his spirit would be ever nigh to bless and to protect us." "O, Karadan!" replied Iarine, "with his dying voice he urged that suit; yet even now, could I restore him to life by granting it, the little word might not be spoken." Karadan remained silent for some time after Iarine had uttered these words, kneeling by the side of the bed; then he clasped his hands, and looking up, with a face of deep anguish, "Yes, yes!" he exclaimed; "it was fated long ago! I see that thou art never to be mine! Thou couldst not consent, even to bring back Anthemmina from exile!" Iarine gazed on Karadan, as if to read his meaning in his eyes, but soon the youth declared that meaning with solemn words and oaths. "Anthemmina yet lives!" he cried; "blame me not that I have concealed this truth till now: hereafter thou shalt know that I am blameless. Anthemmina did not sink beneath the waves, and I can guide thee to the coast, where Feydeleen last night shed balm upon her lonely pillow." Iarine stood rapt, with face upturned and arms outstretched, but motionless; her heart and brain seemed overborne by a multitude of thoughts and feelings which crowded on them at once; a thousand dreams were suddenly realised, and started up from the depths of memory into brilliant light. At last she clasped her hands and rushing to her father's side, "O wake again," she wildly cried, "to hear that my mother lives!" The eyes of him who lay on the couch were open, and he returned her eager gaze. Albinian was not dead: sense and breathing had feebly returned, and he had heard that she whom he had never ceased to love, was yet among the living. He beckoned to Karadan, who stood with eyes fixed on his in amazement. Karadan approached and kneeled by his side. Albinian looked at the maid, then at the youth, and pointed to the silver pitcher now standing on the floor. His lips moved, and Iarine knew, as she bent over her father, that he was entreating her to be the wife of Karadan, and to seek with him for Anthemmina. "Give me thy hand," cried the youth rising: then he whispered in Iarine's ear, "Satisfy the soul of Albinian, and thou shalt be freed from this tie by the time that thou beholdest Anthemmina." "The maid no longer held back, but placed her hand in the hand of Karadan, and the youth, firmly grasping it, said aloud, "Thy daughter has betrothed herself to me, and death only can separate us." Iarine marked not the import of these words, her mind being wholly occupied with the change that came over her father's countenance immediately after they were spoken; for his face, though it wore a happy smile. was now again like the face of the dead. Karadan took the pitcher, and bedewed his body with the charmed liquor supplied by Feydeleen. The effect was marvellous: every wrinkle was removed, soft bloom overspread the cheek, and that body, so miserably wasted by sorrow and sickness, shewed like the corse of some fair and youthful person whose thread of life had been snapped by sudden accident. But this adorning was only for the tomb; Albinian's spirit had fled a moment after Iarine placed her hand in that of Karadan; the empty tenement looked meet to be inhabited, but the soul returned to it no more.

Long did Iarine linger over the corse of Albinian; but, when all hope was gone, having placed her father's remains in a coffin, she went with Karadan to lay them in a hollow among the rocks, where the goatherd promised they should remain in safety till they could be removed to a more august receptacle. That service performed, Iarine besought Karadan to fulfil his promise of conducting her to the abode of Anthemmina, and having mounted a mule, she bade her sorrowful host farewell with many tears, declaring that even when he should cease to be the guardian of her father's body every link would not be severed which bound her to him.

XXXVIII

Phantasmion vainly attempts the destruction of Glandreth, but, entering the bowels of the earth, he meets with one who assures him of victory and vengeance

Phantasmion had hardly set foot in Gemmaura when his guardian spirit appeared before him. "Beware," she cried, how thou proceedest in this district: "the foe has been here before thee. Hast thou no remembrance of the country around?" Phantasmion replied that it scarcely seemed new to his eyes. "Not far from hence," rejoined Potentilla, "is the mansion where thy mother used to dwell with Cyradis, her guardian. After marriage Zalia loved to revisit the spot, and see her little son gambol in those green haunts where she herself had sported when a child; and here in her death-sickness she desired to be buried, feeling like one who longs to lie down in the old accustomed chamber. Her ancient friend survived till an hour ago, but Glandreth and his savage band have murdered him." Then Phantasmion cried aloud, and, flinging himself upon the ground, began to tear his bossy ringlets. "It was rumoured," said the Fairy, "that he possessed a treasure, and was acquainted with rich mines. And so they pierced him with spears, on the tomb of his beloved pupil, which he daily visited; then digging into the ground, discovered no precious stones or metals, but thy mother's coffin, which they are even now carrying away into Palmland. For Glandreth declares that he will hold a solemn feast and burn the relics of Dorimant and Zalia, before all the people, as a sign that the old race of the Palmland kings is utterly abolished." Phantasmion now sprang from the earth, and, grasping Potentilla's robe, implored her either to end his life at once, or to give him the means of sudden vengeance. The Fairy made answer that she could devise but one way of helping him to that for which his soul thirsted, and this was a plan fraught with toil, hazard, and even abasement." Phantasmion exclaimed that he would do and be and suffer anything, if he might but stop his enemies in their outrageous career. "Then listen," she replied; "among the innumerable subjects of my insect realm is one which digs a pitfall in the sand. For nature has so constructed its unwieldly form that it walks backward, and has no other means of catching the nimble creatures which it preys upon. At the farther end of Gemmaura is a wide sandy plain: this thy enemies have to traverse ere they reach the luxuriant Valley of Palms, where their armed comrades are to meet them, and the festival is to be celebrated on the morrow. Thither thou shalt go, and, in the guise of that crafty insect, prepare a gulf large enough to swallow up Glandreth and all his murderous band when they arrive there." The youth embraced this offer, and, having received wings from Potentilla, rapidly followed her through the air, and alighted on a spot suitable for the undertaking, just before the entrance to the Vale of Palms. At a touch of the Fairy's wand his wings vanished, and, in the same point of time, every vestige of his human form disappeared. Led by a natural instinct he forthwith set to work, and traced out circle within circle in the sand, his new body and limbs being his only instruments. Labouring without stop he at length scooped out a deep cavity, of size proportioned to the gigantic form that wrought it: at the bottom of the snare the metamorphosed prince now took his seat, covering himself with sand, so that the upper part of his head with the points of his horrid fangs, which were like two reaping hooks crossed, alone remained visible; and, over the hollow, Potentilla wove a gummy web, on which, when finished, she strewed a light covering of dust and common soil.

By this time the sun was sinking in the west, and the last clump of spiral trees, which Glandreth's company passed on the margin of the desert, cast their lengthened shadows on the yellow sand. The leader had fallen back to the rear, and was deep in discourse with a chieftain, richly apparelled, to whom he was vaunting his triumphs, and describing how he meant to rule the state of Palmland. Some way in advance were those that bore the remains of Zalia, and the younger men went riding on before. No sooner had these youthful warriors, who were mounted on prancing steeds, arrived at the sandy plain, than for their own sport and that of their horses, they resolved on running a race. Their friends behind warned them to beware of the old quarries which lay on the right: but, confident and careless, off they started, avoiding those excavations only to fall into an equally destructive gulf. Within a few seconds of each other all arrived at the abyss which gaped to receive them. At the edge of it they rushed upon a loose bank of pebbles and sand, thrown up by the fabricator: against this the horses stumbled, and, losing their balance, fell headlong into the trap. The men behind wondered to see them suddenly disappear in the distance, and strained their eyes to look after them. It was quite dark ere the company that brought the coffin reached the pitfall, so that, leisurely as they came, all rolled over the shelf and joined their comrades in the hollow. There the mingled crowd were lying crushed and mangled, with broken arms, legs, ribs, and sculls, some over their steeds and some under them, while those horses which still had power to move kicked and plunged and trode their masters to atoms. He who had dug the huge pit kept quietly at his post, somewhat oppressed by the weight of one man's body, nigh the centre of the gulf, but eagerly expecting the arrival of Glandreth. Glandreth however was destined to escape that snare. "The moon is not yet up," he cried to his men, "and we shall have a stream to cross in the Valley of Palms. Kindle the torches that we may see our way." The conqueror was obeyed, and, by the light which the flaming pine branches cast around them, he and his companions descried the heaped and the gaping pitfall. Seized with alarm and astonishment, Glandreth snatched one of the brands, and went with the rest to look down into the gulf, where he beheld a crowd of mangled bodies and heard the groans of the dying. Phantasmion plainly discerned his enemy, on whose horror-stricken visage the torch-light cast a fierce glare, gazing into the pit and narrowly eyeing the scythe-formed weapons of his head which stood out from the centre of it. Another face gleamed beside his, beneath a jewelled head-dress: it was that of treacherous Magnart, whom the indignant youth immediately recognised. After a while the two brothers and their attendants drew off toward the Vale of Palms, when with some difficulty, Phantasmion dragged himself out of his den, bringing up his mother's coffin along with him. He had been miserably bruised, and now feeling all eagerness to be divested of his hideous mask, would have cried aloud for the Insect Fairy, but found himself unable to utter any articulate sound. He looked about and saw not her whom he sought in woman's form, yet surmised that she must still be near him, because a large moth, having the figure of a scull depicted on the upper part of its body, kept flitting around his head, ever and anon uttering a shrill piteous cry, then sinking down beside him. "She deserted Dorimant!" thought he; "perhaps she will leave me also to my fate." But soon he keenly felt the wretchedness of being disabled either from facing his enemies or escaping from them by fleetness; when a band of soldiers armed with arrows and javelins, and lighted by torches, came to take the bodies of their companions out of the pit. One of them, looking over the plain, espied the monstrous form under which Phantasmion was disguised, lying stretched upon the sand. He pointed it out to the rest, who feared to approach, but from a distance discharged their missiles, many of which struck like porcupine quills about the ungainly carcase, and caused the youth such anguish that he believed he should expire that night. "Miserable man that I am," he exclaimed, "or rather miserable spirit of a man, imprisoned in a frightful crust, to what dire extremity have I been driven by mad rage! I have cast away my human form and faculties only to perish unavenged by arrows from mine enemy's quiver!" Still dragging his mother's coffin, he crawled along in hope to gain the shelter of some rocks, and there to find at once a death-bed and a sepulchre. The moon had now risen, and cast her light upon those rocks by the time that Phantasmion reached them; but exhausted with fatigue and pain, he was unable to command the motions of his monstrous body, his eyes grew dim, he came unawares to the verge of a stone quarry, and moving backwards, lost his balance, so that he tumbled to the bottom. Here, when he recovered, sense and motion, which his fall at first suspended, he found himself lying under a vault of stone, with large fragments of rock scattered on all sides. The moon cast her beams wherever they could find entrance amid the lumber of the quarry, and all around was an interchange of blackest shade and soft silver reflections. But the attention of the miserable transformed youth was drawn toward a darksome hollow, whence he heard low sounds proceed; and, after listening a little while, he distinguished two voices, one deep and sepulchral, the other slender and sweet as that of a solitary wren which pipes a faint strain when the blast is silent, and the sun shines on its cushion of snow. "Nevertheless, O save my son!" exclaimed that softer voice. It seemed as if the tones of the second speaker came from under ground, while those of the first descended through the air. "What have I to do with the son of Dorimant?" was the reply. "I have expiated my disobedience, great Spirit of the Earth!" rejoined the voice from above. "I perished through that marriage against which thou didst warn me." "What is Phantasmion to me?" again the Earth Spirit replied; "he hath a helper of his own: and even here, in my domain, she hath presumed to practise her witcheries?" "But thou hast triumphed, O Valhorga," the second speaker replied: "now therefore, I beseech thee, suffer Potentilla to restore my son." While Phantasmion listened to this colloquy, his soul was filled with indescribable tumults, and the silence that succeeded to the last words caused him the most agonising suspense: he felt as if his strong emotions must rend and break to shivers that disproportioned case which lay on the earth, lumpish and uncouth as the half hewn stones around it. But now the hideous dream has vanished, and once more Phantasmion stands erect in his own noble form, splendid as the palm trees, with their leaf-crowned heads and gorgeous clusters, graceful and majestic as the darker cypress. The first object that met his eye was Potentilla, whose wand had just wrought the change, flitting away in the air, her wings growing transparent, her head triagonal, and her whole body more and more minute, till she had changed into a dragon-fly, the gay colours of which twinkled for a moment in the moonlight. She is gone! but what pale shadowy form is that which occupies her place, and gazes with such melancholy tenderness on the renovated youth? Phantasmion looking intently before him remembers the fair and gentle countenance of his mother. An hour ago how ill could he have brought to mind the face of Zalia; that face which, ever beaming in his presence with maternal love, had been to his young mind the very symbol of maternity. Now he not only recognised her features, but saw his childish self placed outwardly before him. The time when he lay in sickness on his little couch, and saw that soft mild countenance still shining in betwixt delirious dreams, now occupied his mind with such intensity, that all which had since occurred seemed dim and faint in comparison; as when a distant moonlit building attracts the eye, all the intervening space looks indistinct and shadowy because that has been rendered so conspicuous. Filled with inexpressible yearning, Phantasmion leaned forward to embrace the form of Zalia; but ah! no living mother watches over him now, and she who has done him this maternal service is but an impalpable phantom. "Blessings on thee, my son!" whispered the spirit; "restore my bones to their resting place, and lay those of my ancient guardian in the same grave!" Phantasmion eagerly promised to obey, and then she related that Valhorga once made her mistress of those precious mines, the report of which induced Dorimant to marry her; that no sooner had she accepted his hand than the gift was withdrawn. While Phantasmion listened, darkness fell upon an opposite rock, which had reflected the full light of the moon from its humid front. He looked and saw what seemed to be the shadow of a giant, leaning forward from a recess hard by. "Dorimant could never find those mines," Zalia continued. "Alas! it was but iron and gold that he sought in seeking me!

The Earth Spirit knew this and frustrated his purpose." "I too need metals!" exclaimed Phantasmion. "Come then!" his mother cried, "and I will show thee where veins of iron have lurked for ages, undisturbed by the hand of man." Phantasmion rejoiced at these words; but now he bethought him of Iarine, and, hoping that he might learn where she abode from the kind spirit, he kneeled down, and, looking earnestly in her face, "Mother!" he said, "knowest thou her to whom I have given thy coronal, the daughter of Anthemmina?" As he uttered that name a mournful displeasure darkened Zalia's countenance, and her face, which hitherto had shone in the moonlight pure as a fleecy cloud, now appeared to be flecked with purple. "What means this fearful change, my mother?" exclaimed Phantasmion, "and O! why dost thou look so mournfully?" The shade of Zalia was silent; Phantasmion held up his hands in earnest supplication, but now his mother's form gleamed upon him no longer, and the moonbeams enlightened only the solid walls of the quarry.

A dawning sun tinged the landscape with its first pale beam, when Phantasmion heard the voice of the Earth Spirit calling him from underground:—"Son of Zalia! follow me!" it cried, "and thou shalt be avenged on Glandreth!" "Shall I leave the light of day!" thought the youth, "and venture below with one who may keep me there for ever?" While Phantasmion hesitated, he heard a thundering sound, and at the same time the masses of rock and walls of stone began to quiver, as if seized with an ague. The tumult having subsided, he beheld an opening in the earth, and from that passage the voice of the Earth Spirit issued and spoke thus:—"If thou wilt be avenged on Glandreth, follow me." Then Phantasmion thought that if Valhorga willed his destruction, he had but to shake the earth a little more forcibly, and straightway he must lie defaced and mangled among the fragments of the quarry. No sooner had he taken this resolve than hope led him onward, and all the dark images which fear had summoned were dissipated in the brightening atmosphere of his soul, like smoky fumes in the transparent ether. He entered the hollow way, and groped along, till the last faint glimmering of light had disappeared, and he stumbled in utter darkness. Awful noises now assailed his ears, and, as he proceeded, they grew louder and louder; but his courage never deserted him, he went right on, till the passage widened, and brought him to an open space with a firm but glassy footing. Here he groped a little way, then stopped, overcome by the seeming weight of darkness, and the utter vacancy on every side:

when, at once, his eyes were attracted by sparks of light kindling in the blackness above, and soon myriads of fresh stars shone out. In another moment these fiery points shot upward, and swelled into volumes of flame, which disclosed the ruby lamps that held them, and a new heaven with gems and numberless constellations glittering over his head. Below that sapphirine dome, the ground was of jasper, embossed with a thousand flower-like jewels; and full in view were lakes of crystal, emerald groves, and towers and spires of diamond, which rose from a golden city, built on many hills, and stretched away in the distance far as the eye could reach. Over against where he stood, at the entrance of this gemmy vale, which, by its over brightness, caused the eye to ache for milder daylight, Phantasmion beheld a swarthy and gigantic figure, leaning on an implement of iron; his limbs were muscular, his cheeks ploughed with furrows, and his eyes deep sunk beneath black beetling brows. "Valhorga!" exclaimed the youth, "it is not gold and jewels that I seek from thee, but brass and iron; give me sharp swords to pierce the impious hearts of my enemies, and let all thy brilliant possessions reflect no other light than that of these subterranean fires!" Valhorga's stern brow relaxed, and he smiled upon Phantasmion. "Thou shalt have iron and brass enough," said he, "to make thy armies glitter in the sun, like glaciers on the bosom of the mountain. Conduct them to the volcano behind the house of Malderyl, and there they shall be fitted out to encounter the troops of Glandreth." Phantasmion's heart exulted in this promise, but, casting his eyes around the sparkling scene, he beheld that stony likeness of a pomegranate tree, whence his mother's coronal had been taken; it grew beside a crystal lake, which reflected the sapphire vault, and stars of carbuncle and ruby, their flames appearing to quiver on its firm smooth face. Then Zalia's mournful image came back into his mind, and he besought Valhorga to explain the meaning of her sudden change. The Earth Spirit made reply:—"Malderyl persuaded thy mother to taste poisonous berries, averring that they were sent by the Flower Spirit, and would render her beloved in the eyes of her neglectful spouse. Zalia still clings to the error which haunted her dying bed, and believes that Feydeleen sought her life for the sake of Anthemmina." Then Valhorga disclosed the ancient feud which had rendered Malderyl and Melledine bitter enemies, both to the house of Thalimer, and the race of Palmland, and Phantasmion found that Dariel, whose scarf he still wore across his bosom, was the brother of Ulander, and had been sent by the Tigridian queen to work his ruin.

This discourse inspired him with fresh desire to encounter his foes, and fresh hope that he should prevail against them ere long, by Valhorga's aid. The Spirit of the Storm he feared not. "Anthemmina's dying day," thought he, "is long since past, and her vow to serve Glandreth must have expired." With a joyful heart he quitted that sapphirine sky, and pursued another dark winding passage, till it led him up into the light of day. When he emerged, the sun was shining in meridian splendour, and he found himself in the midst of Penselimer's army, with the numerous bands of Gemmaurians and fugitives from Palmland, who had flocked around him. They had assembled on the sandy tract, and were greatly at a loss to know what had become of the young monarch, scouts having been sent on all sides to look for him in vain. Great was the astonishment of Penselimer when he beheld the earth gape a little way from the place where he stood, and Phantasmion come forth in helmet, shield, and breastplate of diamonds, which sparkled like icicles in the sunshine, though not to be melted by the hottest ray. "This jewelled armour," cried the king of Palm-land, "is a pledge from Valhorga, the Spirit of the Earth: soon it shall be exchanged for a more serviceable suit, and every soldier of our numerous host shall receive the same harness as myself. Let us march to the volcanic mountain of Tigridia, there to be equipped for battle and victory." Acclamations rent the sky, after the silence of amazement which his first reappearance occasioned: Phantasmion showed himself to his whole army in his brilliant array, so that all were inspired with confidence, and eager to start for the mountain of Malderyl. Phantasmion delayed their march, while he interred his mother's remains, with the body of her faithful guardian, in a secret but honoured grave: those rites performed, the united armies set forth on their distant expedition.

XXXIX

Arzene wanders in search of Karadan to a bay, whence he has just set sail with Iarine

"The spring returns, and balmy budding flow'rs
Revive in memory all my childish hours,
When pleasures were as bright and fresh, though brief,
As petals of the May or silken leaf.

But now when kingcups ope their golden eyes,
I see my darling's brighten with surprise,
And rival tints that little cheek illume
When eglantine displays her richest bloom.

Dear boy! thou art thy mother's vernal flow'r,
Sweeter than those she loved in childhood's hour,
And spring renews my earliest ecstasy,
By bringing buds and fresh delights for thee."

With tearful eyes Arzene murmured this song, and seemed to see the childish, form of Karadan sporting before her, as when she sang it first. No one gave tidings of her son at the hamlet where she had spent the night, but the goatherd had expressed a belief, from inquiries which the youth made, that he and his fair companion were bound for the Tigridian coast, and thither she directed her steps. At mid-day she entered a sunny field, where the reapers were busy at work, and women were binding sheaves. There she sate below the shady fence to rest, and saw a little boy collecting corn poppies, which the sickle had cut down, while his sister was busy in gathering the scattered ears. "Idle child!" cried the laden girl, "what hast thou gleaned, I pray? will those gaudy flowers make bread?" "Bread for bees!" replied the urchin. "If thou art a busy bee, thou canst make bread of flowers." So saying, with a laugh, he flung his posy at the chider's face, and a shower of the profitless blossoms fell down into her armful of corn. Arzene thought of her own playful Hermillian and young Arimel, who loved to forestall womanhood, and step into her mother's place, till the golden crop and the bending groups swam through her tears, and, starting from her seat, she resolved forthwith to seek no more for him who scorned her anxious love, but return to her other children. In this mind she turned her face from the village, whither she had intended to proceed, and, having partaken of the reapers' fare, which they charitably offered, she travelled on in another direction till the day was far spent. Then, sitting down again to rest, she heard the wind sigh dolefully, and saw the black shadow of a tree on a smooth green slope wave slowly up and down. Arzene was thinking with deep sorrow of her truant son, and now she seemed to hear his voice, and to see his image reproaching her change of purpose. She arose, and again resolved to seek along the coast for Karadan. Scarce hoping to reach the sea that night, she journeyed, however, towards it, till she entered a field that was bathed in the clear melancholy sunshine, and contained a clump of dark holm oaks, about which a rivulet wound like a silver chain. Just across that brook, a shepherdess was sitting, while her flocks nibbled the green grass on its margin. Arzene would scarce have seen her among the trees, but the notes of her song, while the words were inaudible, came across the field to her ear, and she went up to the place where the maiden sate, with the intention of begging a shelter for that night. "Go on with thy sweet song," said Arzene, courteously, when the damsel rose at her approach: "I will sit beside thee on this fallen log." The shepherdess renewed her melody, and these were the words of her song:

> Full oft before some gorgeous fane
> The youngling heifer bleeds and dies;
> Her life-blood issuing forth amain,
> While wreaths of incense climb the skies.
>
> The mother wanders all around,
> Through shadowy grove and lightsome glade;
> Her foot-marks on the yielding ground
> Will prove what anxious quest she made.
>
> The stall where late her darling lay
> She visits oft with eager look:
> In restless movements wastes the day,
> And fills with cries each neighbouring nook.

She roams along the willowy copse,
Where purest waters softly gleam:
But ne'er a leaf or blade she crops,
Nor crouches by the gliding stream.

No youthful kine, though fresh and fair,
Her vainly searching eyes engage;
No pleasant fields relieve her care,
No murmuring streams her grief assuage.

The words of this song struck painfully on the sad mother's heart. Her face was bathed in tears, and, while she drooped forward, absorbed in bitter thought, the light-hearted shepherdess gathered her flock, and went away. After awhile, Arzene remembered that she had not where to take her rest that night, and strove to overtake the damsel, but, having followed her for some time, she became exhausted, and laid her down to sleep in a waste field. The sun had just risen, and turned the dew drops around Arzene's bed into diamonds, when Karadan entered the field where his mother slept. From the top of a lofty mullein a goldfinch piped beside her, and soon his new-fledged offspring, led by their other parent, alighted on tall plants around, buoyantly swaying back and forward as they pecked the winged seeds. Arzene saw not the gleeful group: in dreams she had wandered back to her own deserted little ones, and knew not, that he for whose sake she had left them was weeping over her. While the youth still gazed on his mother's face, Iarine came beside him. He started, and would have drawn her away, "Come," he said in a low voice, "our path lies yonder. I bade thee wait till I had explored this field." But Iarine had recognized the features of her who slept, and wondering much at the behaviour of Karadan; "Wilt thou leave thy mother alone in this strange land?" she said. Anguish was depicted on his face, but he answered firmly, "We must leave Arzene, or thou may'st forego all hope of beholding Anthemmina." "She is come in search of thee from her distant home," said the maid; "wilt thou not stay till she wakes, and tell her thy purpose?" "Then it would never be effected," Karadan replied. "Take thy choice; return with Arzene, or seek Anthemmina." Iarine looked at the youth's countenance of woe, and guessed that if the mother beheld her son, she would never suffer him to pursue his journey. With a sorrowful heart she quitted the field, accompanied Karadan to the sea-shore, and there remained in a fisherman's hut, while he went in quest of a vessel. But Iarine knew only that she was to await the youth's return; for so strict a silence had he kept, and enjoined on her, concerning their errand, that she knew not whether her mother's abode were to be approached by sea or land.

After some hours he returned, placed her on the mule, and, holding the reins, led it by rugged paths over a ridge of rocks, from the top of which Iarine beheld a skiff anchored in a little bay. Still carefully guiding the mule, Karadan descended, and soon he had entered the vessel with his companion. "Does the wind blow favourably?" inquired the maid, as she helped him to unfurl the sails. She heard not the reply, but a gurgling sound of laughter issued from under the waves, circling all round the vessel, and prolonged by a succession of fainter and fainter echoes. As a pebble, thrown by a dexterous hand, repeatedly touches the water, then sinks out of sight, even so the sounds were many times renewed till they died into silence. Iarine looked aghast, but heard no comment on that ill-boding mirth from her companion, whose countenance did not regain its gloomy composure ere the skiff had cleared the bay. Smoothly then it sailed, till land was again in sight, and Iarine's countenance glowed, while that of Karadan became livid as a corse. On a sudden, however, an impetuous gale arose, and drove back the vessel from the point toward which the melancholy helmsman was steering; having impelled it far into mid-ocean the wind relented, but rose again as often as the skiff approached the shore. Karadan knew what power was frustrating his efforts, and in a presentiment of this delay, had stored the ship with provisions. The damsel prayed that the elemental strife might cease, but Karadan would have rejoiced could this state of things have lasted for ever.

Meantime Arzene tarried in the creek whence her son had sailed, vainly expecting his return. Scarce had the youth and maiden left the field where she lay, than the deserted mother awoke, and saw Feydeleen weeping by her side. "Why weepest thou, fair one?" Arzene cried; "Shall I never again behold his face?" "Thou shalt behold his face again," the mild spirit answered; but still the tears were trickling from her soft blue eyes upon the flowery sod. "Where shall I find him?" exclaimed Arzene. Feydeleen replied, "Not far from hence there is a narrow bay, encircled by rocks, where a hermit dwells nigh the sea shore. There, after some days, thou shalt behold thy son. When that time comes I will again be with thee, and will bring my choicest gifts to preserve him from all future harm." The spirit vanished, and Arzene, going to the sea shore, learnt from an old man who dwelt in a cave of the rock, that a youth and damsel had lately sailed from the narrow bay in a skiff brought from another part of the coast. Confiding in Feydeleen's assurance, she took up her abode with the hermit, and, from morn till eve, continued to watch the restless ocean, oft reverting in thought to this strain, which had been sung in happier days amid the blooming bowers of Polyanthida.

> *See yon blithe child that dances in our sight?*
> *Can gloomy shadows fall from one so bright?*
> *Fond mother, whence these fears?*
> *While buoyantly he rushes o'er the lawn,*
> *Dream not of clouds to stain his manhood's dawn,*
> *Nor dim that sight with tears.*
>
> *No cloud he spies in brightly glowing hours,*
> *But feels as if the newly vested bowers*
> *For him could never fade:*
> *Too well we know that vernal pleasures fleet,*
> *But having him, so gladsome, fair, and sweet,*
> *Our loss is overpaid.*
>
> *Amid the balmiest flowers that earth can give*
> *Some bitter drops distil, and all that live*
> *A mingled portion share;*
> *But, while he learns these truths which we lament,*
> *Such fortitude as ours will sure be sent,*
> *Such solace to his care.*

XL

The allied forces are equipped with armour in the heart of the volcanic mountain

While Phantasmion was conducting his forces through Tigridia, Malderyl sate in her ancient tower full of angry thoughts. After the murder of Dorimant's queen, as she traversed Gemmaura in her chariot, she had fallen into the power of the Earth Spirit. But Valhorga, who hated Dorimant, released the witch that she might accomplish her projects against him: at the same time he gave her two dwarfs, endowed with wondrous powers, intending on a future occasion, to fetch both her and them into slavery. Malderyl despatched an emissary to Palmland, who planted so many sweet but baleful herbs in Dorimant's domain, that the honey of the bees was infected with it, and the king, regaling himself thereon, was poisoned. But Phantasmion was now beyond the reach of her vengeful arm, while Zelneth and Leucoia, whom she once hoped to enslave, had both escaped her snares. Swartho crouched at the queen's feet, grinning maliciously as he viewed her knitted brows; for he knew that Valhorga had espoused the cause of Zalia's son, and that soon he should return to serve his ancient master.

That evening Malderyl went forth to visit the ancient castle where Phantasmion last beheld Oloola. Gloomy thoughts possessed her soul as she ascended the tower whence her husband and her son, by Glandreth's command, had been cast upon the flagstones below. There she stood, while the twilight was deepening into darkness, and saw the ghosts of Helmio and Sylvalad fluttering about the parapet, and beckoning, with earnest gesticulations, as if they invited her to throw herself down. She watched them till her head grew dizzy, and she almost felt tempted to obey the summons. Their motions were like those of swallows teaching their young to fly. One after another, each gleaming ghost would perch on the battlements, a little way off, look eagerly towards her, then plunge into the court beneath. As they flitted away in a curving line, both swept by Malderyl, looked in her face reproachfully, and pointed to the horizon, just as the moon, emerging from clouds, cast a clearer light upon the landscape, and enabled her to descry an army encamped upon the plain. Then back she hied to her house upon the hill, and commanded Swartho to raise pictures on the wall, and show her what was coming. He obeyed, but when she looked to have seen chariots and horses, and men in armour, mockery flames quivered around, and she stood in the midst of a seeming furnace. Malderyl shrieked, and, rushing forth, beheld the mountain crested with fire. Twice did a pyramid of flame burst forth from a lofty eminence above the mansion, twice it sank back, as if slicked in by a mighty force: the third time it remained, a steady blaze, which made the moon and stars appear to shine in vain. As fast as her tottering limbs could carry her she descended the skirt of the hill, and would have made her way through a plantation of firs and pines, but started when suddenly she beheld all the trees before her glowing with fire, the trunks and branches and every needle leaf appearing red hot. Meantime, with a crash like thunder, the ancient mansion was levelled with the ground. Torrents of fire gushed down the ravines above, and Malderyl saw that she must soon be overtaken by the flames. Again she looked at the plantation of firs, thinking to rush through the midst of it; but in front of that fiery grove stood the towering form of Valhorga, whose wild locks and rugged cheeks looked awful in the glare of the conflagration. "Fear not the flames, Malderyl," he said, with a grim smile; "thou shalt ply thy burning tasks unhurt." So saying, he touched her with his iron mace, when she became fire proof, and seeing that she was now condemned to endless toil in the bowels of the earth, she repented not having thrown herself down from the tower, that her spirit might wander at large with the ghosts of Helmio and Sylvalad. She followed Valhorga through the glowing pine grove, and at the other end of it beheld the army, which she had seen at a distance, approaching the volcano, while Phantasmion, radiant with diamonds, led them on. They had descried the conflagration, and believing it to be a signal from Valhorga, resumed their march at midnight. And this was not the only host which the light of those flames had attracted: from the woods of Nemorosa came Ulander, conducting his troops of tiger hunters, clad in shaggy skins, and armed with bows, arrows, and javelins.

Valhorga waved his hand, and the flames, which looked like a billowy sea, now rolled away, curling upwards to the top of the mountain, and there forming a fiery coronal. By the light of that blaze Phantasmion beheld a vaulted passage, occupying the place where Malderyl's mansion had stood. He beckoned to Phantasmion, and, as the youth followed him through the avenue, which received light from within, he heard a chaos of sounds, and soon entered a vast cavern hollowed out in the heart of the mountain. At the farther end was a huge hill of fire, whence smoke and flame rose up through a chimney that formed the crater of the volcano. Innumerable swarthy labourers were ranged in this vast smithy, row within row: one company softened the blocks of metal, then quenched them in vessels of water; another fashioned them on the anvil; every process in the formation of armour was going on, and every thing used in war was made in this workshop. The roaring of the flames and bellows, the hissing of the metal when plunged in water, the clattering and jingling of hammer and anvil, produced a din which almost deafened the ears of Phantasmion. Malderyl took her place among the toiling crew, and helped to make the shield which was afterwards worn by the son of Dorimant. As fast as the suits were made ready, the bands of warriors entered to fit them on, and ere the morning dawned, they were all equipped except Ulander. For he had espied Malderyl, as she followed her master into the cavern, and, guessing that her time of punishment was come, felt loth to witness it. The whole throng of artificers had withdrawn to the haunts whence the Earth Spirit had summoned them, and Phantasmion was the only warrior that remained in the mighty dome. At one end of the cavern Valhorga leaned against a rock, resembling the gigantic effigies which some nations carve in the sides of mountains. "Why does Ulander tarry?" cried the king of Palmland, as he looked at the shield of one last suit which Malderyl was polishing. "Ay! why does Ulander tarry?" repeated Valhorga, with a stern voice; "tell him that his armour is finished, and that he must fetch it, ere it be too late." But now the Nemorosan chief appeared entering the cavern, and soon began to doff the tiger's hide which he wore on his shoulders. The ancient queen arose when she saw her kinsman; and laying hold of his garment, besought him, for his father's sake, to procure a mitigation of her doom. Then Phantasmion, at Ulander's treaty, besought Valhorga that Malderyl might be permitted to die, and join the shades of Helmio and Sylvalad. The Earth Spirit smiled carelessly, and answered, "Be it as thou wilt." Malderyl, having heard these words, sprang into the midst of the blazing fire, when the flames rose up around her, and she looked like an image of bronze which they blackened but vainly attempted to destroy. Valhorga touched her with his mace, then down she sank upon her fiery bed and was consumed in an instant While they yet gazed on the flames the warriors heard a strange unnatural sound, that seemed to express pain or grief, and, looking about, they espied Swartho in a corner of the cavern, his bright eyes gleaming like jewels set in rusty iron. Though sorely oppressed by the heat, he had lingered behind all the other slaves to see what would be done with Malderyl, and was grieved to the heart that she should escape the insults by which he had hoped to repay her former tyranny. Ulander, recollecting his treatment of Leucoia, was about to pierce the livid breast of the dwarf with the spear he had just received; but Phantasmion, laying hold of his arm, bade him beware how he touched a servant of Valhorga, whose mighty form was yet visible in a recess of the cavern. Then the two chiefs issued forth into the daylight, and beheld the united armies ranged upon the plain, their burnished armour shining coldly in the light of the newly-risen sun.

XLI

Iarine finds her mother in the sequestered peninsula

While Phantasmion and his allies were conducting their armed force to Rockland, driving along with them troops of sheep and kine formerly plundered from the land of Palms, and followed at a distance by a train of wolves and tigers, which seemed ready to brave any danger for the sake of obtaining a share in the booty, Karadan still contended with the impetuous gale. At length it sank and was no more renewed; the voyagers gained the coast and silence reigned on sea and land while the dark youth placed Iarine on the beach. He told her how she was to find the dwelling of Anthemmina, and tears streamed from the maiden's eyes when he declared that she must seek it alone. "Farewell!" cried Karadan passionately; a ray of joy, at sight of those tears, brightening his sad face. "More than betrothed thou canst not be to any one but him who owns this charmed vessel, and thou hast been betrothed to me!—Alas! that wreath upon thy brow!—When next we meet may it be there no longer! Then thou wilt know that I have ventured for thy sake as he who gave that pledge will never dare to do." Sorrowful indeed was the parting of Iarine and Karadan, while each had a heart full of the gloomiest forebodings; but little did either suspect what worse calamity awaited the other. Karadan stood at the vessel's prow and watched the maiden, hurrying with tremulous feet, along the rocky coast; again and again she turned to wave her hand, and beheld him still keeping his station; at last she disappeared, and her garment, fluttering behind her, vanished out of sight. Then Karadan fastened the pitcher securely to his body, steered away his skiff into the deep water, and looking to the sky, beheld, just dawning into view, a winged form, which, since he first beheld it, had a thousand times been present to his nightly slumbers. He waited not to see the dreaded shape more fully revealed, but plunged into the waves and perished, the charmed vessel remaining still bound to a heart which fear and love could agitate no longer.

Unconscious of his miserable fate Iarine pursued her way to Anthemmina's abode. No living creature met her eye as she hastened on amid sickly herbage or blighted bushes, and the sky wore a leaden hue even more melancholy than that of the plain. Once she looked up and beheld a flight of swallows, which soon descended, like a shower of dappled stones, and lay dead on the ground before her. The farther she advanced the more pining and desolate the face of nature appeared. Beyond the cliffs of the shore she journeyed over a perfectly level plain, and, after a time, the turrets of a solitary dwelling came within view amid the tops of spiral cypresses. Just such a landscape Iarine had beheld in mournful dreams, and she hurried on, hoping by quick motion to escape the sad feelings which the scene re-awakened. After passing a collection of low mounds like graves, she gained the cypress wood, and, advancing through it, soon found herself in front of that mansion which she had seen at a distance. The door stood open, and Iarine entered, but no one greeted her at the threshold. She traversed many empty apartments, all such as would have befitted a palace; they were decorated with black marble and costly hangings, but the colours of the drapery had fled, while the ornaments and utensils around were tarnished and rusty. She visited a small chamber which contained a bed, hoping to find some tokens of living inhabitants; the bed was occupied, the body of an old man being laid out there, and branches of cypress mixed with yew arranged over the head of the corse. This solemn sight assured Iarine that some one yet survived in the house or its neighbourhood. She retraced her steps, quitted the mansion, and having crossed the grove that extended behind it, descried two figures, standing beside a boundless sheet of sluggish, lurid water. On she went, and beheld a stately lady all hung over with blue garlands of star-shaped blossoms, her long black tresses floating wide, and her head and neck adorned with strings of pearl. An aged woman, who held a basket, seemed to be contending with her, while she persisted in throwing cakes of bread afar into the marsh with an air of sullen fierceness: her companion, having tried in vain to stop her hand, let fall the empty basket, and crossed her arms in all the tranquillity of settled despair.

On Iarine's approach the women in humble apparel turned about and looked at her in astonishment; but the majestic lady continued to gaze upon the marsh. The maiden felt unable to speak, but, perusing her face with deep anxiety, felt assured that she beheld her mother. The outline of her form and features was grandly beautiful; but her cheeks were white as wax, her blue eyes spectrally bright, and her delicate arms and fingers wasted to the bone. There was something wild and ghastly in her countenance, and strangely it was contrasted with that of her companion, who seemed benumbed by misery, but not bewildered. "Who art thou?" said the feeble creature, "and why hast thou come hither to see us perish, and to perish thyself when we are gone?" "Art thou not Dorna, my mother's nurse?" replied the damsel, "and is not this Anthemmina, the wife of Albinian?" "Woe is me! thou sayest true," replied the aged woman; "and surely thou art the sweet Iarine, whom this wretched lady left in the Palace of Rockland, when she quitted it never to return." All this time Anthemmina remained with her eyes fixed upon the stagnant water, speechless and motionless. The damsel related who she was, and how she had come to that coast, tenderly addressing her mother, but obtaining not a word, nor even a single glance, in return; till at last, she took her hand and implored her to break this fearful silence. Then she who was so gaily bedecked looked up, and, beholding the wreath of jewelled flowers, gazed at it with an astonished countenance. "Zalia," she cried, at length, her eyes kindling with frenzy; "art thou come instead of Dorimant?" Then, with a wild shriek, she snatched the chaplet from the maiden's brow, and trampled it under her feet. Heart-stricken and overpowered, Jarine sank upon the ground at the feet of the once gentle and captivating Anthemmina. She had found her mother, but alas! in what state! Here was the goodly fabric, to outward view still perfect: all the wondrous materials were yet in being, but the springs within had failed, and the whole was a wreck.

"We are starving!" Dorna cried; "no fresh provisions have been sent us for many months, and our last remnant of food now lies in yonder marsh. Alas! my mistress feels no trouble concerning things like these. Sorrow and the noxious vapours of this pool have turned her brain, and daily she decks herself, as when she first came hither, still expecting to be visited by Dorimant, king of Palmland." "How came she hither?" Iarine exclaimed. "By the arts of Glandreth," Dorna answered, "a storm drove our vessel to this desolate coast, but that storm was raised by Glandreth's power. In those days the wicked chief was enamoured of my mistress, and, I doubt not, beguiled her with feigned tales, saying that Queen Zalia was near her end, and that, when she died, Dorimant would carry her into Palmland. So she trusted herself with him, and, never consenting to become his wife, has remained his wretched captive. I will tell thee more while we repair to the beach: let us go in haste lest thy conductor should sail away." "He bade me return to my own country by land," replied the maiden; "saying that this peninsula could scarce be a day's journey from the chief palace of Rockland." "If he is gone we must all perish!" Dorna replied; "there is no passage hence by land. The place is separated from Rockland and Tigridia by this vast marsh, the exhalations whereof are so baleful that any birds which attempt to wing their way high in the air above it are sure to perish. All our household have died, one after another, of lingering maladies; the last survivor expired yesterday, and strength will fail me, I fear, to dig his grave." During this discourse Anthemmina sate upon the ground, weaving a fresh garland, and sometimes raising her head to cast sullen glances at the unhappy maid. Dorna hied away to the sea shore, hoping yet to hail Karadan's vessel, while Iarine stood beside her mother absorbed in silent grief.

XLII

Phantasmion and his allies join battle with Glandreth in the valley of the Black Lake

S truck with consternation at sight of the united army, the people of Rockland had offered no resistance, but had forthwith despatched messengers to Glandreth, and while Phantasmion was gazing on the Island where Iarine used to dwell, it was announced that the conqueror was about to enter the valley of the Black Lake with his victorious forces. Soon afterwards the foremost bands of the enemy were descried at a distance, and were hailed by the men of Palmland with this chant:—

> *Their armour is flashing,*
> *And ringing and clashing,*
> *Their looks are wild and savage!*
> *With deeds of night*
> *They have darken'd the light,*
> *They are come from reckless ravage!*
> *O bountiful Earth,*
> *With famine and dearth,*
> *With plague and fire surround them;*
> *Thy womb they have torn*
> *With impious scorn;*
> *Let its tremblings now confound them!*
> *Our cause maintain.*
> *For as dew to the plain,*
> *Or wind to the slumbering sea,*
> *Or sunny sheen*
> *To woodlands green,*
> *So dear have we been to thee.*

> *The new-blown flowers,*
> *From thy fairest bowers,*
> *Their rifling hands have taken;*

And the tree's last crop,
That was ready to drop,
From the dews have rudely shaken;
Through deep green dells,
Where the bright stream wells,
Like diamond with emerald blending;
Through sheltered vales,
Where the light wind sails,
High cedars scarcely bending;
Through lawn and grove,
Where the wild deer rove,
They have rush'd like a burning flood;
For mornings beam,
Or the starry gleam,
Came fire, and sword, and blood.

Then lend us thy might,
Great Earth, for the fight,
O help us to quell their pride;
Make our sinews and bones
As firm as the stones,
And metals that gird thy side;
May the smould'ring mountains,
And fiery fountains
Inflame our vengeful ire,
And beasts that lurk,
In thy forests murk,
Their tameless rage inspire;
While from caves of death
Let a sluggish breath
O'er the spoilers' spirits creep,
O send to their veins
The chill that reigns
In thy channels dark and deep.

But if those we abhor
Must triumph in war
Let us sink to thy inmost centre,
Where the trump's loud sound,

Nor the tramp and the bound,
Nor the conqueror's shout can enter;
Let mountainous rocks,
By earthquake shocks,
High o'er our bones be lifted;
And piles of snow
Where we sleep below,
To the plains above be drifted;
If the murderous band
Must dwell in the land,
And the fields we loved to cherish,
From the land of palm
Let cedar and palm
With those that rear'd them perish.

Phantasmion knew so well how the land lay in this mountainous region that Penselimer desired him to take the lead in all orders and dispositions of war; he had already shown the herdsmen how they might drive their bleating and lowing troops across the hills into Palmland, and he now joyfully proceeded to marshal the allied armies and conduct them to the most advantageous post. Flanked by the lake and its deep banks on one side, and on the other by a woody brow, they were soon drawn out in order of battle; the long winding files were quickly transformed to squares, clothing every inch of green turf and purple heather with brass and steel as fast as a painter's brush invests a pannel with new colours. The ground covered by the front line rose gradually at either end, toward the lake and toward the mountain, so that the troops were ranged in form of a semicircle. The centre of the van was occupied by Phantasmion with his light Gemmaurian cavalry, whose helmets were surmounted with carbuncles representing ruddy flames; but the young monarch's own crest was of diamonds, and displayed the figure of a damsel holding a pitcher. The Nemorosan spearmen were placed on either wing, Ulander commanding the division flanking the hill. His foresters wore casques crested with the grim visage of a gaping tiger. The king of Almaterra divided his large force into two squadrons, taking charge himself of that which held the middle ground, while Delmorin, son of Sanio, commanded the rear. Some companies of archers, wearing stag's horns on their helmets, were posted by Phantasmion among fir trees on the slope of the hill, where fan-shaped branches, growing close to the ground, kept them in ambush, though now and then their sylvan crests peeped out amid the leaves.

Meantime Glandreth was rapidly advancing and filling the plain opposite to that narrower space which Phantasmion's front line occupied, and which looked like the contracted girth of the valley. His force appeared innumerable, and had been swollen by accessions from Palmland, together with certain well-ordered battalions brought by traitorous Magnart, whom the mighty promises and mysterious hints of Glandreth had persuaded to strengthen the strong cause, and desert that of Albinet. The chief now sate beside his brother in a stately car which preceded the army, and listened to his talk with deep attention; Glandreth pointed to the sky, and Magnart seemed more bent on watching the appearances there than on surveying the ground and the enemy's array of battle. The aspect of that well-accoutred host, reflecting a bright sun from burnished armour, was indeed an unwelcome surprise to the mighty general; and, though his own was still more numerous, he could not hope to surround and overpower his opponents with multitudes of horse, by reason of their having secured so advantageous a position. Nevertheless, Glandreth was free from even a shadow of dread, and beheld the furious onset of his foes, when the battle began, without concern; for it was not in sword and buckler, nor in stout hands and hearts, that he reposed his trust; he had summoned other powers to his aid, and a dark massy cloud which followed his course, or paused with him, right over his head, while the cope of heaven around was crystal clear, assured him of victory.

Phantasmion saw that cloud and his heart was troubled; seen indeed it must needs have been by every one present, but he of all the assembled multitude alone surmised that it was aught more than a collection of vapours, he alone imagined that it contained such an ally of Glandreth as no mortal power might withstand. Perplexing conjectures engrossed his mind; he thought of Oloola's doubtful conduct at former junctures; he strove to think that she was no real enemy to his cause; he believed that Anthemmina's dying day was long since passed; yet why did that black cloud continue to hover above the head of Glandreth, and what did it portend? While the other chiefs, animated with the most confident hopes, were performing feats of valour, Phantasmion's brow was overcast, and, for a little while, the buoyancy and ardour of his temperament appeared to have forsaken him.

Soon, however, the young monarch roused himself from anxious speculation, and led on the troops with all his wonted energy. Phantasmion eagerly desired to encounter Glandreth; but lo! the chieftain, conspicuous by his long white plume and lofty stature, resigns the command to Magnart, who leads the vanguard, and, retiring from the fight, ascends a bare rock, just apart from the conflict, whence he obtains a full view of the hills above and of the plain beneath. Triumphantly from that eminence he cast his eyes around, having reason to believe that, in a few moments, every object he beheld would be absolutely subjected to his power. Below where he stood were the contending armies, the flashing of armour, the tramp of horses, the clang of sword and shield. On the green hill side he observed the numerous sheep and herds which now belonged to his adversaries: with scarce perceptible motion they were stealing onward, while ever and anon their conductors turned about to look upon the field of combat.

Part of the flocks had already disappeared, having wound their way into a rocky gorge, while the rest were following. Glandreth's heart swelled with scornful exultation as he looked upon them. "Now," thought he, "ere those flocks are out of sight the plunderers shall have felt my power; at one stroke I will change the scene, and my enemies shall be crushed for ever." At this moment success appeared inclining toward the less numerous army; Magnart had fallen by the hand of Phantasmion, and his body was trampled under foot by the throng; Penselimer, with his heavy armed troops, powerfully supported the Gemmaurian cavalry; and the archers placed behind the fir trees, like a herd of armed deer, came rushing down to attack the enemy in flank. Glandreth beheld Phantasmion; after he had given Magnart his death-blow, pressing onwards and striving to win his way to the place where he stood. Then he lifted up his glittering blade and shouted, "Come on, Phantasmion!" The rocks were still resounding that cry, when a far different echo came from the cloud over his head. "Phantasmion!—Phantasmion!—Come on, Phantasmion!" was uttered from above in a tone more shrill and piercing than that of the chieftain, more like the sound of the wind than that of any human voice; it prevailed over the din of battle; every ear heard it; every eye was fixed on the black mass, and every weapon was suspended. But the dense, pitchy cloud remained unchanged and motionless, and had a preternatural appearance alone in the pure blue sky.

Phantasmion gazed at it, as he listened with awe but not with terror to that aerial challenge; an eye of intense light now became visible in the centre of the darkness; it grew and spread till he seemed for a moment to perceive the indistinct lineaments of a dazzling face, and at the same time a hand glanced forth and beckoned him. Feelings akin to frenzy possessed the young warrior at that sight; he resolved to know his fate, and not to die without having essayed at least to punish the iniquitous transgressor; he spurred his horse, and began to drive right onward through the ranks, which made way before him. Then once more Glandreth raised his sword, and pointed to Phantasmion, while he cast up his face to the sky, and called upon Oloola. The call was heard; a gush of lightning burst from the cloud, quivered adown the uplifted blade, and clothed, as with a robe of fire, the mailed body of Glandreth. A moment he stood enveloped in flames; the blasted corse then tumbled from the rock, and, just as Phantasmion arrived, rolled down at the feet of his courser.

No noisy peal followed this vengeful lightning; no cry was uttered at the fall of Glandreth; silence was in the sky, amid the mountains, and on the motionless lake, and the armed multitudes, lately engaged in the turmoil of conflict, were still as the stones and rocks. Arrow-shaped particles of innocuous flame were diffused around; each combatant beheld them gliding over the polished helm and breastplate of his neighbour, and all fell terror-stricken with their faces to the earth. Phantasmion alone was exempted from the blinding glare; silent, yet calm, he sate on his unmoving steed, which hung his head, and like all living things around, seemed stupified with amazement. Unappalled he sate, his head thrown back to gaze on the dark cloud, which slowly ascended and gradually brightened, as if some luminous body within were eating away its coal-black shroud. That shroud became thinner and thinner, revealing more and more of a winged form, till at last, when it was perfectly transparent, the floating locks and outspread pinions of Oloola, ere she disappeared in the upper sky, were dimly visible.

XLIII

Anthemmina dies in the presence of Iarine and Phantasmion

Phantasmion was still gazing upward, when he discerned in the sky that angelic vision which first made him long to soar aloft; at the same time a well known voice whispered in his ear, "Come, and find Iarine." Then he felt himself enabled to quit the earth, and, rising buoyantly into the air, pursued Iarine's image over hill and dale. But when at last the apparition melted away, he saw his guardian Fairy flitting on before him; swiftly they traversed the Land of Rocks, passed the Diamanthine Palace, and flew above the waves till they descried an empty vessel drifting about at random. Phantasmion followed Potentilla when she entered the skiff, and no sooner had they alighted on the deck than the pinions of both disappeared, and the Fairy, sitting at the helm, appeared like some ancient pilot. "In this boat," she said, "Karadan conducted Iarine to the place of her mother's exile: in this boat thou shalt bear Iarine away, but death alone can release Anthemmina." The Fairy then disclosed what Oloola's power had long forced her to conceal, how Albinian's first queen had been tempted by Glandreth, how she came to the Lost Land which was cut off from the neighbour countries by an impassable marsh, and shunned by seafarers on account of fearful traditions and predictions connected with its name. "On that dreary coast she roamed," continued Potentilla, "till at length every cloud, which hung about the sun's globe and steeped its fleece in splendour, seemed growing into the likeness of Dorimant, every changeful mist that rose from the wave seemed about to take his form. Thus she fared till not a vestige of her former being remained but that one miserable dream. Glandreth meant to have sailed with fresh provisions the day after the battle; but Anthemmina, in frenzy, had cast the scanty remnant into the water, and by hastening the day of her death released Oloola from a vow long repented of: thus was she enabled to punish the wickedness of Glandreth, and thus hath his cruelty recoiled on his own head." "But Karadan," inquired the youth, while the skiff went forward with a favourable breeze, "how knew he where to find Iarine's mother?" "Karadan," she replied, "was visiting his fair young cousin in the Land of Rocks, when Glandreth laid his plan for carrying off the queen. By way of a childish frolic, he hid himself in the lower part of the ship, and remained unseen by the chieftain till he was about to sail away from the peninsula. Then coming forward, he fearfully exclaimed, "Where is the queen? O where is all the crew? Thou wilt not leave them on this barren coast?" While he spoke thus, Oloola made herself manifest in thunder and lightning: his young spirit was filled with terror, and he took solemn oaths never to reveal Anthemmina's abode. 'The day that any one through thee finds this peninsula,' said Glandreth, 'that day will be the last of thy life.' Karadan knew not that at the very hour when he brought Iarine thither, Oloola was released from her vow to Glandreth, and free to serve him whom she had ever loved since first she saw him on the mountain's top." "And the silver pitcher?" exclaimed Phantasmion. "That was stolen from the hapless queen by Seshelma," replied the Fairy, "and afterwards transferred to Karadan, who knew that Iarine's fate depended on it, and was beguiled by the waterwitch to hope that she might in the end be his." "But O, where is it now?" the youth eagerly demanded. Potentilla replied not, but pointed to the coast of the peninsula, where Dorna was joyfully hailing the vessel. Phantasmion gained the shore, and, guided by the aged woman, crossed the bleak waste which his betrothed maiden had lately traversed; then, hurrying through the cypress grove, he came in sight of the marsh, just as the sun was throwing a red gleam over that livid pool, in which, on the far horizon, he seemed ready to sink and quench his flaming tiara. When he had passed the wood, Phantasmion stopped and beheld Iarine kneeling beside her mother, who lay on the margin of the lake, and seemed nigh unto death. Now that life was waning, her senses had fully returned. She had recognised her sweet Iarine, and they had wept together; could such tears have rained upon her blighted cheek before they might have kept away a fatal malady. "Dear child," she said, "thou wast a glimpse of soft blue sky between the clouds of my tempestuous life. Now that it beams forth once again, my day is closed." Just as Anthemmina had spoken thus, and had begun to lament over the wretched pass to which Iarine was brought, she heard approaching footsteps, and, casting up her death-stricken eyes, beheld Phantasmion. "Dorimant!" she faintly exclaimed; and Iarine, clasping her hands, cried, "Yes! the son of Dorimant! Phantasmion! He is come to save and to protect us!" Then, while the youth kneeled by her side, and told his tale, Anthemmina saw how she had been deceived by the watery vision, and whom the figures there portrayed did truly represent. She was glad to depart herself, and thankful to find that her child was destined for happiness, which had ever been a mere vision to her. "But the silver pitcher, given me by the guardian spirit of our race, that is still wanting!" So thought Anthemmina when she joined the hands of the youthful pair, and blessed their union. The mists of death had now begun to darken her eyes, but, ere they were closed for ever, she caught a glimpse of the charmed vessel, gleaming amid the cypress trees, and just discerned a train of aerial figures, which had glided thither from the sea, and were now pausing in silence amid the shadows of the grove. Her head then sank upon its earthy pillow, and, with a smile on her countenance, the mother of Iarine expired. The maiden closed her eyes, kissed her wan cheeks, and sank in a swoon upon her bosom. Phantasmion goes to raise her in his arms, but pauses on seeing another mourner come to weep for Anthemmina. It is Feydeleen, the Spirit of the Flowers; softly she rises from amid the lilies of the pool, her head wrapped in a hood, white as those lovely blossoms, while the ends of her shiny green mantle float away on either side of her bending form, and rest upon the surface of the water. And now she droops in sorrow over Anthemmina and the fainting maid; tears drop from her fair eyes on the faces of both, and her yellow locks, light as gossamer, fall down and mingle with the dark tresses of Anthemmina. At length she raised her head, and throwing back the snowy hood which had concealed her face, disclosed her bloomy cheeks and golden tendrils to Phantasmion. Feydeleen pointed to the silver pitcher, then to Iarine, and, softly smiling, whispered, "She is thine!" Hues of life were drawing on the maiden's cheek while Feydeleen retired among the white and azure blossoms. She veiled her head, and bowed it on the surface of the pool, as a water-lily closes her cup and lowers her flexile stem, when the sun is on his downward path. In a few moments, none but the heads of the lilies glimmered on the darkening waters of the marsh.

As Feydeleen disappeared, Iarine rose from the earth, supported in the arms of Phantasmion, and then the train of sea-nymphs, with feet glancing in the twilight, fair as foam that twinkles on the crest of a billow, poured forward like a soft advancing tide. The foremost of them brought the charmed vessel and placed it in the maiden's hand; they who came last bore the corse of Karadan; they paused among the cypresses, and Iarine held up the silver pitcher to hide the tears which flooded her drooping face. But ere those tears had ceased to flow, Phantasmion received it from the willing hand of his gentle-hearted maid.

The nymphs now surrounded Anthemmina's body, taking the weedy coronals from their heads to scatter them on that fair corse. Those who formed the outer circle blew melancholy notes through many a wreathed shell, attuning them to this farewell strain which their sisters chanted:

> Ah, where lie now those locks that lately stream'd
> 'Mid gales that fann'd in vain that fever'd cheek?
> Low let them rest, ye winds,
> The heart now rests in peace.
>
> How vainly, while the tortur'd bosom heav'd,
> Restless as waves that lash'd her sea-beat haunt,
> We strove to cool that cheek
> Which death too quickly chill'd!
>
> Like wreaths of mist, that some lone rock o'erhang,
> And seem intent to melt the crags away,
> While with soft veil they hide,
> Its tempest-riven head;
>
> We hover'd round thee on the lonesome beach,
> And sought to calm thy brow with dewy hand,
> Thy wild unquiet eye
> With pitying glances met.
>
> "O fly with us," we whisper'd; "from glad hearts,
> From mirthful bands that meet on moon-light shores,
> We came to watch thee pace
> This melancholy strand.
>
> "A captive thou, an exile here confined;
> But fatal passion to more galling chains,
> To exile more unblest,
> Thy blinded spirit dooms.

"O fly with us; no dangerous choice we know,
Mild heavenly influence guides our gentle lives,
Obedient as yon tide,
Sway'd by the circling moon.

"O fly with us, free, free, as ocean gale,
To roam at large, releas'd from sorrow's power."—
Ah no!—far happier scenes,
More blissful change, be thine!

Through fields of radiance let thy spirit stray,
While these fair relics, shrin'd in ocean's depth,
Shall gleam like purest pearl,
Caress'd by winds and waves.

SARA COLERIDGE

XLIV

Phantasmion and Iarine are wafted to
the narrow bay, whence they sail with
Zelneth and Leucoia to Rockland

While the procession moved along the wood with Anthemmina's
body, one of the many garlands that hung about it fell to the
ground, which Iarine took up, and fondly twined amid her own tresses.
Phantasmion observed the pomegranate wreath at a little distance
glittering on the borders of the marsh; he went to fetch the relic, and
placed it in his bosom, resolving to keep the memorial for his mother's
sake. In the stillness of the air, as he stooped beside the pool, a mournful
sound, like the boom of some distant bittern, came to his ear across the
waters. It was the voice of Seshelma; just as Karadan expired, the witch
was about to seize on his corse and the pitcher along with it; but Oloola
had descended in a whirlwind, and, bearing her aloft, had plunged
her in that pestiferous bog which bounded the Lost Land. Thence she
dared not return into the sea, but ever after continued slowly roaming
from one part of the fen to the other; while her moans and wailings,
heard sometimes on the side of Tigridia, sometimes toward the Land of
Rocks, augmented the horror with which the people of those countries
regarded the marsh and the peninsula beyond it.

The moon was up when Phantasmion and his fair princess gained
the beach, and espied Dorna sitting in the vessel with the seeming
pilot. They entered it, and, when they had put out into the deep, no
cloudlet was ever driven along the sky by the keen winds of March
more swiftly than that skiff was made to fly over the ocean plain. After
awhile, Phantasmion discerned before the vessel's prow a shadowy form
which seemed to be guiding it on its way. Iarine saw not what he saw,
for her eyes, from which the tears had scarcely ceased to flow, were
now heavy with sleep, and at last she lay in slumber on Phantasmion's
cloak upon the open deck. Then the phantom rose up from the waves,
and turning about, revealed to him that still watched the face of Zalia.
While she murmured blessings on his head, he pointed to the sleeping
maid: "O bless her too," he cried, "who makes me blessed." The shade
of Zalia bent toward Iarine, but soon recoiled, gazing with a sad look on

the blue lilies which now lay withering on the damsel's stainless brow. But when Phantasmion removed Anthemmina's garland and placed the jewelled wreath upon the maiden's head, again the face of Zalia grew softly bright, and, bending over Iarine's tearful cheek to breathe a benison, she seemed like the moon shedding benign influence on some dewy flower.

When the stars faded in heaven, Zalia, too, disappeared, but first she pointed to a group of figures now in sight upon the margin of the narrow bay, and sighing said, "Awake, Iarine! thou hast fellow mourners! Lo, Zelneth and Leucoia weeping for their mother and for Karadan!" With that voice sounding in her ear, Iarine awoke: the shade of Zalia had vanished, but she beheld the daughters of Magnart kneeling on the beach beside two prostrate forms. Nigh them a fair shape was pouring liquid on those lifeless bodies, but when Iarine approached the mourners, it disappeared, leaving behind a fragrant atmosphere. Feydeleen had been performing the last kind office for the mother and the son: Arzene had watched and waited for Karadan in the bay till those same sea nymphs who bore his pale corse to the peninsula, transported it thence to her feet, then falling senseless over it, she was drowned by the advancing tide. The same vessel in which the son of Magnart sailed from these shores, received his embalmed body, with that of his mother. Iarine, Zelneth, and Leucoia, closely united in sorrow, entered the skiff with Phantasmion, and were driven by steady gales to the Rockland coast, not far from the Diamanthine Palace.

Leaving the fellow mourners at that royal abode, Phantasmion rejoined his kingly allies at the capital city of Rockland, and learned that Glandreth's army had submitted to their united forces without striking another blow, so that the whole country was subdued. Albinet with his mother Maudra had disappeared; for no sooner was the fatal end of Glandreth generally known, than the principal men of Rockland had revolted against the widowed queen, declaring that they would neither endure her sway nor that of her sickly child. To escape their hands, she had fled with young Albinet, no one knew whither, and the chiefs placed their crown at the disposal of the allied monarchs, signifying a desire that he who should espouse the daughter of Albinian might reign over them. Phantasmion was not eager to embrace this proposal, but caused diligent search to be made for Iarine's brother, whose rights he resolved to uphold. At this time it was announced that mines of iron, as well as of copper, had been discovered in Gemmaura, and in a part of Palmland adjoining that district.

While Ulander was restored to his ancestral throne, the blooming Hermilian inherited Polyanthida. Meantime Penselimer and the sylvan chief found their fair consorts at the Diamanthine Palace, and heard how, in obedience to the voice of Feydeleen, they had followed their mother to the narrow bay, where they found her corse on the beach beside the body of Karadan. Afterwards Leucoia made known to Ulander that the witch's cavern was destroyed on the night when the volcanic mountain filled the heavens with smoke; and Zelneth told her kingly spouse that the bleak waste around his castle had begun to smile with verdure, while the black cloud no longer rested on the horizon. "It is reported," said she, "that the dim vale has been freed from its diurnal canopy by the Spirit of the Blast, and that Melledine has drowned herself in a mountain pool which lies in deep shadow."

Phantasmion caused the remains of Albinian to be brought from Nemorosa under the care of the faithful goatherd, and to be interred in Rockland with fitting pomp. Magnart's body could never be certified among the heaps of slain which had been defaced by the trampling throng; but the obsequies of Arzene and of Karadan were solemnly performed, and splendid monuments were raised to their memory. Anthemmina had no share in these funeral honours; her relics could not be entombed beneath a solid marble pile: but the face of the deep, with its changeful hues and emotions, for the mind of Iarine, was her mother's monument, and strains like these she dedicated to her memory:

> *Poor is the portrait that one look portrays,*
> *It mocks the face on which we loved to gaze;*
> *A thousand past expressions all combin'd,*
> *The mind itself depictured by the mind,*
> *That face contains which in the heart is shrin'd.*
> *Yet, dearest mother, if on lasting brass*
> *Thy very self to future times might pass,*
> *Ill could I bear such monument to build*
> *For future times with dearer memories filled.*
> *Ah no! thy fadeless portrait in my breast*
> *From earth shall vanish when I sink to rest;*
> *But, ere to join thee on glad wings I go,*

Thy sun-like influence, beaming here below,
In sorrow's hour, when earthly hope betrays me
To heaven above, my hope's best aim, shall raise me,
In hours of bliss when heaven almost seems here.
For thy sweet memory claim the tribute tear;
So yon bright orb doth tearful incense gain
From glittering lake, sweet rill, and humid plain,
Yet dries the spray that trembled in the shower,
And shines reflected from each dripping flower.

SARA COLERIDGE

XLV

Iarine finds her brothers in the grove where Phantasmion first saw Potentilla

When the days of mourning had expired, all the children of Magnart, with the kings who had espoused Zelneth and Leucoia, accompanied Phantasmion and his betrothed princess to Palmland, that they might be present at their nuptials. The country palace where the young monarch had always resided lay in their way, being at no great distance from the confines of Rockland; and here it was resolved that the company should sojourn, while preparations were made for the wedding in the principal city. There was a strange look on earth and sky when Iarine entered that regal domain, a hot sun being veiled by bluish mist; her cheeks glowed and her breath laboured with the stifled heat and with eager anticipation, for she expected shortly to behold her long lost infant brother. Eurelio was to be lord of Gemmaura, so Phantasmion had declared; but how could she rejoice over him without grieving for Albinet? And alas! where was Albinet to be found, or how could she discharge toward that beloved boy her promise to his father? With beating bosom she hastened onward, and entered the grove where Potentilla first showed herself to Phantasmion. There she espied a child just old enough to run alone, caressing a poor boy in tattered clothes, and presenting him with fruits, toys, and fragments of cake from a basket where all were mingled together. Close by was a woman who wore a beggar's garb, and seemed in woeful plight; she sate upon the ground, her head inclined against a tree, watching that fair child and his pale comrade, who ate the dainties given him by the rosy little one as if he were well nigh famished. Her looks were full of misery, but not a tear-drop glittered down her ghastly cheek. Iarine knew at once that the younger child was Eurelio, and flew to embrace her darling charge, twice lost, and now twice found. While she held him in her arms, the sickly boy wept, and, catching her robe, exclaimed, "O sister, wilt thou not speak to me? art thou, too, turned against me?" Startled by the sound of a well known voice, the lady looked at him steadfastly, and saw that he was her father's heir, the poor rejected Albinet. Then she gave Eurelio to his nurse, who had come up in breathless haste, and tenderly caressed her weeping brother, shedding tears herself while she wiped the big drops which fell from his eyes.

But soon his face beamed with happiness, though wan as frosted roses, and, turning to the wretched woman, who vainly strove to rise, "Mother," he cried, "our griefs are ended now: here is Iarine. Sister, didst thou find that healing well? If thou hast any of the water left, I pray thee give it to my mother." By this time the gentle princess had recognised Maudra's altered face, and, kneeling beside her, whispered words of consolation, declaring that she herself would be protected, and Albinet restored to his rights, by the generous king of Palmland. Tears now gushed in torrents from the eyes of Maudra, but still she could make no reply; her evil counsellor, whom she had met on the sea-shore, after the destruction of Glandreth, and frantically strove to punish, had stricken a deadly chill into her frame and rendered her speechless. And now Phantasmion was seen holding up the charmed vessel among the boughs of the pomegranate tree, which stood a little way back within the grove. Potentilla sat in the shadow, while Feydeleen, less hidden by the foliage, was pouring a fragrant liquid from her chalice into the pitcher: and just as Zelneth and Leucoia, with the rest of the company, arrived, he shed the flower-spirit's balmy gift on the head of Albinet, whose body gradually changed as the precious drops trickled over it, till by the time they reached the ground he stood erect in blooming health and vigour. His limbs, on which the ragged garments had before hung loose, now muscular and shapely, filled them out to their full stretch; his form was upright, and his cheeks, though not so round and soft, were blooming as those of Eurelio. Maudra had witnessed the change with flushed cheek and gleaming eye, but could not utter a word of joy or thankfulness. Albinet flung his arms around her neck; "O mother!" he said, "why art thou not healed of this dire malady?" But Maudra scarcely thought of him or that; for now again her eye was fastened on Eurelio. Iarine observed that look, and blamed herself that she had so long delayed to place the lost one in his mother's arms. In haste she brought him to her side, and gently whispered, "This is thy rescued babe, thy sweet Eurelio!" Joy lighted up the face of the dying woman at these words; she strove to clasp the smiling child to her bosom; but, ere she reached him, her sight failed, and, sinking backwards, she expired in the arms of Albinet.

A little while afterwards Phantasmion looked down into the grove, and saw the heir of Rockland leaning against a tree, with his weeping eyes fixed upon the ground. The Flower Spirit gleamed beside him in the hazy light, and seemed to smile, as she bent forward, like a sapling swayed by a gentle breeze, to crown his drooping brow with thornless roses. Eurelio was too young to weep the death of Maudra; he thought she slumbered when silently and softly she was borne away. With Potentilla's wand he struck a hollow trunk of sycamore, and sweetly his childish laughter rang through the grove when myriads of bees came crowding forth, and shone with all the dyes of the opal, as they hung from a branch above his head. Phantasmion felt as if he had dreamed of years, not lived them; the fairy looked as old and upright as when she first appeared to him; the trees around all seemed as green and flourishing; the grove was filled with just the same soft insect murmur, and that bright swarm hung dazzling as of yore.

But lo! the sun has broken through its hazy veil, and Feydeleen's soft cheek, as if it faded in the brilliant light, is seen no more among the blossoms; Albinet raises his head, from which the airy chaplet melts away, and with wonder-stricken eyes Eurelio gazes upward, for Potentilla has risen from his side. A moment yet the wings of her insect steeds are painted against the background of one lingering cloudlet—but now they disappear, while earth below, suffused with splendour, becomes a softened image of the heavens themselves.

Phantasmion looked round in momentary dread, lest Iarine should have proved a spirit and vanished like the rest; but there she stood, her face beaming bright as ever in full sunshine, the earnest that all he remembered and all he hoped for was not to fade like a dream.

A Note About the Author

Sara Coleridge (1802–1852) was a British writer, editor and translator born in Keswick, Cumberland, England. She was the only daughter of English poet Samuel Taylor Coleridge and his wife, Sara Fricker. As a child, she was greatly influenced by her uncle whose vast library exposed her to the Greek and Latin classics. As an adult, she embarked on a literary career starting with translations such as *Account of the Abipones* in 1822. This was followed by lighter fare inspired by her growing family. Coleridge notably wrote *Pretty Lessons in Verse for Good Children* and *Phantasmion: A Fairy Tale*.

A Note from the Publisher

Spanning many genres, from non-fiction essays to literature classics to children's books and lyric poetry, Mint Edition books showcase the master works of our time in a modern new package. The text is freshly typeset, is clean and easy to read, and features a new note about the author in each volume. Many books also include exclusive new introductory material. Every book boasts a striking new cover, which makes it as appropriate for collecting as it is for gift giving. Mint Edition books are only printed when a reader orders them, so natural resources are not wasted. We're proud that our books are never manufactured in excess and exist only in the exact quantity they need to be read and enjoyed.

bookfinity™

Discover more of your favorite classics with Bookfinity™.

- Track your reading with custom book lists.
- Get great book recommendations for your personalized Reader Type.
- Add reviews for your favorite books.
- AND MUCH MORE!

Visit **bookfinity.com** and take the fun Reader Type quiz to get started.

Enjoy our classic and modern companion pairings!

Classic & Modern

Printed in the USA
CPSIA information can be obtained
at www.ICGtesting.com
JSHW022321140824
68134JS00019B/1217